THE LOST QUILTER

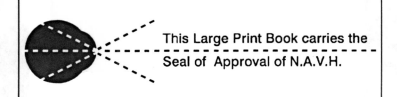

This Large Print Book carries the
Seal of Approval of N.A.V.H.

THE LOST QUILTER

JENNIFER CHIAVERINI

LARGE PRINT PRESS
A part of Gale, Cengage Learning

GALE
CENGAGE Learning™

Detroit • New York • San Francisco • New Haven, Conn • Waterville, Maine • London

GALE
CENGAGE Learning·

LIBRARY OF CONGRESS CATALOGING-IN-PUBLICATION DATA

Chiaverini, Jennifer.
   The lost quilter : an Elm Creek quilts novel / by Jennifer
Chiaverini.
     p. cm. — (Thorndike Press large print core)
   ISBN-13: 978-1-4104-1402-1 (alk. paper)
   ISBN-10: 1-4104-1402-7 (alk. paper)
   1. Compson, Sylvia (Fictitious character)—Fiction.
2. Quilting—Fiction. 3. Quiltmakers—Fiction. 4. Quilts—Fiction.
5. Genealogy—Fiction. 6. Domestic fiction. 7. Large type books.
I. Title.
PS3553.H473L67 2009
813'.54—dc22   2008048665

ISBN 13: 978-1-59413-357-2 (pbk. : alk. paper)
ISBN 10: 1-59413-357-3 (pbk. : alk. paper)

Published in 2010 by arrangement with Simon & Schuster, Inc.

ED016

To my husband, Marty
Forever my beloved

ACKNOWLEDGMENTS

Many thanks to Denise Roy, Maria Massie, Rebecca Davis, Dina Siljkovic, Aileen Boyle, Kate Ankofski, Mara Lurie, Melanie Parks, and David Rosenthal for their contributions to *The Lost Quilter* and their support for the Elm Creek Quilts series through the years.

Hugs and thanks to Tara Shaughnessy, the world's best nanny, who plays with my sons so I have time to write.

I am indebted to the Wisconsin Historical Society as well as their librarians and student workers who provided excellent resources for this book. I am also grateful to Geneva Keating of the Historic Charleston Foundation and to Gretchen Smith of the Edisto Island Museum for their invaluable help with my many questions about life in Charleston and Edisto Island during Joanna's day. I am especially thankful to Ann Craigmile for her thorough reading of the manuscript and insightful comments.

Thank you to the friends and family who have supported and encouraged me from the beginning, especially Geraldine Neidenbach, Heather Neidenbach, Nic Neidenbach, Virginia Riechman, and Leonard and Marlene Chiaverini. Thanks also to my teammates from Homeland Insecurity, Just For Kicks, and Oh-Thirty for providing me with awesome workouts, great camaraderie, patient coaching, essential stress relief, and only one broken bone during the writing of this book.

Most of all, I thank my wonderful husband, Marty, for showing me what true love means every day, and my sons, Nicholas and Michael, for filling my life with laughter and joy.

PROLOGUE

On a clear, brisk October morning, Sylvia Bergstrom Compson descended the stone staircase from the veranda of Elm Creek Manor and set out for the barn, where the estate's caretaker awaited her. High above, an arrowhead of Canada geese crossed the cloudless sky and disappeared behind the gold and scarlet forest encircling the estate, their fading sentinel cries warning of winter's approach. A gust of wind carried the scent of wood smoke from a distant fire.

Sylvia smiled and tucked her hands into the pockets of her navy wool cardigan, her sturdy shoes crunching dried leaves that had fallen upon the rear parking lot, empty except for the Elm Creek Quilts minivan and the red pickup belonging to Sarah and Matt McClure, two of the manor's few permanent residents. Curiosity had compelled Sylvia out of doors that morning, as the note Matt had left on the kitchen counter had not explained why he wanted her to meet him in the barn. It didn't matter. Sylvia was glad for any excuse to wander that way and enjoy the estate's glorious autumn beauty before winter took hold.

She crossed the bridge over Elm Creek and followed the gravel road to the two-story red barn that her great-grandfather, Hans Bergstrom, had built into the side of the hill shortly after founding Elm Creek Farm in the late 1850s. Since then the barn had served as a shelter for farm animals, a garage, a plant nursery and toolshed, and more recently, as a woodshop for one of the manor's newest arrivals, Joe Hartley, the husband of Elm Creek Quilt Camp's newest teacher. A former steelworker forced onto disability decades earlier by a devastating injury at the mill, Joe had made quite a name for himself in the furniture restoration and carpentry business both in Ambridge, his hometown on the Ohio River, and throughout Pennsylvania. When his wife Gretchen's new job brought the couple to Elm Creek Manor, Sylvia had been pleased to offer Joe the empty half of her great-grandfather's barn for his flourishing business.

In Sylvia's opinion, her generosity had already proven to be as rewarding for her as it was for Joe. Within days of his arrival, Joe had begun searching the manor's cluttered attic for long-forgotten antiques — chairs with broken spindles, bureaus with drawers that stuck — heirlooms that when they were no longer usable were moved into storage because they were too beloved to be discarded. Joe's careful ministrations had already restored her great-aunt Lydia's bureau and her grandmother's favorite rocking chair to perfect condition. Sylvia, who had found the task of clearing the attic of clutter too daunting, often thought that in hiring Gretchen as a teacher and offering her and her husband accommodations within the manor, Elm Creek Quilts had gained not one new staff member but two.

As she approached the barn, Sylvia recognized voices within — Matt, the estate's caretaker; his wife, Sarah, Sylvia's dear young friend and cofounder of Elm Creek Quilts; and Joe himself, probably hard at work on another newly discovered heirloom from the attic. Entering through the large double doors, Sylvia discovered her friends in Joe's woodshop examining an antique desk that had evidently been well used by its original owner.

"This is why you summoned me from my warm house on this chilly autumn morning?" Sylvia inquired. "I expected nothing less than a treasure chest stuffed full of the long-lost Bergstrom jewels."

From kneeling to examine the bottom of the desk Matt sat up so quickly that he grazed his head on a drawer. "There are lost Bergstrom jewels?" he asked, rubbing his forehead and wincing.

"She's kidding, honey," Sarah said, patting his shoulder, then placing a hand on her tummy and gazing heavenward as if praying that the twins she carried would have more astute senses of humor than their father.

"To me, the desk itself is the treasure," said Joe. "This is solid cherry, quarter-hewn, and look at the detailing on the side panels. It's a bit scuffed and scratched, but I can take care of that, no problem."

"Well, then, please go right ahead," said Sylvia, surprised. "You should know by now that you don't need to ask my permission. You haven't disappointed me yet and I doubt you ever will."

"This desk needs more than a little sanding and stain," Joe warned, indicating a drawer on the right-hand side. "This drawer is locked, and the keyhole's so corroded from rust that the tumblers are fused solid."

"So we probably couldn't unlock it even if

we had the key." Sarah threw Sylvia an inquiring glance. "Which I assume we don't, unless it's dangling from a master key ring that I don't know about?"

"I don't think so, and even if there were one, I wouldn't know where to look for it." Sylvia drew closer and peered at the rusty keyhole. It did indeed seem permanently fixed shut. "Well, it's still a lovely desk even without the use of one drawer. Those two on the left side should suffice. My suggestion is not to worry about it."

"I'd think so, too, except —" Sarah beckoned to Matt. "Show her, honey."

Matt nodded, rose, and lifted the side of the desk. Sylvia distinctly heard something slide over the wood and thump softly against the interior wall of the drawer. When Matt set the desk's legs back on the floor, the sound came again, whispery and dry, like old paper.

"I can pry off the drawer front to get at whatever's inside," Joe said, "but not without damage. I checked the other drawers and they were made solid, with dovetail fittings. I can repair the drawer after, but it won't be as strong, and I can't promise that I won't scrape up the wood. And anything I do will lower its value as an antique."

"But that's the only way to find out what's

inside." Sarah had clearly already formed her own opinion of what should be done. "You weren't planning to have the desk appraised and sold anyway, were you, Sylvia?"

"There might not be anything important in there," cautioned Matt. "I doubt it's a wad of hundred-dollar bills. You might ruin the desk only to find an old pocket dictionary or a pad of blank paper."

"Or you might find an important piece of Bergstrom history," said Sarah, shooting her husband a pointed look. "Maybe another memoir, like the one your great-grandfather's sister Gerda wrote. Or maybe a bundle of letters. Or maybe the original deed to Elm Creek Farm! Wouldn't that be an amazing find? We could frame it and display it in the foyer."

"My great-grandfather won Elm Creek Farm from a drunkard in a horse race," Sylvia reminded her. "Somehow I doubt he ever held anything as formal as a deed."

But the desk's scratches and worn places suggested that it had seen a great deal of use. Someone — or perhaps generations of someones — had read and written letters at that desk, had kept ledgers or balanced accounts, had saved receipts and bills and children's report cards. Matt could be correct; the drawer might contain nothing of value. On the other hand, it could also shelter something that documented a part of the Bergstrom family history, a small clue that would illuminate a new facet of her ancestors' lives.

The potential for discovery overruled any concerns she might have had about damaging the desk.

"I don't think I could walk past this desk day after day without wondering for the rest of my life what that drawer contains," she declared. "Joe, please do your best to minimize the damage, but don't keep us in suspense too long."

Joe retrieved tools from the pegboard above his workbench and set himself to the task. Within minutes he had pried off the drawer front, brushed off a thick layer of dust from the inside, and set the carved cherry panel on the desktop. Stooping over, he reached deep into the recess, tugged hard on something Sylvia couldn't see, and grimaced when the drawer didn't budge. He knelt down to get a better angle, filed off a thin sliver of wood from the right side of the drawer, and reached into the opening again. The old wood creaked and groaned in protest, but little by little, Joe forced it open until at last he yanked it free. "Stubborn piece of junk," he complained cheerfully. "The wood must've swelled with moisture. It was fused so tight, the lock was unnecessary."

"One of my ancestors must have thought it was necessary once," Sylvia pointed out, coming closer to see what had been locked away for so many decades.

There within the broken drawer lay a stack of yellowed envelopes, bound together with a frayed, faded ribbon.

"Careful," Sarah murmured, though Sylvia did not need the warning to know to proceed cautiously. Gently she picked up the bundle, but when she tried to untie the ribbon, it crumbled to dusty fragments beneath her fingertips. Softly she blew the tattered bits aside and fumbled for her glasses, which hung from a silver chain around her neck.

The envelope on the top of the stack was addressed to Miss Gerda Bergstrom, Elm Creek Farm, Creek's Crossing, Pennsylvania.

"Creek's Crossing?" Joe asked, peering over Sylvia's shoulder.

"Yes. Waterford was called that long ago." Sylvia set the stack of letters on the desktop and gently thumbed through them, counting ten in all, arranged with the earliest

16

postmark on top. The second letter was also addressed to Gerda Bergstrom, but the other eight were addressed to the Bergstrom Residence. The fifth had been returned to the sender, who had evidently crossed out the words Creek's Crossing, written Waterford below it, and affixed a new stamp over the one that had been canceled. The remaining letters had been sent to Waterford. The return address on the first letter was from Virginia, while the others had been mailed from various towns in South Carolina, none of which sounded familiar.

Sylvia carefully opened the top envelope, which was thankfully far less brittle than the ribbon had been. She withdrew a single sheet of yellowed paper, gingerly unfolded it, and began to read aloud:

February 21, 1868

Dear Miss Bergstrom,
   Please accept my sincere apologies for sending but a single letter in response to the great many you have sent to my family. It is unfortunate that your remarkable perseverance and prolifigacy as a letter-writer will have been in vain, for I regret that I do not have the answers you seek. I cannot dispute that my husband once

kept a servant named Joanna in his service, but I have no idea what became of her after she left us. My husband customarily brought chastened, wayward servants back to our plantation at Greenfields in order to impress upon our other negroes the sad fate of the runaway, but these unfortunate few would remain with us only a short while after that. Since servants proven faithless were useless to him, my husband would be obliged to sell them, usually to our relations in Georgia or South Carolina. I confess that I do not recall whether the servant named Joanna faced these consequences; my husband kept so many negroes that I did not know them all, and I doubt I would have recognized the one in question in any case.

I regret that I am unable to offer you more help in your search. It saddens me to chasten your enthusiasm, but every letter you may send us in the days to come, no matter how heartfelt or elegantly phrased, will meet with the same result. I have nothing to tell you about Joanna, nor shall I in the future. If I may say so, delicately, perhaps the time has come for you to abandon your fruitless quest before the perpetual disappointment takes its toll on your health.

I remain most cordially yours,
Mrs. Josiah Chester
Formerly of Greenfields Plantation,
Wentworth County, Virginia

Sylvia's voice caught in her throat each time she read the familiar names: Joanna, a runaway slave who had found refuge at Elm Creek Farm. Josiah Chester, her cruel owner. Wentworth County, Virginia, the land Joanna had fled, and to which she had probably been returned upon her recapture.

Sylvia's great-great-aunt Gerda Bergstrom had recorded the story of Joanna's daring escape and tragic recapture in her memoir. Gerda had also told of her own long, obsessive, ultimately unsuccessful search for Joanna after the war, and in the last pages of her memoir she had described a letter very much like the one Sylvia now held.

The reason for the locked drawer was suddenly clear: Gerda had known secrets about the Bergstrom family she intended to conceal forever, even from her own descendants. Perhaps especially from them.

"Mrs. Chester obviously didn't want to hear from Gerda again, but someone else was willing to write," Sarah prompted, indicating the other letters.

Sylvia cleared her throat, returned Mrs. Chester's letter to the envelope, and picked up the second from the stack. "This one was mailed from South Carolina," she said, opening it. "Perhaps Gerda was able to track down some of the relatives that bought the Chesters' recaptured slaves."

May 14, 1896

Dear Miss Bergstrom,

I am writing on behalf of my grandmother to inquire after the health of a gentleman, Mr. Douglass Frederick, whom she met when she enjoyed your kind hospitality at your farm in 1859. She would be very grateful for any information you could provide about him, especially his current address so that she may write to him directly.

Yours sincerely,
Mrs. Lenore Harris

"Who's Douglass Frederick?" asked Matt. "Who's Lenore Harris, for that matter?"

"I've never heard those names before," said Sylvia, shaking her head and returning the letter to the envelope.

"Could she have meant Frederick Douglass?" asked Sarah. "Did he ever visit Elm

20

Creek Farm?"

The Bergstroms and their closest friends had been abolitionists who ran stations on the Underground Railroad, so it was not entirely out of the question. "I don't believe so," said Sylvia. "I'm sure Gerda would have recorded such an event in her memoir. As an abolitionist she considered Frederick Douglass one of her heroes, and she mentioned his autobiography."

The third letter, written almost exactly a year later, was similar to the one before it:

May 12, 1897

Dear Miss Bergstrom,

At my grandmother's request, I am writing to request any information you might have about Mr. Douglass Frederick, a gentlemen she met when traveling through the Elm Creek Valley in early 1859. For many years she has been interested in resuming their acquaintance, and she hopes that you may be able to assist her in this regard. My grandmother is aged and in failing health, so time is of the essence.

Sincerely,
Mrs. Lenore Harris

Sylvia frowned, puzzled. "The first families of the Elm Creek Valley are well known. I don't recall the surname Frederick among them."

"She's asking about a runaway slave, not a neighbor," said Sarah. "Think about it. 'Douglass Frederick' is obviously code for a slave who found freedom, and Lenore Harris's grandmother had reason to believe Gerda would know whom she sought. Who but a runaway slave would have been visiting Elm Creek Farm in early 1859?"

"My great-grandparents and great-aunt were running a station on the Underground Railroad then," mused Sylvia. "Mrs. Harris's grandmother could have been trying to find a runaway who passed through here. That might explain why her letter is so vague. Perhaps she was a loved one left behind, trying desperately to discover what became of him, and yet still determined to protect his identity."

"But why would she need to protect him in" — Matt glanced at the top of the page — "1897? Slavery had been abolished. Even if he had once been a slave, Douglass Frederick would have been a free man by then."

"Yes, but as my great-great-aunt Gerda wrote, giving a people their freedom did not grant them their equality. They had a long, hard fight ahead of them." Sylvia thought for a moment. "It's possible that Lenore Harris didn't know why her grandmother was so curious, so insistent, and that's why the letters lack a certain directness."

"Or her grandmother was deliberately vague," said Sarah. "According to Lenore, her grandmother met Mr. Frederick here, at Elm Creek Farm. It's obvious who she's looking for." Sarah looked around at the others, incredulous. "Oh, come on! Who else do we know who visited Elm Creek Farm in early 1859 and then wound up in South Carolina? Lenore Harris's grandmother must be Joanna!"

"And 'Douglass Frederick' is an alias for the infant son she left behind?" Sylvia shook her head. "It's highly unlikely, my dear."

"No, it's not," Sarah insisted. "All the pieces fit. The year. The location. The grandmother's presence at Elm Creek Farm and later in South Carolina. The absence of pertinent details. Notice that she doesn't ask about an African-American man, just in case he was passing as white. Joanna and her son were light-skinned, remember? They were going to use that to their advantage as they traveled from Pennsylvania to Canada. Lenore's grandmother had to be circumspect or she might give away their ruse."

"I suppose it's possible," said Sylvia. "The letters arrived after Gerda's death. If Lenore's grandmother was indeed Joanna . . ."

To think that the answers Gerda longed for had come too late.

"If Gerda had already passed on, who locked the letters in the drawer?" asked Joe. "Someone knew they were worth saving."

"I have no idea," said Sylvia. Another puzzle. Perhaps the remaining letters would provide more clues. She read each one carefully, only to find echoes of the same request for information about Douglass Frederick. There was nothing to suggest that anyone from Elm Creek Manor had ever responded, even to say that they knew nothing about the man Mrs. Harris's grandmother sought. Perhaps someone had responded, but the grandmother — Joanna? — had persisted despite the denials, knowing that the Bergstroms offered her last and best connection to her lost son.

"Joanna Frederick," said Sarah. "Joanna Frederick from South Carolina. We have a name and a location now. We might be able to discover what became of her."

Sylvia's pulse quickened, but experience had taught her not to entertain false hopes. "After all this time, dear? And with our best historical researcher away at graduate school?"

"It won't hurt to dig around a bit more, even without Summer to guide us. We won't know if we don't try." Sarah's eyebrows arched. "You can't tell me you're not curious."

Sylvia smiled back. "You wouldn't believe me if I did."

After receiving Joe's assurances that he would do his best to repair the drawer and return the desk to its original beauty, Sylvia returned to the manor and climbed the grand oak staircase to the second-floor library. At her touch, double doors swung open into a room spanning the entire width of the south wing. Early morning sunlight spilled in through tall diamond-paned windows on the east wall, casting long rectangles of light on the rugs and hardwood floors. Oak bookcases filled the spaces between the windows on the east, west, and south walls, their shelves bowing slightly from the weight of leather-bound volumes and framed sepia-toned photographs of Sylvia's ancestors and the manor's earliest decades. She expected Joe would find more books and photos in the attic as he searched the accumulated possessions of four generations of Bergstroms for more furniture to restore.

The remnants of the previous night's fire lay in the stone fireplace that dominated the south wall. To the left of the mantel hung the Castle Wall quilt her sister Claudia and sister-in-law Agnes had pieced as a memorial to Sylvia's first husband, James; to the right were nine display rods arranged three by three. From seven of the rods hung sections of the Winding Ways quilt Sylvia had made for her friends using fabrics that represented each woman's unique qualities. The mosaic of overlapping circles and intertwining curves, the careful balance of dark and light hues, the unexpected harmony of the disparate fabrics and colors created a wondrous design of many winding paths meeting, intersecting, parting, offering the illusion that the separate sections formed a single quilt. The illusion was broken by the missing sections in the lower right corner and the left middle side — Judy's portion and Summer's. When the two founding members returned to Elm Creek Manor, they would hang their nine-block sections in their proper places. Until then, the empty spaces served as a reminder that although they had left the beloved circle of quilters, they had not been forgotten.

Sarah's dog-eared copy of *What to Expect When You're Expecting* lay open on one of the two armchairs drawn up to the hearth. Other chairs and sofas formed a square in the center of the room, awaiting the return of the remaining Elm Creek Quilters, who for the most part had scattered at the end of the season and would not return until March. Sylvia wondered what her friends would think of the bundle of letters discovered in the antique desk. She wished she had Summer's historical insight, Gwen's wisdom, and even Diane's sarcastic cynicism to guide her, to balance Sarah's headstrong enthusiasm. The Elm Creek Quilters' varied opinions rarely failed to help Sylvia gain clarity as she pondered a mystery.

The mystery of the letters was far from the most uncertain or the most troubling of those her ancestors had left behind as their legacy. Foremost among the unanswered questions of her life were the truth of her heritage — which until a few years ago she had never had reason to doubt — and the fate of one runaway slave.

Her first name was Joanna, and if she had any other, Sylvia did not know it. She knew nothing about Joanna except for the precious few details recorded in the handwritten memoir of her great-grandfather's sister,

Gerda Bergstrom.

In January of 1859, Joanna had sought refuge at Elm Creek Farm, a fugitive slave lost in the night, driven from her intended route north by a fierce snowstorm. Her destination was the neighboring farm, but when she spotted the signal quilt hanging on the Bergstroms' clothesline, she assumed she had reached a safe haven. Little did she know that Anneke Bergstrom had copied an abolitionist neighbor's pattern, unaware that the design carried a secret message to travelers along the Underground Railroad.

Unexpectedly thrust into the clandestine world of runaways and stationmasters, the Bergstroms sheltered Joanna — injured, exhausted, and pregnant — throughout the winter. They concealed her from roving slave hunters, all too aware that their own lives and freedom hung precariously in jeopardy until Joanna gave birth and she and the baby were strong enough to continue north. Fearing for her family's safety, Anneke betrayed their secret, and Joanna was captured and thrown back into slavery. The slave hunters did not know about Joanna's son, whom she had been forced to leave behind in the Bergstroms' care.

For a long time after Joanna's recapture, an anguished Gerda tried to find her. She wrote to Joanna's master, Josiah Chester, but he did not respond even before the Civil War disrupted mail service. Undaunted, she pursued other leads without any success. Gerda eventually abandoned the search, believing that Joanna must have died before she could make another escape attempt, before emancipation would have enabled her to travel freely. Surely if she had lived, she would have returned to Elm Creek Farm after the war to be reunited with her son — who, in his mother's absence, was raised as a Bergstrom.

Joanna was light-skinned, and the father of her son was her white master, so the Bergstroms' unsuspecting neighbors had been easily fooled. Or perhaps willing to be fooled. Anneke Bergstrom, the woman Sylvia had always known as her great-grandmother, had given birth to her first child within weeks of Joanna. Anneke claimed the boys were twins and found a sympathetic doctor to create false birth certificates confirming the deception.

For reasons of her own, Gerda had been unwilling to reveal within the pages of her memoir which of the "twin" boys was Anneke's and which was Joanna's, which of the boys was Sylvia's grandfather and which was her adopted great-uncle.

In her heart of hearts, Sylvia knew that the question of her identity as a Bergstrom did not depend upon whether her grandfather was Anneke's child or Joanna's. An adopted child was as much a part of a family as a child born into it. She would always consider Hans and Anneke her great-grandparents, nothing would ever change that, and yet —

It was difficult to contemplate that the woman who might have been her great-grandmother had been so cruelly separated from her child, that she had grieved, suffered, died — all without knowing the fate of her son. Even if Joanna was not her biological ancestor, Sylvia found it unbearable to imagine her last years.

But not knowing what had become of her was even worse.

Sylvia settled into the tall leather chair behind the broad oak desk that had belonged to her father, pulled out the second drawer, and withdrew a small bundle wrapped in soft ivory flannel. She hesitated before removing the protective cloth. So many times she had returned to Gerda's memoir hoping to discover an overlooked clue, but no matter how often she puzzled over cryptic phrases or asides that could be potent with meaning if only she understood the historical references, she never stumbled upon the answers she longed to find.

Sylvia had found the journal in an old steamer trunk in the attic, wrapped in a Log Cabin quilt with alternating dark and light rectangles encircling a black center square. This was the quilt made famous in Bergstrom family lore, the quilt that had supposedly served as a signal assuring runaway slaves that they had found a station on the Underground Railroad. That detail turned out not to be true; Gerda had made the Log Cabin quilt in memory of Joanna during the long years of waiting and praying for her return. The other two quilts in the trunk, a scrappy strip quilt and a Birds in the Air crib quilt, had been the real signals; the first was Anneke's creation, the second, the work of Gerda and Joanna, made in haste after the first signal was compromised. A fourth quilt that had joined these three was now in protective storage in an unused room of the manor: another, larger Birds in the Air quilt, dilapidated, worn with time and hard use, made hundreds of miles away but unmistakably linked to the quilts made on Elm Creek Farm.

Though it had belonged to her family for generations, a quilt camper named Margaret Alden had given the quilt to Sylvia after

Gerda's journal helped them discover a possible connection to Sylvia's family estate. Known by the elder members of the family as both the "Elm Creek Quilt" and "the Runaway Quilt," its fragmented three layers were held together by quilting stitches depicting scenes from the Elm Creek Valley — the southern pass over the Appalachians, the original farmhouse that became the west wing of the manor, and several others, some Sylvia did not recognize. After Sylvia learned that Joanna's owner and Margaret Alden's great-grandfather were brothers, she concluded that Joanna herself had pieced the Runaway Quilt, concealing images of landmarks from her ill-fated journey so that one day she could return to Elm Creek Manor, to freedom and her son.

But of course she had no proof, only sketchy details connected by thin threads of faith. Even this did not answer the questions that had tormented Gerda until the end of her life: What had become of Joanna, and why had she not returned to the Elm Creek Valley?

Sylvia unwrapped the memoir and set the soft flannel aside. The slim volume's brown leather was worn and cracked with age, and though Sylvia opened the book carefully, the spine crackled from strain and sent up a whiff of old paper. Gerda's elegant script covered the unlined pages in fading ink, and here and there, she had written a chapter heading and date in larger letters. Gerda had begun her story in the spring of 1856, Sylvia noted as she turned the brittle pages, but Joanna had not entered the narrative until nearly two years later.

A piece of paper fell from the book and tumbled to the desk.

In a moment of panic, Sylvia thought Gerda's pages had come loose from the fragile binding. Just as suddenly, she realized that the thickness and color of this paper was different from that which Gerda had written upon, though it seemed no less delicate. Setting the memoir on top of the flannel, Sylvia took up the page by its corners and gingerly unfolded it, recognizing a handbill she had seen before, when she first read Gerda's story:

$20 REWARD!

For the capture and return of a Negro woman, runaway or stolen from me two days after Christmas. She is of medium height and build; she may attempt to pass as White or Free but you will know her by the fresh mark of a flatiron, which I made on her right cheek. She is an expert with the needle and may have in her possession a silver thimble and needle case, which belonged to my late Mother and which the Negress has stolen. The above reward of twenty dollars will be given upon return of the said Negress to me or my agents, and an additional ten dollars will be provided for the restoration of my stolen goods. Josiah Chester, Wentworth County, Virginia, December 29, 1858.

Twenty dollars for a person, ten for a needle case. Fighting her disgust, Sylvia scanned the handbill for pertinent details. Josiah Chester had wasted little time in seeing that his handbills were distributed as far north as central Pennsylvania; he obviously considered Joanna a valuable slave even if he had been unaware that she was carrying his child. Oddly, though, he never mentioned her name, or even her age, and to say that she was medium height and build was vague enough to be entirely unhelpful. He must have counted upon the scar to identify her — the scar he had made and spoke about almost indifferently, as if cruelly burning a woman's face did not burden his conscience. Josiah Chester's words said more about him than they did about the woman they were intended to describe.

Sylvia herself might be descended from that hateful man. Perhaps that was why she had not begun her own search for Joanna sooner.

For she knew she must pick up the thread of Gerda's thwarted search or, like her great-great aunt, she would be haunted by unanswered questions until the end of her days — Joanna's fate, her heritage, the astonishing letters discovered in the locked desk drawer.

The handbill provided a sketchy description, a date, and a possible location. The slave catchers who had taken Joanna from Elm Creek Farm had almost certainly returned her to the Chester plantation in Wentworth County, Virginia. Based upon Margaret Alden's story of the Runaway Quilt, Josiah Chester later sold Joanna to his brother, Margaret's great-grandfather. After that, Joanna's trail disappeared into history. She had been lost to Gerda and to her son forever.

Unless Sarah was correct — and Mrs. Lenore Harris's grandmother was the lost quilter Gerda had searched for but had never found.

Sylvia resolved to call her favorite historical researcher, Summer Sullivan, a founding Elm Creek Quilter and newly enrolled graduate student at the University of Chicago. If Sylvia were to have any hope of picking up the thread of Joanna's life, she must know the location of the Chesters' plantation. If anyone could track down that information using only the scant details in the old letters, Summer could. Sylvia would enlist the help of her favorite quilt historian too, longtime friend Grace Daniels, a curator at the De Young Museum in San Francisco. Together those two clever, resourceful women might help her discover what had become of Joanna's former masters. And if the Chester family's personal papers had survived the Civil War, perhaps they mentioned a certain slave woman, an incorrigible runaway worth keeping only because of her incomparable skill with a needle. Perhaps some diary or ledger or letter had recorded her fate.

Perhaps Sylvia and her friends would find the answers Gerda had been unable to discover.

CHAPTER ONE

1859
From Pennsylvania to Virginia

The first warning was the sound of the front door bursting open and slamming shut, and Hans's boots hitting the wooden floor as he ran. Upstairs, Joanna and Gerda exchanged a startled look over the bed where Joanna's son kicked and waved a chubby fist, surrounded by the layette they had sewn for him in preparation for the journey to Canada. Then Hans's voice rang out, terrible with warning: "There's trouble coming!"

"Go," Gerda barked, her thin, plain face hardening into a mask of fury and fear as she shoved Joanna toward the hidden alcove. Without thinking, Joanna scrambled through the rough entrance Hans had cut through the plaster and drew her legs up to her chest, pressing herself against the back wall. Gerda set the false door in place and dragged the treadle sewing machine in front of it. Just as the baying of dogs reached her ears, Joanna remembered her son, cooing and kicking on the quilt in plain sight. Faint with horror, she pressed a shaking hand against the plaster, barely visible in the dusty darkness.

"Bergstrom, open up!" came a muffled shout from downstairs, then a crash as the front door was forced open. There was a creaking of bedsprings, Gerda's footsteps quick on the floorboards. Surely Gerda had taken the baby with her. She would find another hiding place for him.

Joanna said a silent prayer, her eyes fixed on the thin crack of light outlining the false door. Somewhere downstairs, men shouted and Anneke screamed. Boots pounded, swift and heavy on the stairs. Dogs barked, frenzied from the hunt, closer and closer. The sewing machine scraped across the floor, plaster crumbled, and the false door fell away.

"We got ourselves a nigger, boys!"

Arms reached in, seized her, dragged her from the hidden alcove. Joanna fought and scratched and kicked as rough hands tore her clothes and tangled in her hair. Suddenly Gerda flew into sight like a terrible bird of prey, clawing at the men, screaming an unearthly howl of rage. Suddenly Joanna found herself free.

"Run, Joanna," Gerda screamed. One of the men lashed out with his fist and struck Gerda across the face. Her eyes rolled back and she crumpled to the floor.

Joanna ran for the door, but the other man caught hold of her skirt and yanked her off her feet. "You're done runnin', girl," he snarled close to her ear, his breath reeking from tobacco. She struggled, but his grip tightened on her upper arm. His companion seized her other arm and together they wrestled her from the room and down the stairs, kicking and fighting. Through tears and blood, she glimpsed Hans sprawled motionless on the floor, his wife Anneke on her knees, reaching for him, weeping. Two other white men stood nearby. One of them nudged Hans with his muddy boot, but he did not respond. Frantic, Joanna looked around for her son, but before she could catch sight of him, the men dragged her from the house and into the yard, where they flung her to the ground, muddy and cool from a recent spring rain.

Four horses stood at the hitching post. Numb, her ears ringing, Joanna staggered to her feet and tried to run, but the larger of the two men caught up with her in two strides. "Fetch a rope," he barked. The other man took a long coil of rope, bound Joanna's wrists, and lashed the other end to the pommel of his saddle.

The sharp fibers cut into her skin. "Please," she said, an involuntary moan. "Please."

The second man slapped her hard across the mouth. "Hush up." He nodded to his companion. "Let's head out. I want to clear the pass before sundown."

Joanna tasted blood and dirt. Desperately she strained against the rope, but the knots held fast. The men mounted their horses. Frantically Joanna tore at the ropes with her teeth, but the man dug his heels into the horse's side and she was yanked into a stumbling run. She threw one last look at the farmhouse and glimpsed Gerda in the doorway, clutching her side, her face gray with pain and despair. Then the horse broke into a trot and Joanna tore her gaze away as they splashed across the creek and climbed the opposite bank. Soon the dark wood closed around them, and the farmhouse disappeared, as completely as if it had never existed.

Her captors did not have her son. She clenched her teeth against sobs. Had he been left behind intentionally? Those other two men — had they come for him? Would they take her baby somewhere else, sell him somewhere else?

For miles she half ran, half stumbled after the horses, blinded by tears, dizzy with grief. They had been so close to freedom. The false papers, the horse and carriage Hans had promised her — they would have carried her and her son to Canada. But now all was lost.

Where was her son?

Hours passed in a blur of pain. She lost sensation in her hands, a bitter mercy. Her wrists were scraped raw until the rope that bound them became soaked with blood. She lost a shoe, one of the good, sturdy shoes Gerda had given her, fit to walk miles in. They could have seen her all the way to Canada and freedom, but instead, instead one was lost and one would take her back to Virginia, back to that plantation, to certain punishment, to the lash —

Her stomach rebelled and she was sick. Ahead of her, one of the men cursed and the other laughed.

"That's a right ugly scar on her face, ain't it, Peter," the shorter man remarked to the other, who grunted a reply. "Say, girl, how'd you get that? Horse kick you?"

"That's a burn," Peter said. "Didn't you

read the handbill, Isaac? Mr. Chester did it with a flatiron."

When the shorter man nodded and said no more, Joanna understood. He couldn't read. She could. Gerda had taught her. All those winter months trapped indoors, hiding, waiting for the baby, for spring — she had put the time to good use. But it was dangerous for a slave to possess such forbidden knowledge — dangerous, and maybe fatal. If Marse Chester discovered she could read, he might kill her for it, but maybe, maybe he would never find out. The slave catchers had to sleep sometime. She could get free, disappear into the night —

The horse quickened its pace and nearly pulled her off her feet.

Reeling, Joanna fought to stay conscious. The men wouldn't pause if she fell; they would drag her behind the horses if they had to. As long as she made it back to Greenfields alive, they would get their money. Broken or sound, as long as she lived, it made no difference to them.

She had to get away.

Every step sent shooting pains up her right leg; her lifeless arms strained as if they would be torn from their sockets. She longed to let her mind drift free of her body, but she dared not — she had to remember the way back. Her eyes darted, seizing upon landmarks, noting forks in the road. She made a verse of them and repeated it to herself, a song set to the pace of the horses' hooves, adding new lines as they passed significant features. Her memory could not fail her. She had to find the way back.

The farther south they traveled, the longer her return journey would be. Each mile put her son in greater jeopardy. It might already be too late. The other two men might already have sold him off into slavery so far south that Joanna might never find him.

The miles and hours passed in a blur of pain. Landmarks became more difficult to distinguish from the endless similarity of rocky road, forested glen, and burbling creek. When the sun lay low on the horizon, Peter allowed them to stop and set up camp where a stream crossed a clearing. Joanna drank her fill, but Isaac did not untie her hands and they gave her nothing to eat. Her milk had soaked through the front of her dress, all but indistinguishable from the sweat and filth of the road. She pictured her son's sweet red mouth and felt her milk let down. She turned her back on the men and folded her arms across her chest, pressing hard against her nipples to staunch the flow.

The slave catchers had not mentioned her son, not once, not to goad her about her loss, not even to speculate about the price he would fetch when the other two men sold him into slavery. Maybe they did not know about the baby she had left behind.

Days passed. Sometimes the shorter man, Isaac, tied her hands and feet and made her ride flung over his horse; other days he bound only her hands and made her walk behind. It was Peter's choice, and Joanna never knew what he would choose until he said it. As much as walking exhausted her, she bitterly hated riding, for the horse carried her more swiftly away from her son.

One hazy morning as the sun beat down, raising spectral waves over the hard-packed dirt road, as the horse shook flies from its mane and Joanna rode with her cheek against its sweaty shoulder, half dozing, light-headed from the heat and from hunger, she was startled fully awake by the sound of gunfire.

"Fireworks," Peter remarked, jerking his head to the east and patting the horse's neck to steady it. Joanna craned her neck and spied a yellow farmhouse in the middle of a wheat field, a puff of white smoke rising into the sky behind it.

"Happy Independence Day, Peter," said Isaac.

"Same to you."

"Say, Peter," Isaac said, "why don't we stop in town and do a little celebrating? Chester don't know we got his girl. He ain't expecting us, so he won't know if we bide our time."

"I'd rather get rid of her and get our pay."

"A few hours here or there won't matter none. Come on, Peter, it's unpatriotic not to pause and reflect on Independence Day. It's been a long ride and I'm parched for a real drink."

Peter eyed him skeptically, but then allowed a slow smile. "Well, I daresay if you're buying, I could use a drink myself."

"Let's drink to our country and to the health of that pretty little thing who turned in this here wench," said Isaac. "Such sweet lips ripe for kissing, and best of all, she don't speak a word of English."

As the two men laughed, Joanna went cold and numb. Anneke. They could mean no one else. Anneke had betrayed her.

The road took them past a few more farms, and then they came to the town, a few rows of houses and stores tucked into the fork of a river. Joanna automatically added the town to her list of landmarks, but she had been able to observe very little of the landscape during the miles she had lain on her stomach across the horse, and there were great gaping silences in her song. In her darkest moments she despaired of filling them, but then she remembered the feel of her son's curly head in the crook of her arm, remembered his sweet baby scent as she held him, and remembered how she had made her way north once without knowing the way. Landmarks would help guide her, but she did not have to rely on them alone.

Peter and Isaac took the horses to a livery stable on the western edge of town and paid to have them watered and fed. They left Joanna lying bound hand and foot in the straw on the floor of Isaac's horse's stall and went off in search of a tavern. Fearful of the horse's hooves, Joanna dug in her heels and pushed herself to the far corner, where she managed to sit up and take stock of her surroundings. Dim sunlight filtered in through the open stable door, and the sweet, pungent smell of manure lingered in the air. From somewhere unseen came shouts of celebration and the popping of fireworks; a fly buzzed, and the horse's ear twitched.

With the stall door firmly latched, no one passing through the stable would see her or suspect she was there. The stable master knew, of course, because he had seen the men bring her in and had charged Peter extra for her. But the stall door hid her from view, and until Peter and Isaac returned, she could work on the ropes unobserved.

Her mouth was dry; her stomach rumbled. She longed for a dipperful of cold water. She glanced around for a stone, a tool, anything, and spied a bent nail protruding from the wall a few feet away. Inching toward it, she flinched as Isaac's horse stomped a hoof and whickered nervously. "You just settle down now," she said in what she hoped was a soothing tone. She pushed herself up onto her knees and strained to reach the nail. Back and forth she scraped the ropes against the nail, over and over again, until her arms ached and her back was drenched with sweat, until at last some of the fibers broke and the knots loosened.

Furiously, she sawed away on the ropes until they fell away. Heart pounding, ears straining for the sound of approaching footsteps, she tore into the ropes binding her feet. How long had the men been away? One hour? Two? They could return at any moment. Should she steal Isaac's horse? She would make better time on horseback, but she was not a good rider and the theft would draw the stablehands' attention. Better to slip away quietly and stay out of sight.

When her shaking hands failed to loosen the knots, she strained against the ropes, wrenching them up her calves and exposing the buttons on her remaining shoe. Quickly she undid the fastenings and yanked off the shoe — and the ropes went slack around her ankles. She kicked herself free, took a steadying breath, and rose shakily to her feet. Her head spun; she clung to the wall until her vision cleared. Isaac's horse whinnied and tossed its head. Joanna crept around him and cautiously peered over the stall door. A white man in work clothes passed outside the entrance to the stable, but he did not glance her way. Her eyes fixed on the sun-drenched stableyard, Joanna reached over the stall door and lifted the latch.

The door swung open with a creak.

She slipped out of the stall, closed the door behind her, and silently stole toward the open doorway. She heard men approaching before they appeared; she ducked behind the door until the men passed and their voices faded.

She longed for the cover of night.

She took a deep breath, murmured a

desperate prayer, and cautiously peered around the door. Three men stood in the stableyard, resting casually against the fence and watching holiday revelers pass. No one looked her way. She took one step into the yard, and then two, silent, careful steps along the side of the stable, her gaze locked on the workers. When she reached the corner, she peered around it but saw no one. Everyone must be in the town, distracted by fireworks and speeches. Ahead of her stretched a broad cornfield cut by a road, the pale green shoots knee-high; beyond it a hill sloped toward a thick cluster of trees.

She took one last look around and broke into a run.

She raced across the cornfield, stumbling in the furrows, bare feet sinking into the soil, ears straining for the shouts of alarm that would surely come at any moment. Her breath came in raw gasps, tearing from her lungs. The sun shone fiercely, turning the road into a bright glaring line, impossibly far away.

She heard the wagon before it emerged from the trees. She flung herself to the ground, knowing the green shoots would hardly conceal her. Exposed, she held perfectly still, digging her hands into the moist earth as if to fix herself in place. The sounds of jingling harness and clomping hooves grew louder, passed, faded, until only the hum of insects and the distant popping of fireworks remained.

For minutes Joanna could not move except to tremble.

She dragged herself to her feet and sprinted for the road. Her filthy skirt clung to her legs, threatening to trip her up. Panting, she yanked it out of the way and dashed across the road, dirt and pebbles hot and sharp against her bare feet. Another acre of corn, and then she reached the grassy slope. She flung herself down the hill, half running, half falling, the trees ahead of her cool and dark and beckoning. Branches scratched at her hands and face as she broke a path into their shade. She pushed through the underbrush until she could not see the cornfield, until the fireworks fell silent behind her. Only then did she sink to the ground at the base of an oak, gasping for breath, limbs shaking, a cramp stabbing her side. "Praise Jesus," she sobbed between gasps, but she knew she was far from safe.

She plunged ahead on the trail, straining her ears for the sound of pursuit. All she heard was birdsong, and her own jagged breathing, and the blood pounding in her ears. The woods were cool and shaded, a blessed relief, but her mouth was dry, her stomach hollow. It took all her strength to stay upright and moving.

After a time, the woods thinned ahead of her and she slowed her pace, reluctant to cross an open meadow. All too soon the trail ended at the edge of a wheat field, the pale green shoots rustling in an intermittent wind. About a quarter mile ahead, she spotted the back of a tidy white farmhouse with a wraparound porch. A barn and two smaller outbuildings stood several yards away, and beside the barn she spotted an iron pump with a trough. Horses milled in a nearby corral, and the wind carried to her the lowing of a cow and the clucking of chickens. On the sunny, southeastern corner of the house, a large kitchen garden thrived, and a few paces away, two quilts hung on a clothesline strung up between two trees. Joanna recognized the patterns, a Rose of Sharon and an Economy Patch, neither of which were the secret designs that indicated she had reached a station on the Underground Railroad. For all she knew, those patchwork symbols carried meaning only in the Elm Creek Valley. When she had journeyed north months before, no other stations had used a quilt to tell a weary runaway that she had found sanctuary. Each family had made themselves known in a unique manner that she was told only as she departed the station before. Now the order and nature of those symbols were so jumbled in her memory that she had no hope of sorting them out. Even if she could, Peter had chosen a different route south than the one Joanna had followed north, and she did not know how to find her way back to the Underground Railroad. She wasn't even sure where she was, how close to the Pennsylvania border or how far.

There were no slave quarters here that she could see, but that was no guarantee that the folk were abolitionists. It was a small farm, and perhaps they could not afford any slaves. Light-headed, wavering, Joanna watched from the woods, but she detected no sign of any people, no movement except the horses grazing and the quilts swinging back and forth in the breeze. It was late afternoon, the sun still high in the summer sky, and she knew she ought to press on and wait until nightfall to approach a dwelling. But she also knew she might not come upon another source of water before she fainted from exhaustion.

She waited as long as she could bear, her gaze returning again and again to the pump.

Then, praying that this family too had gone into town to enjoy the Independence Day celebration, she crossed the wheat field and approached the back of the house, ready to flee at the first sign of danger.

When she reached the pump, she worked the handle with shaking hands until water gushed from the spout. She cupped her hands beneath the clear, cold water and drank her fill, pausing only to pump the handle and start the flow again, the iron handle creaking like a song of joy. When her thirst was quenched, she pumped more water to wash her feet and face, laughter bubbling up like the water from the hidden spring. Refreshed, almost gleeful, she wiped her eyes with the back of her hand and shook the droplets from her fingertips —

And froze at the sight of a small boy standing on the whitewashed porch.

He stared at her, openmouthed and motionless.

For a long moment she stared back in silent panic. "Why, hello there, young man," she finally said, trying her best to sound like a woman of quality. "I hope it weren't no trouble that I refreshed myself at your pump."

The boy stared.

Joanna took a step backward, her bare toes

squishing in the mud. "I'll be on my way now."

"Pa," the boy shouted. Joanna stumbled backwards and broke into a run. "Ma! Come quick!"

She bolted around the corner of the house, straight into the solid form of a man. The impact knocked her to the ground, and as she scrambled backwards away from him, he recovered from his surprise and quickly caught up with her. He seized her around the arm and lifted her kicking and struggling to her feet as the boy continued his cry of alarm.

"Settle down, now," the man said as Joanna frantically tried to peel his fingers from her arm. "Settle down."

Behind him, the front door burst open and a small, fair-haired woman stepped out. "Mercy, Miles," she cried. "What on earth —"

"I found her, Ma." The boy had come running from the back of the house. "She was drinking at the pump."

"What's your name?" The man closed his beefy hands around her upper arms. His voice was gentler than his grip. "What are doing out here, all alone?"

With a sob, Joanna ceased struggling, knowing she would never break the man's iron hold. Her gaze fell upon the boy, who had dared draw a few paces closer and stared back at her with eager curiosity. She looked away.

"For heaven's sake, Miles, the poor thing's terrified." The fair-haired woman descended the steps and lifted her skirts over her shoe tops as she crossed the yard. A deep crease appeared between her brows as she inspected Joanna, her sure gaze taking in Joanna's bare feet, her soiled clothing, her matted hair, and the burn scar on her face.

"What's your name?" The man gave her a little shake, but such was his strength that it rattled her teeth. When she did not respond, he shook his head and said to his wife, "I've never seen her before. Do you think she's simple? Maybe she came in to town for the celebration and wandered off from her family."

"Don't be silly, dear," said the woman. "She's colored. She's on the run, no doubt, or why else would she drink from the pump instead of knocking on the door like decent folk?"

The man studied Joanna, perplexed. "This here's a white woman. Look at her skin. She's as white as me."

His wife laughed. "And you're as dark as an Indian yourself, in the summertime."

He shook his head, still disbelieving. "Maybe she's one of them Italians. They put their women out to work in the fields."

"Look at her hair. She's colored." The woman took Joanna's chin in hand and turned her face to examine her scar. "My, my. She's been ill-treated, this one. No wonder she ran off."

"Are you a runaway, girl?" the man asked.

"I am colored," Joanna said. "But I'm no runaway. My name is Constance Wright. I'm a freedwoman from the Elm Creek Valley in Pennsylvania. My husband is Abel Wright, a freeborn colored man who owns his own land."

"How'd you find yourself here in Maryland?" the man asked.

Maryland. A slave state.

Joanna took a deep breath. "Some slave catchers passed through our town. When they couldn't find the runaways they were after, they snatched me instead. I told them I was no runaway, but they didn't care. They say they can sell me anyway." She began to sob, real tears, for herself and her dream of freedom, slipping away. "My husband don't even know where I am. My two boys probably think I'm dead."

The husband and wife exchanged a look. After a moment, the man's grip relaxed.

"Come on," said the wife, taking Joanna's arm. "Let's get you inside and get some food into you. Johnny, go fill the bathtub."

"But it's not even Saturday," the boy protested.

"It's not for you. Go." She pointed to the doorway, and Johnny ran off. "My name is Ida Mary Dunbar. Mrs. Miles Dunbar." She beckoned for Joanna to follow her into the kitchen, where she pointed to a wooden bench next to a table and indicated that Joanna was to sit. "We'll have to get word to your husband so he can come fetch you."

"My husband can't leave the children, or the farm," said Joanna. "Thank you kindly, but I'll make my own way home."

"You can't go on foot, not all the way to Pennsylvania." Ida Mary took a loaf from the breadbox and cut two thick slices, which she buttered and placed on the table. "Tomorrow my husband can take you into town. You could send a telegram to your husband and ask him to wire money for train fare."

Joanna forced herself to take small, ladylike bites of the bread. "I don't want to put your man to any trouble."

"It's no trouble." Ida Mary set a tin cup of milk and a dish of sweet pickles on the table. "But you can't go like that. None of my dresses would fit you, but we can wash the one you're wearing." She glanced at Joanna's feet. "You'll need shoes. My neighbor's daughter is about your size. She might have an old pair that will do until you get home."

"Please don't tell anyone I'm here. If those slave catchers find out . . ."

Ida Mary's eyebrows rose. "All right, then. I'll tell her my feet are swelling from the heat and my own shoes pinch me. That's no lie."

Joanna thanked her and finished every crumb of the meal. She could not remember ever tasting anything so fine. Afterward, Ida Mary sent her son to the neighbor's for the shoes, and her husband went outside so Joanna could bathe in the copper tub. Hidden from the rest of the kitchen by a white bed sheet draped over a string, Joanna sank blissfully into the cool water, letting exhaustion and the heat of the day dissolve from her body. The water eased the soreness in her engorged breasts. Soon, unless she made it back to her son, she would have no milk for him.

Closing her eyes against tears, she let her head fall back against the rim of the tub, praying that her son was safe, that when she returned to Elm Creek Farm, she would find him there. Perhaps even now Gerda held him, snuggled within the soft folds of the Feathered Star quilt Joanna had sewn for him as she awaited his birth. Perhaps Gerda whispered stories of his brave mother, promising to find her and help them make their way to freedom in Canada. Gerda would not let her son forget her.

Her hopes restored, Joanna rested and planned, her stomach almost unpleasantly full. She would see her son again. When night fell, she would fill her pockets with food and set out on foot, and by the time the Dunbars woke, she would be far away.

On the other side of the draped sheet, Ida Mary had set out an old cotton shirt and trousers belonging to her husband, as well as some undergarments that Ida Mary must have worn when she was expecting little Johnny, because they surely would not fit her now. The soft cotton undergarments fit loosely but they would do. After Joanna rolled up the pant legs and sleeves and pinned the waist of Miles's borrowed clothes, she felt comfortable for the first time since she left Elm Creek Farm. Ida Mary had washed Joanna's garments while she bathed, and by the time Johnny returned with the shoes, her dress and underclothes were hanging on the line. Though the sun shone brightly, the air was thick and humid, and Joanna doubted they would dry by nightfall. She would have to don them nevertheless. It was sin enough that she planned to steal the Dunbars' food. She would not add the theft of clothing to her crime.

"Why don't you sit down?" called Ida Mary from the kitchen, and Joanna realized that she had been in constant motion since stepping out of the bath, moving from the kitchen to the front room and back, peering out each window, searching the road and the distant trees. "Even if those men track you down here, they can't take you against your will, not if you're a freedwoman."

Joanna forced herself to stop pacing. "That didn't matter to them back in Pennsylvania. I think it'll matter even less here."

"Perhaps they didn't believe you when you told them you weren't a runaway." Ida Mary gave a little laugh and tied on an apron. "I confess I'm having some difficulty believing you myself."

Joanna went cold, but she forced herself to appear calm. "If even good people like you and your husband doubt me, I can see why men of low character like them slave catchers wouldn't believe a word I say."

"You must admit that it does sound a bit

fanciful, two men willfully breaking the law by taking a free woman into slavery."

Joanna forced a smile and gave an acknowledging nod, and spared a glance out the window. She spotted Miles working in the barn, Johnny at his elbow, likely getting in the way rather than helping. She could not see the road from that window, but she dared not arouse Ida Mary's suspicions by resuming her anxious lookout. Joanna knew there was nothing fanciful about what she claimed Peter and Isaac had done. Slave catchers were lazy folk, and to them, one colored person was as good as another if they couldn't find the one they sought. A white person's word that a free Negro was really an escaped slave was all that the law required. No white lawman would believe a colored person's protests that the slave catchers had lied.

"Your speech is very much like that of the colored folk hereabouts," Ida Mary remarked. "I should have expected you to sound . . . different. More like a northerner."

"My mother was from Virginia. I expect I sound like her."

Ida Mary nodded as if her curiosity was satisfied. "Sometimes cooking three meals a day can be so tiresome," she said, laying a bunch of green-tufted carrots on the cutting board and taking a knife from a drawer.

"May I help?"

"How kind of you to offer. There's a way you can make the time pass more agreeably." Ida Mary nodded toward the front room. "My book of psalms is on the knickknack shelf in the parlor. Would you read to me while I work?"

"Of course." It was a test, but not a very good one. Everyone knew slaves were not permitted to learn to read, but even some white folks couldn't. Joanna went to the front room and found a small book bound in green leather. Thanks to Gerda and her lessons, Joanna would pass Ida Mary's test, but would she be safe even then? If Ida Mary was suspicious enough to test her, Joanna should not wait until nightfall to flee. She should set down the book and keep walking, right out the front door. But her clothes, still damp on the line, and the concealing darkness, and food for the journey — she could not leave without them. And the wheat field separating her from the woods — Miles Dunbar would spot her as she crossed it, and he could easily overtake her even if she ran as she had never run before.

She had no choice but to wait until the

family slept to make her escape.

She returned to the kitchen, book in hand. "Which psalm would you care to hear?"

"The thirty-second," Ida Mary replied, watching her carefully.

Joanna nodded, found the page, and read aloud, trying to sound like a northerner rather than a slave out of Virginia. The prayer, full of longing, stirred up memories of prayer meetings at Greenfields, sitting on the dirt floor of a slave cabin and raising her voice in a song of worship, a plea for deliverance. And the Lord had heard her. After so many years of suffering, the Lord had opened the door for Joanna, but Anneke had closed it.

Joanna read the final verse with tears in her eyes. She blinked them away and looked up from the book to find Ida Mary regarding her. "It's my favorite, too," Ida Mary said. "I can see you're a good Christian woman. You needn't fear that any low slave catcher is going to keep you from your husband and children. They'll have to get through my Miles, and there aren't many men foolhardy enough to take him on."

"You're very kind," said Joanna, praying that she would not have to put Ida Mary's staunch promise to the test.

Before long, Miles and Johnny washed up

and came in for supper. After helping Ida Mary set out fried chicken, succotash, fresh baked bread, and pickled cucumbers, she hesitated before accepting the seat Ida Mary offered her on the bench across the table from Johnny. She had never sat at a table for a meal with any white folks but the Bergstroms. Smiling to hide her discomfort, she took her place and complimented Ida Mary on the meal.

"It's our own Independence Day celebration." Ida Mary filled their cups with lemonade, set down the pitcher, and took her seat at the foot of the table. "My husband is too industrious to take a day of rest except on the Sabbath. Since we couldn't go into town, we'll have our picnic —" Suddenly she fell silent, frowning.

At the same moment, Joanna heard the distant baying of dogs. Her stomach lurched and she bolted upright. "I got to go now."

Miles rose and went to the window. Over his shoulder Joanna saw Peter and Isaac emerging from the woods on horseback, accompanied by two other men on foot. One was pulled along by three leashed bloodhounds. The dogs led the men straight across the wheat field to the pump where Joanna had drank and washed the mud from her hands and feet. Isaac pointed somewhere out of sight, and Joanna knew he had seen her dress on the clothesline.

Her head spun. She gripped the edge of the table to keep from falling.

"Now, don't you fret," Ida Mary said briskly. "We'll get this sorted out. You won't come to any harm."

"Are those the men who took you?" asked Miles.

Unable to speak, Joanna nodded. She sank down heavily on the bench, her thoughts churning. What now? If she ran out the front door, she would be spotted even if the men stayed out back, and the dogs would be upon her before she could reach the distant trees. She was trapped.

Someone pounded on the back door. "Open up, Dunbar," a man called. "We don't want trouble."

"You stay put," Miles ordered Joanna. He opened the back door off the kitchen but kept his hand firmly on the latch, barring entrance to the two men who stood on the porch. The bloodhounds yelped and slavered at their feet, knowing their quarry was near.

Miles's frame nearly filled the doorway, forcing the two men to crane their necks to peer into the house. The man holding the dogs nudged the other as his gaze came to rest on Joanna.

"Wilson. Boyle," Miles's deep voice boomed. "What brings you fellows out our way?"

"These two men say their slave's run off, and Boyle's hounds led us here." Wilson indicated Joanna with a jerk of his head. "From the look of things, I reckon they earned themselves some nice, juicy bones."

"This unfortunate woman is no runaway," said Ida Mary, standing between Joanna and the men. "Her name is Constance Wright. She's a free woman from Pennsylvania, abducted by these unscrupulous men when they could not find their rightful quarry."

Wilson removed his hat. "Begging your pardon, ma'am, but they tell a different story."

"That there's her dress hung out to dry," bellowed Isaac from the yard. "Bring her out or we'll come in and get her!"

Miles stood a head taller than the largest of the other men, and a single skeptical look was enough to make Wilson and Boyle shift uncomfortably on the doorstep. "Look, Dunbar, they swear she's a runaway," Boyle said apologetically, yanking hard on the dogs' leashes to keep them from bolting into the house. "We won't let them set foot in your home if you say so, but you should hear them out."

"We don't care to listen to liars and scoundrels," said Ida Mary.

Joanna's heart pounded and her palms were slick with sweat. Her thoughts darted, desperate to find an escape, but came to a crashing halt at the sight of Peter at the doorway. "Take a look at this," he said, reaching past Wilson and Boyle to thrust a crumpled sheet of paper at Miles.

A glimpse was enough. Joanna recognized the handbill Josiah Chester had printed up after her escape, the one describing her unmistakable scar. She had seen the handbill before, at Elm Creek Farm. Gerda Bergstrom had torn down one that had been posted outside a shop in town.

Miles studied the paper before holding it out to his wife. As she read it, she grew very still. She drew herself up, mouth pursed, and with a flick of her wrist, she beckoned the men inside. "Take her."

Joanna went cold. "Please, ma'am —"

"Be quiet, Constance, or whatever your name is," Ida Mary snapped as Wilson and Peter entered the kitchen. "You lied to us. Freedwoman, indeed. You're nothing but a runaway and a liar."

"Ma?" Wide-eyed, Johnny clambered off his bench as the two men circled the table.

Joanna darted into the front room, but before she reached the door, Peter seized her around the waist and brought her to the floor, his weight crushing the air out of her. He stank of liquor. She gasped for breath as he and Wilson pulled her to her feet. They wrestled her out the front door and around the back of the house, where Isaac waited with the rope. Kicking, clawing, Joanna fought to free herself, but the men held on, cursing her, and all too soon her hands were bound and the other end of the rope was lashed to Isaac's saddle. She threw one desperate, pleading look to the Dunbars, who stood at the back door watching the scene unfold.

"Don't forget her clothing," said Ida Mary.

Grumbling, Isaac snatched dress and shift down from the clothesline and stuffed them into his saddlebag. She saw money change hands as Peter paid Wilson and Boyle and thanked them for their services. Then the slave catchers mounted their horses and set off for the road south, pulling a stumbling Joanna along behind. A cry of anguish and pain escaped her throat; she tripped and fell, but the horses did not slow their pace. A wrenching pain shot through her knee as she struggled to regain her footing. She collapsed and cried out as the horses dragged her through the dirt and gravel. Swearing, Isaac reined in his horse. "Get up," he shouted, tugging sharply on the rope that bound Joanna's hands. "Get up now unless you want a beating."

Slowly, painfully, Joanna struggled to her feet, and Isaac chirruped to his horse. "We should hobble her," he said to Peter, his words slurring. "That's the only way to cure a runaway."

"That's for Mr. Chester to say, not us."

"She ain't worth it." Isaac shook his head, swaying slightly in the saddle. "No slave's worth all this trouble."

"Chester must think she is. His wife favors her sewing."

The men fell silent as they made their way south. It was nearly twilight before they made camp near the bank of a rushing river. If only she had not given in to her thirst and allowed the Dunbars' pump to draw her out of hiding. She could be free, right now, and miles closer to the Elm Creek Valley and her son. What did it matter now if she lived or died, if she died of thirst on the way to Greenfields or was beaten to death after her arrival? She would never have another chance like the one she had just let slip through her grasp.

It might be better to close her eyes forever

right there on that riverbank, never take another step south, never take another beating. Her son was beyond her reach; she could do nothing to protect him. She was as good as dead to him already. Why live another day as a slave?

Too exhausted for tears, she pulled off the secondhand shoes, which would surely never find their way back to Ida Mary's neighbor now. She washed her feet in the river, slowly and deliberately. In all the years she had lived at Greenfields, Josiah Chester had never hobbled a slave by cutting the tendon joining heel to ankle, not out of kindness but out of concern that the maiming would lower the slaves' value should he have to sell them. But no slave had ever fended him off with the sewing scissors or threatened to tell his wife about his nighttime visits to the slave quarter. No slave had ever fought back, or drawn his blood and then run off. He might hobble Joanna as a lesson to the other slaves. If the wound didn't putrefy and kill her, it would at least make certain that she never ran again.

Behind her came the sound of boots scuffling in the dirt. "Get out of those man's clothes," Isaac ordered. "It ain't proper."

He threw her clothes at her back; they struck her across the shoulders and fell to the ground. Joanna reached behind to pick them up, drawing her feet out of the rushing water.

"Go on, then." Isaac nudged her with the toe of his boot.

Slowly Joanna unbuttoned the borrowed shirt, slipped her arms from the sleeves, and folded it, and set on the ground beside her. The dress was still slightly damp from washing. Despite all it had been through, it was still beautiful. Anneke had cut and fit the pieces, and she had added the lace trim with her own hand. How could the same woman who created such a lovely gift have betrayed her?

"Turn around." When Joanna did not move, Isaac raised his voice. "I said, turn around. Stand up while you're at it."

She knew it would do no good to argue. Concealing the pins in her palm, she unfastened the trousers, let them fall to her ankles, and stepped out of them. Though the summer night was balmy, she shivered as she turned to face the men, knowing that pregnancy had left its telltale signs upon her body. The pins pricked her palm, a small reassurance that she was not defenseless.

Peter stared. "Were you a wet nurse on the Chester plantation?"

"No, sir," said Joanna, trembling. It was

no use to pretend she had been. The youngest of Mistress Chester's children was four years old, and the wet nurse had been sold away long ago.

"Don't she have to have a baby before . . ." Isaac gestured. "Before all that?"

Peter nodded, grim. "Do you have a child waiting for you back at Greenfields, wench?"

Joanna shook her head.

He frowned, and Joanna knew he was counting the months between her escape and her recapture. Not that it mattered when she had given birth, or who the father of her child was. A child born to a slave was a slave.

Unbidden, Joanna dressed herself, pulling the soft cotton shift over her head, slipping the dress over it. Her heart lifted. They had not known about her boy. The other men had not sold him off into slavery someplace far away, and she refused to believe Anneke would. Her son surely was safe and sound on Elm Creek Farm.

"Her child is Josiah Chester's property," Peter said. "If he finds out that we left it behind —"

"He don't ever have to know," said Isaac.

The men fixed Joanna with twin glares. "You can't tell him, either," ordered Peter. "You know that's the only way to keep your baby safe."

"My baby already safe," she retorted. "He on his way to Canada. He set out with an abolitionist lady two days before you caught me. You'll never find him."

As Peter raised his hand to strike her, Joanna darted out of reach. "I might be inclined to forget what I know if I was treated more kindly."

Peter slowly lowered his hand. "Is that so."

Joanna knew she was unlikely to get anything more from the men in payment for her silence. "As far as Marse Chester ever know, I never had no baby."

They crossed the Virginia border a few days later. Joanna would not have known except that Peter announced the news as the horses splashed across a stream. Only a few months before, sheltered by a kind Quaker family in a barn on the Pennsylvania border, she had vowed never to return to Virginia. Then she had dared dream that someday she would live as a free woman in Canada. Now the most she could hope for was that Josiah Chester would not hobble her, she would not be sold off so far south that escape to the free North would be impossible, and that her son would remain safe.

She would wait, and stay alive, and bide

her time, and when the time was right, she would run.

CHAPTER TWO

1859

Greenfields Plantation, Virginia

When they passed the Richardson plantation, Joanna knew they were no more than a half day's ride from their destination — Greenfields Plantation and Marse Chester. She felt a sting of phantom pain as if his knife already dug into the cord at the back of her ankle. If it were severed, she could not run.

Later they crossed Ashworth land, where Joanna had been born. Joanna's mother and four of her brothers and sisters lived there still, if they hadn't died or been sold off. Joanna scarcely remembered them. When she was around five years old, Josiah Chester's mother had come in her carriage to ask Marse Ashworth if he had a young girl to sell, for she needed someone to care for her grandson now that he had started walking. The master's wife promptly offered

Joanna, overcoming her husband's objections with a wordless look of reproachful defiance that Joanna did not understand, except that she had always known the mistress hated her.

Swooping her up in her arms, Joanna's mother fled back to their cabin and hid her beneath a mound of quilts, but the overseer came in swift pursuit. He seized Joanna by the wrist, dragged her outside, and hefted her into the carriage across from her new mistress. When she shrieked for her mother, the gray-haired white lady in the fine dress slapped her and told her to hush, and as the coachman chirruped to the horses, she instructed Joanna in her new duties. She must tend the baby and keep him safe from harm, rock his cradle at night, and change his diapers. She must keep him clean, keep him from crying, and let the younger Mrs. Chester rest.

Joanna did her best, but she was too young for the task. Mason was a good baby as babies went, but all babies cried, and all soiled their clothes. Joanna could barely lift the chubby ten-month-old and she struggled to hold him still when changing his diapers. Her forearms soon became bruised from his strong kicks, and she ran herself ragged keeping him from breaking her mistress's precious trinkets or tumbling from the veranda. She was expected to stay up all night rocking his cradle, but sometimes weariness overcame her and she nodded off, awaking with a jolt when Mason wailed. Instead of picking up her son and soothing him, the mistress would snatch a willow whip from her beside table and beat Joanna on the neck and shoulders to teach her to stay awake.

"She's useless," the mistress complained to her mother-in-law one afternoon when an exhausted, starving Joanna could not run fast enough to prevent Mason from toddling happily into a mud puddle. "I'll thank you to allow me to choose my own servants next time."

Mother Chester's thin lips formed a hard line in her wrinkled face. "Mr. Ashworth assured me she's from excellent stock. Her mother is a strong field hand and she's already borne five children, and at no more than one-and-twenty. The girl only wants training, and she has six months to acquire it."

With a doubtful frown, the mistress lay her slender white hand upon her abdomen, and with that gesture Joanna understood the hints and half-finished conversations of the past few weeks. In six months another young master would join the family, and Joanna would find her duties multiplied. Her heart plummeted. Until that moment she had assumed that once Mason was out of diapers and sleeping through the night, she would be allowed to return home to her mother.

She dreaded the new baby's arrival and longed for her mother and siblings. She endured the sleepless nights and beatings, and she felt herself becoming thinner and weaker as Mason thrived and grew. His chubby arms were thicker around than hers, and once, as moonlight streamed in through the window and her little charge slumbered, her mind took hold of the notion that her skin and flesh and bone were disappearing into his, and as he continued to grow, one day there would be nothing left of her but an empty, worn, homespun dress, crumpled in a heap on the floor.

One afternoon she was straining to lift Mason into his chair when he suddenly lunged for a toy and slipped from her grasp. His head hit the chair with a sickening thud as he fell. For a heart-stopping moment he lay on the floor blinking up at her in surprise. Then he began to scream.

The mistress came running. With a gasp she snatched up her son, and once assured that his skull had not been split open, she handed the boy to her maid and seized Joanna by the shoulders. She shook her until Joanna's teeth rattled, screaming horrible, terrifying threats of what would become of her should Mason die. Joanna felt herself slipping into a faint, but she stayed conscious long enough to hear Mother Chester enter the room and declare, shocked and scandalized, "Caroline, you must control yourself."

The grip on her shoulders eased and Joanna fell to the floor, dazed and reeling.

The mistress prevailed upon Marse Chester to buy a suitable wet nurse to tend both newborn and elder brother. Until such a slave could be found, Mason, who was not injured, was entrusted to Honor, a half-blind elderly slave whose knowledge of herb lore had earned her a measure of grudging respect from whites and coloreds alike. Joanna understood that she was in deep disgrace for dropping the young master, but any hope that she might be sent home for her failure vanished when Mother Chester announced that Joanna would help Ruth, the cook, until she was old enough to be put to work in the tobacco fields.

Ruth's seven children had been sold off to Georgia traders years before, and Joanna quickly became the unwitting beneficiary of their absence. Upon her thin shoulders Ruth poured the love and attention she had been unable to offer her own sons and daughters. Perhaps somewhere far to the south, other bereft mothers did the same for Ruth's children.

No longer forced to stay awake all night, Joanna slept soundly curled up beside Ruth in a small room off the kitchen; it was no more than a walled-in lean-to, but it was more comfortable by far than the slave cabins. She filled out and grew stronger, thanks to Ruth's willingness to look the other way while Joanna stuffed her cheeks with the best of the table leavings before reluctantly scraping the rest into the slop bucket for the hogs.

"Watch me," Ruth admonished dozens of times a day as she cut up chickens and shelled peas, determined to teach Joanna everything she knew. As the months passed, Joanna gradually understood Ruth's urgency: Only if Joanna became essential to the household would she attain any measure of security from being sold south, to Georgia or Florida, where life was hell on earth for a slave. Ruth's status on the plantation had not protected her children, nor would it protect Joanna, her favorite, who had thus far proven to be a poor investment.

If anyone's position at Greenfields was secure, it was Ruth's. Joanna once overheard another slave say that Ruth hadn't been beaten since childhood, since coming into her own as mistress of the kitchen. A popular legend around the slave cabins contradicted that claim. The story said that shortly after Ruth's youngest son was sold to pay off Marse Chester's gambling debts, a pound of salt pork and a rope of sausages went missing between the smokehouse and the kitchen. Marse Chester didn't believe the theft could have occurred without Ruth's tacit approval, but when she insisted she knew nothing, he ordered the overseer to give her five lashes. After that, Ruth's cookery took a sudden turn for the worse: the soup was slightly too salty, the chicken a trifle underdone, the biscuits flat and stale. Marse Chester reprimanded her, but when he threatened another beating, she seemed to lose even more of her vaunted skill. On the eve of a grand party, it was said, the mistress begged her husband to make amends with their offended cook or the Chesters would be shamed before the finest families in Virginia. No one knew how Marse Chester had mollified Ruth, but her cooking suddenly returned to normal and from that day forward no one dared beat her or accuse her of dishonesty.

When Joanna asked her if the stories were true, Ruth was silent a moment before she said, "I fight my battles the only way I know how. You need to learn your own way."

When Joanna turned seven, Marse Chester decided she was old enough to join the other children in the fields, picking hornworms off the tobacco leaves. Ruth pleaded with him to reconsider and even begged the mistress to intercede, but the mistress had never forgiven Joanna for dropping Mason — and blamed the girl for provoking her own hysterical reaction, so unbecoming a lady. The mistress would just as soon have her mother-in-law's regrettable purchase out of her sight, so a place was found for Joanna in the slave cabins.

Ruth was ordered to take her to her new home. "Don't you fear," Ruth said, her eyes red-rimmed. "I'll get you back in the big house soon. Just wait till they see how I can't get by without your help."

Joanna missed Ruth, but in a way it was a relief to be out in the fields, away from the white family. The work was hard and hot with the sun beating down, but she didn't have to be so careful, so fearful of spilling a pan of beans or breaking a dish and drawing Marse Chester's ire. They sang as they worked, and sometimes a slave, granted leave to visit a spouse at Mr. Ashworth's plantation, would return with news of Joanna's mother and siblings. She didn't eat as well, of course, though sometimes Ruth was able to slip her the end of a loaf of bread and repeat in whispers her promise to find a way to convince the Chesters that Joanna's place was in the big house. Joanna believed her less with each repeating.

They were picking the tobacco plants for the third time that season when Ruth came running out to the fields. She seized Joanna by the shoulder, called to the overseer that she was wanted up at the big house, and urged Joanna into a trot. "Just do as she say and mind your tongue," Ruth instructed. "Watch old Mrs. Chester's hands and do what she do. I already know you got sharp eyes and nimble fingers. Can you tie a knot?" When Joanna nodded, she breathed, "Good girl. Good girl." Joanna had never seen her so agitated.

They stopped at the pump, where Ruth hurriedly washed Joanna's hands and face. Before Joanna knew it, she was standing in the fancy parlor before the two Mrs. Chesters, eyes downcast, wishing she were back in the hot, dusty tobacco rows, far from the white ladies' scrutiny.

"This here girl can sew," Ruth said, placing a hand on Joanna's shoulder, then quickly removing it as if she didn't want to seem too fond.

"I thought she was your kitchen maid," said the younger Mrs. Chester.

"She was, but when we all done cleaning up after supper, she help me with my mending."

Joanna held herself perfectly still, betraying nothing. She had never done anything of the sort.

The elder Mrs. Chester peered at her myopically. "Come here, girl." Obediently Joanna stepped forward. "Let me see your hands." Joanna held them out for inspection. "Remarkably clean, for a field hand."

"She wash up before she come in," said Ruth. "She know better than to soil your pretty fabrics."

The mistress gave an elegant, skeptical sniff and reached for a pair of silver scissors sitting on a table at her side. She snipped off a length from a spool of white thread, withdrew a slender silver needle from an intricately embossed case, and beckoned to Joanna. "Thread this needle and knot the end."

Joanna bobbed a nod and took needle and

thread, careful not to touch the mistress's smooth white hands with her own. She sensed Ruth watching over her shoulder, longing to instruct her but unable to speak and reveal her lie.

Joanna had seen women piece quilts and mend clothes in the slave cabins, so she knew more or less what to do, although she had never tried it herself. On her second attempt, she poked one end of the thread through the needle's eye, then stuck the needle between her teeth while she tied a small knot at the other end. She held the threaded needle out to the younger mistress, who recoiled in distaste. "She had that in her mouth," she said, incredulous. "I'm not going to touch her spittle."

Quickly Ruth stepped forward and took the threaded needle. "I'll wash it for you. She do it right next time."

As Ruth hastened away, the mistress turned to her mother-in-law to complain, but before she could speak, the elder woman said, "If you had given her a pincushion, she needn't have used her mouth. She'll do, Caroline."

"She smells."

"A bath will cure that. Let her stay with Ruth instead of returning to the slave quarter. You know very well that's what

Ruth desires, and if you don't want our friends to starve at your quilting party, you'll grant her this one favor."

Resigned, the mistress dismissed Joanna with a distracted wave of the hand. Joanna hurried back to the kitchen to tell Ruth, who cried out for joy and embraced her. But the promise of more food, easier work, and Ruth's happiness did not settle Joanna's mixed feelings. The mistress was as determined to find fault with her as Marse Chester's mother was to prove that she had been right to purchase Joanna. Joanna would rather work bent over in the hot sun than caught between those two women.

Two days later, carriages arrived bearing masters and mistresses from plantations throughout the county. The Ashworths came with their eldest daughter, who was to be married soon and for whom the party had been arranged. While the men talked and smoked, the women layered pieced and appliquéd tops in a long wooden frame on the veranda and finished the quilts for the bride's trousseau. Joanna was on her feet all day, threading needles, tying knots, snipping loose threads so the ladies needn't interrupt the rhythm of their work. Deftly, they soon covered the elegant tops in intricate patterns — bows, flowers, crosshatches, feathered plumes, and fans, all created with the finest, most delicate stitches Joanna had ever seen. The ladies chatted and gossiped and exchanged advice as they worked, forgetting or ignoring Joanna's presence except to beckon her to snip a thread on the underside of the quilt or to pass them a new, threaded needle. They spoke about the upcoming wedding, praised the advantageous match, speculated about the new household, and despaired of the difficulties the newlyweds would face in obtaining good, loyal, trustworthy servants. Times had changed, they sighed. Nowadays slaves were so lazy and dishonest it was hardly worth the trouble to feed and clothe them, especially since they took ill so often — or stayed abed shamming illness — and had to be supported into their old age when they could no longer work to earn their keep.

"It is our responsibility and our Christian duty," said the elder Mrs. Chester, bending over the quilt to inspect her work closely. "We are enslaved every bit as much as they are and we must resign ourselves to it."

The other ladies nodded and murmured their agreement.

Thanks in no small part to Joanna's hard work, the quilting party was a success. At the end of the day, twelve beautiful, soft, warm quilts were completed for the betrothed couple and packed away until they could adorn the new house being built for them on the northern acres of the Ashworth plantation.

Since Joanna had proven herself useful, the Chester ladies began summoning her whenever they had sewing of their own to complete. As she grew older, she worked in the kitchen less and in the ladies' sitting room more often. She learned to piece simple quilt blocks, to mend torn clothing, to hem a gown, and to assemble a shirt from pieces the mistress cut out. She knew as if by instinct how to cut the fabric so that it draped most becomingly, how to take apart and reassemble geometric shapes so that quilt pieces fell together in a new and delightful pattern. By the time she was fourteen, she could piece, appliqué, and quilt as beautifully as any of the ladies who had attended the quilting party, and she could design, cut, sew, and fit a dress beginning with nothing more than the mistress's description. Eventually almost all the household sewing fell to her, from coarse homespun clothes for the slaves to a fine summer suit for Marse Chester himself. She trembled as she took his measurements;

Marse Chester endured the imposition on his time good-naturedly, complimenting Joanna on her work while the mistress looked on sharply. He must have known he frightened her, for he spoke kindly while she fit the suit, adjusting the length of the trousers and the sleeves. "Mother did well to bring her to the household," he declared to his wife when the suit was finished, admiring himself in the mirror. "We're the best-dressed family in the county, and rightly so." The mistress, observing them over her needlepoint from a chair near the window, agreed, if only because she wouldn't dream of contradicting her husband in front of a slave.

A few months later, the mistress arranged to hire out Joanna to Mrs. Richardson, who had much admired Mrs. Chester's newest gown and requested Joanna's services, since her arthritis made fine sewing impossible. It was the first time Joanna had left the plantation since arriving as a young child, and she packed her sewing basket with mounting excitement. Marse Chester's trusted groom was instructed to deliver Joanna to the Richardson plantation and fetch her home in a week's time. But Joanna saw little of her new, temporary surroundings, for from the moment she arrived, she measured and cut and sewed, all too aware that she had only seven days to finish the task. By day she sewed, pausing only for scanty meals of coarse gruel and a bit of pork; at night she slept on a folded quilt on the floor near the cookstove. She set in the last lace panel two hours before Marse Chester's groom arrived with the wagon. Delighted with her lovely new gown, Mrs. Richardson paid him Joanna's wages and instructed him to thank Mrs. Chester for the gracious lending of her seamstress. To Joanna she gave a small bundle of leftover fabric, "For quilts, or whatever other use you may have for it." Joanna, who had never had even the smallest scrap to call her own, stammered out her thanks and offered to come back whenever Mrs. Richardson needed her and Mrs. Chester permitted.

On the ride home, Marse Chester's groom told her she was a lucky girl. A slave who brought in outside wages was even more valuable than one who worked only on the home plantation, especially with the master's gambling habits throwing the family into occasional precipitous debt. "If you can earn more for him than he could get selling you to the Georgia traders," the groom said, "then you in a very good spot."

Joanna nodded to show she understood,

but she knew she would only be allowed to earn outside wages at the mistress's discretion. The mistress was so proud of her finery that she would not be inclined to help other ladies acquire a wardrobe as varied and as pretty as her own.

"Sometimes, if you work hard and mind yourself, Marse Chester maybe let you keep some of your wages," the groom added. "You could buy something good to eat, something pretty to wear, maybe save it up and buy your freedom someday." Even as Joanna's thoughts seized upon that revelatory idea, the groom slowed the horses a trifle and gestured to a gang of slaves laboring in the tobacco rows in the distance. "This here's Ashworth land. See that pretty woman with the shawl? That's my wife. The little one next to her, that's your mama."

Joanna's heart leaped. She shaded her eyes with her hands and studied the distant figure, but she was too far away to see the woman's face clearly. "And my daddy?" she asked the groom eagerly. "Is my daddy out there, too?"

The groom regarded her incredulously. "Girl, your daddy's Marse Ashworth. Everybody know that." He chuckled and shook the reins, urging the horses to resume a faster pace.

■ ■ ■ ■

She was fifteen when Marse Chester began watching her from the doorway while she sewed. Sometimes he would ask her to fetch him something to eat from the kitchen and bring it to him in his study; other times he would merely eye her silently for a few moments and move on. She knew white people hated to see a slave sitting down, so when his gaze fell upon her, she made an effort to appear as busy and industrious as she could. He made her so nervous that she often had to pick out stitches after he left, and she dreaded the sound of his footsteps on the floorboards, knowing the distraction would make her fall behind schedule. She expected the two Mrs. Chesters to scrutinize her work, but why would a man take an interest in a slave's sewing? Maybe, she dared hope, he contemplated hiring her out to Mrs. Richardson or another mistress, and maybe if she did well, he would let her keep some of her wages. Maybe one day she would be able to buy her freedom, and her mothers' and siblings' too. Maybe they could reunite in the North, in Canada. Her brothers could grow tobacco, her mother and sisters could keep house, and she could earn wages taking in sewing. They need never fear beatings or Georgia traders, and no one would ever separate them again.

Her hopes died a few days later, when Marse Chester brushed the length of his body against hers as she stood in the kitchen, chopping carrots for soup. Ruth said nothing, not even after he left them alone in the kitchen, so although Joanna felt sickened and unsettled, she pretended it hadn't happened.

But that night a shadowed figure appeared in the doorway of the little room Joanna shared with Ruth. She held herself perfectly motionless and silent, feigning sleep, but Marse Chester groped beneath the quilts and seized her arm. Before she could cry out, she felt Ruth's strong arm encircle her waist, restraining her. "You want something to eat, suh?" Ruth said, her usually sure voice quavering. "I fetch it for you."

Marse Chester pulled on Joanna's arm until she gasped from pain. "Go back to sleep, Ruth."

"Suh, she's just a girl. I . . . I can take care of you."

"Ruth, if you know what's good for you, you'll hush up and go back to sleep."

Ruth said nothing more. Marse Chester hauled Joanna out of bed and propelled her, stumbling, out the kitchen door, past the smokehouse, to a grassy hollow some distance from the big house. She struggled, but he was much too strong. He held his hand over her mouth to muffle her cries of anguish and pain.

When he finished, he stood up, brushed the grass from his knees, tucked in the shirt she had sewn for him, and held out a hand to help her to her feet. She wrapped her arms around her waist and rolled over onto her side away from him. "Very well. Lie here alone, then," he muttered. She heard the grass rustle as he strode back toward the house, but soon the chirping of crickets drowned out the sound of his footfalls.

She tried to sit up, but her stomach rebelled. She vomited up everything she had eaten that day, until bile burned her throat, until she shook with dry heaves. Suddenly she felt strong hands on her shoulders. A scream strangled in her chest as someone wiped her face with a cool, damp cloth. "Hush, baby," Ruth murmured. "It's gonna be all right."

But it wouldn't. Joanna knew that. She would never be all right again.

When Marse Chester came for her again a few nights later, Joanna kicked him and thrashed and clung with both fists to the quilts so he could not drag her outside again. Before long he either decided she was not worth the effort or feared waking the mistress, for he stormed off, muttering curses.

The next night he was prepared for a struggle. He pinned her arms against her sides and hauled her out of bed before she had a chance. Outside he pushed her down into the same grassy hollow, and when she scrambled to her feet and tried to run, he seized her skirt and hauled her back. Again when he was through, he offered a hand to help her up; again she ignored him. Alone, she made her way to the pump and washed up before heading back to the small room off the kitchen where she knew Ruth waited anxiously. Brushing grass from her clothes and hair, she smoldered with resentment and rage — against Marse Chester, who deserved it, and unreasonably, unfairly, against Ruth. She knew Ruth couldn't have protected her from Marse Chester, couldn't have prevented what had happened — and yet, to her shame, she wished the stout cook had risen from the bed, snatched up her cast iron fry pan, and split his skull with it. But it would have ended the same. Marse Chester would have had his way, and Ruth would have earned herself a beating that probably would have killed her. No slave who valued her own life attacked a white man, especially her own master.

He came for Joanna at least twice a week. She gave up fighting him, knowing it was useless, knowing she was only dragging things out and delaying her return to her own warm bed. After the fourth time, Ruth told her that she ought to see Honor for the herb that would keep her from getting Marse Chester's baby. "Don't waste any time," Ruth urged. "Honor's cures won't do nothing once the baby's in you."

"Maybe I should get a baby," said Joanna bitterly. "Once the mistress knows what her husband's doing —"

Ruth set down her spoon with a sharp whack. "You think she don't know? She know. You think you the first? As long as she can pretend he's a good, faithful, Christian husband, she overlook a lot of sins. But you wave a big belly in her face, you find yourself worked hard in the tobacco rows until your baby come, and unless it at least as dark as you, it'll be sold down south as soon as it's weaned."

What did she care what happened to the master's baby, a baby she never wanted? But she had seen how other mothers changed their minds once they held their unwanted babies in their arms, and she couldn't be sure the same wouldn't happen to her. Nor did she want to risk the mistress's ire or, worse yet, death in childbirth.

Later that day, she slipped away from the house and hurried down the hill to the rows of ramshackle cabins that made up the slave quarter. Hot and stifling in summer, frigid in winter, the cabins were bordered by small kitchen gardens Marse Chester allowed them to cultivate on their own time. Young children — mostly unclothed, although a few wore shirts too big for them, the hems past their knees — toddled in the dusty footpaths between the cabins and stared at her in frank curiosity as she passed.

Honor's cabin was the last in the row, nearest the stream and farthest from the privy. In front of her door lay offerings of dried apples, bundles of cloth, a chipped cup — gifts made in gratitude for cures bestowed or curses lifted. The woman herself — thin as a cornhusk and bent with age — was around back directing a pair of girls as they weeded her garden. Within a year, Joanna estimated, they would be in the tobacco rows picking hornworms.

Honor turned a pale, cloudy eye upon her as she rounded the cabin. "You that girl who sews?" she called. "That Joanna from the

Ashworth place?"

Joanna had been at Greenfields so long that the reminder she had come from somewhere else startled her. "I'm Joanna."

Honor beckoned her closer and grasped her forearm, looking her up and down as if trying to study her through thick cotton wadding. "Well, you're all right for now but you should have come seen me sooner."

They went inside, Joanna unsure whether she was guiding the old woman or she was being led. "You know why I come?" she asked uncertainly, glancing around the dim room. Bundles of roots and herbs hung above the fireplace, and in the corner was a crude table set with a chipped plate and a mortar and pestle.

"Course I know. All the pretty girls need old Honor sooner or later." Honor shuffled to the fireplace and felt among the dangling bundles for two plants Joanna did not recognize. She separated them on the table, placed a few sprigs of each in the pestle, and crushed them together. She tapped out the blended herbs onto a scrap of cloth, twisted it into a small pouch, and tied the ends shut. "Brew this into a tea. That shouldn't be hard for you, working in the kitchen as you do. Drink one cup every morning, and another cup at night if you don't feel your courses coming on at the right time. When you run out of leaves, come for more."

Joanna accepted the pouch and gave Honor a thin slab of pork and two biscuits Ruth had wrapped in cheesecloth. But instead of taking the gift, Honor closed her hands around Joanna's. A knowing smile spread across her face. "That's not all you wanted from me, is it?"

Joanna freed herself, closed Honor's grasping hands around the bundle of food, and backed away. Honor's smiled deepened, and she tapped her lips with a gnarled finger. "Of course I have what you need," she said in a voice scarcely above a whisper. "And you so close to the kitchen — it would be easy to do. But poisoning the marse — even if you only make him sick, they kill you for it."

"I know that," said Joanna. That's why she hadn't asked for the poison; that's why she had only brooded in vengeful silence. But somehow Honor had known. "How did you —"

"I hear him with you at night. Course you want him dead."

"Maybe they kill me for it, but at least he'd be gone too."

Honor cackled. "And after that, you think

his widow set us all free? No. We just get a new marse, maybe worse than the marse we got now. You only thinking of yourself, only thinking of today. Ruth the cook. They blame her, too, if Marse Chester die of poisoning. Maybe blame her *instead* of you. Ever think what they might do to her?"

"No," said Joanna. "I didn't think —"

"You right you didn't think." Honor tapped Joanna on the temple. "Use your head, girl. I know you got one. You ever want to be free, you got to think. And drink that tea." Honor turned away from her to put away the bundles of herbs. "When you run, and you *will* run, you won't get very far with a baby in your belly."

Without replying, Joanna stumbled from the cabin into daylight. Blinking from the sudden glare, clutching the pouch of herbs in her fist, she hurried back to the big house before the two Mrs. Chesters realized she was gone.

Less than a year later, there was only one Mrs. Chester to placate, to please, and to fit for dresses. In February Marse Chester's mother caught the grippe in her chest, wheezed putrid fluid for a week, and expired. She had left instructions in her will for her personal maid and loyal groom to be freed and paid the sum of twenty dollars apiece, but Marse Chester and his lawyer concluded that she must have been delirious from fever at the time she amended her will, so her heirs could legally ignore her request. When he realized he was not going to be freed, the groom ran off and hid in the woods, but since he came back the next morning, Marse Chester did not order a whipping. "He missed two meals and slept on the cold, hard ground last night," Joanna overheard him tell the mistress. "That's punishment enough."

The slaves were of two minds regarding the groom's return. Some congratulated him for avoiding punishment after annoying the master and said that he had done right to return after he had made his point. Others thought he should have stayed in the woods until the master agreed to abide by his mother's deathbed wishes. Joanna thought he never should have lit out for the woods in the first place. Wasn't he the Chesters' most trusted slave? Wasn't his word law in the stables? He should have hitched up a wagon, set out for the northern road as if sent on an errand, and kept going until he crossed over into freedom. "Think," she imagined Honor saying. "You ever want to be free, you got to think."

The younger Mrs. Chester — the only Mrs. Chester anymore — wasted no time ordering yards of black crepe and wool for her mourning garments. By the time she cast them off a year and a day later, her regular wardrobe was hopelessly out of style. Weeks of poring over fashion magazines and contemplating different designs followed, and Joanna spent nearly every waking moment with needle in hand, fitting bodices, adjusting hems, offering her opinions on everything from the quality of a cotton lawn to the most flattering color for the mistress's complexion. Often Joanna's duties included listening and nodding agreeably while the mistress chattered on about household matters or whatever county gossip had managed to find its way to the plantation. While the two Mrs. Chesters had not always gotten along, as the only two white ladies for miles, they had been forced into companionship. With her mother-in-law gone, the younger Mrs. Chester had no one to talk to save her husband, who was rarely available, or her children, who had little interest in her favorite topics of conversation, or her slaves, who alone could be relied upon to listen and flatter, if not understand as an equal might.

As the years passed, in a turnabout Joanna

never could have imagined, she replaced Marse Chester's mother as the mistress's favorite confidante. She learned more than she cared to know about Marse Chester's tragic weakness for cards and horse racing, about Mason's struggles in school contrasted with his younger brother's impressive aptitude, and about her daughter's growing beauty. To Joanna's amazement, though she did little but echo the mistress's own words back at her when obliged to reply, the mistress seemed to think of her as sympathetic to her concerns. If she had known what bitter retorts Joanna concealed behind an impassive face, she would have had her supposedly dutiful slave beaten day and night. If she had only known how often her husband dragged Joanna from her bed, how often Joanna choked down Honor's preventative remedies, Mrs. Chester would have sold her loyal confidante so far south Joanna would have been unable to even dream of freedom. But instead she gave Joanna all the leftover fabrics from her dressmaking to sew quilts for herself and for Ruth, and when she hired Joanna out to neighboring plantations, she allowed her to keep ten percent of her earnings. Then came an evening — Joanna's eyes straining in the fading light, her neck and shoulders aching from hours of tedious fine stitching — when Mrs. Chester told Joanna that she was writing her last will and testament.

"You ill, ma'am?" Joanna asked, as relieved for an excuse to look up from her work as she was surprised by the news.

"No, I'm perfectly sound, but none of us knows when the Lord will call us home." Mrs. Chester gazed out the window and sighed. "You have been a good and loyal servant, and you shall be rewarded. Upon my death, you will be manumitted."

Joanna reminded herself that a reply was in order. "Thank you, ma'am."

As if expecting a different reaction, Mrs. Chester turned away from the window to study her. "That means you will be granted your freedom."

"Yes, ma'am. Thank you, ma'am." Joanna busied herself with her sewing, fighting back a scowl of rage. If Mrs. Chester wanted to reward her so much, why not free her now? Promises in a last will and testament were next to useless unless her son and heir chose to honor them. What if by then Mason Chester had a wife who wanted pretty dresses? What if he weighed fulfilling his mother's last wishes against the money Mrs. Richardson and others would gladly offer for Joanna's services? And what if Mrs.

Chester passed on before her husband? Marse Chester would never let Joanna go.

Mrs. Chester should ask the family's loyal groom what deathbed promises were worth. She should ask her mother-in-law's favorite maid, who was married to a freeman but still a slave herself. They knew how it killed the soul to wait years and years for freedom that was ultimately denied. And now, even though she knew better, just like them, Joanna would wait and hope and end up disappointed.

Sick at heart, Joanna bent over her sewing and blinked back tears. No matter how firmly she tried to talk herself out of hoping for the impossible, she knew she would await the reading of Mrs. Chester's will as if her life depended upon it — for it did. Even though she had seen how blithely the family had ignored the wishes of the elder Mrs. Chester, even though she expected nothing, she could not shut off her hope. She knew she would be devastated when Marse Chester or Mason inevitably found a reasonable way to avoid freeing her. It would have been better if the mistress had never told Joanna her intentions.

Joanna was nineteen or perhaps already twenty when Marse Chester chose a new favorite, a girl around fifteen, a field hand. For nearly two months he strode off to the slave quarter at night instead of dragging Joanna from beneath the quilts she had pieced with the scraps of his wife's dresses. She sometimes heard him slip out the kitchen door, but he never once paused in the doorway of the small room off the kitchen Joanna and Ruth shared. Ruth had promised her his interest would fade; she herself had been his favorite once, but he had not sought her out that way in more than twenty years. Although Joanna felt sorry for the other girl, she was even more guiltily relieved that the master had found someone else and left her alone.

By that time she had become the plantation's laundress as well as its seamstress, and she rarely helped in the kitchen anymore. A new little girl assisted Ruth, a spindly little thing whose sharp elbows and knees poked Joanna in the back when they curled up under the quilts at night. Joanna tried not to think about how unlucky the little girl would be to grow into womanhood within Marse Chester's sight, and how one day he would tire of the field hand and seek out a new favorite. Sometimes, though, as the girl bolted down leavings from the family's dinner, Joanna's eyes met Ruth's, and she knew the cook shared her worries about the child's likely fate.

Joanna hoped and prayed to be far from the plantation when that day came. She had already saved up nearly five dollars of her own, which she carried day and night in a small pouch pinned within her clothing. She was going to buy her freedom and later that of her mother, whom she had not seen since she was last hired out to the Ashworth plantation nearly four years before. Though she had only been granted a few minutes in the slave quarter, Joanna had memorized every detail of her mother's features as she hungrily caught up on the news of her brothers and sisters. She would never forget her mother's face, no matter how much time or distance separated them in the years to come.

It was two days after Christmas, and the big house was quiet in the wake of the departure of the Chesters' holiday guests. Mrs. Chester had taken to her bed, exhausted from the effort of entertaining, and had sent down word that Joanna was to begin her new gown without delay. Joanna was in the sitting room, cutting the silk Marse Chester had given his wife for Christmas, when she heard a familiar footfall in the doorway. "Do you need to do that here?" Marse Chester asked, more curious than angry.

Joanna quickly set her work aside and rose, head bowed. "The mistress told me to, suh," she said. "This here silk is fine, and she don't want it to catch on nothing rough."

"Where is your mistress?"

"She's upstairs, suh. She indisposed."

"Is that right?" He studied her, and when he stepped into the room, she knew her time of respite was over. Her heart caught in her throat. Was the marse crazy? It was broad daylight, Ruth was not far away in the kitchen, and though the mistress was upstairs in bed, she was not sleeping.

"Please, suh," she said. It was unbearable that he should do this now, after two months of peace. As he lunged for her, she ducked out of reach and seized the shears. "You leave me be," she said, leveling the sharp points at him, "or I'll tell the mistress what you do at night. I'll tell her how you go to the slave cabins when you say you going riding."

With a snarl Marse Chester brought his fist down upon her hand, knocking the shears to the floor. As she reached for them, he grabbed her, put his hand over her mouth, and shoved her against the wall.

Struggling, Joanna groped for the scissors, for a lamp, for anything — and her hand closed around something hard and metallic. She struck at him with all her strength, scratching his face, drawing blood. He swore and drew back, wiping blood from his face, but as Joanna tried to scramble away, he snatched the flatiron from the fire and pressed it against her cheek. Searing pain, a terrible odor, a piercing shriek, and then all went dark.

When Joanna came to, she was lying alone on the sitting room floor, her skirt hiked up above her knees, her face throbbing with heat and pain, her loins echoing another pain. She called out weakly for Ruth, but Marse Chester must have sent the cook away or she would have already been at Joanna's side. Ruth would have heard everything, would have known how badly Joanna needed her.

Gingerly Joanna sat up, her limbs aching. Grasping the arm of a chair, she pulled herself to her feet, straightened her clothes, and took the mistress's warmest shawl from the back of a chair. Wrapping it around her own shoulders, she made her way to the empty kitchen, where a basket of apples sat on a table. She tucked two into her apron pocket and went outside, walking steadily but as if in a dream. She set out on the road she had often taken when hired out to neighboring plantations. She passed the young mistress riding her pony and returned the girl's wave; she passed slaves working around the stables and outbuildings, and heard distant singing, a mournful, familiar lament about crossing over Jordan. She walked on, and no one paid her more than a passing glance or asked her about her business. They were too far away to see the fresh angry burn on her cheek, too far away to see the emptiness in her eyes. From where they stood, there was nothing to distinguish that day from any other Joanna had been sent on an errand for Mrs. Chester.

She walked for hours and hours, until evening fell and she could not make her way along the road without stumbling. They would have discovered her missing by now. With a tremor of apprehension — the first stirring of emotion she had felt since setting forth — she hastened across some farmer's field and hid inside a haystack. The day had been unseasonably warm, but with the setting of the sun, all warmth had fled. Catching her breath, shivering in the thin December air, listening for pursuit, she suddenly realized that she still held the object she had used to strike Marse Chester.

It was the mistress's elegant silver needle case, hinged and lined with wine-colored velvet, with five sharp needles and an embossed silver thimble tucked inside. One corner was red with Marse Chester's blood, or perhaps her own.

She slept fitfully and woke the next morning, ravenous. She devoured the two apples and hid within the haystack until nightfall, dozing off and starting awake at the slightest noise. When darkness descended, she crept from the haystack and continued north, straining her ears for the distant baying of slave catchers' dogs.

On and on she had traveled, day after day.

With the help of her hard-earned five dollars and a stroke of good fortune that guided her into the Underground Railroad, she had made her way to Pennsylvania, a free state. By that time it was winter, and since she had not thought to bring Honor's pouch of herbs with her, the evidence of her master's crime had been growing in her belly.

The Bergstroms had sheltered her, had seen her safely delivered of her child, and had devised a scheme by which she and her son would travel in disguise to freedom in

Canada. With forged documents, new clothes, and a borrowed horse and carriage, at that very moment Joanna and her son should have been embarking upon new lives in freedom. Instead her son was lost to her, and she was back where she started, back at Greenfields, further from freedom than she had ever been.

Marse Chester's slaves paused in the tobacco rows and watched in silence as the two slave catchers and their quarry passed. The overseer let them take in the lesson of Joanna's failure before urging them back to work.

Isaac and Peter brought their horses to a halt in the stableyard. Marse Chester had heard them approach and waited on the front veranda of the big house. Joanna's heart gave a lurch. Even from that distance she recognized his proud, angry, self-satisfied stance. Mason stood at his side, tall and sturdy, glaring at her as if he still remembered the poor care she had given him as a child. He was wearing a shirt she had sewn months earlier; she knew the fit of the collar as her own work. She had no time to wonder why the mistress had not come outside to witness the spectacle, for Isaac yanked her down from the horse, propelled her across the dusty yard, and shoved her to the ground at the foot of the stairs to the veranda.

"We got your girl, Mr. Chester," said Peter. There were other words exchanged and fees paid, but Joanna's ears rang and she took no notice of them. Her mind was far away as the slave catchers rode off with their purses fattened and the overseer seized her by the shoulders and dragged her off to be beaten. As her back was torn open by the overseer's whip, her last thoughts before darkness claimed her was that at least her son was safe, at least he would never be beaten or sold down south or have his dreams of freedom crushed like a flower underfoot.

When she woke, she was lying on her stomach on a bed of worn quilts in a slave cabin, her back aching and throbbing with such searing pain that she gasped aloud. She heard bare feet scuff the dirt floor, and then a familiar voice spoke close to her ear: "Just lie still. You not fit to sit up yet."

It was all she could do to stay conscious; sitting up was out of the question. Joanna swallowed back her nausea and said, "How long I been here?"

"Ten days almost," replied Honor. Joanna felt an unexpected coolness as Honor placed wet tobacco leaves on the raw flesh of her back; the pain eased almost imperceptibly before welling up again. "I gave you something to dry up your milk so the swelling won't grieve you so much. Did you have a boy or a girl?"

Joanna licked her dry, cracked lips and tried to think. Honor cackled at her hesitation. "Oh, don't be afraid, girl. I saw the signs, but I've kept bigger secrets than yours from Marse Chester. It was a boy, wasn't it?"

Joanna managed a nod.

"What's his name?"

"Frederick." Joanna closed her eyes, longing to slip back into oblivion. "Frederick Douglass North." Her name in Canada was going to be Joanna North. She'd die before she let anyone call her or her son Chester. "I name him after a great man."

"I told you to drink my tea. Didn't I say you wouldn't get far with a baby in your belly? Maybe you'll listen to the old conjure woman from now on."

"But I did get far," Joanna murmured, too exhausted to defend herself for not remembering the pouch of herbs when she fled the plantation.

"Not far enough. Where's your boy now?"

Free in Canada, she prayed. "I don't

114

know. The slave catchers left him behind."

"Well, that's a mercy." Honor bustled around the fireside. Joanna drifted, half-awake, until Honor roused her by pressing a warm cup to her lips. She lifted her head slightly to drink, and when she dropped back upon the quilts, exhausted from even that small effort, she glimpsed Honor overturning the empty cup upon the hearth. "I don't see your boy here," she said, studying the patterns in the damp leaves. "I don't see him a slave at all. Long as you keep quiet so no one knows where to look for him, he should grow up free."

"Will I ever see him again?"

Honor hesitated and brushed the leaves into the fire. "Leaves don't tell everything."

An evasive reply that meant no. Joanna's throat constricted around a moan of anguish. She must not put too much into the old conjure woman's words. Honor didn't know everything.

"Mr. Linney want you in the fields as soon as you're able," said Honor, selecting herbs, working with mortar and pestle to make a concoction for some needy slave. "He left it up to me to say when that is, but two more weeks about as much as you get out of an overseer like him. Look like no more big house for you."

Joanna nodded to show she understood. She would have to find someone with room in their cabin for one disgraced runaway. It would be a relief to stay out of Marse Chester's easy reach. Ruth and the new little girl would continue to have the room off the kitchen to themselves. "Ruth come to see me since I been back?"

Honor hesitated, the mortar making a sharp clink against the pestle. "Ruth gone."

"She run away?" Joanna's heart clenched. "Marse Chester sold her?" It couldn't be. Not even a man as vile as Marse Chester could have blamed Ruth for Joanna's escape.

"Yellow fever sweep through here last February," said Honor. "I did all I could. Ten slaves got taken. Young Marse Billy, too. The mistress hasn't been right since."

"Ruth's dead?"

"You ask me, she was ready to go." The clinking of stone against stone told that Honor had resumed her work. "She blame herself for everything bad happen to you. Folks talk when they got the fever, and I hear everything. Ruth say that if she had just let you be in the fields, if she hadn't tried so hard to get you back in the big house, Marse Chester maybe never lay a hand on you. Course, we both know he don't mind walking to the slave cabins for what he want, but Ruth too heartsick to listen to sense."

Joanna's head swam. Ruth, dead and gone, wrongly blaming herself for Joanna's misfortune. "Her blood on Marse Chester's hands."

"So much blood on his hands already. He don't care about another drop more."

"I care."

"But you can't do nothing about it."

Joanna clenched her teeth and squeezed her eyes shut against tears of grief and rage. Maybe Honor was right, but someday, somehow that man would pay for all the evil he had done in life, if not in this world, then in the next. He had lost one son to the same sickness that had taken Ruth, but the scales were far from balanced.

Ten days later, Mr. Linney ordered Joanna to the tobacco fields. The effort of stooping and bending to pluck the leaves opened the newly forming scars on her back until her dress soaked through with blood and dried stiff beneath the hot sun. Back in the slave cabins that evening, she cried out as Honor peeled the fabric from her skin and applied a salve to her wounds. She sank into sleep immediately upon lying down, and in the morning she woke to find that Honor had washed her dress. It was still slightly damp when she put it on and reported to the fields, where the wounds once again tore open and bled. But each day they bled a little less as her skin knit together and hard ropes of scars formed. The tree of life, slaves called the pattern of branching scars. When only pinpricks of blood dotted her dress at the end of the day, Honor declared that she was healed. Joanna understood that to mean that she had to find another place to sleep at night and leave her pile of quilts to whoever next needed Honor's tending.

Two other slave women with three children between them agreed to take her in, but Joanna almost refused because the very sight of children wrenched her heart. But she told herself she would get used to constant reminders of her absent son and accepted their welcome. Whenever a baby's cries interrupted her sleep, she instinctively reached for Frederick and was jolted anew to discover him gone.

She would get used to it, she told herself.

But before that day came, a little girl came running to the tobacco fields with a summons to the big house. "Mistress want to see you," she prompted breathlessly when Joanna merely stared at her for a moment, her heart turning over. She had not seen

the mistress since before she ran off. Perhaps Mrs. Chester wanted Joanna to start a
new dress for her, though her year of
mourning for her youngest son would not
end until midwinter. More likely she needed
help with the household sewing and laundry, and her need outweighed her husband's
determination to see Joanna punished with
the hardest work on the plantation.

Full of trepidation, Joanna followed the
little girl to the parlor. She stopped short in
the doorway and dropped her head, not only
out of habit but also to conceal her shock.
For a moment, as she first glimpsed the
black-clad woman by the window, she
imagined she looked upon Marse Chester's
mother. The mistress's hair had gone gray
and grief had etched deep grooves around
the corners of her mouth and between her
brows. Draped in mourning black, she sat
gazing out the window with such resigna-
tion that Joanna knew she had not been
brought there to fashion a new gown.

She stood silently until the mistress addressed her. "So, you've returned to us."

"Yes, ma'am," said Joanna, although the
mistress's words suggested Joanna had
come of her own volition.

"You left us in quite a poor state, with the
slaves' winter clothes only half completed.

Most of them had to do without, thanks to your disobedience."

"Yes, ma'am. Sorry, ma'am." Let the mistress understand that as she pleased. Joanna *was* sorry if anyone had to suffer through the cold because of her, but she would never be sorry she had run away.

"You're sorry." Mrs. Chester turned away from the window, and as her gaze lit upon Joanna, she started. "Good heavens, Joanna. Your face!"

Instinctively Joanna raised her hand to cover her scarred cheek.

"My husband said you had injured yourself, but I had no idea . . ." Quickly Mrs. Chester composed herself. "From the look of your scar, I take it you burned yourself?"

How could she tell the mistress what had really happened? She kept her eyes on the braided rug, and Mrs. Chester took her silence as assent. "Very well. You'll keep that scar for the rest of your life as a reminder of your foolishness." The mistress's expression hardened to iron. "I trusted you, Joanna. You wanted for nothing. You had plenty to eat, money of your own, a bed in our own home — all a slave could aspire to. I never raised a hand to you, even when you were cheeky, even when you dropped Mason. And how did you repay me?"

Joanna did not respond. Could the mistress not remember the many times she had struck Joanna with the willow branch when baby Mason's wails interrupted his mother's sleep? Did she truly believe Joanna had forgotten?

The mistress's thin, spotted hands grasped the arms of her chair, tightening and releasing. Joanna remembered how smooth and pale those hands had once been. "I've certainly learned my lesson, although my husband says I'm still too forgiving for my own good. It was all I could do to persuade your master not to hobble you. He said a seamstress doesn't need to walk, but I insisted that a laundress does, hauling water and hanging up clothes and so forth. You were fortunate I was able to convince him to settle for a beating."

"Thank you, ma'am," said Joanna, barely audible.

"Your gratitude is too little, too late." The mistress clasped her hands in her lap and regarded Joanna sternly. "I cannot abide an untrustworthy servant, and neither can my husband. Now that the harvest is nearly over, you're going to be sold."

Joanna could scarcely breathe. "To the Ashworths, ma'am?"

"Heavens, no. The whole county knows

121

the trouble you've given us. No amount of fine stitchery could ever convince our neighbors to overlook your deceitful nature. As soon as we can arrange to transport you, you're going to the only master who will have you — my husband's brother in South Carolina."

CHAPTER THREE

1859
Charleston and Oak Grove Plantation, South Carolina

Joanna begged for one last visit to the Ashworth plantation to say good-bye to her mother and siblings, but although the mistress promised to ask her husband's permission, Joanna knew she would never see her mother again. Marse Chester would never agree to make extra work for his horses and groom just so a disgraced slave could exchange farewells, and he would never trust her to make the three-mile journey on foot alone.

When a band of Georgia traders came through a few days later, Marse Chester hired them to carry Joanna to his brother's plantation. Sick at heart, she closed her eyes as a white man barely older than herself locked iron bands around her ankles and forced her into a cage of solid iron bars on the back of a wagon. Another man ran a heavy chain through loops in the iron bands around her ankles and around those of the other six slaves already on board, binding them together. When the traders thrust her into their midst, the other slaves held out their hands to cushion her fall. As the horses started up, they begged her for food and water. She had no water, but the food she had hidden in her apron was quickly divided up and devoured. Joanna wondered how long it would be until she ate again.

As she watched the big house and the outbuildings disappear around a bend in the road, her head swam with despair. She might never be closer to her son than she was at that moment, and every thud of the horses' hooves took her farther from him.

The hot, dry days stretched into weeks. The Georgia traders rarely passed food through the bars and twice a day drove their prisoners out of the cage and forced them to jump up and down for exercise. Sometimes they would stop at a plantation to sell a slave, but more often than not, when money changed hands, a new slave was crowded into the cage, sometimes weeping, sometimes stoic, often numb with disbelief and despair.

A few of the slaves had come from far-off

Kentucky and had been with the Georgia traders for months. Most, like Joanna, were from Virginia. As they traveled ever southward, Joanna heard stories as heartbreaking as her own: A man who had pleaded with his master not to sell off his wife only to find himself sold instead. A husband, wife, and six-year-old daughter from Maryland sold off to cover a widow's debts. A mother whose three-year-old child had clung so tightly to her skirts as she was forced into the wagon that the traders had been obliged to buy him, too, only to sell him away from her at the next town. Two young brothers, about ten and twelve, who had no idea where they were from or why they had been parted from the only home they knew. A young field hand who had been afraid to join his brothers when they ran away upon hearing that they were to be sold; he would never know their fate, but it had to be better than his. "Should've gone with 'em," he said glumly, squinting up at the sun. "Even if they dead, they free, more free than me."

"I ran away once," said Joanna softly, and a few of her companions roused from their numb lethargy to peer curiously at her. "I made it all the way to Pennsylvania."

"That a free state," said an older man with gray in his hair. "How you end up here?"

Joanna dared not tell him about her son, the reason she had lingered too long, the reason she had been captured. "Bad luck," she said instead. "Bad luck and slave catchers."

After many, many days, when Joanna had lost hope that she would ever know any life but the endless jostling in the crowded, fetid cage, with sun and rain beating down and hunger constantly gnawing at her belly, the wagon rolled into a city larger than any they had yet passed through. She overheard the traders mention Ryan's Mart, and Chalmers and Queen Streets, but those places meant nothing to her. Throughout the long journey, the traders had never let any potential buyers inspect her, not even the most persistent. She assumed that was because she was not really for sale; Marse Chester's brother owned her now. Now she wondered if the traders had been saving her to earn a higher profit in the city. But what did it matter where she was sold? One master was as bad as any other. And yet the thought of auction made her tremble. If the older Marse Chester were cut from the same cloth as his brother, Joanna was likely to be as miserable with him in South Carolina as she had been in Virginia, but how much more terrifying it would be to be sold at auction to a complete stranger, about whom nothing would be familiar.

The sun was high overhead when the wagon came to a stop on a busy square — more buildings, more people and horses and carriages and wagons than Joanna had ever seen. Overwhelmed by the assault of heat and noise and unfamiliar odors, Joanna kept her eyes on the cobblestones, dizzy from hunger and thirst. One of the traders disappeared into a building lined with tall white columns, and after he returned, the slaves were herded indoors, into a brick building the younger trader called a barracoon. There the cuffs and chains that bound them were removed, but they were driven into cells, families and friends clutching one another so they would not be separated. Soon they were locked up again behind iron bars and stone walls, and at the sound of the door slamming shut, the youngest boy broke down in sobs. Wordlessly Joanna held him, rocked him in her lap, and stroked his head until he fell asleep.

The next morning the slaves woke to the sound of the Georgia traders approaching, their voices full of confidence and humor. "Guess they slept well," muttered the young field hand who constantly berated himself for not running off with his brothers.

"Why wouldn't they?" said the older, gray-haired man bitterly, pushing himself stiffly to his feet from where he had slept on the cold stone floor. "And us without a bite to eat. Serve them right if we faint dead away on the auction block and they can't get a dime for us."

"Who want a gang of sickly slaves?" murmured another.

Joanna stayed out of the talk, knowing it would do her no good to sham illness just to spite the Georgia traders. The little bit of injury she would do them was not worth ripping open her back again. But before the plotting could begin in earnest, the smell of their long-delayed rations cut through the filth of the prison, and the group pressed forward against the bars. Joanna made sure the two young brothers received their share of bread and cold salt pork before settling down with her own portion. It was the best meal they had been offered in weeks, and the barracoon was silent except for the sound of ravenous eating and the distant sounds of the city on the other side of the wall.

It seemed only minutes later that the traders took them from the cell and back outside. Blinking in the sunlight, Joanna shaded her eyes and regarded the busy street corner with only a small stirring of the nervousness that had struck her the previous day. The colored folk passing by were better dressed here than in the country; some carried the tools of their trades, some wore tin or brass badges engraved with names and numbers pinned to their jackets, and others walked with the confidence of free men. Perhaps they *were* free, Joanna thought, remembering her old plans to earn enough money with her needle to buy her freedom. Perhaps such dreams were possible here.

"Where they taking us?" she asked the older man with gray in his hair as they were led toward a building with a high arched entryway flanked by octagonal pillars.

"Do it matter?" he retorted as they passed through a large iron gate and entered the market proper, a single large room with a high ceiling. "This here's Charleston, and this here's the auction block."

"But . . ." Joanna glanced from the trader at the head of their group to the one following behind. Neither paid her any attention, and she did not want to call attention to herself, so she looked away despite her misgivings. "I ain't supposed to be here."

The older man snorted. "I ain't supposed to be here neither. I'm supposed to be in my cabin in Virginia, with my wife cooking me up something from her garden. But here I am, and here you are, and that's that."

Her heart pounding, Joanna expected to find a crowd of eager buyers waiting for them, but the market was empty except for one slave boy who sat on the ground cradling a drum. At a signal from one of the traders, the boy began to beat out a rhythm, and the slaves were ordered to dance and jump up and down.

Bewildered, Joanna complied, watching the Georgia traders through downcast eyes and shying away from the strange paddle they used instead of a whip on any slaves who did not exert themselves sufficiently. Less than an hour later, she and the other slaves were herded back into the barracoon, where rations were brought to them, more food than she had been given at one sitting since leaving Elm Creek Farm. While they devoured the meal, a doctor came around and inspected them, one by one. The doctor's cool gaze lingered on her scarred cheek, but he told the Georgia traders there was nothing he could do for an old burn. After the doctor left, the slaves were left to themselves until evening, when they were again taken to the market and made to exercise, and again brought back indoors for a full if plain meal.

Day after day they were put through the same routine. The wounds the cuffs and chains had left on Joanna's ankles healed, and her dress no longer hung slack. Looking upon the others as they danced and jumped to the sound of the beating drum, their muscles toned and skin gleaming, Joanna saw few lingering signs of their journey south with the Georgia traders, and she knew that potential buyers were not meant to know how roughly the slaves had been treated.

Then a day came when the Georgia traders inspected them carefully, ordered gray hairs plucked from some of the older slaves, oiled the young girls' hair, and gave the most raggedly dressed among them new clothes. Joanna's dress was washed and returned to her, and she submitted to having her hair neatly braided. Two of the Georgia traders studied her scar glumly, shook their heads, and agreed that nothing could be done.

Again they were led from the barracoon and through the high arched entryway of the market. Joanna's heart pounded, for this time she heard a babble of voices within. As they passed through the octagonal pillars, the older slave, his gray hair now dyed black, took her elbow and spoke close into her ear. "You a pretty, yellow thing except for that scar. You maybe got a chance. You look out for a nice-looking gentleman, one who got his wife with him. If he's gentle and kind to his wife, he might be good to his slaves. You be sure to smile nice and tell him you a good worker. If you cry and moan and say you don't want to go, well then he won't take you, and you end up with some surly fellow who beat you day and night."

Before Joanna could reply, the slaves were lined up near the wall and told to face the center of the room, where white men and a few white ladies had gathered. In the midst of the crowd, a man with a loud, booming voice invited the whites folks to inspect the slaves as thoroughly as they wished before the auction began. As the prospective buyers approached, Joanna glanced around frantically for the Georgia traders and spotted them climbing the stairs to a long platform on the far side of the room opposite the entrance. Engrossed in their preparations for the auctions, they had forgotten her.

All around her, white men — some dressed in fine suits, others in sturdier clothes, but all in their best whatever their station in life — examined likely purchases. Their ladies looked on from a discreet distance, apart from the fray, murmuring to one another, offering a deferential opinion to their husbands when asked. Joanna's companions were ordered to show their teeth, to walk back and forth, touch their toes, stoop and bend, while the whites studied them sharply for hidden defects. Some of the white men looked coolly indifferent as they inspected the merchandise; others looked stern or suspicious as if wary of being cheated. One portly middle-aged gentleman wearing a gold watch on a chain strolled past the line of slaves with his wife on his arm. Laugh lines creased the corners of the woman's eyes, and when she stumbled on a loose stone, her husband quickly steadied her and said something to make her smile warmly up at him.

Beside her, the man from Maryland drew himself up and stepped forward. "Look at me, sir," he called to the portly white planter. "Name's Elijah. I got a strong arms and a stronger back. You won't find any man here better than me, and that's the truth, sir. I pick tobacco nearly twenty years, since I was a boy, and I done a little smithy work too."

The portly planter had only glanced his way at this declaration, but at a word from his wife, he stopped and looked Elijah over.

"You've worked as a smith, you say?"

"Yes, sir. Little bit of carpentry too. This here's my wife, Sarah." Urgently he beckoned her forward; she bobbed a quick curtsy and gave the couple a trembling, apprehensive smile. "She's a fine cook and a laundress."

The planter shook his head regretfully. "We're only in need of a strong field hand or two."

"Sarah'll give you a full day's work in the fields good as most men," Elijah burst out before the planter could move on. He reached behind his wife and pulled their young daughter to the front. She seized her mother's hand and peered up at the planter fearfully. "This our girl, Molly," he said, placing his hands on her shoulders. "She's just a little thing now but she's strong. She already know how to hoe a garden and mind babies. She's a good girl, sir, and she don't eat much. Please, marse, sir."

Suddenly Joanna felt a sharp pinch on her arm as a thin white man with sunken cheeks tested the thickness of her muscles. "Thin, but strong," he remarked, opening her jaw with two calloused hands to inspect her teeth. "You have the manner of a house slave, but you seem strong enough for field work."

"I done both, sir," she said faintly when he let go of her face. Was he a kindly man, like the one Elijah so boldly addressed? How could she possibly know for sure so quickly? "I pick tobacco in Virginia."

"Ever work a rice field?"

"No, sir."

"I expect you could learn. What happened to your face?"

"I . . . I fell on a flatiron, sir."

"Is that so?" He peered at her scar. "Are you a laundress, then? Our old laundress took sick and died last spring. My wife would be pleased if I brought home a new one."

"Yes, sir, and a seamstress. I can sew anything from fine dresses and suits to slave clothes. I do quilting, both fine and plain."

"My wife likes to do her own quilting. If she had someone to do the plain sewing, she would have more time for it." The planter turned her around, studying her hips. "Do you have any children?"

Involuntarily Joanna glanced at the ten-year-old boy, who was being looked over by a man and woman dressed in somber black while his brother stood nearby, shifting his weight from foot to foot. She forced herself to look away. "No, sir."

Just then one of the Georgia traders hurried over. "I'm afraid this one's spoken for, sir," he said, his drawl smoothly apologetic.

"But the auction hasn't even begun," the thin man protested.

"Sorry, sir, but she belongs to Mr. Stephen Chester of Edisto Island. If you want her, you'll have to take it up with him."

A flash of annoyance crossed the other man's face. "Well, why the hell did you bring her out to the block if she isn't for sale?"

"Terribly sorry, sir." The trader seized Joanna's arm and propelled her back through the iron gate to the cobblestone street. "It's back to the barracoon for you, girl."

Trapped once more behind iron and stone, Joanna waited for news of the others, straining her ears for sounds from the auction block. Would any of them return or would they all be sold? She hoped that Elijah would persuade the portly planter to take his whole family, and she hoped the two young brothers would somehow stay together. Should she have tried harder to impress the thin white man? Would she have been better off with him than with Stephen Chester? She would never know.

Suddenly she had a terrible thought: The thin white man needed a seamstress and laundress, and the kindly planter needed only field hands. With Joanna unavailable for purchase, Elijah's family could have already been divided between the two white men.

Exhaustion overcame her and she fell asleep, stretched out on the cold stone floor. It was twilight when the sound of voices awakened her — the two Georgia traders, congratulating each other on the handsome profits won at the auction. Quickly Joanna sat up, eager to see if any unsold slaves had brought back news, but the traders were alone. They opened the barred door long enough to slip a tin plate of cornmeal porridge and a small tin cornboiler full of water inside, then left for a celebratory drink, locking the door behind them.

The traders' cheerful banter faded behind them as they left. As the darkness of the barracoon enveloped her, Joanna groped in the darkness for her plate and cup. Alone, she ate every last morsel, dreading what the next day might bring.

In the morning the traders brought her slapjacks, which she ate outside as they prepared the wagon for departure. Since they had brought her a second cup of water, she slipped the tin cornboiler they had left behind the previous day into her apron pocket, hoping the Georgia traders had forgotten it. She could not imagine caring so little for something so precious. It had an arched, fixed handle on the side to hold on to while drinking, and a second, thinner handle of curved wire so the cup could hang from a belt or a pack. The hinged, tight-fitting lid had a loop on the top so it could slide onto a spit held over a fire. The slave hunters that had brought her back to Green-fields Plantation had each carried larger versions made of copper, and Joanna had seen them use theirs for everything from drinking water to making coffee to boiling up cornmeal porridge. She had never owned anything so useful, not even the stolen embossed needle case and thimble, though they were made of more valuable metal.

She waited for the Georgia traders to notice their cornboiler was missing and to tear her clothes apart searching for it, but they took her from the barracoon, ran a chain through her manacles, and thrust her back into the wagon cage, all without mentioning it. It was not theirs, she realized. The cornboiler belonged to whoever ran the barracoon, and maybe, maybe, by the time they realized it had disappeared with their most recent prisoner, she would be far away.

Riding alone in the wagon cage, wondering what had become of her former companions, she found a strange reassurance in the cornboiler's weight and smoothness, the tight, secure seal of the hinged lid, as if ownership of something so useful and perfectly crafted provided its own protective magic, as if concealing a secret from the Georgia traders meant she had triumphed over them.

After a half day's journey through the marshy South Carolina low country, past rivers and plantations where slaves labored in fields over unfamiliar crops, the wagon boarded a ferry and crossed a river. Though the trip across the water was not long, the lurching motion unsettled Joanna, and she could not shake off the thought of the horses suddenly taking fright, toppling the wagon, and sending her to the bottom of the river still trapped within the iron cage. She breathed a prayer of thanksgiving when the ferry reached the opposite shore and the Georgia traders drove the wagon onto land, even though she knew she was on the wrong side of the water from everyone and everything she held most dear. The river imprisoned her more than chains and manacles, for she could not swim.

Eventually the wagon turned off the main

road and passed through an iron gate with six red brick pillars, above which hung a sign bearing the name Oak Grove. The name suited, for tall oak trees lined the drive up to the big house. Joanna had always heard that Stephen Chester was the more successful of the two brothers, and the grandness of the residence seemed to prove the stories true. The white weatherboard-clad house stood two and a half stories tall on a raised red brick foundation, with four gabled dormers and a wraparound porch. Tall red brick chimneys flanked the structure, surely indicating massive fireplaces within that slaves wore themselves out tending in winter, all to keep their white owners warm. She saw no sign of the slave quarter, but she surmised that rows of cabins lay at some distance from the big house beyond the towering oaks, out of sight and out of mind, too far away to offend.

The traders brought the wagon to a halt in a stableyard, where two young slave boys clad in shirts and frayed trousers raced out to greet them. A man followed at an easier pace, removing his hat — not, it seemed to Joanna, in deference, but merely to mop his brow. The traders ordered him to tend to their horses, and although he nodded and said, "Yessuh," something in his expression said that he would do so for the horses' sake, not their owners'.

As the traders headed to the big house, the man unhitched the horses and passed the reins to the two smaller boys, who led the horses to a watering trough. The man walked around the wagon as if inspecting it for necessary repairs, but Joanna felt his eyes upon her and she raised her head to glare defiantly back at him. His eyebrows rose and he let out a chuckle. "Oh, is that how it's gonna be?" he said. "I thought I'd water you while I water these horses, but now I don't know."

Joanna's mouth was parched, and the very thought of water made her dizzy. "I'd like some water," she said flatly, remembering to add, "please."

The man looked around, patting the pockets of his clothes. "Wouldn't you know, them Georgia traders didn't leave me the key. I can't get you to the trough."

Joanna withdrew the tin cornboiler from her apron pocket and wordlessly passed it through the bars. The man hesitated for only a moment before flashing a grin, taking the cup, and filling it with water from the horses' trough. Joanna drained the cornboiler in three gulps and handed it back to the man. He refilled it a second time, then quickly looked over his shoulder at the sound of the front door to the big house swinging open and shut. "Put that away before they take it from you," he advised, joining the boys at the trough and taking the horses' reins to lead them into the stable.

Joanna drank quickly, shook the few remaining drops into the matted straw at the bottom of the cage, and returned the cornboiler to the safety of her apron pocket before the Georgia traders returned. The man who had given her water looked on from the stable doorway as the traders pulled her from the cage and led her up the veranda stairs.

"Should've cleaned her up first," the younger trader muttered to his companion as they passed through the tall front doors and crossed the foyer.

"Don't matter," the older man replied. "She's already bought and paid for, or at least half paid for."

The men took Joanna into a small, walnut-paneled study where a brown-haired woman in spectacles sat writing at a secretary. A neatly attired colored man looked on from a respectful distance, hands clasped in front of him. "Missus Chester," he murmured when the white woman did not look up from her work. "They back. They brung her."

"Yes, I know, Augustus," the woman replied, but she finished another few lines before setting her pen aside and blotting the ink on the page. Resting her chin in her hand, she looked Joanna up and down speculatively, her gaze lingering on the ugly scar on Joanna's cheek. Joanna was surprised to see that her new mistress's face was unlined, her hair without a trace of gray, as if she were only a handful of years older than Joanna herself. She had expected this Mrs. Chester to be as old as the one she had left behind in Virginia.

"Well, she's here, although from the look of her she's had a rough journey." The woman's tone was brisk and her accent crisp, more like that of the Quakers who had sheltered Joanna in Pennsylvania than any plantation mistress she had ever known. "You did feed her once or twice along the way, I trust?"

Joanna felt a surge of angry pleasure. So the Georgia traders' efforts in Charleston had not fooled this woman, at least.

"Yes, ma'am," the senior trader replied, clutching his hat. "Begging your pardon, ma'am, but the other Mr. Chester paid us only half. He said to collect the other half from your husband upon delivery."

"My husband is away on business, so you'll have to be content to collect your fee from me." She gestured to Augustus, who promptly brought her a leather purse from a cabinet near the window, where heavy damask curtains barely stirred in the breeze. She paid the men, thanked them for their services, and told Augustus to show them to the kitchen for a bite to eat before they departed.

Only then did she address Joanna. "My sister-in-law writes that you have a fine hand with the needle but you're impertinent and untrustworthy." She sighed and spared a longing glance for her pen as if Joanna were a distasteful but necessary problem to solve before she could return to more appealing work. "Once again we rescue my brother-in-law from an ill-advised investment. The question remains, what are we to do with you?"

She regarded Joanna expectantly for so long that Joanna realized she was meant to provide an answer. "I don't know, ma'am."

This unexpectedly young Mrs. Chester raised her eyebrows. "That's a very silly answer. My husband's brother didn't send you to us because you're useless but to keep you from running off again. You'll sew for

144

us — although you'll make fewer fancy ball gowns than I suppose you're accustomed to — and you'll tend to the laundry. I suppose you should learn to pick and card cotton as well, since that is what brought my husband his fortune." She glanced up and smiled as Augustus returned with a steaming cup of tea. "I brook no insolence from my servants, so keep a cheerful disposition about you. You'll find that Oak Grove is much different from your former home, and you needn't entertain any foolish notions of running away. No one in our black family has ever deserted us. All of our servants are quite happy, aren't they, Augustus?"

"Yes, ma'am. Yes, we are," said Augustus promptly. Even after the mistress had turned back to Joanna, he did not flicker as much as an eyelid to suggest dissent. *You good,* Joanna thought. She had never learned to hide her feelings so well.

"The housekeeper will give you a new dress and apron. See that you take care of them. We issue our servants new clothes each Christmas, but I see no reason to make you wait" — the mistress's nose wrinkled in distaste — "given the circumstances. Of course you should not expect anything new until next year. You shall share living quarters with Leah and her daughters. The kitchen girl can show you the way. There's a stream not far from the cabins. Bathe yourself and burn those rags you're wearing before you settle in, lest you introduce vermin into the quarter. Come to me here first thing tomorrow morning and I will have work for you."

"Yes, ma'am," said Joanna, as her new mistress took her pen in hand and dismissed Joanna with a nod.

Augustus beckoned her to follow him from the study, out the back door, and to the kitchen building, separated from the big house by several yards. Inside, the heat and smells of roasting pork and stewing vegetables made her head swim. The heavyset cook, her ebony skin gleaming with perspiration from the stove fires, took one glance at her and passed her the end of a loaf of bread. Joanna finished the last crumb before the housekeeper arrived with her new clothes, but when she threw the cook a hopeful, pleading glance, Augustus gestured to the door and told her she would have to wait for the evening meal like everyone else.

Carrying her new dress and apron, she followed the kitchen girl down the hill and through the woods where four rows of cabins stood in a clearing between tall, moss-covered oaks. They were out of sight from the big house but not, Joanna discovered, from another, considerably smaller residence, which surely belonged to an overseer.

Leah was in the cotton fields, so the kitchen girl took Joanna to the cabin and pointed out the general direction of the stream. Joanna found it not ten yards through the thicket, and once assured she was alone, she sloughed off her old, dusty dress and waded into the water, scrubbing herself clean as best she could, missing the smooth cakes of soap Ruth boiled up at Greenfields, mixing the lye and tallow and ash twice a year, in spring and autumn.

Ruth.

Joanna inhaled sharply and ducked her head beneath the water, cooling her scar, which always seemed too warm to the touch. Eyes closed, she saw Ruth quartering a chicken, wiping her hands on her apron, squinting suspiciously as she examined sweet potatoes for mold. She heard Ruth snoring in the darkness of the little room off the kitchen, felt Ruth's strong arm around her waist. Ruth had tried to protect her, but now she was gone, and Joanna was in South Carolina, incomprehensibly far from freedom.

Joanna held her breath until she thought

her lungs would burst. Finally she rose, gasping, and reached for her old clothing, lying in a heap on the creek bank. She scrubbed the dress and wrung the water from it; it seemed stained but not worn through, but she would know its condition better after it dried. She had never owned two dresses and could not bear to burn this one, despite the mistress's orders. Mrs. Chester might never see Joanna in it if she wore it only on Sundays, when the colored folk were left to themselves in the slave cabins — unless here slaves worked the Sabbath, too. Until she knew the way of things, she must be careful.

She shook water from her limbs and hair and pulled the new dress over her head, feeling the familiar scratch of the rough cloth against the tree of life scars on her back. After tying on her apron, she rolled the damp, old dress around her tin cornboiler and tucked the bundle under her arm. She followed the sound of children's voices back to the slave quarter, where she found Leah's cabin still empty, the door closed. She pushed it open and stepped inside the single room with floor of swept earth. Two pallets lay beside the wall opposite the fireplace, spread neatly with string-pieced quilts — linens, linsey-woolseys, but mostly cottons.

The small, worn, mismatched fragments of one quilt had been stitched together into long vertical columns that reminded Joanna of the barracoon. She preferred the quilt on the other makeshift bed, where the scraps had been shaped into squares of varying sizes and sewn together in a riot of faded color, as if those same bars had exploded outward. She thought of the fancy quilts she had pieced at Greenfields and of the intricate Feathered Star she had sewn at Elm Creek Farm while awaiting Frederick's birth, quilts that required ample amounts of the same fabric. She wondered if she would ever have the means to create such a quilt for herself again, or if she would from that day forward sleep beneath quilts fashioned from the narrowest strips salvaged from clothes worn to rags.

She had no quilt to call her own anymore, neither fancy nor plain, and nothing to sew one with. Until she could gather needle and thread and build a store of scraps, she would have to hope that this Leah and her children would share. She glanced around for a place to hide her dress and cup and found herself suddenly immobile, unable to decide. This cabin was her home now, but not one inch of it was hers. She was rooted to the spot by the impossibility of finding a safe hiding place within it.

"Whatch doin' in here?" piped up a voice behind her.

With a start, Joanna spun around to find a young, bare-legged girl standing in the doorway. "I'm Joanna," she said. "Mistress told me I should stay with Leah."

"Leah's my mama." The girl peered up at her curiously. "I'm Lizzie. You talk funny. What happen to your face?"

"My old marse burn me with the flatiron. That's why I run away."

The girl's eyes widened. "They chop off your foot when they catch you?"

Joanna lifted her skirt enough to show her feet, scarred but whole. "No. They just beat me and send me here."

"No one ever run away from Oak Grove," Lizzie said. "Anyone try, and all the slaves get beat and don't have no ration drawing until the runaway come back."

"So for the loss of one slave Marse Chester beat the rest and let them starve to death?"

"He don't beat the babies," Lizzie amended. "Just everyone old enough to work. That's why when anyone even think about running off, the others talk him out of it or tell Aaron. He the driver. He almost as yellow as you." She eyed Joanna's bundle with interest. "What you got there?"

"Just an old dress I need to spread out to dry."

"Hang it on a bush by the creek," the girl advised, pivoting around one bare foot in the doorway. "Put it out of sight so no one take it. I got to go watch the babies. Dinner coming soon." And with that she darted off.

Alone, Joanna hesitated before concealing her tin cornboiler under a corner of the nearest quilt and hurrying back to the creek, where she draped her dress over a low branch of a shady tree. The creek was wide there and rocky, the current too swift to cross on foot. Joanna wondered how deep it ran, and if a woman on horseback could cross to the other side safely. She shook her head and headed back to the slave quarter. Better she should learn to swim than dream of a swift horse to carry her off. Hans Bergstrom had promised her a fine mare and a carriage; Gerda would have provided the false papers that would ensure her and Frederick safe passage to Canada. But she had no allies here.

From a distance, she heard the shrieks of children, and she instinctively quickened her pace. Following the shouts, she found the children gathering in the widest row between the cabins, pushing and shoving to reach two colored women in aprons and headscarves carrying a large black kettle. Through the push of thin limbs and dark bodies Joanna glimpsed a long wooden trough into which the two women emptied the kettle. The children immediately swarmed the trough to scoop up cornmeal mush with wooden plates or chipped tea cups or hollowed gourds or bare hands, and Joanna, after a moment of shock, hurried back to Leah's cabin for her own tin cornboiler.

But when she lifted the corner of the quilt, the cornboiler was gone.

Joanna flung back the quilt and patted it down in case the cup had rolled beneath its soft folds, but she found nothing. She was certain she had concealed it beneath the quilt of squares, but just to be sure, she checked beneath the stripy quilt, too. Nothing.

Her tin cornboiler was gone.

Taking quick, deep breaths to hold her anger in check, Joanna strode from the cabin and searched the throng of hungry children for Lizzie. "You give me back my cup," she ordered, seizing the girl's arm.

"What cup?" Lizzie tore herself free, balancing her wooden plate carefully so as not to spill a morsel of her supper. "I don't have no cup."

"I left it in your mama's cabin. Now it's gone."

"Well, I don't got it." Scowling, Lizzie backed away just as three girls who looked to be her age came to stand with her, unsmiling, their eyes fixed on Joanna. "Didn't I tell you to hide your things?"

The dress. Her hunger momentarily forgotten, Joanna raced back to the creek to find the low branch in the shade bare but for leaves and branches.

She stared at it for a long while, disbelieving, until gnawing pangs of hunger drove her back to the slave cabins. The two women had left, taking the kettle with them, and the wooden trough had been wiped clean of even the smallest grain of mush. Instinctively she ran a finger along the bottom of the trough and brought it to her lips, but only the fragrance of cornmeal and stewed greens lingered.

Joanna heard whispers and muffled laughter as she found a seat alone on the ground beneath a moss-veiled live oak. Exhausted, stomach growling, she sat in the shade with her back against the tree, watching as the children devoured their scanty meals and ran off to play under the watchful eyes of Lizzie and the other big girls. From a cabin doorway, an elderly man called out, "That food ain't for you, yellow girl. We eat when the field hands come in."

Faint from hunger and exhaustion, Joanna sat and waited for the day to end. The sun was setting when men and women finally trooped in wearily from the cotton fields. As their children ran to them, Joanna caught snatches of greetings and jokes, all in a bewildering, unfamiliar dialect she could scarcely understand. She nodded politely to other women casting her sidelong glances as they passed on their way to gather water and firewood. Heart sinking, she realized that they were preparing their own evening meals, using rations that must have been distributed perhaps days before her arrival. Her wait for the women to return with another full kettle had been in vain.

A woman was approaching her from across the dirt path, her jaw set so resolutely that Joanna knew she must be Lizzie's mother. Joanna absently smoothed her apron and feigned indifference as Leah halted only inches away, planted her hands on her hips, and glared down at her. "My girl Lizzie say you call her a thief."

Joanna blinked up at her, needing a moment to untangle her dialect. "I left my cup in the cabin and my dress by the creek like she told me to, and now they gone."

"My Lizzie didn't know nothing about no cup, and anybody could've seen your dress hanging out to dry. My girl don't want your old rags."

"*Someone* took my things."

"Not my Lizzie. You probably never find out who and never get 'em back." Turning away, Leah added in an undertone Joanna wasn't sure she was meant to overhear, "Stupid yellow girl. Might've helped you find your things, but not after you show up on your first day and call my daughter a thief. Like you know anything about her."

"If Lizzie didn't take my cup," Joanna called after Leah angrily, "then someone else went into your cabin while you in the fields and found it. How that make you feel, someone going through your quilts when you out working?"

Leah halted and turned back around, and for a moment it seemed that the focus of her anger had shifted. Then she frowned and shook her head. "Nothing of mine is missing, so it don't matter to me. Anyhow, no one but you ever saw this cup — if you ever had one. Bet you didn't." She strode off, calling back over her shoulder, "You can find somewhere else to sleep."

Joanna watched her go, ignoring the stares

and smirks of the few remaining onlookers. Twilight had fallen, and most of the hands had withdrawn to their own cabins — to rest, to eat, and to tend to their own chores, forced aside until the master's work was done. It was the same everywhere, on every plantation Joanna had ever known.

She quickly counted more than fifty men and women walking between the cabins, but she reckoned their real numbers to be at least three times that, including the children and house slaves and those who had already gone home. She saw now that clusters of men and women shared foodstuffs — flat-bread, carrots, sweet potatoes — and some-where someone was cooking meat. How had someone come by meat? Her mouth watered at the smell of it; she wished she had something to offer in trade. All her worldly possessions had been lost, and evicted from Leah's cabin, she had no ration to share. Her only hope was that tomorrow the cook would take pity on her and give her some-thing to eat when she reported to the big house in the morning. It would be a long, hard, miserable night until then.

"You can stay with us."

Joanna looked up to find a woman aged maybe not quite thirty years helping a bent-shouldered old woman down the path.

Joanna didn't think twice, didn't wait for the invitation to be snatched away. "Thank you," she said, scrambling to her feet. "I'm Joanna."

"I know. You the runaway." The woman smiled and beckoned Joanna to follow. "I'm Tavia. There's five of us in our place, six counting you — me, Auntie Bess here, and the children. It wasn't smart to pick a fight with Leah. She one of Aaron's favorites, one of the best pickers. She fast and can work all day without tiring. After she pick her quota, she fill her friends' bags, too — one boll for her, one for each of them."

"She usually help new folks, so they don't get a whipping." Auntie Bess offered Joanna a toothless grin as they made their slow progress down the row of cabins. "I don't expect she'll help you, not after what you said about Lizzie. That child from her real husband, not the man Marse Chester pick for her. She won't hear nothing bad about that girl."

"Lizzie's a good child," said Tavia, stopping near the end of the row and pushing open the door to a cabin. "I don't think she stole from you."

Joanna too was beginning to think she had accused Lizzie too quickly, anger and fatigue having overcome her better judgment. But what Leah had done was worse — humiliating Joanna in front of everyone, casting her out of the cabin as if the mistress's orders didn't matter. Maybe they didn't. The Georgia traders and Augustus had obeyed Mrs. Chester readily enough, but maybe, out of sight of the big house, the slaves made their own rules.

"I won't need Leah's help, at least not tomorrow," said Joanna defiantly as she followed Tavia and Auntie Bess into the cabin, where three children — a toddler, a girl almost grown, and a boy halfway between the two — played a game with cornhusk dolls on a bed in the corner. Joanna marveled upon discovering that it was a real bed, with four oak posts strung with taut rope supporting a double layer of rough, worn blankets. Two other, smaller beds lined the other walls, leaving a small space in the center of the earthen floor to stand.

"You won't need help?" Tavia regarded her with surprise. "You pick cotton before? I hear Marse Chester's brother grow tobacco."

"You're not the first of his slaves to come to us," said Auntie Bess, lowering herself onto the bed closest to the fireplace. "We get all his runaways and troublemakers. Aaron break them all."

She spoke matter-of-factly, but Joanna still felt a chill. She resolved to avoid Aaron's notice as much as possible. "The mistress told me to come to her tomorrow for my work. I sew and do laundry, mostly, though I work the tobacco fields some back in Virginia."

"Aren't you a lucky thing, having easy work in the big house," said the oldest girl, strong and broad-shouldered. Joanna guessed she had been working the fields for almost half her life.

"I don't know about that." Joanna thought of all the nights Marse Chester had dragged her from her bed. "Sometimes it's best to stay out of the white folks' sight."

"Ain't that the truth," said Auntie Bess. "I cook for them since I was younger than Pearl here, till I get too old to lift the stock-pot to the stove. Listen good, Joanna. The new mistress think herself a kindly, Christian woman, but she just as bad as the rest of them. Don't cross her."

"The new mistress?" echoed Joanna. Marse Chester's mother had lived in Virginia forever and had never been the mistress of Oak Grove. Maybe the plantation had come down through the wife's family, not Marse Chester's. "You mean Mrs. Chester's mother?"

"No. None of us ever seen her," said Tavia. "Marse Chester's first wife died of consumption two winters ago. She was a kindly woman — never beat a slave, always saw that we had enough to eat, tend us when we sick. She gone only six months when Marse Chester marry his children's teacher. She come here from a city up north."

Auntie Bess shook her head. "Lived all her life in a free state, but she took to slave owning as quick as if she born to it."

"And here we been thinking we got ourselves a new abolitionist mistress," said Pearl.

"Hush, Pearl," admonished Tavia, glancing at the door. "What if Aaron walk by and hear you?"

Pearl shrugged as if unafraid, but she sat down on the edge of the largest bed and clasped her hands tightly in her lap.

"The new mistress only four years older than Marse Chester's eldest girl, and Miss Evangeline hate her," said Auntie Bess. "She'd bite her tongue off before she'd call the new mistress Mama. Don't get caught between them two."

"Keep quiet and do as you told and you be all right," said Tavia, passing Joanna a small, flat sweetgrass basket holding a slab of hoecake and a piece of dried fish.

Joanna thanked them for the warning and devoured every bite of her meal, hoping that the next drawing day wasn't far off. When the mistress assigned Joanna to Leah's cabin, she hadn't given the household extra rations. It was little wonder that Leah had taken the first opportunity to send her away so that feeding her would be someone else's problem. Joanna hated to think of Tavia and the others spreading their scarce rations even thinner on her account.

The women's warning lingered in her thoughts as she picked the last crumbs from the bottom of the basket. She would never forget how, as a child, she had sought refuge in Ruth's kitchen when the tension between the two Mrs. Chesters from Virginia escalated, and how the younger mistress had disliked her on sight simply because she was her mother-in-law's purchase. If she did something to please one mistress, she earned the enmity of the other, but if she did nothing, she angered both and paid a double price.

Joanna never understood why some white ladies couldn't get along with one another. If they had their choice of companions, maybe they could afford to bicker and squabble with the women of their households, but plantations were so far apart that most white ladies rarely saw any others except members of their own family. Back in Virginia, the younger Mrs. Chester had spoken well of her mother-in-law only after her death. If white women were torn from their mothers and sisters in childhood, or lived with the daily threat of losing daughters to the Georgia traders, maybe then they'd learn to cherish their women kin while they remained among the living.

In the darkness, Tavia sorted out the sleeping arrangements, assigning two to a bed — herself and her son Paul in one, Auntie Bess and the youngest daughter in another, Pearl and Joanna in the largest. Joanna had not slept off the ground since Pennsylvania, and as Pearl offered her one of the rough blankets, she asked how they had come to have three beds. "My uncle Titus made them," Pearl told her, her voice growing faint as fatigue overcame her. "My mama's younger brother."

Joanna drifted off to sleep, heart pricked by envy. She thought she could have borne a thousand seasons picking cotton if she could have lived with her mother, if she could have known her uncles. That, she realized, was how the Chesters of Oak Grove kept their colored folk from running away.

The older Marse Chester knew what his brother never learned, perhaps because his own family life was so miserable. It was difficult to run away, but harder still to leave beloved relations behind, especially knowing they would bear the runaway's punishment. How could a husband abandon a wife to beatings and starvation, a mother her child?

Unless the whole family ran off at once, they must all stay put. It was a trap, an impossible trap, one she could escape only if she never allowed herself to care about anyone at Oak Grove.

But she knew it was already too late for her to turn her heart to stone. The kindness of the women who had taken her in, who had made room for her in their crowded cabin, had seen to that.

It was still dark in the cabin when Pearl shook her awake the next morning to gather firewood and fetch water. Outside, the sun was low in the sky, the forest of live oaks a dark, moss-draped silhouette in the east along the river. Other figures moved in the shadowed mists — shawl-wrapped women, slender girls, half-naked children — hunger urging them on. Joanna collected dry, dead branches while Pearl dipped a tightly woven sweetgrass basket into the swift-moving stream. They worked in silence, slowly waking up to the day — another long day picking cotton in the hot sun for Pearl, a day full of strange newness and unknowns for herself.

Back at the cabin, Tavia quickly packed two sweetgrass baskets with corncakes and salt pork. Covering each with a tight-fitting lid, she distributed the last of the corncakes between Pearl, Joanna, and herself. "You'll get your noon meal at the big house," she told Joanna between bites, handing one basket to Pearl and tucking the other beneath her arm. "Can you help Auntie Bess lay a fire so she can make the children their mush? Mistress won't be up yet, so you got time. Me and Pearl got to get to the fields before Aaron do."

She didn't need to explain why. Joanna agreed, glad for something to do to thank them for their kindness. Pearl touched her arm in passing as she and her mother hurried out the door. "We'll eat better tonight. Uncle Titus going hunting."

"Hunting?" Joanna asked Auntie Bess after the other two women were gone. The younger Marse Chester had forbidden his slaves to hunt. "With what? Sticks and stones?"

Auntie Bess shrugged, searching through a pile of sacks in the corner for the cornmeal. "Some of the men use sticks and stones, if that all they got. Titus, he borrow the marse's old hunting rifle. Sometime he take possum or squirrel, sometime he get a deer. But today I think it'll be rabbit. He say he set some snares yesterday."

Joanna stared at her in disbelief. "Marse Chester give his slaves guns?"

"Not any slave. Just Titus. And Aaron, and one or two others." Auntie Bess cackled through a toothless grin. "I know what you thinking. Why not just shoot Marse Chester? Well, what Titus gonna do then? Where he go? What happen to Tavia and her children after he run off? Girl, you gonna make that fire so I can feed these children or not?"

Quickly Joanna laid the dry sticks in the fireplace, but before she could light the tinder, Auntie Bess waved her off and urged her to hurry on up to the big house. "Mind yourself," she cautioned as Joanna hurried out the door. "Tell Sophie you Tavia's friend and she look after you."

Munching the dry corncake, Joanna hurried up to the big house, her nervousness tempered by the comforting thought that Sophie, whoever she was, might help her find her way in the unfamiliar household as a kindness to Tavia.

When Joanna reached the house, she found the stout cook outside at the pump, panting heavily as she worked the handle with one thick arm and held a large pot beneath the spout with the other. "You there," she said, spotting Joanna. "Come help me."

Joanna quickly complied, holding the pot beneath the cool, gushing water while the cook threw her weight against the stubborn, creaking pump handle. "Would it kill Marse Chester to let me oil this thing?" she grumbled, pausing to catch her breath and wipe her brow with the back of her hand. Then she beckoned impatiently to Joanna. "Don't just stand there, girl. Bring it to the kitchen."

"I'm Joanna," she said, following the cook inside.

"I know." The cook gestured to the cookstove. "Leave it there."

"Do you know where I can find Sophie?" asked Joanna, hefting the heavy pot onto the stove and shaking water droplets from her apron.

"She usually in the kitchen." Then the cook sighed and added grudgingly, "All right. I'm Sophie."

"Oh." Joanna watched hungrily as Sophie

brought out a jar of sourdough starter and a sack of flour. "I'm living with Tavia now, and since they didn't get any rations for me, I thought maybe —"

"You living with Tavia?" Sophie interrupted. "Augustus say Mistress put you with Leah."

"Leah . . . didn't have enough room."

Sophie harrumphed. "Oh, but Tavia, she got lots of room." Shaking her head, she reached into a cupboard for a mixing bowl. "Leah already took your ration. You want it, you got to get it from her."

"When did Leah come for my ration?"

"This morning before sunup."

"And you just let her take it?"

Sophie shot Joanna a warning look. "She your head of household, as far as anyone tell me."

"How am I supposed to get it back?" Joanna asked. "She's not likely to give it to me if I ask nicely. What am I supposed to do? Steal it from her cabin while she in the fields?"

"Not unless you a lot stronger than you look," retorted Sophie. "Your ration gone, girl, but since you Tavia's friend, I'll see what I can find for you. No sense in them children going hungry on your account."

Joanna knew it was the most she could

hope for. "Thank you."

"You best get on. Mistress'll want you ready for work before breakfast even if she don't give you nothing to do. Wait out back for the housekeeper."

Joanna nodded and hurried off to the back door of the big house. The housekeeper, neatly attired in a calico dress, starched white apron, and white cap, opened the door as quickly as if she had been watching through the window for her. She led Joanna to a parlor and admonished her to stand and wait for the mistress.

Alone, Joanna waited, rocking from her heels to her toes when her feet grew tired. A clock chimed on the mantelpiece; from another room came the clinking of china as someone set a table. Overhead, floorboards creaked, followed by the sound of voices and footsteps on the stairs. Joanna stood alone in the parlor while the Chesters ate their breakfast and was standing yet when a young woman with clear blue eyes and long blond curls piled on top of her head swept into the parlor.

"You must be the new seamstress," she said, then raised a hand to her throat as her gaze lit upon Joanna's scarred cheek. "Good heavens. What happened to your face?"

"Burn scar, miss."

"Is it a brand? I've heard they sometimes brand runaways." She waved a hand dismissively to indicate she didn't require an answer. "No matter. You've come just in time. I'm spending most of the spring and summer with my aunt in Charleston to avoid the malaria season, and Daddy's bought me some delicious fabrics for my wardrobe. No matter what Mrs. Chester says, don't let her talk you into finishing her dour old dress before starting my new gown. Understood?"

"Yes, miss," said Joanna, ducking her head. What did the young lady expect her to do if the mistress wanted her dress completed right away? Should she sew the dress with one hand and the gown with the other?

The young woman's eyebrows arched. "You agreed so quickly that you must not be aware of the risks involved." She lowered her voice and drew closer. "Don't let my stepmother know that you've set her dress aside in favor of mine. Her first two husbands died under mysterious circumstances."

"I won't, miss," Joanna replied shakily. Mrs. Chester didn't look old enough to have already gone through two husbands, but she would heed the young woman's warning —

and finish her stepmother's dress first. Why risk upsetting a murderess?

"Good." The young woman, who appeared to be sixteen or seventeen, looked her over speculatively. "How long do you intend to stand there idle — what was your name?"

"Joanna, miss. Until the mistress come, miss."

"That will do, Evangeline," said Mrs. Chester, appearing in the doorway. "You have reading to attend to."

Evangeline pursed her lips, inclined her head gracefully to her stepmother, and glided from the room with a soft rustling of rose silk. Mrs. Chester sighed quietly and turned her attention to Joanna. In sharp contrast to her stepdaughter, she wore a dress of somber brown, her hair parted in the middle and pulled back into a smooth knot at the nape of her neck. Her round spectacles caught the light as she led Joanna to a small closet off the kitchen where a sewing basket and pile of mending as high as her knee awaited.

"Attend to your master's clothes before the children's. When you've completed the mending, I want you to finish my dress." The mistress gestured for Joanna, who stood a head taller, to take a bundle of blue-

and-brown plaid wool down from an upper shelf. Joanna unfolded it to find pieces cut for a dress — a skirt basted to a bodice, two sleeves with white cuffs pinned in place, a collar creased from folding. Joanna quickly saw that whoever had begun the dress fashioned garments much differently than she did. Although the dress was nearly half-finished, it would take Joanna at least as much time to redo poorly sewn seams and properly align the bodice than if she had started from scratch.

She hid her dismay from the mistress, who continued, "You may work in here if you like, or outside in the yard where the light is better. If my stepdaughter badgers you about her new gown, you have my permission to remind her that if she does not finish her Greek translations to my satisfaction, there will be no visit to her aunt in Charleston, and no need for a new gown. Her father may indulge her vanity, but not I. Her constitution is no more delicate than her younger brothers', or my own. I daresay that if we can brave the risk of yellow fever and malaria, so can she."

"Yes, ma'am," said Joanna, though she wouldn't dare say any such thing to Miss Evangeline. Just as she had feared, she had found herself exactly where everyone had warned her not to tread — caught between the demands of two mistresses. The Bible said a man could not serve two masters, but Joanna thought serving two masters would be easy compared to serving two jealous mistresses.

She sewed all morning beneath the shade of a live oak not far from the big house, mending torn trousers and popped seams. She guessed the ages of the three younger children from the size of their clothes — two boys and a girl, of whom the youngest was about four. As she sewed a button on a young boy's Sunday suit, she imagined her own son wearing it proudly as he rode in the carriage Hans Bergstrom had arranged to carry them to Canada, and then she gasped aloud as shock struck her with the force of cold water.

She could not remember her son's face.

Squeezing her eyes shut, she frantically searched her memory. She could feel his mouth on her nipple, his curly head against her unscarred cheek, his soft baby smell, but her mind's eye glimpsed nothing, not even the faintest image of his sweet face. He had a perfect, broad nose, she reminded herself. Round, full cheeks like her mother's. Clear, wide, guileless eyes. Bit by bit, she pieced together her memory of individual features she had once gazed upon so lovingly, so carelessly, but it was all a patchwork of glimpses that she doubted resembled her child at all. How would she recognize him if she ever found her freedom? What horror to think she might pass her own son on a crowded street in Canada and not know him!

"Joanna," came a distant shout. "You all right?"

Startled, Joanna shaded her eyes and spotted Sophie outside the kitchen. "Yes," she called back. "Just got sun in my eyes."

Sophie frowned, bemused, but did not question her. "Marse's family done eating. Come on inside and have yours before it's gone."

Joanna did not need to be asked twice. Gathering the mending and the sweetgrass sewing basket, she hurried to the kitchen, where the house slaves were already eating bowls of rice, beans, and okra, on foot or sitting on the floor, quickly, so they might fill their empty bellies before the Chesters summoned them back to work. Sophie twice filled a bowl for Joanna, who barely tasted the unfamiliar spices and textures in her hunger, and cut her a thick slab of cornbread. Without shame she picked the crumbs from her apron and ate those too, and if Sophie had not already ordered the kitchen girl to scrub the pot, Joanna might have begged to lick it clean first.

She sewed for the rest of the afternoon, but she was unable to finish all the mending and was thus spared choosing between Mrs. Chester's dress and Miss Evangeline's gown. "Mistress want you in the study," the housekeeper informed her as she separated the mended clothes from those unfinished in the small closet off the kitchen. Through the window Joanna spotted the field hands trooping slowly from the white-flecked cotton fields and she knew Tavia would soon begin supper. Hoping the mistress intended to give her her ration, even a half ration, she hurried to the study.

As before, the mistress sat at the secretary writing on creamy ivory paper. Joanna waited for her to speak, forcing herself not to fidget, her thoughts fixed on Tavia's hearth and Uncle Titus's hunting. She could almost smell roasting rabbit.

"I understand that you disobeyed my instructions," the mistress said suddenly, dipping her pen in a bottle of indigo ink and signing her name to the bottom of the page.

"No, ma'am," said Joanna, surprised.

"I told you to share Leah's cabin." She set

174

down her pen, lifted the sheet, and blew gently on the rows of small, elegant script. "Instead it has come to my attention that you are living with Octavia and her family. Were you somehow confused by such simple instructions?"

"No, ma'am."

The mistress set down the paper and regarded her sternly. "Did Leah forbid you to enter her cabin?"

"I did go into her cabin, ma'am," said Joanna, with perfect honesty. "Tavia had more room and she ask me to stay with them. I help Pearl fetch firewood this morning so she and Tavia could get to the cotton fields sooner."

The mistress pondered this and did not seem displeased. "Did Leah give you your rations?"

"Not yet, ma'am." Nor would she ever, but Joanna would endure a whipping before she carried tales to the white folks about a slave, even one as mean as Leah. "There wasn't no time. I haven't seen her since yesterday."

"See that you collect it. The next drawing isn't until Saturday. You may stay with Octavia's family, but I must warn you that in the future, you must ask Aaron before you make any changes to your living arrangements. There's no need to make his job more difficult than it already is."

Joanna hoped to avoid meeting Aaron as long as possible. "Yes, ma'am. Sorry, ma'am."

"Did you finish the mending?"

"About halfway done, ma'am."

The mistress's eyebrows rose. "Only halfway? It seems my sister-in-law over-praised your sewing skills. Be here all the earlier tomorrow morning. It's washing day."

Shaking her head as if she should have known Joanna would disappoint, the mistress turned back to her letter. Joanna made a quick curtsy and returned to the kitchen, where Sophie was nearly finished preparing the Chesters' supper. "Take that when you go," she said, jabbing a spoon in the direction of a sweetgrass basket with two woven handles. "Bring the basket back in the morning."

Murmuring her thanks, Joanna snatched up the basket and hurried outside before Sophie could change her mind. Glancing into the basket as she left the big house, she glimpsed a sack that probably held corn-meal, a tin of molasses, and a slab of salted pork. It wasn't much to sustain her for three days, but it was more than she was likely to get from Leah, and it would make her less of a burden to Tavia.

Auntie Bess and the children must have collected more firewood during the day, for when Joanna reached the cabin, a fire already crackled in the fireplace. "We'll have sweet potatoes with our rabbit," Auntie Bess announced, poking a stick into the ashes where four large sweet potatoes roasted.

"Uncle Titus caught one?" said Joanna, setting Sophie's basket on the floor and snatching up the one Pearl had used to fetch water.

"He and Tavia are skinning it now. If you pass them on your way to the creek, tell them to hurry. Pearl's getting the children and I bet they all about to faint from hunger."

Joanna promised she would. She had only taken a few steps from the cabin when she saw Tavia coming up the dirt path, smiling as she talked with a tall, broad-shouldered man carrying a skinned rabbit. She stopped short at the sight of him, he looked up, and a smile spread across his face.

He was the coachman who had filled her tin cornboiler with water and passed it to her through the bars of the cage.

"You Uncle Titus?" she said. It seemed impossible he should be Tavia's brother. Ta-

177

via was all goodness, while Titus had mocked her in her thirst.

He shrugged. "I suppose I am to some, but you don't got to call me uncle."

Tavia slapped him lightly on the arm, but her eyes shone with pride. "Don't tease." To Joanna she added, "Hurry back with the water, won't you? Sooner we eat, sooner we can turn in."

As Joanna nodded, Titus said, "You need your rest. Washing day tomorrow."

Joanna made a tight smile and hurried off to fetch the water. He was mocking her again, pointing out how Joanna's worst day in the big house was better than his sister's easiest day in the fields. Of course it was true, but the same could be said for him. The coachman's job was one of the most prized on the plantation, or at least that was how it had been in Virginia. And wasn't Titus allowed to hunt with the master's own rifle? Most field hands suspected that house slaves were spies and shills for the white folks, but Titus was no field hand, and from the sound of things he was more privileged by far than Joanna. He had no call to mock her.

She almost forgave him after that first bite of rabbit, meat so tender it fell off the bone. The younger children were more spirited than she had ever seen them, begging their uncle to tell them stories while they licked meat juices from their fingertips, scrambling for the best seats on the ground beside him. Then, when she had almost taken a liking to him, Titus spoiled it by eyeing her curiously as she tried to drink water from the lid to a jar that Pearl said had once held pickled cucumbers. "What happened to that fine tin cup with the lid and handle you brought from Virginia?" he asked. "You lose it already?"

"I didn't lose it," she said shortly, swallowing her last bite of sweet potato and carrying her makeshift cup into the cabin. She heard voices murmuring outside, and she supposed Tavia, Pearl, and Auntie Bess were telling him about her losses and her disagreement with Leah. She didn't care, except it would give him one more thing to laugh about.

She was in the washhouse putting the master's trousers through the mangle when she next saw Titus. How long he had stood in the doorway watching her before knocking his boot against the frame to catch her attention, she did not know. She glanced up, locked eyes with him, and frowned to hide her sudden stir of embarrassment and anger, emotions he seemed to inspire in her without trying. She didn't pause in her work, but she had never been good at hiding her feelings, and she wasn't sure she had succeeded this time either.

As he approached, she saw from the corner of her eye that he carried a bundle of calico under his arm. "So at Oak Grave the coachman carries dirty laundry for the mistress?" she said, trying to put enough contempt in her voice to carry over the cranking complaints of the mangle.

"I can't see the new mistress wearing this," he said, lifting a faded sleeve and letting it fall. "It'd drag on the ground unless she stood on a chair."

Joanna released the winch and turned to face him, hesitating at the sight of her old dress. Carefully Titus unfolded the sleeves, unrolled the skirt, and revealed her lost tin cornboiler.

"Where did you find them?" She knew he was not the thief.

"It don't matter. What matters is you got them back."

"It matter to me."

"It wasn't Leah. Or Lizzie." Titus draped the dress over her shoulders like a shawl and closed her hands around the cornboiler, all without a trace of mockery. "The thief won't trouble you no more."

She knew she would have to be content with that. "Thank you." The cornboiler was cool and smooth in her hands, but already beads of condensation were forming on the rounded sides. She was suddenly conscious of her flushed face, her hair frizzed and kinked into a wild, dark halo from the humidity. She turned away and draped the dress over the flatiron board and set the cornboiler upon it.

As she took hold of the winch again, Titus gestured to her scar. "Your old marse do that to you?"

Joanna nodded and inhaled sharply, remembering the smell of her own seared flesh. "Flatiron, right out the fire."

"How far you get?"

"What?"

"When you run away, how far you get?"

"Pennsylvania. A town called Creek's Crossing."

"That near Philadelphia?" said Titus. "The new mistress from there. Don't expect you'd find a lot of buckra kind to runaways in Pennsylvania."

"Buckra?"

"White folks."

"But I did," said Joanna. "Quakers, mostly. They hate slavery. But it wasn't just white folks who help me on my way. Free coloreds gave me shelter too. There was one family —" She took a deep breath, tears pricking her eyes at the memory. "A farmer in the Elm Creek Valley — Abel Wright and his wife, Constance. He grow wheat, raise goats, make cheese. He born free, and he bought his wife's freedom. They have two sons who never knew the sting of the lash. They give me food, clothing, shoes, hope, but I don't know what's happened to them. When I got caught, the man who sheltered me got taken by the police. His sister, too, maybe. Maybe everyone who helped me in jail right now. I don't know."

"You sold down south, your friends in trouble . . . You sorry you ran?"

"No," she said, without needing to pause and consider. Wasn't her son better off? "But if I ran again, some folks I wouldn't trust a second time."

"Some day I gonna run." Titus spoke with such fierce determination that she didn't doubt him for a moment. "Sometimes Marse Chester hire me out to his friends need to deliver foals, break horses. He give me a portion of my wages to keep, and I save every cent. If I can't buy my freedom by the time I'm thirty, I'm gonna take a horse and ride north."

"Where you gonna go?" asked Joanna. "What about Tavia and Auntie Bess and the children? I hear Marse Chester set Aaron on a runaway's kin."

"I'll take them with me," said Titus, undaunted. "They hide in the carriage, and I drive. You can come, too."

"Me?"

"Why not? You in Tavia's household. You think I leave you here to get beat and starve? Besides, you the one who know the way. You know folks who can help us."

"I don't know the way from here," Joanna said, glancing at the open doorway and lowering her voice. "I know the way from Greenfields, the other Marse Chester's place in Virginia."

"I'll get us that far. I travel a long ways driving Marse Chester, I hear buckra talk, I learn things. I talk to other coachmen." Suddenly Titus seized her arm. "Say you'll help us. I can't die a slave. I'm a man, Joanna. I got a mind, a soul. I won't die a slave."

Joanna took a deep, shaky breath. "You know they gonna have their eye on me. I'm a runaway, remember? They just waiting for me to run off again so they can beat the running out of me."

"Then you just gonna have to make them think you happy here."

183

Joanna shook her head. "Unless they stupid, they never believe it."

"Buckra want to believe we all happy, loyal servants. Don't the mistress call us her black family? They see what they want to see." Just then, Titus glanced down and seemed startled to find himself still clasping her arm. Abruptly he let go. "Meantime, you got to fix the way north in your mind. Draw a map if you can, but hide it good."

"Draw a map," said Joanna, skeptical. "Where'm I gonna get paper and ink?"

"Mistress's study."

"And if I get caught stealing?"

He shrugged and grinned with his familiar insolence. "Don't get caught."

Before she could protest, he left the wash-house, pausing in the doorway to throw her one last mocking grin over his shoulder. "You nothing like your sister," Joanna called after him, and heard his answering laugh. She wondered if Tavia knew of his plans, or if Joanna was his first and only confidante.

As she hung the wash out to dry — colors in the cooling shade, whites in the harsh sunshine, in a reversal of the usual order of things — she mulled over Titus's words. He was right to say she must fix the details of her journey north in her mind, but she did not see how she could draw a map. She had never held a pen except for those brief months in the Elm Creek Valley when Gerda Bergstrom had taught her to read. She remembered landmarks, not the number of miles or acres she had followed from one hiding place to the next.

While the laundry waved in the breeze, Joanna finished the mending and began ripping out ill-made seams of the mistress's half-finished dress. After trimming a narrow strip of blue-and-brown plaid from the bodice so that it would lie smooth, she was tempted to slip the scraps into her apron pocket, but then she thought of Aaron, whom she had thus far seen only from a distance, and decided it was not worth the risk. Instead she carefully saved all the scraps in the sewing basket, and at the end of the day, when she put away the washing and gave the mended clothes to the house-keeper, she went to the study, where she found the mistress reading.

"I didn't summon you," said Mrs. Chester, marking her place with a finger and closing the book.

"No, ma'am, but I have to tell you that before I can finish your dress, I need to fit the bodice and check the length of the sleeves."

"Very well. Tomorrow morning after

breakfast."

"Yes, ma'am." Joanna hesitated. "Mistress Chester, I also wanted to know what you like to do with the scraps from the sewing, if you or Miss Evangeline save them for quilting."

"My reading and writing keep me too busy to quilt, and Miss Evangeline cares little for needlework save embroidery." The mistress pursed her lips, thinking. "You may keep the scraps if you can find a use for them."

"Yes, ma'am. Thank you, ma'am."

Joanna slipped away to the washhouse to collect her tin cornboiler and the dress she had worn on the journey south, the dress she would never again wear, for she had discovered a more important purpose for the faded calico. With the fabric from the dress and the scraps she collected from the household sewing, she would create a quilt, the most important and necessary quilt she had ever made.

With needle and thread she would fashion Birds in the Air blocks like those she had made with Gerda Bergstrom during her brief winter in Pennsylvania, Birds in the Air for freedom and a swift flight north. When the top was complete, she would quilt the three layers with stitched portraits of landmarks she had encountered along the way from Greenfields to Elm Creek Farm. She would disguise the quilted symbols with fine stipple work and crosshatches and feather plumes so the clues would be invisible to a casual observer. No master or mistress would examine a slave's quilt, ridden with filth and vermin and the stink of the slave quarter. Its secrets would be invisible to the Chesters, whose own cast-off clothing furthered their deception.

Joanna would create the map Titus wanted beneath the Chesters' oblivious scrutiny, and one day it might lead them all to freedom, and to her lost son.

CHAPTER FOUR

1860
Oak Grove Plantation, South Carolina

Joanna was forbidden to wash the other slaves' clothing or to mix her own laundry in with the Chesters', but a few days before Titus meant to speak with the marse on their behalf, she soaked his best coachman's jacket and trousers in the same tub as the buckra family's, scrubbed out every stain, and hung them to dry out of sight of the big house and Aaron. She fixed a loose button, mended a torn hem, and pressed everything carefully with the flatiron. Titus polished his shoes himself, with grease meant for the horses' tack and saddles.

"How do I look?" he said, tugging on the lapels of his jacket, turning in the small space between beds in Tavia's cabin, showing off for his sister and the children.

"Remember the fancy coachman who drove that cotton buyer from Atlanta last month?" Joanna asked.

Titus grinned, pleased. "The fine-looking fellow who was too good to sleep in the stable? The one who pretended not to understand Gullah talk?"

"That's the one. You don't look nothing like him." Over the children's laughter, Joanna added, "He was silly, all puffed up like a rooster with a new flock of hens. You look like a man to reckon with."

"Marse Chester already knows what you look like," warned Auntie Bess, stirring the children's cornmeal mush over the fire. "Clean clothes don't change nothing. You still smell like horses."

"If Joanna don't care, you shouldn't."

"It don't bother me," Joanna said, taking his hand. She was so nervous, her heart fluttered against her breastbone. She knew, even if Auntie Bess refused to see it, that clean clothes might make all the difference. Titus had to look like a man of business to do business with a man like Marse Chester.

Titus had chores in the stable, so after a quick kiss, Joanna hurried off to the big house to finish darning the children's socks before meeting Miss Evangeline in her bedroom for a dress fitting. Joanna would be relieved to put the last stitch in a gown that had been nothing but trouble even before she made the first muslin pattern. Miss Evangeline had slapped Joanna after she saw her stepmother wearing the blue-and-brown plaid dress she had ordered Joanna to defer in favor of her own. Joanna's stammered explanation that she had feared that if she angered the mistress, she would face an untimely death like the mistress's first two husbands incensed Miss Evangeline all the more. "Even an ignorant nigger like you should have realized my stepmother was fortunate to beguile one man into marriage, but three?"

Joanna soon discovered that she was not only the target of Miss Evangeline's deceptions, but also an unwitting subject. When visitors came to the plantation and glimpsed Joanna's scar, Miss Evangeline spun stories of how Joanna had flung herself in the fire in a spiteful attempt to lessen her value before going to the auction block. Sometimes the burn was a brand, marking her as a slave who had tried to poison her master, and another time it was the imprint of a horseshoe glowing from the forge, where she had hidden during a thwarted escape attempt. The story Miss Evangeline repeated most often claimed the burn was a tribal marking inflicted upon Joanna in childhood in a primitive rite that involved the worship of idols and the drinking of blood.

"What would they think if I told them Miss Evangeline's own uncle done this to me?" Joanna said bitterly one night in Tavia's cabin, after the young mistress had humiliated her before a crowd of friends and admirers. "My scar might not be so funny if they knew the truth."

"Our mother bore the marks of her tribe," said Titus. "A row of scars across her forehead — cuts, not burns. Her grandmother did it to her when she came of age, but after her mother and grandmother died, there was no one left to remember the name of the tribe or where it come from. No one was left to mark Tavia when her time came."

"I thought our mother's scars were beautiful," said Tavia softly, and Titus nodded.

Joanna smiled to thank them, but she could not take comfort in their words. Her scar stood for violence and rage, marking her as nothing more than the property of a man she hated.

"At last we shall see what this new seamstress can do with finer cloth," Miss Evangeline remarked when Joanna first cut into the blue silk Marse Chester had bought Miss Evangeline for her new gown. It was true he had bought a finer and more luxurious fabric for his daughter than for his wife, but Mrs. Chester had probably chosen the plaid herself; Joanna had never seen her in silk.

With the mistress's blue-and-brown plaid dress out of the way, Joanna was able to devote all her attention to Miss Evangeline's gown, except on washday or days when Mistress Chester filled her basket with mending or darning. Soon, when Miss Evangeline saw how beautifully Joanna fashioned the blue silk, she seemed to conclude that it would be well worth the wait. She apologized for striking Joanna and insisted she keep the silk trimmings for her patchwork. The gift would have meant more had the mistress not already promised Joanna all the scraps from the household sewing, and Miss Evangeline's words, meant to please, troubled Joanna. In all her life she had never received an apology from a Chester. She feared Miss Evangeline might mention the apology to her parents, who could send Joanna to Aaron on some pretense to make sure she didn't get above herself.

Joanna's eagerness to be done with that troublesome gown was not why she raced through the darning, glancing down the hill to the stables from the shade of a live oak, determined to finish before Titus came to the big house to speak to Marse Chester.

Miss Evangeline's bedroom was above the study, and Joanna hoped to listen in on their conversation through the open window. The housekeeper, Dove, had promised to arrange it so Miss Evangeline was ready for her fitting before Marse Chester left to ride the cotton rows. Dove's careful plotting would be for nothing if Joanna weren't there on time.

It was only a few weeks after her arrival at Oak Grove that Joanna had discovered what a friend and ally she had in Dove, who had been assigned the laundry chores after the previous laundress had died in childbirth. Dove hated the steam burns and the smell of lye even more than she resented the extra work, and she had found in Joanna her deliverance from the hot, steamy washhouse, barely tolerable in winter, unendurable in summer. Dove was quick to agree to almost anything that would keep Joanna content and industrious, anything to spare herself a return to waterlogged hands and backaches.

Joanna finished the last sock, packed her basket, and returned to the big house just in time to see Titus leaving the stable, brushing straw from the sleeve of his dark coat. She waved to him, swinging her arm in great arcs above her head until he saw her, but she dared not shout to him, to bridge the distance between them with words. There were too many ears listening, too many people who would thwart their plans out of spite rather than allow anyone to be contented where they were not. One in particular made Joanna wary.

"Miss Evangeline upstairs in her room, reading," said Dove quietly when Joanna slipped in through the back door, "but she say she going riding before midday. If you want to catch her, you best hurry."

Whispering her thanks, Joanna hurried to the closet, traded the pile of darned socks for the pieces of blue silk that shimmered like water in sunlight, and hurried upstairs to Miss Evangeline's bedroom. She rapped twice on the door. "Miss Evangeline?" she called. "You like me to fit your new gown now?"

"Come in," Evangeline cried, tossing her book on the bed as Joanna entered and closed the door behind her. "Hurry, get me undressed. Wait until Charlotte sees me in this. I don't care if her gowns are from Paris; they won't hold a candle to mine." As she spoke, she spread the gown upon her bed to better admire the graceful lines, and then repeatedly bent forward to move a sleeve or a cascade of lace. "When Robert sees me, he'll want to go speak to my father that very moment, if Jonathan doesn't beat him to it."

"Miss Evangeline," Joanna said, struggling to unfasten the buttons down the back of her wool riding dress, "if you could hold still a moment —"

Miss Evangeline laughed and complied as Joanna undressed her and slipped the new gown over her head. As Joanna fastened up the back and pinned the gown where it needed to be taken in, Miss Evangeline offered up a steady stream of praise for the exquisite mother-of-pearl buttons her aunt Lucretia had sent from Charleston, the blue silk that perfectly matched her eyes, and the various shades of green her friends would turn when she made her entrance at the next dance. Whenever it seemed required, Joanna murmured perfunctory agreement, straining her ears for sounds from the drawing room below. At last she heard voices, and she was certain she recognized Titus's, but she could not distinguish the words or even the temper of the discussion.

She gave up in frustration, frowning around pins held between her teeth as she adjusted the length of the skirt and the fit of the waist. "You've outdone yourself, Joanna," Miss Evangeline praised, admiring herself in the mirror. "I've never worn a finer garment."

"Thank you, miss," said Joanna, just as a knock sounded on the door.

"Who is it?" called Miss Evangeline sharply, in the voice she used only for her stepmother.

"It's Dove, miss. Marse Chester wants to see Joanna downstairs."

Miss Evangeline's eyebrows rose. "Whatever would he want you for?"

"I don't know, miss," said Joanna, fighting the urge to dash downstairs. "Should we finish here first?"

"No, if he wants you, you best go to him." Miss Evangeline's gaze returned to her own slender figure in the mirror. "Send Dove in to help me undress, and you can come back for the blue silk when Papa's finished with you. I hope you aren't in any trouble. I need my gown finished by next week."

Joanna excused herself and a few moments later stood outside the drawing room, hands clasped in front of her apron, eyes downcast the way the master preferred them, until Marse Chester beckoned her inside. Titus stood before the master's mahogany desk, coachman's cap in hand, but he flashed Joanna a quick smile as she lingered in the doorway.

"You ask to see me, Marse Chester?" she said.

"Indeed. Come in." He regarded her speculatively, dark blue eyes curious in his heavy face, hair the color of faded corn silk growing thin on top, thicker in the beard and sideburns and flecked with gray. "Titus tells me he would like to marry you."

Joanna nodded, eyes on the pattern of nicks on the edge of his desk. She recognized the book that lay open on the polished surface — his ledger, where he recorded every penny earned or spent on Oak Grove. Her own name was inked on one of its pages, her name and age and the price she would likely fetch if he decided to send her to auction. "Yes, sir."

"Do you want to marry him?"

"Yes, sir, I do."

"Titus is a fine man. You'd be a fool not to." Marse Chester sat back in his chair, frowning thoughtfully and stroking his whiskers. "It's not a match I would have considered, but I see no reason to object. Very well. You have my permission to marry."

Titus took Joanna's hand. "Thank you, Marse Chester, sir." Marse Chester nodded, benevolent but bemused, and dismissed them. They left before he could change his mind.

In the hall, Titus glanced around to be sure they were alone before sweeping Joanna into his arms and pressing his lips to hers. Joanna melted into his kiss, but then she pushed him away. The younger Chester children might be listening around the corner. "He didn't say anything about where we should live," Joanna said.

"I didn't want to ask and give him a reason to refuse. I'll stay in the barn for now and you can stay with Tavia. Sometime after harvest I'll ask him if I can build us a cabin. If we need to." He always said things like that when they were alone, hints that running off was never far from his mind. Suddenly, like a lamp extinguished, his good humor vanished. "I hate asking him to let me marry you. You already my wife."

"But he don't know that." No one outside the slave quarter knew Joanna and Titus had jumped the broom three months before, on New Year's Eve, and no one but Tavia and Auntie Bess knew they were expecting a child by autumn. "Tavia's right. We have to do it this way so he don't marry us to no one else."

He nodded, but his mutinous look remained. Joanna hoped he would remember to mask it before Aaron or the Chesters saw and beat it off him.

Joanna longed to run to Tavia and share their good news, but after one last, hasty kiss, Titus had to leave for the stable and Joanna for Miss Evangeline's bedroom. Dove must have guessed from her shining eyes what Marse Chester had decided, but she knew better than to ask in front of the young mistress. Instead Dove offered a small smile of congratulations when Miss Evangeline wasn't looking.

"What did my father want?" asked Miss Evangeline as Joanna gathered up the blue silk gown and packed her sewing basket.

"Titus ask permission to marry me, and Marse Chester said yes."

"The coachman?" Miss Evangeline's blue eyes widened in wounded surprise. "Why, Joanna, you never said you fancied him. If you wanted to marry, you should have come to me. I would have sorted it out with Daddy."

"I couldn't," Joanna blurted without thinking.

"Why ever not?"

"Because — because I didn't know if he fancied me."

"Oh. Of course." Miss Evangeline nodding knowingly and donned her riding cap. "Sometimes it's difficult to understand a man's intentions. But all's well that ends well. Congratulations, Joanna. I hope you'll be happy."

She didn't add that she also hoped to announce her own engagement soon, because white marriage was so unlike slave marriage that it could not be mentioned in the same breath. Belying her good wishes, the tight set of her mouth made her annoyance plain. Unless Miss Evangeline married soon, a simple slave would accomplish what she had not. That was why Joanna never would have asked Miss Evangeline to intercede on their behalf with her father. She had seen Miss Evangeline ruin the marriage plans of a onetime friend by spreading tales about the young woman's unspecified "indiscretions," not because she wanted the man for herself, but because she was offended that he had not asked her first. If that was what she did to another white girl, Joanna could imagine how she might crush a slave.

Joanna didn't understand Miss Evangeline's determination to rush headlong into something that seemed unlikely to bring her any happiness. Miss Evangeline adored her father and wept whenever he left on an extended journey, and Joanna had often heard her declare that Oak Grove was the loveliest place on earth. After she married and moved away, she would rarely see father and home again. She loved flirting and dancing but took no interest in managing the household, preferring to leave such dreary tasks to her stepmother except when Mrs. Chester's decisions thwarted her pleasures. Although she craved the admiration of the young men who visited Oak Grove and vied for her attention, she didn't seem to love any one of them in particular. Auntie Bess had said Miss Evangeline would go where her father wanted to put her, which he would do as soon as he found where the greatest profit could be made. No one would dare say Miss Evangeline was going to be sold off to the highest bidder, but that's how it sounded to Joanna. If Miss Evangeline were not so demanding, so apt to strike out with quick flashes of temper when displeased, Joanna might have felt sorry for her.

A few days later, Joanna was putting away clean clothes in the younger boys' bedroom when she heard the master and mistress talking in the foyer below. "What's this I hear about your coachman marrying my laundress?" asked Mrs. Chester, in a voice that managed to be both direct and deferential.

The silence could have been a nod, or just

as easily a frown. "Titus sought my permission and I granted it. It's true that I had planned to breed her with another buck, but Titus is strong and healthy, and he'll do just as well."

Joanna shivered at the thought of their narrow escape. Holding her breath, she drew closer to the door.

The mistress lowered her voice. "I wonder if it's wise to reward that runaway. She hasn't been with us long and I'm still not certain we can trust her. If she believes we are too lenient, she might try to run again."

"On the contrary, a marriage she and Titus both desire will settle her down," replied Master Chester, with none of his wife's fear of eavesdroppers. "Especially after children arrive. She won't want to leave her husband, and she can't run away with a baby on her hip."

"If she does, you'll have to buy me a new laundress," said the mistress lightly. "Speaking of expenditures —"

"Martha, dear, if this is going to be another reproach about finery for my daughter —"

"Not a reproach, but a caution. Last season's harvest was your most profitable in years, but we can't expect such abundance every year. If the harvest is less than what you expect, or, God forbid, there should be a drought this summer —"

"Now, Martha, don't worry." Joanna heard a noise like a dry kiss on a soft cheek. "Dresses and hair ribbons and amusements for Evangeline and her young friends are an investment, one that should pay off soon."

"I understand, dear, but prudence —"

"Martha." With a word, he commanded her silence. "Don't worry. Our creditors have been paid, the new crop will be put in soon, and if I need to raise cash, I can sell a slave. All the more reason to encourage Titus to marry your laundress, eh? The more affectionate they are, the more they'll increase our wealth."

The mistress murmured a reply, and from below came the sound of footsteps as master and mistress parted. Joanna finished putting away the clothes, a cold knot in her throat. Master Chester was wrong. Marriage would not settle her down, force her to thrust roots into mounded-up furrows of earth and push out children the way cotton plants offered up their long, silky fibers. She had run with a baby in her belly once; she could run with one in her arms. How could she not? Marriage would not protect Joanna or Titus from being sold off, nor would it protect their child.

Titus often vowed that he would not die a slave. Joanna was determined that their son or daughter would not live as one, nor would their family be parted on another man's whim.

In the evenings Joanna pieced Birds in the Air blocks until her water-wrinkled, pin-pricked fingers shook and her neck ached. She cut shimmering blue silk and blue-and-brown plaid wool and faded calico into triangles, paired them off to form squares split diagonally into dark and light halves, and gathered them into blocks. One large dark triangle pointed the way north; three smaller dark triangles followed behind. She sewed until the light failed her, until exhaustion overcame her. While she sewed, she fixed the landmarks in her mind, blocking out the curious sidelong glances and the muttered remarks about the runaway who had lost her mind, who sewed all day for the master and all night for herself.

Fixing her mind on the journey north, she blocked out gnawing pangs of hunger that never seemed to leave her. Dove slipped her extra food whenever she dared risk it, but Joanna hid whatever would not spoil and brought it back to Tavia's cabin to share with the family. Whatever she ate seemed to vanish somewhere between her mouth and her stomach, for she never felt full, never felt her hunger ease. She began to wonder if she were not pregnant after all, if instead her monthly blood had stopped because she was starving. She had seen it happen to others, at Greenfields and in the Georgia traders' wagon. Until she felt the child stir in her womb, she did not know for certain. After that, she imagined each movement as a death throe, not the testing and stretching of growing limbs but the desperate thrashing of a starving child.

Piecing the quilt set her mind adrift from the anchor of fear that threatened to hold her down on Oak Grove, forever afraid, forever without hope, forever a slave.

Joanna wasn't in the cotton rows to witness the terrible scene unfold, but Tavia and Pearl saw everything.

Late winter and early spring meant sowing cotton for harvest later that summer. Earlier the fields had been laid off in rows three feet apart and striped with ridges formed by two furrows of the turning plow. Slaves walked the lines with a shovel plow to put a trench down the center of each ridge, and into it other slaves tossed the seeds saved from the last season. Last of all came the mule pulling the board that gently scraped the top of the ridges, covering the seeds with a thin layer of soil.

Miss Evangeline was out riding with Robert Harper, an army officer and distant relation from Charleston visiting Oak Grove on the pretense of determining the advantages of cultivating Sea Island cotton versus hirsute varieties. Joanna had heard the truth from Miss Evangeline while fitting her new riding dress: His family had made its fortune from rice, and since Colonel Harper was a military man, neither he nor his brothers stood to benefit from his study of cotton. He had come on an entirely different errand — to see if Miss Evangeline's beauty was equal to its descriptions and to win the esteem of her father. As far as Joanna could tell, no one had made much of an effort to conceal his real purpose from Miss Evangeline. "Charleston would be a lovely place to live," she said to her reflection as Joanna slipped pins into the hem of her dress. "It's fashionable, and not too far from home, and Aunt Lucretia knows everyone who matters."

Miss Evangeline and her unacknowledged suitor were riding the cotton rows just ahead of the sowers when Colonel Harper noted the slave women's physical prowess.

"They're as vigorous as some of my soldiers," he remarked, with the authority of a man ten years the pretty belle's senior. "Note the musculature, designed for brute strength rather than grace, endurance rather than beauty. In physical form, they more closely resemble the male of their own race rather than the female European."

Miss Evangeline nodded, in perfect agreement. "Underneath, as well, as I'm sure you know."

"Underneath?" said the colonel. "You mean, in the heart? In the seat of the soul?"

"No, silly." When he peered at her, uncomprehending, she tossed her head and laughed. "Oh, you're incorrigible. You won't be satisfied until I say it aloud, will you? You know perfectly well that I mean underneath their skirts."

"Miss Evangeline!"

She gave his forearm a playful swat. "Don't pretend to be shocked, Colonel, and don't pretend you don't know for my sake. I'm not a fragile magnolia blossom, and you're a man of the world. Your family owns many slaves. I'm sure you've dallied."

"Never," he said, then added, "Never with a negress."

She put her blond head to one side and studied him. "I do believe you're telling the truth. You're like my father in that regard. Well, then, I am embarrassed that I ever spoke of it."

When she pulled the reins to lead her horse away, the colonel stopped her. "You can't leave it at that. Surely you don't expect me to believe that colored women —"

"Possess a pistil as well as a stamen? Why do you think it so impossible? You can find such examples throughout God's creation. Look upon this very cotton field in a few months' time and you will see thousands of plants possessing both the male and female parts of reproduction."

Joanna had seen the young mistress weave similar tales and could imagine how guileless and innocent Miss Evangeline's blue eyes had been as she had cast her net of words around her prey. Even so, the colonel was not so easily taken in. "You're mocking me, Miss Evangeline. I have never called a lady a liar before, and I won't do it now, but I do not, I cannot believe you."

"You force me to prove it to you." Miss Evangeline singled out Leah from among the sowers. "You, there. Come here."

With a glance at Aaron, the overseer, who was busy chastising the slave leading the mule for not keeping a steady pace, Leah adjusted her seed bag on her shoulder and left the line. She stopped a few yards away from the horses and looked up at Miss Evangeline, expressionless.

"This isn't necessary," said the colonel.

"Indeed it is. If you won't take my word, I must show you the proof." Miss Evangeline gestured impatiently to Leah. "Go on, then. Lift your dress."

Leah stared balefully back at her and did not move.

Miss Evangeline's rosebud mouth turned in a frown. "I've seen you in the yard and I know you're not deaf and dumb. Show the gentleman what you carry beneath your skirt."

Leah's steady gaze grew stonier, but still she did not move, not even to shake her head in refusal.

"Your field hand is either very disobedient or very well trained," the colonel remarked. "I wouldn't be surprised to learn that you've rehearsed this entire scene. She can't raise her skirt, or she'll expose your lie. Well done, Miss Evangeline."

"I assure you, this is no act." The young woman's usually velvet voice was like ice. "You. Field hand. Raise your skirt or I will have it torn off."

Leah's fists tightened around the seed bag slung over her shoulder. "I never raise my

209

skirt for no buckra man, and I won't raise it for no buckra woman either."

"You watch your tongue," the colonel barked, all mirth vanished. "You'll address your mistress with respect."

Leah waved a buzzing insect away from her ear and shot him a look of poorly veiled contempt. She didn't work for him, the look said.

The colonel, who was accustomed to seeing his orders carried out without question, climbed down from his horse. Aaron looked up from cuffing the mule driver and started down the cotton rows toward them, his hand on the whip coiled at his belt. The other slaves kept putting seeds in the furrow trenches, watching from the corners of their eyes, concealing their worry or fear or outrage behind impassive masks, pretending to see and hear nothing.

Aaron held one of Leah's arms while the colonel held the other. The colonel tore off her skirt, ripped off her thin muslin shift, spread her legs, and inspected her. He found only the same parts every buckra woman had, below a thin belly soft from carrying two children for the man she loved and four more for the man the master had bred her with.

"You're right," the colonel said, releasing

Leah so suddenly that she tumbled backwards upon the overturned earth, spilling seeds. "She's more man than woman, more beast than man. She belongs in the stable with that mule."

"Papa wouldn't want to distress the mule," said Miss Evangeline, managing a tight smile. They wheeled their horses around and trotted off between the furrows.

When Joanna left the big house that evening, not yet knowing what had happened in the cotton fields, she froze at the sight of Leah in the yard — naked, squatting on the ground where the children gathered chestnuts, wrists bound together in front of her shins, a long stick thrust behind her knees and in front of her elbows. The stick and the ropes held her in the squat, digging her feet into the mud for balance while Aaron uncoiled his whip. Leah's first, terrible scream jolted Joanna from her paralysis. Trembling, she forced herself to place one foot in front of the other, the hairs standing up on the back of her neck, ears filling with Leah's screams.

The quarter was not far away. Joanna kept her eyes fixed on the last cabin in the row so that she would not see Aaron's strong copper arm draw back, so she would not see the welts and blood on Leah's back.

Aaron's whip was seven feet of cowhide with a sturdy oak handle at one end and a small lead weight on the other, the better to bruise and scar the flesh. Joanna had never felt his whip on her own skin, but she had kissed the marks it had left on Titus. Another scream; she gasped and kept walking.

Evening came. Voices were subdued in the slave quarter as hungry workers prepared meals or were fed. No one could remember Aaron ever beating his favorite. Going to the stream for water, Joanna passed Leah's cabin and overheard sobbing and low, soothing voices within. Leah's was not among them. Aaron had looped ropes around her neck and staked them to the ground, holding her in her squat between the chestnut trees. If she fell asleep, the jerk of the rope would wake her; if she fainted, she would strangle herself.

"Maybe that's what they want," said Pearl. "They could say she killed herself. Then her death won't stain their pure Christian souls."

"Don't say such things," Tavia said, scraping the last bits of rice from the pot onto the children's plates. "Aaron's arm isn't so worn out that he won't give you a beating, too."

"She'll need tobacco leaves for her back."

Joanna watched the fire without seeing it, remembering Honor's ministrations. "Fresh picked is best. It'll help the healing and ease the pain."

But not much. Joanna would never forget the throbbing, stinging pain, the humiliation, the slow healing as reopened wounds brushed against rough homespun. Instead of a lead sinker, the driver at Greenfields had a piece of hooked wire at the end of his whip to cut and tear the flesh. She did not want to find out which felt worse.

"No one here has tobacco leaves," said Titus quietly. "Just dried tobacco for a pipe."

"I don't think that work the same way." Even if it did, Joanna doubted they could barter for enough to mix into a salve. She rose, wrapped a cornmeal dumpling in a scrap of cloth, and picked up one of the tightly woven sweetgrass baskets they used for water.

"Where you going?" Tavia asked. "You can't go to her when she's in the buck. Aaron will be watching."

Joanna stepped through the cabin doorway. "I can't leave her there."

"Titus, go after her," she heard Tavia say, and Titus said something in reply, but he did not pursue her. Night had fallen, and those not kept awake by the sound of Leah's children sobbing had already dropped off into an exhausted sleep that would end too soon with the ringing of the work bell in the morning. If Leah fell asleep that night, she would not see another sunrise.

Clinging to the shadows, Joanna made her way to the creek by moonlight, by the sound of the rushing water, and by the feel of the well-worn dirt path beneath her bare feet. Every sense alert, she carried the dripping basket behind the rows of slave cabins, through the moss-draped oaks, and across the clearing — suddenly immensely broad and exposed — until she reached the cluster of chestnut trees. Leah crouched beneath them exactly as she had when Joanna had passed hours before.

Half-conscious, Leah let the water dribble from her lips to the dirt when Joanna held the basket to her mouth. Then, spluttering, she drank, nearly tumbling over in her instinctive lunge for the water. Joanna steadied her, gripping her around the waist where the whip had not cut her, supporting Leah's weight until she had drained the basket. Joanna broke off a piece of cornmeal dumpling and placed it in her mouth, but though Leah tried to swallow, she coughed and retched and spat the yellow crumbs onto the ground.

"You . . . best go," Leah mumbled. "Aaron —"

"Aaron's asleep," Joanna said, although she could not be sure.

"My children?"

"They're fine."

"I can't feel my feet." Leah choked out a sob. "So tired."

"I know." Joanna drew closer. "Listen. It'll hurt, but you can lean up against me and rest."

"The ropes —"

"I'll hold you up. You won't strangle."

"If they see you —"

"Once you've slept a bit I'll go."

Joanna sat down on ground damp from blood and sweat, her knees bent, her back to Leah's. Leah eased her back against Joanna's, gasping as her gashes pressed against the rough fabric of Joanna's dress. In the darkness Joanna could not see the blood, but she smelled the metallic slickness as it seeped into her own clothes. She dug in her heels and braced herself as Leah slipped into unconsciousness and let her full weight fall against Joanna.

Joanna watched the moon set and the sky brighten in the east beyond the oak forest, her ears ringing from the song of cicadas and the strain of listening for Aaron. Hours passed. Once she thought she heard horse's hooves on the road to the slave quarter, but no one passed by the big house or the chestnut trees. One by one the stars went out and the sky grew pink, the clouds lit up from below as the sun rose. When Joanna could not bear the threat of discovery any longer, she nudged Leah awake. She was so slow in coming to that for one panicked moment Joanna feared she had died. But at last Leah groaned, shifted her weight back to her own feet. "Keep my children away from here," she asked faintly. "Don't let them see me."

Joanna agreed and fled to the slave quarter.

Titus lay on the grass outside the cabin waiting for her; there was no room for him in any of the beds inside. "I'm fine," she said as he leaped up, before he could scold her.

His eyes were red and bleary from lack of sleep. "Did Aaron see you?"

If he had, Joanna would be staked down in the buck beside Leah. "I don't think he left his cabin all night."

"Around midnight he circled the quarter twice on horseback."

Even in darkness, Titus could identify every horse on the plantation by sound.

Joanna shivered. "It's a good thing I went to her when I did, before he came to stop anyone from leaving."

"Joanna." Titus caught her by the arm before she could duck into the cabin. "Why? You don't even like Leah."

Joanna couldn't explain how she felt, how she could not have done anything differently. "Because I *am* Leah."

Titus studied her, uncomprehending, and let her go.

Inside, Tavia was rising from bed, where she had no doubt drifted in and out of sleep all night, waiting for Joanna's return or for shouts of alarm warning that she had been discovered out of the slave quarter. "How's Leah?" she whispered. The work bell would wake the others soon enough.

"She's strong, but she won't last a second night in the buck."

"Marse Chester never keeps anyone in the buck more than one — Joanna, your back," Tavia gasped, grabbing Joanna's shoulder and spinning her around.

Glancing over her shoulder, Joanna spied the crosshatch of bloodstains on her dress. "It's not mine. It's Leah's."

"You can't go up to the big house like that. As soon as they see this —" Tavia shook her head, thinking. "What about your old dress?"

Joanna gestured to the pile of Birds in Air blocks and scraps in the corner farthest from the fire. "Cut up for quilts."

"She can wear mine," said Pearl, tossing off her coarse blanket and sitting up.

"No," said Tavia and Joanna at the same time. Joanna added, "I won't have you take a beating in my place."

"I'll have the seed bag on my back to cover the stains."

"Joanna's dress is too long for you," said Tavia. "It'll drag on the ground."

"I'll hike it up around my waist and hold it in place with a pin. You got a pin, don't you, Joanna?"

Reluctantly, Joanna nodded. It was no use pretending she didn't. Whenever she pieced her Birds in the Air quilt, she brought out the four pins she had taken from the big house, slim pieces of bent brass the mistress would never know were missing. That didn't mean Joanna wouldn't be beaten for stealing if any Chester ever caught her with them.

Quickly Joanna and Pearl switched dresses. Tavia's brows knit together in worry; Auntie Bess shook her head but said nothing. The work bell rang. Pearl and Tavia snatched up cold cornmeal dumplings cooked over the fire the night before, grabbed the sweetgrass baskets with their lunch ration, and ran off for the fields.

Titus was nowhere to be seen when Joanna hurried off to the big house after feeding the younger children their cornmeal mush. She did not know whether to be worried or relieved when she saw only bent grass and scuffed earth beneath the chestnut trees. Worry won out. She ran for the kitchen building and burst in on Sophie, fixing breakfast.

"Aaron left Leah there until all the hands passed on their way to the fields," Sophie told her, reading the question in her eyes as she caught her breath. "After they all took a good look, he untied her, gave her back her clothes, and let her drink before sending her to work."

"She's out in the cotton fields? Now?"

Sophie shrugged. "Cotton got to be planted."

"How's she even keeping her feet? After the beating, and the buck, and no food —"

"That's what Marse Chester asked Aaron." Sophie returned to the work Joanna had interrupted, kneading dough on a floured breadboard. "Marse Chester say she must have rested last night, but how she did that without pulling up the stakes or strangling herself, he don't know. He thinks someone helped her somehow. Aaron say he'll be watching the hands today to see if anyone's more tired than they should be."

With a stab of alarm, Joanna remembered Tavia's restless night and Titus's bloodshot eyes. She wished she could warn them, but she couldn't, not without drawing Aaron's scrutiny their way. A laundress never had good reason to be in the cotton fields or the stable. "We're always tired," Joanna said shakily. "We wake up tired and go to bed tired. If that's all he has to go on, he must think there was a big crowd underneath those chestnut trees last night."

"Talk like that and they'll think *you* helped her," warned Sophie. "Except that you and Leah hate each other."

"I don't hate her."

"That's not what I heard. Maybe for a little while you should let people think you do." Sophie sighed and pounded dough. "Aaron said Leah's his best picker and ought not to be treated so hard. Marse Chester said she'll be healed fine by picking time and she can keep those scars to remind her to treat her mistress with respect. If you ask me, the buck wasn't Aaron's idea."

Joanna was not so willing to absolve him. Aaron had a large cabin to himself and drew extra rations every Sunday, privileges won because he kept the other slaves in line by force. Joanna had not been on Oak Grove long and tried to stay out of his sight, but it seemed to her that each day cruelty came easier to him. Even his warning that Leah should not be treated so brutally was spoken not from mercy but from concern that an injured worker could not carry as many pounds of cotton to the scale.

Aaron was in a fury from daybreak to twilight, Tavia and Pearl reported wearily after they dragged themselves home from the cotton fields at sundown. His whip was never out of his hand, and all day long he snapped it in the air near the face of any slaves who slowed their pace. They gobbled their noon meal standing up in the fields, feeding themselves with one hand and placing seed with the other. Leah he mostly ignored, though she lagged behind the others, stumbling and spilling seed on the sides of the furrows instead of in the trenches. Twice she fainted, and both times he left her there to lie in the dirt until the mule caught up to her, then he gestured impatiently for the nearest slave to pull her to her feet. She finished the last furrows for the day as nothing more than dead weight, arms slung over the shoulders of friends, feet dragging. They would have finished more of the field had he left her where she lay, but Aaron insisted she work with the others, even after she no longer had the strength to reach into her bag of seed.

"She's broken," Titus told Joanna when they slipped away from the others after supper, the only time when they could be alone. "Her body will heal but not her spirit."

"She's only weak from the beating and the buck," said Joanna, interlacing her fingers with his. "She'll get her strength back. By summer she'll be as prideful as ever."

But Titus shook his head. "You didn't see her eyes."

It was true. In the darkness beneath the chestnut trees, she had not looked into Leah's face, and she did not know what Titus had seen there. On Sunday, she understood. Leah sat listlessly in the doorway of her cabin, her face turned toward her children playing with sticks in the dirt, but she did not seem to see them. The stir of excitement that flowed through the quarter as the ration drawing approached did not touch her, and when it was time for the heads of household to pick up their families' weekly supply of cornmeal, molasses, salt pork, and potatoes, Leah's sister went in her place.

Summer passed, and still Leah seemed remote, as if she looked upon Oak Grove from the opposite side of a great crevasse. When the cotton bolls burst forth, she no longer picked her quota with time to spare and then spent the rest of the day goading the others as she filled her friends' bags. Instead, Tavia said, she shuffled through the rows as if her limbs were half-frozen, sometimes meeting her quota, sometimes not. She did not cry out when Aaron whipped her, nor did the beatings propel her any faster through the fields.

Once Joanna tried to talk to her, but Leah's gaze drifted past her and she walked away as if unaware that Joanna was still speaking. Then one morning, Leah was gone. She did not come to the fields when the work bell rang, and when Aaron seized Lizzie's shoulders and shook her, the girl burst into tears and admitted that she had not seen her mother since she had left for the cotton fields the previous morning.

The alarm went out; the patrollers and their dogs were summoned. Every slave in the quarter over the age of seven received three lashes, except for Leah's sisters and her husband, who received ten. On Sunday Marse Chester canceled the drawing, and when Titus asked permission to go hunting, he was denied. Some men, Titus among them, stole off at night to fish or check rabbit snares; the women shared the harvest of their gardens. Joanna felt her baby stirring faintly and feared that it would starve, despite Sophie's stolen gifts from the kitchen. "How long will Marse Chester cancel the drawing?" she asked Titus. "He can't let us all die. Who pick his cotton?"

"No rations until they catch Leah," Titus said, a muscle in his jaw working. Day after day he swallowed back his bitterness and anger until it festered in his belly, and Joanna knew he could not hold it forever. He was a man. He would not let his family starve. Joanna feared what he might risk to keep them alive, to keep her and her baby alive.

But on Friday, when every sack of cornmeal in the quarter was empty and slaves swayed on their feet beneath the hot sun and the too young and the too old collapsed and had to be carried into the shade, word spread that Leah had been found. The slave who drove the wagon that brought her body back to Oak Grove said that she had been discovered floating facedown, tangled in reeds where the Edisto River emptied into the ocean.

No one knew whether she had drowned while trying to escape or if she had walked into the deepest part of the creek and let the waters close over her.

Two days later, the heads of households collected their weekly rations as if the drawing had never been interrupted.

Miss Evangeline spent spring and summer in Charleston with her aunt Lucretia, so instead of sewing for her, Joanna was set to work sewing rough "Negro cloth" into clothing for the slaves, though they would not receive their new garments until Christmas. As the first harvest came in, Marse Chester, figuring Joanna had little else to do with the young mistress away, ordered her to set the slave clothing aside and sort cotton instead.

All summer long, except on washdays and mornings when Mrs. Chester had mending for her, Joanna joined several older women in the outbuilding where the clattering cotton gin separated the seeds from the silky fibers. They sat on the floor, mounds of ginned cotton piled up around them and across their laps, dividing the pure white fibers from those discolored a faint yellow. The pure white cotton fetched a better price at market, but one yellow speck discovered within the bale could mean the difference between a grade of "Fancy" and "Good Middling." On her first day, Aaron cuffed Joanna upside the head for allowing a few fibers with a minuscule amount of yellow into the white pile, then cuffed her again when she overcorrected and included a few fine white strands in with the yellow. Eventually she caught on, and by July she could sort cotton as swiftly as the older women, whose thin, leathery hands fairly flew through the piles.

If she lived long enough, she would become one of those old women, she realized, once her hands grew too stiff to work a needle and her arms too weak to haul wash water. This would be her fate if she reached old age before freedom. The Chesters of Oak Grove needed every slave and hired no one out, so she couldn't earn any money to buy her freedom. Some days she woke from dreams of Elm Creek Farm so despondent she could hardly rise from bed, knowing Marse Chester would name her child and put him or her in the stable or the big house or the fields as he saw fit. Then an image would appear in her mind's eye — Leah tangled face down in the reeds, bobbing in the current that might have carried her across the ocean to the land of her ancestors. She thought of Leah and forced herself to rise, to eat, to report to work, to duck her head and avoid the eyes of the white buckra. She lived for the moments when she could be alone with Titus. His arms and his dreams of freedom, so tightly interwoven with her own, were her only solace. Titus and the Birds in the Air quilt reminded her of a world beyond Oak Grove, a world where she imagined her firstborn thrived and where one day his little brother or sister would play by his side.

But freedom seemed an increasingly elusive dream the larger her belly grew.

One evening about two months before she expected her second child to enter the world, Joanna sewed the last row of Birds in the Air blocks to the bottom of her quilt. She had made twelve blocks more than necessary, thinking to piece them into a smaller quilt for the baby, but a quilt for her child would have to wait until she finished the quilt that would record the clues that might one day lead her family to freedom.

The next washday, Joanna approached Mrs. Chester in her study and asked if she might have some of the lowest-grade cotton to fill a patchwork quilt.

"I'll ask my husband if he can spare it,"

the mistress replied, sizing up Joanna's belly. "How much longer?"

"About two months, missus, I think."

"That's fortunate. You'll have that all out of the way before Miss Evangeline returns. She would be quite distressed if you were unable to prepare her trousseau."

That was how Joanna learned that Miss Evangeline was to be married. She thanked the mistress and hurried back to the wash-house, heart sinking as she realized that the slaves' new clothing would be pushed aside once again. Joanna would be needed to sew a wedding gown and fine dresses suitable for an officer's wife in Charleston — if she had guessed correctly and Colonel Harper was Miss Evangeline's intended husband. Most of the field hands had worn through the clothing distributed the previous Christmas, and Joanna sometimes mended torn seams and patched holes in exchange for food. But she could not repair what had been completely worn away.

A few days later, the mistress granted Joanna's request for cotton. "But only enough for one quilt," she cautioned, "and only the lowest grade." It made no difference to Joanna; a middling grade, yellow batt flecked with hulls would keep her as warm as the purest white. She filled her apron with sweepings from the floor around the cotton gin and stashed the bundle in the cabin until she could collect enough large pieces of fabric to piece together into a backing. Until then, her quilt would have to wait while she worked on the slaves' clothing. If she did not finish, many of the 170 men, women, and children the Chesters owned would go naked in winter while Miss Evangeline wore fine wools and furs.

Later that week, Mrs. Chester announced that Miss Evangeline was returning home from her aunt Lucretia's house in Charleston earlier than planned so that they could begin preparing for the wedding in earnest. Joanna helped Dove air out the young mistress's room and change the linens, but she rushed through the chores so she could resume sewing clothing for the slaves. Even the simplest shirts and dresses took at least a day to complete, and although Joanna despaired of finishing before the distribution at Christmas, she pressed on. Basting shirtsleeves and hemming trousers, Joanna longed for Anneke Bergstrom's sewing machine, which she had learned to use during her single winter in Pennsylvania. If only Mrs. Chester would buy one for Oak Grove, but she was too frugal to spend money on something that did not benefit her. Mrs. Chester already *had* a sewing machine — Joanna. Why waste good money on another?

When Miss Evangeline returned, Joanna resolved to convince her that a sewing machine would allow Joanna to sew a finer seam and produce more pretty dresses in a fraction of the time. Never one to turn away from any opportunity to acquire more finery, Miss Evangeline might persuade her father that a sewing machine would be a good investment.

In the meantime, Mrs. Chester found her own solution to Joanna's impossible workload.

She was heating water in the washhouse when Lizzie appeared in the doorway. "Mistress says I'm supposed to help you," she said sullenly, as if she still resented Joanna's accusation that she had stolen the tin cornboiler. "You supposed to teach me everything you know."

Joanna could not look at Lizzie without imagining Leah tangled in the reeds. "Why you? You don't act like you asked for this job."

"All the bigger girls are picking cotton." Lizzie put her head to one side and thrust out her chin, eyes narrowed and fixed on Joanna's face as if she were daring herself not to flinch at Joanna's scar. "I'd rather be with them in the fields than in here with a stupid yellow girl who thinks I'm a thief."

Joanna emptied soap in the wash water and stirred the steaming brew with a long wooden paddle. "You only say that because you never had to work the fields."

Lizzie tossed her head. "What would you know about it, house slave like you?"

"I pick tobacco back in Virginia," Joanna retorted. "Girls and boys younger than you weren't playing in the slave quarter, watching the little ones. That was a job for old women. Soon as a child five or six years old, they out in the fields picking hornworms off the tobacco leaves. The driver follow behind looking over your row, and if he find any hornworms you missed, he make you eat them."

Lizzie looked ill. "Well, I wouldn't miss any."

"Everybody miss some, specially at first."

"Not me."

Exasperated, Joanna shook water from the paddle and thrust the handle toward Lizzie. "Here. Try not to burn anything or Aaron might decide you old enough to pick cotton after all."

Grumbling, Lizzie snatched the paddle and did as Joanna said.

231

That day's work took twice as long as usual, but as the week passed and Joanna shared what she knew as patiently as she could, she discovered that Lizzie had a quick mind to go with her saucy tongue. She could remember, word for word, Joanna's recipes for different soaps — one for clothes, another for skin, several different mixtures for different kinds of stains — and although she wasn't strong enough to empty a full bucket of water into the washtub or haul a basket of damp laundry out to the line, she could still feed wet clothes into the mangle while Joanna cranked the winch, or stir the soaking clothes with the wooden paddle so Joanna could turn a few pieces of coarse homespun into a dress for a girl in the quarter. The more the girl learned, the more Joanna discovered to teach her.

If Lizzie had any care about her future, Joanna thought, she would learn to do the washhouse work quickly and well. Field work would be the death of her. Her sharp tongue was no match for Aaron's whip.

Sewing, mending, washing, sorting cotton. Awaiting Miss Evangeline's return. Awaiting the arrival of her child. Bartering sewing services for food; rejoicing when Titus came home from hunting with a rabbit or a squirrel. Slipping away from the quarter to be alone with him; whispering of the day they would run off, all of them, leaving only an empty cabin behind. Wondering if they were only sharing wistful dreams rather than plans, real plans, plans they intended to carry out.

Then one night, Titus drew her off into the woods near the creek, where the rushing water would cover their voices. "What do you say we run off sooner rather than later?"

For a moment, Joanna could only stare at him. "I haven't finished my quilt yet" was her first, foolish response.

"You don't need the quilt. You got everything fixed in your mind."

"How soon?"

"Next week. Sunday." He clasped both her hands in his. "Marse Chester is sending me to Charleston to fetch Miss Evangeline home."

"He's not going with you?"

"He got too much to do here with the harvest and his buyer coming, so he's sending me alone."

"But don't Miss Evangeline need an escort?" White ladies rarely traveled anywhere without a husband, father, or brother to look after them.

"Her cousin Bartholomew's coming back with her — or he would be, except we won't be going that way." A rustling in the bushes silenced him, until he saw it was only a squirrel. "Listen. You, Tavia, Auntie Bess, and the children can hide in the coach until we well out of sight of the ferry and anyone who might know me or Marse Chester's horses by sight. I know a blacksmith in Charleston — a slave, but he can write. He'll make us passes all the way from Charleston to Philadelphia."

Joanna thought it over, took a deep breath, and shook her head. "No one would believe us, not even with a pass. What reason would seven slaves have to be driving themselves all that way alone?"

"Not seven slaves. One widowed white lady, her trusted driver, and her five slaves."

Joanna's heart hammered. "Titus —"

"You know you can pass for a white lady if you wear a fine dress and bonnet. Didn't you tell me that was the plan to get you from Pennsylvania to Canada? We'll say you a white lady whose husband died from measles. You don't have any kin here, so you going back to home to your mother to have your child. We'll paint spots on your face so no one will want to get too close and ask you questions."

"But when you don't show up in Charleston —"

"By the time Miss Evangeline gets word to her father that I never show up, we got ourselves a good head start. They'll be looking for runaway slaves, not a poor, sad, sick white lady in a coach."

"Aaron won't miss us, not on a Sunday," said Joanna, mulling it over. "Not until Tavia don't show up for the drawing."

"We can say she sick, ask someone else to get her ration. That'll buy us a little more time."

"And then Monday morning, when she and Pearl don't show up at the fields, whoever got her ration for her will get beat." Joanna shook her head. It couldn't be done, not without bringing down punishment upon others. "Everyone will get beat, and everyone will go hungry."

"I'll hunt every day between now and then so that everyone has a little meat put away. They can have our garden. We won't need it." He squeezed her hands tightly and pulled her close. "I know you hurt whenever anyone else hurts, but sometimes you got to think of your own. Marse Chester won't starve them to death, and he won't let Aaron beat everyone to death. If they kill us all, you think they gonna send Miss Evangeline and her brothers and sister out to the fields to pick that cotton? They need us or they lose everything."

Joanna pressed her lips together and nodded. She didn't want anyone to suffer on her account, but if the alternative was to stay forever a slave, to bear her child into slavery —

"It might work," she said. "It could."

"Once we get to Philadelphia, first thing we do is send word to your friends and find your son," Titus promised. "I'll raise him like he's my own."

Joanna burst into laughter, tears in her eyes. "He don't look nothing like you."

"I don't care." Titus raised her hands to his lips, eyes shining with hope and pride. "You a brave woman. I knew that when you first glared at me through the bars of that wagon. I know it won't be easy to travel so close to your time, but it'll be easier than running with a newborn who always pick the worst time to cry, who make noise just when you most need him to be quiet."

She knew he was right, and that a chance like this might never come again.

They went over their plan every night in the cabin while the children slept. Tavia clasped her hands in her lap, eyes wide and anxious whenever Titus described the dangerous route north, but she agreed that this was their best chance for freedom. Pearl, eager and determined, offered to help pack food for the journey and promised to keep the children quietly occupied on the long drive north. In vain they all tried to persuade Auntie Bess to come along, but she insisted that she was too old to travel so far, that she would slow them down if something went wrong and they had to abandon the coach and travel on foot. "Didn't you say you need someone to draw the ration on Sunday?" she said. "If I do it, no one else needs to know what you got planned. That'll buy you an extra day, almost."

"If you stay behind, they'll punish you," said Tavia.

Auntie Bess cackled. "What they gonna do, beat an old woman?"

"They done it before," said Pearl.

"Even if they do, it be worth it to get you almost an extra day head start."

"Come with us, Auntie Bess," Titus urged. "Live the rest of your days a free woman."

"Tell you what," she said. "You get free, then you get yourself a good living and buy my freedom."

Nothing they said would persuade her. All Titus could do was to promise to buy her freedom someday, leaving unspoken how unlikely it was that he could ever do so, how many years he would have to work to earn enough wages, how impossible it was to imagine him persuading Marse Chester to sell one of his slaves to one of his runaways.

Joanna stole one of the mistress's old dresses, one left in the mending basket so long the mistress had forgotten it. One night she let out the hem, ripped out seams, and made it over to fit her belly. If anyone noticed that the fabric didn't match, she hoped they would pity her as a newly impoverished, frugal widow. She was counting on the painted measles spots to keep people at a distance. As for her burn scar, she had no idea how to explain it away except as a symptom of the same disease.

Auntie Bess used up the last of the cornmeal baking biscuits for them to take on their journey. When they protested that she ought to keep some back for herself, she retorted, "Next week I'll have the whole ration to myself."

"After that, you'll be lucky to get a ration at all," said Titus, still confounded by Auntie Bess's refusal to run. "You best eat your fill Sunday night, because Monday morning they'll take everything you got left."

"I'll hide it in the woods in a basket," she said airily, so Titus let her be.

They counted down the days and slept restlessly at night, full of eagerness and worry. The children sensed something was coming, but they were accustomed to uncertainty and did not fuss. Some mornings Joanna awoke from nightmares of slave hunters and bellowing dogs, shaking from fear and tasting bile. Other days she fairly flew from the big house to the slave quarter, counting down the number of times she would swing the washhouse door shut, pass the chestnut trees, cross the dusty road between the cabins. Dread and excitement haunted her; anticipation spurred her to plan for an uncertain future: This time next month, they might be crossing the border into Pennsylvania. This time next year, they could be building a home in Canada, with rooms for them all, her older boy and her new baby taking his first steps, her husband and his kin.

This time next week, they could all be in the buck, bound down in a squat, backs split open and seeping blood. This time next week, they could be dead.

Friday came — their last Friday on Oak Grove, the women murmured to one another as they prepared to leave Tavia's cabin for the day. Two more days to prepare; two more days to worry, to think of a million reasons to change their minds. Joanna rolled Mrs. Chester's altered dress into her Birds in the Air quilt top and tucked her carefully hoarded pins, the needle case she had fashioned from a piece of worn linsey-woolsey, and her tin cornboiler into the bundle. Tomorrow she would leave the big house with the sewing shears and add them to her belongings. She figured she had earned them.

But as she was leaving the kitchen building after the noon meal, she spotted Titus striding up the road to the big house, his face contorted from the effort to conceal his fury. Instinctively her hand went to her belly to comfort her child, and when she caught Titus's eye, she nodded and moved off behind a stand of live oaks so they could speak unobserved.

"What is it?" she asked as he took her hand and led her even farther into the thicket.

"Marse Chester change his plans," he said, his jaw clenched so hard he could barely get the words out. "He's sending me tomorrow to fetch Miss Evangeline. Not Sunday, tomorrow."

"What?" Suddenly dizzy, Joanna reached for his strong arm and held fast. "Why? Why tomorrow? Does he know we mean to run?"

"I don't know. I don't think so, or we'd be feeling the lash right now." Titus held her by the shoulders and locked his eyes on hers. "We can still run. We still got the coach, we still got this chance. We just got to figure out how to do it."

Numbly, Joanna shook her head, trying to clear it. "How?" Titus could hide the children in the coach before sunrise, and maybe, maybe she could slip away from work since no one but Mrs. Chester knew from day to day whether she would be sorting cotton or sewing, but what about Tavia and Pearl? "Maybe Auntie Bess can tell Aaron that Tavia and Pearl sick."

Titus shook his head bleakly. "Aaron always checks to make sure no one's shamming. If they wait in the cabin until Aaron come by, someone might see them going from the quarter to the stable."

And if Aaron didn't believe they were sick and sent them out to work anyway, they couldn't simply drop their bags and walk off the cotton fields when the time came for Titus to depart in the coach.

"Maybe —" Joanna took a deep, shaky breath. "Maybe when they take their full bags to get weighed, instead of going back to the fields —"

"Aaron can see everything from the farthest edge of the fields to the scales," Titus broke in. "If they out of sight for more than five minutes, he'll know they run off."

Joanna knew he was right — and that she was watched almost as constantly as Tavia and Pearl. The buckra might not notice her absence as quickly, but before the day was out, everyone would realize that Joanna had disappeared. If the fugitives managed any head start at all, it would be a matter of hours or minutes, not days. A man on horseback with a rifle could overtake them before they reached Charleston, before they could collect the forged passes, their only measure of protection from patrollers and slave hunters.

If Joanna disappeared while Titus was out with the wagon, Marse Chester would know exactly where to search. He would punish them severely, sell them away from each other — or sell their child and keep Joanna and Titus, the better to punish them for the rest of their lives.

But Titus might never get another chance like this one.

"You got to go alone," she told him.

"Joanna —"

"You got to. We can't come with you, but you can still get away."

"What would Tavia say if she hear you

talking like this?" Titus placed a hand on her belly, and she laid her hands on his. "She wants freedom for her children as much as we want it for ours."

"Tavia would say I'm right and you know it." Titus shook his head, but she hurried on before he could argue, before he could persuade her that it had to be all of them or none. "Your friend can write a pass saying you been sent to fetch someone back to your master, someone in his family — make it his old mother, who can't travel alone. Patrollers'll believe that before they believe a coach full of slaves and one white lady with measles and a burned face. Soon as I talk, or if they see my hair, they'd know I'm not white anyway."

Anguished, Titus embraced her. "No. I can't do it. I can't leave you and Tavia and the children. Not when you about to have my child."

Joanna fought back tears, tears she could not explain away when she returned to the big house, tears that would arouse the mistress's suspicions. "You got to go." She pressed her hand to his cheek, to the dear face she loved to look upon. "After you get to Philadelphia, you make your way west to the Elm Creek Valley. You find Gerda Bergstrom at Elm Creek Farm, and you find my son. Keep him safe until you can buy my freedom."

She buried her face in his shoulder and felt him nod, his tears hot on her skin.

Saturday morning. Tavia looked so frightened, Pearl so bitterly disappointed, that Joanna implored them to keep their faces turned away from Aaron or he would know something was wrong. They had said their good-byes the night before, after supper, knowing it would be too difficult on the day of their parting. Titus had told his young niece and nephew only that he was going to Charleston to fetch Miss Evangeline, hoping that the children would not be punished too severely if, when questioned later, they knew nothing of his escape. As if they had sensed that their uncle would be gone much longer than he claimed, they had held on to him when he tried to go, begging him to stay until they fell asleep. He agreed, and sat on the edge of their bed stroking their backs until their eyes closed. Then he kissed them, embraced each of the women in turn, and gave Joanna one last, lingering kiss before he gathered up the food set aside for the journey and ducked out of the cabin.

The next morning the sun shone brightly in a clear blue sky, but Joanna was insensible to anything but grief and fear. If Titus could not get the forged pass or if it wasn't convincing, he could be shot on sight as a runaway and Joanna would never know what had become of him. Even if he made it to freedom — *when* he made it to freedom — he might not be able to send word to them. She would wonder for the rest of her life if the father of her child were living or dead.

She was sewing beneath the oak trees when she heard the coach rumble out of the carriage house, her husband high upon the driver's seat, reins in his hands. He turned around once to look back, and she knew, although he gave no sign that he had seen her, that as long as he lived he would remember how she had looked as he had driven away, resting her sewing upon her ample belly and watching him go.

Then he turned back around, and she could only sit and watch his tall, straight back as he disappeared down the road behind a curtain of moss-draped oaks.

Suddenly hatred surged through her. What was one day to Marse Chester? One day to spoil their plans, to ruin all their hopes, to separate her from the only man she had ever loved. Titus was her only happiness, and now he was gone.

Shaking with rage, she flung her sewing aside and pressed her hands to her face. The baby stirred and kicked within her. After a moment, Joanna lowered her hands and pressed them to her abdomen, answering the baby's silent call, pressing gently upon the little feet that explored his little world. If only he could drift there forever, and never know discomfort, never know loneliness or grief or pain.

The Bergstroms would help Titus raise the money to buy their freedom. If the Bergstroms were not dead or in prison for helping her, they would help her husband.

The thought was a fragile thread holding her last hopes together, and if she tugged upon it, all would unravel.

Sunday passed, dull and heavy. When the time came for heads of households to draw the weekly ration, Joanna lined up behind Tavia and asked for Titus's share. "Don't you live with Tavia?" asked Aaron, eyeing her skeptically.

"Only because Miss Evangeline don't want me to sleep in the barn." She had stayed with Titus in his corner of the hayloft for the first few weeks of their marriage — after their second ceremony, the one the Chesters knew about — until Miss Evangeline complained that she smelled like horses. Then it was back to Tavia's cabin and stolen moments alone beside the riverbank.

She met Aaron's gaze boldly, ignoring the whip coiled on his belt. She would be feeling its sting soon enough. They all would. "I'm head of household while Titus gone to Charleston to fetch Miss Evangeline. He could get his ration himself when he gets back, but you always say if we miss the drawing, we got to wait until next week. He can't go without food until then."

"All right. Take it." Aaron set out Titus's portion on the ground, and Joanna quickly scooped up everything and carried it back to the cabin before he changed his mind. She knew he would not have bent the rules for anyone but Titus, the most trusted slave on Oak Grove after himself. Titus's betrayal would enrage the Chesters the way the escape of a mere field hand never could. Her throat constricted whenever she imagined what Marse Chester would do to Titus if he were captured. And if they didn't catch him, those left behind might starve to death, no matter how much Marse Chester needed them to bring in the cotton. She would have to hoard every scrap of food she could in preparation for the coming famine.

In the meantime, only Joanna, Tavia,

Pearl, and Auntie Bess knew what awaited them. They could not warn the others without exposing Titus's escape, and if Aaron overheard even whispered rumors, slave hunters would be sent in pursuit as soon as Marse Chester could summon them. Joanna envisioned Isaac and Peter dragging Titus, bound and bleeding, behind their horses; she pictured the Georgia traders hauling him from the barracoon to the auction block. Dizzy and sick, unable to drive the horrible pictures from her mind, she ran off to the riverbank and wept, pressing her hand to her mouth to strangle her sobs. Hunger and exhaustion eventually drove her back to Tavia's cabin, where the other women put their arms around her and held her. In the center of their intertwined arms was Joanna's child, all that remained to her of the man she loved.

A storm struck the next day, driving rain and thunderclaps that shook the big house and turned day into night. Bored, Elliot Chester, the eldest son, terrified his two younger siblings with tales of a giant sea monster roaring and thrashing in the ocean to the east, furious at the humble planters who disturbed its rest by casting ships upon the waves above his watery kingdom. Joanna jumped at each flash of lightning, praying that Titus was far north of the storm and that the impassable roads would delay a messenger sent from Miss Evangeline's aunt.

The storm subsided by nightfall and the next day dawned warm and sunny. While listing Joanna's duties for the day, the mistress wondered aloud what could be keeping Miss Evangeline. "Her father should have gone to fetch her," she said, piling boys' trousers into Joanna's mending basket. "Likely she wanted to linger another day to enjoy the shops and parties, and if her aunt agreed, what could Titus do without an express command from his master?" Suddenly she paused and peered into Joanna's face. "You needn't be troubled. We don't blame Titus. Evangeline ought to know better."

Joanna composed herself and nodded. Until Aunt Lucretia sent word that Titus had never arrived, the Chesters would invent one excuse after another for the delay. Each day took her husband farther and farther from their reach. She prayed for the horses to be swift and strong, speeding him northward. She prayed that the Bergstroms would offer him work and a place to stay so that he could earn enough to buy his family's freedom. They raised horses;

they could use a man like Titus.

She prayed that when Marse Chester punished the slaves who remained because he could not touch the one who had escaped, his vengeance would not cause her to lose Titus's baby.

She was sitting in the doorway of the washhouse when the clatter of hooves and rumble of carriage wheels came from down the front road. "They're here," she heard the youngest Chester boy shout, and her heart suddenly plummeted. The aunt had not sent a man on a swift horse with the news of Titus's escape but had hired a driver to bring Miss Evangeline herself. Joanna could not imagine a worse messenger. Miss Evangeline would flee to the safety of her father's arms, and with blue eyes shining with unshed tears and chin trembling bravely, she would weave a tale of an innocent maiden abandoned in the dangerous city, betrayed by a deceitful, ungrateful slave. Each embellishment would fan the flames of her father's wrath.

Clutching her sewing, Joanna closed her eyes, but she could not sit there forever. Packing up her mending basket, she grasped the doorframe and hauled herself to her feet. Supporting her belly with one hand and balancing the basket on her hip, she left the solitude of the washhouse for the kitchen building, where Sophie had stepped outside to watch Miss Evangeline's homecoming.

The coach rounded the bend — and even from a distance Joanna recognized it as Marse Chester's own coach, and the road-weary man on the driver's seat as her own Titus.

Her knees gave way. Sophie saw her crumple too late to break her fall. "Joanna," she exclaimed, hurrying to her side. "You all right? Is it the baby?"

"No," Joanna managed to say as Titus pulled the coach around to the front veranda. Quickly Augustus appeared to open the door and help Miss Evangeline descend. Holding her skirts out of the mud, a smiling Miss Evangeline floated up the stairs and into the big house, followed closely by a man who looked to be a few years older, dressed in a perfectly tailored suit and mopping his round, bland face with a white handkerchief. After Augustus and Titus unloaded Miss Evangeline's belongings, Augustus carried the trunks and parcels inside while Titus drove on to the stable to care for the tired horses.

Leaving the mending scattered on the ground, Joanna hurried to the stable, where she stopped short in the doorway, fighting to catch her breath. Titus was unhitching the horses when her shadow broke up a patch of light on the floor. He looked up and held her gaze, but she was frozen in place and could not throw herself into his arms.

"I couldn't do it," he said, in a low voice only she could hear. "I couldn't leave you to be beaten and starved. I couldn't leave you to have our baby alone."

"You could've gotten free," she choked out, forgetting to look around for Aaron. "You could have bought our freedom."

"That could take years."

"I would've waited."

"Joanna." He spoke her name like a caress. "You my world. You my life. Aaron and his whip, that crazy Miss Evangeline — and any day Marse Chester could sell you off where I'd never find you. We're together now, you, me, and the baby. When we run, we run together."

Tears slipped down her cheeks. "We might never get another chance like that one."

"We get another chance." He patted one of the horses on the flank and came to her, and she flew the last few steps to cross the distance that separated them. "I know you glad to see me even if you don't say it."

"I am glad to see you," she said, her voice muffled by his shirt. She had sewn it for him, wishing with every stitch that she dared make it from the same fine cotton she used to make shirts for the master, so that the coarse slave cloth would not chafe the scars on his back. She had given him up forever, and now here he was, holding her.

She could not be sorry he had returned.

Miss Evangeline had brought home yards of ivory taffeta, silk ribbon, and lace for her wedding gown. The day after her return from Charleston, she summoned Joanna to her room, spread several magazines open on her bed, and showed Joanna tinted fashion plates of demure, elegant white ladies in fine dresses. She instructed Joanna to take the bodice from one pattern, the sleeves from another, the neckline from a third, and the skirt from a fourth to create a gown lovelier than any of those pictured, lovelier than any gown ever before seen. "Please me in this manner," she said, smiling brightly as she handed Joanna the stack of *Godey's Lady's Book*s, "and I'll see that you are well rewarded."

Joanna nodded and carried the magazines to the closet off the kitchen, heart fluttering. Some buckra would beat a slave for even glancing at words written on a page, and Miss Evangeline had blithely ordered her to walk away with a pile of magazines. It was better not to have the temptation. Titus and Tavia knew her secret, but no one else could discover she knew how to read. But it was impossible to keep her attention fixed on the pictures of white ladies with long, slender necks and plump hands when the words drew her eye. After skimming the patterns in the Practical Dress Instructor sections, she read a poem about a young woman taking her ease in her garden, a favorable review of a new novel titled *The Hand but Not the Heart,* a treatise on the proper education for young girls, and a letter from the editor admonishing her readers not to discuss politics "as was becoming the fashion among the younger set," because men did not like such "mannish ways" in their wives and daughters. It was silly and foolish enough to make Joanna stifle laughter, and yet she hungered to decipher the meaning of every line. Too many months had passed since Gerda Bergstrom's lessons, reading Frederick Douglass's *Autobiography* while recovering from her difficult journey through the pass into the Elm Creek Valley. She had forgotten a great deal, but with practice it might come back to her.

She held on to the magazines as long as she dared, explaining to the young mistress that since she could not draw, she had to look at the pictures from time to time to make a pattern in her mind. Whenever she was sure she was alone, she set fabric and thread aside and slowly read a page, over and over, figuring out the meaning of an unfamiliar word by the words around it and by the pictures, if there were any. Some of the articles offered practical advice for dressmaking that aided Joanna as she struggled to pull together what Miss Evangeline admired about her favorite fashion plates. She memorized tips about making patterns and fitting dresses but doubted she would be able to put her newfound knowledge to practical use. How could she make several different sizes of patterns with pleats already in place when she was forbidden paper and pen? How could she measure carefully along the many different seams when she was limited to a long piece of string rather than a measuring tape? How could she try anything new without piquing the young mistress's curiosity and leading her to the conclusion that she could read? Joanna needed the magazine's advice and patterns to create the dress Miss Evangeline envisioned — a six-tiered skirt of ivory taffeta trimmed with wide bands of rose silk, a wrap bodice with a basque waist, a neckline that bared much of the shoulders, gathered puff sleeves — all while maintaining the pretense that she did not know her letters and numbers, that she could assemble complicated garments simply because she was ordered to do so.

Joanna marveled that a girl as sharp as Miss Evangeline didn't suspect the truth.

The struggle to use what she had learned while pretending to know nothing slowed her progress, but when Miss Evangeline grew impatient, Joanna explained that she had to take her time lest she make a mistake and waste the precious fabrics and trims. "That's none of your concern," snapped Miss Evangeline. "Let my father worry about the expense. You should worry about pleasing me."

Afraid of arousing suspicions, Joanna returned the magazines, having learned all she could from them. The dress came together swiftly after that, and Joanna began to hope that she might finish the rest of Miss Evangeline's trousseau soon enough to complete the slaves' clothing in time for Christmas.

She felt her first pains while crawling on the floor in Miss Evangeline's room, measuring the fall of the tiers with a long piece of yarn. "Whatever are you grunting about?" Miss Evangeline asked.

"The baby," said Joanna, sitting back on her heels as another wave of pain seized her. "It think it's coming."

"Well, don't have it in here." Miss Evangeline snatched the luxurious folds of fabrics out of Joanna's reach. "Go outside. Go to the slave quarter." Then the young mistress's composure returned. "You have my permission to return to your cabin until your child is born."

Joanna thanked her and left, not bothering to mention that it could be hours before her child entered the world. If Miss Evangeline knew that, she would keep Joanna sewing until the moment she had to set down her needle to catch her own baby on the way out.

Joanna went first to the stable, but one of the little boys who mucked out the stalls told her that Titus was out exercising the horses. Her discomfort sharply increased as Joanna made her way to the slave quarter, pains increasing so rapidly that she could only shuffle in the dirt, clutching her belly. Labor had not come upon her so suddenly a year and a half earlier when Frederick was born, but then she had relaxed in a comfortable bed, with plenty of food and rest, and Gerda's attentive care. The Bergstroms had sent for their friend, a doctor and fellow abolitionist, when her labor had taken a dangerous turn. What would Joanna do if something went wrong this time? She had never known the Chesters to summon a doctor to the slave quarter.

Auntie Bess was sitting in the doorway of the cabin weaving a sweetgrass basket when Joanna arrived, but one glimpse of Joanna's painful grimace stilled her hands. "It your time?"

Joanna gasped and nodded as a clenching fist of pain seized her. "It's not like before," she said, panting, after the fist released.

"Second babies sometimes come faster." Auntie Bess rose and beckoned to her. "Come on, daughter. I'll take care of you."

They walked by the stream in the cooling shade, Joanna leaning on the older woman, pausing to stand and breathe when she could not walk. A blur of hours passed, a pain both worse than her worst beating and more bearable. She cried out for Titus, for Ruth, for Honor, knowing they could not come to her aid but that Auntie Bess was there, murmuring encouragement, wiping her brow, promising her that her child would be well and strong.

When her daughter came, she came quickly — a sudden wrenching and then it was over. Murmuring words Joanna did not comprehend in her exhaustion, Auntie Bess bathed the child, swaddled her in a worn flannel blanket, a discard from the big house Joanna had made over with her finest stitches around the edges.

When Joanna felt rested enough, Auntie Bess guided her back to the cabin and sent a child running for Titus. Soon he was there, embracing Joanna and cradling his daughter in his arms. Tiny nose, tiny dark eyes, dark, dark hair, strong tiny hands to curl around a fingertip.

"I want to call her Ruth," Joanna told him. "After a woman who cared for me back in Virginia."

He glanced at her, and she saw the question flash through his mind: Why not name their daughter after Joanna's own mother? Just as quickly, she saw understanding: Joanna did not know her mother's name.

"Ruth a good name," he said. "I promise you, little Ruthie, one day you gonna be a free woman."

Tears pricked Joanna's eyes. Titus saw, and he reached for her hand. He laced his fingers through hers, the palm of his hand callused and strong. "Now do you see?" he asked her softly. "Now you see why I couldn't leave the two of you behind?"

Joanna had a day of rest in Tavia's cabin, nursing Ruthie, dozing, walking stiffly around the cramped space when Auntie Bess chided her out of bed to take a few easy paces around the cabin. The next morning, not long after Tavia and Pearl hurried off to the cotton fields, Lizzie brought word from the big house that Joanna had to come tend to the laundry.

It was washday; Joanna had lost track. "I'm coming," she said, hauling herself out of bed, wincing at a twinge of pain in her abdomen. Shaking her head in resigned disapproval, Auntie Bess helped her fashion a sling out of Ruthie's flannel blanket so she could keep her sleeping daughter close while she worked.

Hurrying to the washhouse, Lizzie's brow furrowed when Joanna fell behind. "Come on," she urged anxiously, racing ahead. "Mistress sent Augustus by twice already asking where you at. I start the fire and fill the washtub all by myself, but that ain't good enough for him. He keep asking for you."

Joanna found herself surprisingly moved that Lizzie had started the laundry on her own, but she could not hurry any faster, not even to ease the girl's worries. As they passed the kitchen building, Sophie leaned out the doorway and called, "Mistress wants to see you. She's waiting in her study."

Lizzie groaned aloud, and Joanna's breath caught in her throat. "But the laundry —"

"Big girl like Lizzie can't do that on her own?"

"Course I can," Lizzie retorted. "That's what I tell Augustus."

"Joanna, you best hurry," said Sophie, ignoring the girl. "The mistress in a fury when she find the washhouse empty and no one watching the fire."

"The mistress came here?" Dismayed, Joanna whirled on Lizzie. "I thought you said she sent Augustus."

"She did! She must have come by after I went to fetch you."

Joanna felt a trickling between her legs and knew she had begun to bleed again, and she hoped that the rags Auntie Bess had given her would be enough to staunch the flow. Dizzy, she wished she could crawl back to Tavia's cabin and lie down.

"You go see the mistress," Sophie urged, "then come back here for something to eat while I hold that baby."

Joanna took a deep breath and nodded,

steeling herself as she made her way to the back door. The housekeeper let her in and urged her to hurry. "Marse Chester's waiting," Dove whispered, giving Joanna a gentle push and gesturing down the hall.

"*Marse* Chester?" she whispered back. "I thought the mistress —"

"They're both there. Now go!"

Heart pounding, Joanna went to the study and found Marse Chester sitting behind his desk, ledger, pen, and ink pot set out neatly before him. The mistress stood to his side, her hand resting on the back of his chair as if they were posed for a portrait.

Head bowed, Joanna waited for them to address her.

"Your child was born alive, I see?" said Master Chester, eyeing the weight of her sling.

"Yes, sir," said Joanna, fighting the urge to turn her back and shield her daughter from his view. "Two days ago, midafternoon."

"Very good." He beckoned her forward. "Let's have a look. Male or female?"

"A girl, marse." She opened a fold of flannel so he could examine the sleeping child. Long lashes curled on a smooth, copper cheek above a strawberry mouth.

"Ah. Pity." Marse Chester took up his pen and opened his ledger. "Still, she's a pretty little thing and capable of learning, I trust."

"Given her breeding, I would train her up as a house servant," the mistress suggested. "She could become a fine housemaid, or a seamstress like her mother."

The master nodded as if he considered that sound advice. "You're certain, Joanna, that Titus is the father."

"Yes, sir," she said, confused.

He peered at her sharply. "It's important that I know the truth. If you've dallied elsewhere —"

"No, sir," she said, more forcefully than was wise. "Ruthie's my husband's child."

His eyebrows rose. "Ruthie? That won't do. Let's say instead . . . Calpurnia. The wife of Caesar." He turned to his wife. "This one must be above reproach, isn't that so, dear?"

The mistress smiled, so he must have made a joke, although Joanna didn't find anything amusing. "Perhaps it's a bit much for such a little one," the mistress replied demurely.

"Something simpler, then. Julianna? No. Julia."

Just in time, Joanna remembered not to protest. She held herself perfectly motionless while the master dipped his pen, turned the pages of his ledger, and wrote, "Julia, quadroon female. Sired on Joanna by Titus. Value twenty dollars."

"You may go, Joanna," said the mistress before the ink had dried.

The date for Miss Evangeline's marriage to Colonel Harper was set for the first Saturday in October, after the last cotton harvest but before the weather turned too unpleasant for travel. Joanna's hands were in constant motion — sewing, fitting, washing, mending, pinning, draping the ivory taffeta, embroidering handkerchiefs and linens with the young mistress's new monogram — every day from the moment she set Ruthie into her sling and hurried to the big house until twilight when she made her weary way back to the quarter, for food in Tavia's cabin and comfort in Titus's arms. On washdays, Lizzie amused Ruthie while Joanna hauled water or when she worked close to the fire, but on every other day but Sunday, Joanna carried her daughter in the sling when she worked indoors or let her lie on her blanket on the soft grass when she sewed outside. Always, always, she kept Ruthie close, remembering not to call her by her true name if any of the Chesters were nearby.

The sling was too cumbersome to wear while she stretched and bent and stooped to fit Miss Evangeline's garments, so she would fashion a makeshift bed out of her mending basket and set the baby in a safe place somewhere in the room, out of the way but still near. At first Miss Evangeline indulged her, won over by the novelty of a baby in the house, but before long she declared Ruthie's coos and soft wails "tiresome" and insisted that Joanna leave her in the housekeeper's care during dress fittings. Dove was happy to hold a sweet baby girl, her own children having grown up, died, or been sold off, but Mrs. Chester was less amenable. "Dove has her own work to attend to," she said, after Ruthie's hungry cries interrupted her reading. "Surely one of the old women in the quarter can look after her."

From then on, Joanna left Ruthie with Auntie Bess, her breath catching in her throat as she shut her ears to her daughter's cries and went to the big house alone, feeling strangely bare and unprotected without the comforting weight of the sling. At first, Auntie Bess carried Ruthie up to the big house several times a day to nurse, but although the thin old woman didn't complain, Joanna knew the walk was difficult for her and doubted she would be able to keep it up as Ruthie grew. The mistress did not permit her to find out. When Ruthie was little more than a month old, Mrs. Chester told her to either wean her child or find someone else to nurse her, because "Julia" was distracting her from her duties.

Rage flared up within Joanna, and she stifled a sudden urge to shove Mrs. Chester backwards so that her head cracked against the corner of the master's desk and her spectacles shattered. She could not obey. She could not give her second child up to suckle at another woman's breast. Back in Tavia's cabin, she swore she would not do it, so to spare her a beating, Titus found a woman whose newborn had died a few days before of a fever and promised her regular meat and fish in trade for her milk. "She'll get the comfort of a child to hold, Ruthie will have a full tummy, and you'll be all right with the mistress," Tavia said, gently taking the baby from Joanna's arms. "It's only while you up at the big house. Nights, Sundays, she's yours alone, yours and Titus's."

Joanna knew she had no other choice, but every day her milk grew thinner, and every day Ruthie minded her leaving a little less. Then came an afternoon when Ruthie wailed when Joanna took her from the other woman's arms. Later that evening, she would not calm down until Auntie Bess cuddled her and sang a song in Gullah talk Joanna didn't understand.

"She won't know me this way," Joanna fretted as she and Pearl gathered water.

"She'll know you," said Pearl. "My mama had to do the same thing when I was born, but I don't remember that. I remember everything that came after, and the same will be true for Julia Ruth."

"Just Ruthie," Joanna murmured automatically. She hoped Pearl was right and that she would have many years to remind her child who her real mother was.

The last week before the wedding was a frenzy of preparation. Guests arrived, bringing horses that needed tending and clothes that before long became soiled and needed washing. Joanna and Titus hardly saw one another for all the work that needed to be done, but Ruthie was content, and they looked forward to the two days of rest the Chesters had promised them after the wedding guests departed. In the meantime, there were too many buckra to please, too many ways to send Miss Evangeline flying into a temper. Joanna dropped into bed at night with Ruthie curled up beside her, barely waking when the baby latched onto her breast and suckled hungrily, dropping off to sleep while she nursed.

The day came. Miss Evangeline glowed in her ivory brocade, more beautiful than any fashion plate. Joanna dressed her before the ceremony and joined the other house slaves at the back of the gallery, the finest room in the big house, while the bride and groom exchanged their solemn vows before the preacher. He was a different preacher than Mrs. Chester sent to lecture the slaves on Sunday morning each month; that preacher had tufts of gray hair fringing a bald pate and smelled faintly of drink as he exhorted the slaves to go about the master's and mistress's business as dutifully as they would their Heavenly Father's business. This preacher smelled of lemon water and was far jollier, almost overcome with tears of joy as he praised the married state. Joanna's thoughts drifted to the day she and Titus had jumped the broom, how the quarter had celebrated, how they had spent their wedding night. A crash of cheers and applause brought her abruptly back to the present: Miss Evangeline was kissing the colonel, and now she was married, and soon she would be the mistress of a fine house in Charleston. Joanna would be happy to wave farewell as she drove away.

The wedding party, family, and guests

began filing outside to the piazza overlooking the garden. "What do you think about our Robert joining the family?" a jovial, red-faced man asked Joanna in passing. She bobbed a curtsy and murmured that she liked it just fine, that the marse colonel was a fine man — lies that skipped off her tongue while in her mind's eye she saw the colonel tearing off Leah's dress. Other guests queried other slaves on either side of her; the slaves promptly provided the only replies that were possible or expected in the situation, but the buckra grinned and nodded their heads as if pleased to have their good opinion of the match confirmed.

After the ceremony, Joanna was sent to the kitchen to help Sophie, so she saw nothing of the celebration that followed the ceremony, although she heard the music and laughter drifting on the balmy air and sampled the dishes Sophie prepared — roasted pheasant, sweet sausage, potatoes with sage, cucumber pickles, bread with white flour, oranges — and last of all, a small square of white wedding cake, a confection so light and sweet she devoured it in two bites before it could melt on her tongue.

The next day every house slave and a few field hands who had decent clothes and manners fit for company were put to work, some helping clean up the mess left behind after the party, others assisting the weary revelers as they rose, had breakfast, and departed. Only the next day did all the slaves truly enjoy a day of rest. Although the drawing had been delayed a day, when Augustus finally summoned the heads of households, he gave them double rations as well as coffee, tea, and sugar. "Miss Evangeline should get married every week," Pearl remarked, sticking her finger into the folded paper and sprinkling a few white crystals on her tongue.

The week of celebration would end with Miss Evangeline's departure, which could not come soon enough to suit Joanna. Her hands and wrists tingled from the strain of constant sewing, and she was tired of Miss Evangeline's fanciful stories and flashes of temper. She had a few short months to finish up before the annual clothing distribution at Christmas, and with Miss Evangeline out of the way, she just might be able to do it.

Joanna was in the washhouse pressing Colonel Harper's suit with the flatiron when the kitchen girl came running to announce that Miss Evangeline needed Joanna to pack her trunks. "Why me?" Joanna said without thinking.

The kitchen girl shrugged, and Lizzie remarked, "I guess since you made all those fine things, you the only one who knows how to fold them proper."

"Anyone can fold a dress," Joanna retorted, but she left Lizzie to finish up and took her time going to Miss Evangeline's bedroom. There dresses were spread over the bed and trunks lying open on the floor; shawls and hair ornaments lay scattered about as if a great wind had swept through the room and scattered the contents of the clothespress and bureau everywhere. Joanna couldn't help wincing at the sight of the garments she had so painstakingly made strewn about so carelessly.

"You want all this in the trunks, Miss Evangeline?" Joanna asked, stooping over to pick up an embroidered morning coat.

"You may call me Mrs. Harper now, Joanna," Miss Evangeline said graciously, forgiving her error. "I must thank you for your fine work on my wedding gown. My husband, the colonel, was truly overcome as I descended the stairs. He looked as if he had glimpsed heaven itself when he beheld me."

"That's nice, miss."

"Of course, the trick will be to keep him

feeling so after we've been married awhile and he knows me better." Miss Evangeline sighed and fingered a silk glove lying on the bureau, missing its partner. "I believe those fashion plates inspired you, Joanna. I can only imagine what you would contrive if you could read the patterns."

Joanna carefully folded a pair of stockings, head bowed so the young mistress could not read her expression. "I guess you'll have your choice of fine dressmakers in Charleston, miss."

"I'm sure they think so. Even now they're surely plotting how to extort enormous sums of money from my husband for the simplest frock. I can't say I'm sorry that I shall disappoint them."

"How . . . do you expect to disappoint them, miss?"

"Why, by bringing my own dressmaker with me, of course." Miss Evangeline beamed, delighted with her surprise. "Didn't I say you would be rewarded?"

"Miss?" Joanna managed to say. "I'm going with you?"

"My goodness, why do you look so alarmed? There's nothing to fear, Joanna. I know you're not accustomed to the bustle of the city, but you'll adore Charleston once you've seen it."

"I seen it," Joanna murmured, remembering the slave market, the auction block, the barracoon. She had hoped for extra food, for sewing notions, for an extra day of rest. She had expected Miss Evangeline to forget she had promised Joanna a reward altogether. Never, never had she imagined this.

"I must say I expected a far different reaction." Miss Evangeline's pretty mouth turned down at the corners. "Perhaps you don't understand how much improved your situation will be in the city. You'll have your own bed in the dormitory above the kitchen building, and you'll eat meals prepared by our own cook. No more sharing a pallet of blankets in the slave quarter, no more ration drawing on Sunday and mixing up porridge over a fireplace."

But did Colonel Harper have a woman who could nurse Ruthie while Joanna worked? It was unlikely — which meant they would have to let Joanna care for Ruthie herself. She hardly dared hope some good might come of the sudden upheaval. Tavia, Pearl, Auntie Bess — she would miss them terribly, but she would accept the loss of their company if it meant regaining her daughter. "Titus's been to the city with Marse Chester," she said, slowly warming to the idea. "He likes it fine."

"Titus isn't coming with us," said Miss Evangeline, shaking her head, brow furrowing. "My husband already has a groom. Even if my husband had dozens of horses and no one to tend them, I can't imagine my father would part with Titus. My father relies upon him too dearly."

A sudden roaring filled Joanna's ears. She gripped the edge of the bureau for support. "My baby," she said. "I can bring Ruthie, right, miss?"

Miss Evangeline fixed her with a cool, flinty stare that confirmed Joanna's worst fears.

CHAPTER FIVE

1860
Charleston, South Carolina

"I don't want her sulking all the way to Charleston," declared Miss Evangeline as her husband, resplendent in his uniform, helped her into the coach.

"She's merely frightened," Colonel Harper consoled her. "She'll be fine once she gets used to her new surroundings."

"Do you truly think so? *I* think she's still angry about that baby."

"Negroes don't feel love or sadness the way we do. They may give the appearance of true feeling, but they understand these sensations only in a brute, rudimentary way, such as a dog or horse might. What you see now is fear and stubbornness, as simple as that." As the colonel closed the carriage door, the last Joanna heard from her seat beside the driver was, "However, if her manner doesn't improve, I'll beat the sulkiness out of her."

Joanna heard but did not care. What more could they do to hurt her? They had already done their worst. They had ripped out her heart.

Miss Evangeline had tried to explain that her father had given her Joanna as a wedding gift — not Titus, not Julia — and she was a hard-won gift at that. When Miss Evangeline had first suggested the idea to her father, her stepmother had protested that she could not do without her only laundress, nor did she wish to lose such an accomplished seamstress. But with time, charm, and well-reasoned arguments, Miss Evangeline convinced her father that another strong, young girl could be trained to wash clothes, and she herself needed a seamstress much more than her stepmother did. An officer's wife in the city must be an accomplished hostess so that her husband might impress his superiors and win promotions, and she must have the clothes to play the part. Her stepmother, on the other hand, rarely needed finery so far out on the plantation, and in any event, she preferred plainer attire, dresses she could easily fashion herself. Miss Evangeline could not bear to think that as a new bride in a new city, she would drive her husband into debt purchasing expensive dresses to keep the gossips at bay.

The twin pillars of money and pride supported her argument solidly enough to convince Marse Chester. It would reflect badly upon the entire Chester family if Miss Evangeline were perceived as inferior to the other young wives of Charleston. Thus Mrs. Chester lost her laundress, and Joanna lost her family.

"You must have known you would be coming with me," Miss Evangeline had said, astounded by Joanna's lack of enthusiasm. "What need do they have of a fine seamstress here after I go? Why would my stepmother have you train up a new laundress if you were to remain behind?"

Joanna's heart ached. So this wretched decision had been made months ago, with Joanna none the wiser. She understood Chester logic, understood why they believed she must go and Titus must stay, but she had heard nothing to justify leaving Ruthie behind. It would be years before Ruthie could perform any useful work around Oak Grove. Ruthie meant no more to the Chesters than twenty dollars in a ledger, but she was everything to Joanna. Titus would understand why she had to take their daughter away with her.

"Miss Evangeline — Mrs. Harper," Joanna said, quietly desperate. "Please let me bring Julia with me. She such a good baby, such a sweet child, so quiet you hardly know she's there. She won't be no trouble to you or the colonel. I'll work so hard for you, Miss Evangeline, you never seen someone work so hard as I will —"

"You'll work hard in any case." Miss Evangeline's cheeks were flushed, her mouth tight with displeasure. "You forget I know how easily distracted you are by that child."

"Please, miss, I won't be distracted —"

"Enough." Miss Evangeline shook her head, astounded by Joanna's impudence. "I can't expect an ignorant girl like you to understand what a great privilege it is to be permitted to accompany me to my new household, but I do expect obedience. Pack my trunks, and tonight, gather your own things and say your farewells. We're leaving in the morning."

Instead of obeying, Joanna had fled to the stable. "We'll run," Titus said, holding her as she choked out the terrible news. "We'll run tonight. You, me, Ruthie, anyone else who wants to go. I'll have the horses ready by nightfall."

But Joanna's flight from Miss Evangeline's

bedchamber had aroused her suspicions, and she convinced her father to take back Titus's key to the stable. She also ordered Joanna to sleep in the big house, on the floor of the closet where she stored her mending basket. Pleas to be permitted one last night with her husband and child were met with a slap across the face and threats of a more severe beating if Joanna did not stop ruining Miss Evangeline's last night at home.

Auntie Bess brought Ruthie to see Joanna off; Titus was there, assisting Colonel Harper's groom. Joanna clung to him, with Ruthie sheltered between them in the cradle of their arms, until Miss Evangeline impatiently ordered her to climb up onto the seat beside the driver.

"I'll see you soon," Titus said, reluctantly releasing her.

She hoped he was right; surely Marse Chester would want to visit his daughter before long. But Joanna knew Titus would not be permitted to bring Ruthie with him.

Then Titus pulled her close and spoke in her ear. "If you get the chance, run. Don't worry about us. Just run."

Run. How could she run from Charleston, not knowing the way? If she fled from Colonel Harper, where could she go but back to her husband and daughter?

"The marse colonel's not so bad," Colonel Harper's groom said kindly after she had sat beside him in silence for the better part of an hour. They were retracing the same route she had traveled with the Georgia traders more than a year before, but nothing looked familiar. Even if she finished her Birds in the Air quilt, how would it ever lead her to freedom?

"We always have enough to eat," Abner went on when she said nothing, "and the colonel don't whip no one unless you lie or steal. Charleston's a fine place. Don't be scared."

"I'm not scared," Joanna said. She felt cold and numb, still disbelieving. There was no room for fear or anticipation or hope. Least of all hope.

Ruthie will forget me, she thought. Joanna would become nothing more than a vague memory, fading as Joanna's own mother had to her.

After a while, Abner gave up trying to engage Joanna in conversation and left her to brood. Eventually they came to the city, which Joanna had last seen through the bars of a cage. The streets bustled with gentlemen, planters, tradesmen, and slaves going about their masters' business; horses pulled carts; slave women in headscarves carried baskets to and from the markets. The sights and smells and noises drew Joanna from her dark reverie; sensing the slight shift in her mood, Abner began describing the sights they passed. Another slave market, similar in appearance to the one Joanna had seen before. The church the colonel and all his household attended, slave as well as free, where colored folk stood along the walls at the back and listened to the same gospel as their buckra masters. The best places to buy fish and poultry, should the new mistress send her on such errands. Abner promised her she would learn her way around the streets quickly if the new mistress let her go out and about, but it all seemed a tangled muddle to Joanna, accustomed to few strangers and narrow paths within fixed borders.

The colonel lived on Meeting Street in a three-story red brick building with white stone trim and curved balconies on the second and third floors above the front door. As they passed through the wrought iron gates to the carriage house, Joanna glimpsed shady, white-pillared piazzas overlooking gardens behind the house. Surrounding the entire property was a solid wrought iron fence whose decorative flourishes could not disguise the sharp, menacing spikes at the top of each bar.

"Marse Colonel sure afraid his slaves gonna run off," said Joanna. He couldn't be that amiable a master if he needed to turn his yard into a pretty barracoon.

"Hmm?" Abner followed her line of sight to the barricades as the carriage rumbled over cobblestones. "You mean the fence? That ain't meant to keep people in but to keep them out. Must've been forty years ago they put that up because of the slave uprising."

"What?"

"I wasn't even born yet myself so all I know is the stories folks tell. Denmark Vesey, he was the leader. He bought his freedom with money won in a lottery and open a carpentry shop. He swore he wouldn't rest until all his people were free. In secret he got thousands, thousands of slaves from all over Charleston and on plantations near the city to join him, and they were gonna revolt. They were gonna kill the masters and set everybody free. But rumors got around and the white folks panicked, and Denmark and some others got rounded up before they could strike a single blow."

"What happened to them?" Joanna asked.

Abner shrugged and steered the horse around the broad circular drive in front of the house. "What you think? They all got hanged. Even some buckra who took Vesey's part." He pulled the horses to a halt, frowned slightly, and said, "Listen here. You best not ask about those times. The colonel don't like that kind of talk. The Charleston buckra never been so scared as in those days, and they know there more of us in this city than them. Anyone who even seems like he might be the next Denmark Vesey, he gets shut up real quick."

Abner fell silent as a footman in a dark blue coat hurried down the front steps to open the carriage door. Joanna nodded to show she would heed Abner's warnings; only a fool would not. Buckra lived in constant worry that their slaves might rebel. When Joanna was hired out to Mrs. Robinson back in Virginia, the white-haired mistress often complained that the soup tasted bitter and would warn the others at the table not to eat it for fear of poison. Joanna herself had struck Josiah Chester before she ran off, but only from instinct, and only to save her own life. After she was recaptured, no buckra judge would have punished him if he had killed her outright, rather than only nearly killing her with a beating. Almost always, fighting back against a master meant death. Everybody knew that.

Denmark Vesey had been a free man, and yet he had fought back, though he'd had everything to lose. As for Joanna, everything she cherished most had been snatched from her. A few worldly possessions — her Birds in the Air quilt top, a wad of poor-quality cotton swept up from the floor of the gin house, her sewing basket, the tin cornboiler, the clothes she wore, the dress stolen from Mrs. Chester — were all that remained to her, and they were a cold comfort.

In a fog of sorrow and disbelief, Joanna settled Miss Evangeline into her new home, wondering if she would ever feel anything but unsettled, uprooted herself. Upon the newlyweds' arrival, Colonel Harper's slaves quickly gathered in the front hall to meet their new mistress. They were better dressed than the slaves at Oak Grove, Joanna thought, and they seemed better fed — Sally, the cook; Asa, the colonel's man; Minnie, the housekeeper; George, the blue-coated footman who had run outside to meet the newlyweds' carriage; a young boy named Tommy who, Joanna later learned, raked the yard and kept flies off the food at mealtime; and Hannah, a girl a year or two older than Tommy, who emptied pots from the necessary chairs into the privies outdoors, scrubbed floors, swept fireplaces, and jumped, wide-eyed, to any other task she was ordered to do. Joanna never heard her speak and wasn't sure she could.

Miss Evangeline's aunt had come to stay until her niece became accustomed to her new home. Aunt Lucretia's maid, Dora, slept on the floor of her mistress's bedchamber for the duration of her visit. Abner and the stable boys slept in the carriage house. There were no field hands, of course, since the Harper family rice plantation was across the river on James Island. Minnie explained that the colonel often traveled to the home plantation when he wasn't busy at the South Carolina Military Academy, but even when he was away, his household must remain ever vigilant, for he often returned home unannounced. The colonel boasted that as a master horseman he could travel more swiftly than any messenger sent ahead, but Sally scoffed at this. "He don't send no messenger," she told Joanna, scathingly. "He hope to catch us unawares. He think it so funny to watch us scramble to please him." Sally had reason to grumble, for she was expected to have a hot meal ready for the marse colonel whenever he might unexpectedly appear.

The other slaves, who did not have to worry about food spoiling and accidentally poisoning the master, needed only concern themselves with tending to the master's estate and possessions during his frequent absences. The grounds enclosed within the wrought iron barricade seemed small and cramped to Joanna, who had lived all her life on plantations, but the gardens surrounding the house were lush and verdant, and the workyard just beyond them seemed well maintained and sufficient for the needs of a small household. The dependencies included a two-story structure that housed the kitchen and laundry, the carriage house and stable, two privies, and another building whose purpose Joanna couldn't guess at first glance.

Though the grounds were less impressive than Marse Chester's, the residence itself was larger and more opulent than the big house at Oak Grove. Joanna had never seen so many windows, some curved at the top and some boasting colored glass, or ceilings more than twice her own height, or so many fancy plaster moldings and carvings framing the top of each room. The front entrance had a white marble floor laced with gray marble threads, and a curved staircase with ornate whitewashed spindles that rose gracefully to the second floor. Slaves were not permitted to use the stairs except to sweep the steps or dust the banister, Minnie warned as she led Joanna past the staircase to the back of the house, where a door concealed the servants' stairs, narrow and steep, with a landing and a turn every four steps.

It was while unpacking Miss Evangeline's things that Joanna discovered she was not only to be the seamstress and laundress; she was also to be Miss Evangeline's personal maid. "I don't know nothing about dressing hair," said Joanna, almost dropping the trunk lid on her fingers in her surprise.

"Aunt Lucretia's maid will teach you," said Miss Evangeline airily, refusing to let such trivial matters diminish the joy of her first day as mistress of her own home. "You have my permission to learn as slowly as you dare, without raising my husband's suspicions. Until you can master the curling iron, my aunt's maid will be forced to continue her lessons, and Aunt Lucretia will be obliged to remain with me."

Joanna was not surprised to learn that Miss Evangeline's capricious dishonesty to the marse colonel was to continue past the long, implicit deception of their courtship.

Miss Evangeline and her stepmother had grudgingly shared a maid back at Oak Grove, a young woman who had tended Miss Evangeline since they were children together. Joanna could imagine Mrs. Chester insisting upon keeping the maid since her stepdaughter was taking away her laundress. Joanna wished the young mistress had preferred the maid. She had no desire to play the role of Miss Evangeline's accomplice in her deceptions and capers, to be slapped for unavoidable mistakes and chided for laziness even as she worked herself to exhaustion. She preferred to stay out of sight of the buckra as much as possible, but here at Harper Hall, it seemed that colored folk and white were never far apart.

Joanna dressed Miss Evangeline for dinner and waited outside the parlor while the mistress chatted gaily with her aunt, reminiscing about the wedding and anticipating her first forays into Charleston society as the wife of a dashing officer. Joanna helped Sally serve the meal and helped Minnie clean up. After nightfall, she undressed Miss Evangeline, assisted her in her toilette, and dressed her in a fine cotton nightgown to await her husband. Later, as she finished her day's work, she heard the sounds of their lovemaking through the walls and thought of Titus — his strong arms, the pattern of scars on his back, the scent of horses. Her longing for him brought tears to her eyes as, well after nightfall, she retrieved her small bundle of possessions and followed Sally from the house to the slaves' quarters above the laundry and kitchen building, separated from the house by six feet of cobblestones for fear of fire. If only Titus had been given to Miss Evangeline too, and they were crossing the stones side by side, taking their first glimpse of their new quarters together. If only Joanna had been left behind at Oak Grove with her beloved husband and cherished daughter, the only child remaining to her.

If only she could believe their separation would be temporary, but hoping and praying and enduring day after day of disappointment might demand more strength than she possessed. But the alternative, to resign herself to never reuniting with her beloved husband, her beloved son and daughter, would be a waking nightmare, a living death. She had to believe they would finally be together and free one day or she could not keep going — but maybe it was foolish to want to keep going.

But she had to keep going. Titus — what would Titus think if she gave up now? What would Ruthie think when she was old enough to understand?

So, as a distant bell somewhere in the city warned slaves still abroad of the ten o'clock curfew, she forced herself to keep on going for at least the rest of that day, nearly over — out the back door of Harper Hall, across the cobblestone walk to the kitchen with its adjacent laundry, a place she would surely come to know well in the years ahead. Inside, she followed Minnie up a narrow staircase to the house slaves' quarters, men and women together in one long room that spanned the length and width of the building.

The dormitory ceiling sloped on the two long sides so that Joanna could stand upright only in the center where the slats met. A cupola in the center of the ceiling drew hot air upward to cool the floors below, warming the slaves as they slept in winter, Joanna suspected, but roasting them in summer, and a water stain on the floor suggested that it let in the rain. On each end of the room, a small window offered a limited view of a starlit sky and a few palmetto and magnolia trees, and in the morning with the sunrise, perhaps more. The leaded glass panes did not seem capable of opening. The sealed windows made her wonder about the door at the foot of the staircase, and whether Colonel Harper would come around when he was done bedding his bride and lock it, or whether his slaves were so content or so afraid or so despairing that they did not need a locked door to keep them in. Colonel Harper had no dogs, no overseer, nothing to keep them in the dormitory except fear, the threat of city patrollers, and the lack of anywhere to run.

The narrow beds were arranged side by side a few feet apart, with a thin, wood-and-plaster half-wall partition nominally separating the men's quarters from the women's. When Joanna snorted at the ridiculous nod to propriety, the sound echoed hollowly off the pine boards.

Sally gestured to a rope bed covered with a coarse blanket. "Mary's gone, so it's yours," she said, and Joanna did not have the heart to ask who Mary was or what had become of her. Minnie climbed into Asa's bed and raised her eyebrows in a mild challenge when Joanna's gaze lingered too long. Glancing away, climbing into her own bed, her eyes met George's. She might not have recognized him from their brief meeting upon her arrival except for the blue footman's coat draped neatly at the foot of his bed. He gave her a small, inquiring smile, but she pretended not to see it, rolled onto her side, and stared at the pattern of knots on the pine board walls, barely visible in the moonlight that trickled in through the cupola and windows. She closed her eyes and willed herself to remember Ruthie's sweet baby scent, but all she smelled was old pine, coarse wool, and weary bodies.

Before dawn, Minnie shook her awake to stumble sleepily down the narrow staircase, through the door that was not locked, and back into the big house to attend Miss Evangeline. She and Asa waited outside in the hallway until the master and mistress summoned them into the room. Miss Evangeline was lying in bed propped up on pillows, but when Joanna answered, she tossed off the quilt and told her which dress to select from the clothespress. The colonel held out his arms so Asa could slip him into a white shirt; he did his own buttons up the front while Asa adjusted the collar. As they were dressed and groomed, the newlyweds chatted comfortably, flirtatiously, as if they were alone, as if Joanna and Asa could neither hear nor understand them.

After the colonel departed, Aunt Lucretia's maid, Dora, came in to show Joanna how to heat the slender curling rods over the fire, how to twine Miss Evangeline's golden locks around the hot metal, how to hold the hair in place long enough to form the curl but not so long that the hair scorched, how to release the curl from the iron so that a golden spring bounced into place. Miss Evangeline held perfectly still, occasionally admonishing Joanna to take care not to burn her, as if she could read the temptation in Joanna's thoughts. Joanna followed Dora's instructions carefully, and although her clumsy curls lacked the smooth perfection of the more experienced maid's, at least she didn't burn the delicate pale skin along the mistress's hairline and earn herself her first beating in Harper Hall. At last Joanna set the curling irons aside and watched as Dora gathered the curls in a satin ribbon and handed Miss Evangeline a mirror so she might inspect their work.

"If I had sat here with my eyes closed, I still would have known that Joanna did this side of my head and Dora the other," the young mistress remarked. "Dora, you must tell my aunt that Joanna may need weeks to master your skills."

As Dora nodded, Miss Evangeline's mirthful glance met Joanna's in the mirror. So the mistress thought Joanna had made clumsy curls on purpose, as she had been commanded. If it put her in good humor to think so, Joanna would not reveal the truth.

Waking up before dawn to wait outside Miss Evangeline's bedchamber. Dressing her silently while Asa attended the marse colonel. Helping Sally serve meals. Helping Minnie clean up afterward. Mending and darning when Miss Evangeline or Aunt Lucretia left work in her basket. Laundry once a week, much less of it than at Oak Grove, hanging clothes in the workyard rather than the wide open fields in the shade of the moss-veiled oaks. Hearing the sounds of wagons and horses' hooves and foghorns and ships coming into harbor rather than the melancholy song of the field hands. Climbing wearily to her bed in the slaves' dormitory at the close of day. Weeping silently for her husband and lost children until she sank into sleep.

The days grew shorter, the nights cooler. Back at Oak Grove Joanna would have been sewing coarse cloth into trousers and skirts and dresses for everyone in the quarter, but not in Charleston. A pair of seamstresses on the Harpers' James Island plantation produced enough clothing for the marse colonel's slaves as well as their own, replacing the garments with the change of seasons in spring and autumn instead of annually at Christmas. With no slaves to sew for and Miss Evangeline still enjoying the novelty of her trousseau, Joanna found herself sewing less and less and working as lady's maid, cook's helper, and housekeeper's girl instead. Missing the feel of a needle in hand and soft cotton upon her lap, one Sunday morning Joanna asked Miss Evangeline for the gift of an old muslin sheet to line her Birds in the Air quilt. Miss Evangeline agreed, so after church services, while the other slaves enjoyed the last of the November sunshine in the yard, Joanna carried her bundle from the room above the kitchen to the piazza, where she spread out the yellow, hull-flecked cotton over the lining, smoothed the patchwork Birds in the Air top over both, and basted the three layers together with large, zigzag stitches, just enough to keep the fabric and batting from shifting.

She knew how she would quilt it: crosshatches and feathered plumes, intricate and delicate, fine enough for a mistress's fancy quilt, dense enough to disguise the images she would stitch into the blocks, the landmarks she remembered from her journey to the Elm Creek Valley.

Someday she and Titus and Ruthie would make that journey north, to find freedom and her lost son. Joanna had to believe that to get through the days, through the long, lonely nights. She could not do as Leah had and cast herself upon the waters. She was too stubborn, too afraid.

She quilted the landmarks into the soft, yielding fabric, thinking of the brown hands with cracked and weathered fingertips that had picked each boll, hands of the women she had loved, Tavia and Pearl, and even Leah.

Ruthie. Would Ruthie wear herself out and die young in the cotton fields? Would she be a bright yellow housemaid, too often before the watchful eyes of buckra men who could take whatever they wanted? Miss Evangeline's brothers were coming of age, two of them, and they would have friends, house-guests they would want to indulge with a night of pleasure. A pretty housemaid, close at hand, sparing them a walk to the quarter — Titus would not stand for it. Titus could not prevent it. Ruthie would carry a white man's child, a child she never wanted, a child that could be sold away from her, plunging her into the agony of grief only a mother who had lost a child could understand.

It would be for Ruthie as it had been for Joanna, as it had been for Joanna's mother, as it had been for her mother, mother to mother until the first who had been captured in Africa and shackled in the dark, stifling, suffocating stench of a ship's hold, terrified and sick on the rolling waves, longing for her mother, starving, bleeding from the rusty shackles on ankles and wrists, praying for deliverance, deliverance that never came.

It would never end. Sunrise to sunset, year after year, mothers and daughters caught up in a current that swept them tumbling over and over, unable to take a breath, thrashing about in the waves for some safe refuge that lay out of reach, beckoning from a distant shore.

During her first two weeks as mistress of Harper Hall, Miss Evangeline entertained guests every night — her aunt Lucretia, her cousins Bartholomew and Gideon, numerous James Island Harpers, Governor Pickens, General Beauregard, and so many others that Joanna did not catch half their names as she passed in and out of rooms, waiting on one and then another. At Oak Grove parties, the buckra discussed cotton, fashion, neighbors, and the weather; at Harper Hall, the subjects of conversation were cotton, rice, neighbors, states' rights, the weather, and secession. When talk turned to secession, as it quickly did after crops and weather were hastily introduced and dismissed, the debate sometimes grew so heated that after a while some of the ladies delicately tried to steer the conversation to safer waters. But not Miss Evangeline. She queried general and governor alike on points of constitutional law and the popular belief that the federal government would not contest Southern secession, if it came to that. "Let them confront us if they dare," declared Miss Evangeline, her eyes snapping blue sparks. "I am a South Carolinian first and an American second. I know that with my husband leading them, our boys will have enough fight to withstand any aggression from the North."

Her remarks were invariably greeted with applause, and Joanna overheard other officers congratulating the marse colonel and praising his wife's fiery spirit.

The more guests, the more work for the household, the less sleep for the slaves, the more prone Joanna was to making mistakes. One morning she dropped the curling iron, and before she could snatch it up, it had burned a dark line across two floorboards.

"Be careful," Miss Evangeline snapped, her nerves already on edge. Her uncle had come to dinner the previous evening and had asked, smiling kindly, when he might expect his wife back home, to tend to the business of her own household.

The smell of scorched pine filled the air, and Joanna imagined, strangely, the tall trees lining the road to the old slave quarter in flames. "Sorry, miss," she murmured.

Aunt Lucretia left the next day, and although she lived only a few minutes' ride away in another part of Charleston, Miss Evangeline wept as if her aunt were departing for the western frontier. At supper that same day, the colonel told Miss Evangeline that he intended to spend the next week on the James Island plantation. Joanna could have told him this was a bad idea if he meant to keep his bride in a sweet temper. As Joanna passed dishes and refilled water glasses, she watched from the corner of her eye as it dawned upon Miss Evangeline that she was meant to stay behind. "What a lovely idea," she said, smiling at her husband as if she assumed she would accompany him. "I would enjoy seeing your mother. It would be pleasant to have female companionship again."

The colonel laughed. "My dear, you saw

my mother last week, and your aunt left us only this morning! You can't say you've lacked female companionship."

"But now I shall, and with you away, I know I'll be lonesome."

"You have your books and knitting to occupy you when the duties of the household don't demand your attention. You might also consider befriending some of the officers' wives. I know several who desire to better their acquaintance."

Miss Evangeline agreed to follow his advice, but her voice was oddly subdued.

The next day after her husband kissed her and departed, she watched from the window as he mounted his favorite gray stallion and trotted off through the wrought iron gates, Asa trailing behind on a slower mare with the colonel's satchel. When they were gone, Miss Evangeline wandered through the house as if seeing it for the first time, running her fingertips over the chair rail in the dining room, peering up at the curved windows as if studying how the glass panes had been pieced together. Watchful, Joanna finished the day's mending and began darning the colonel's socks, waiting for an explosion of temper. But the young mistress surprised her. "Get my wrap," she ordered after Joanna cleared away the lunch dishes.

"I want to see more of the city. If it is to be my home, I must know it."

Joanna fetched Miss Evangeline's wrap as well as her own shawl while the mistress waited in the foyer. When George offered to tell Abner to prepare the carriage, Miss Evangeline waved him to silence, declaring that she intended to go on foot, for she had grown sluggish with so little exercise. "Don't forget your basket," she told Joanna as she tied on her bonnet and left the house. Quickly Joanna snatched it up and followed after.

Miss Evangeline strolled briskly down the cobblestone streets, avoiding puddles, wrinkling her nose at the stench rising from an open sewer. Joanna stayed close, afraid of becoming lost in the throng. They found the market, where Miss Evangeline purchased flowers, which she placed in Joanna's basket, and a bag of roasted chestnuts, which she munched as they walked. The smell made Joanna's mouth water.

They strolled along streets lined by row houses awash in pastel hues, and by the harbor where Miss Evangeline looked out at the ships waiting for high tide so they could approach, her gaze lingering on the horizon beyond the white sails and tall masts. She gazed across the water to Fort

Sumter, where the colonel had served before he was posted to the South Carolina Military Academy. The sight seemed to remind Miss Evangeline of her absent husband, for she sighed and turned her back to it, declaring that she had seen enough of Charleston for one day.

The mistress was silent for the entire long walk home. Joanna suspected she was brooding over her husband's absence, until just as they reached Harper Hall, she said, "Those iron barricades will do us little good against an invading army."

Joanna made no reply, because usually Miss Evangeline did not expect one, but the mistress was too lost in thought to notice her maid's surprise. For all her bold words about the courage and strength of her husband and his men, Miss Evangeline was not eager for war.

The front door burst open as they climbed the front steps. "Missus," the housekeeper exclaimed. "The stovepipe cracked and a big cloud of ash puff out all over."

Miss Evangeline stared at her for a moment, uncomprehending. "Well, sweep the floor, then," she ordered, continuing across the threshold.

"I did, missus, but now what do Sally do for cooking?"

Frowning, Miss Evangeline shrugged off her wrap and passed it to Joanna. "Fix the stovepipe, of course, you goose." She beckoned for Joanna to follow her to the sitting room.

"It ain't something I can fix," said Minnie, bewildered, trailing after them. "Won't you come see, missus?"

Barely concealing her impatience, Miss Evangeline went with Minnie to the kitchen, where one half of the stovepipe dangled from the wall and the other lay on the floor beside the stove, split down one long side. Joanna saw that Minnie had indeed swept away every trace of soot.

Miss Evangeline gnawed the inside of her lower lip. "Who fixes such things?" she asked no one in particular. "Could George manage it? The blacksmith? The scoundrel who sold my husband this wretched contraption?"

"I don't know, missus," said Minnie. "It work fine for twenty years. Never needed to fix it before."

From Miss Evangeline's expression, Joanna knew she was thinking that this never would have happened if her husband had been at home, and if it had, he would have known how to fix it. "Joanna, run next door and ask Mrs. Ames what to do," she said.

Joanna threw her shawl back over her shoulders, hurried next door, and quickly returned with Mrs. Ames's reply. The kindly neighbor had sent word to a trusted handyman who took care of such things for nearly every family on the block. The stove could be repaired, but not until the following morning. Lacking pots and implements for cooking over an open fire, Sally made do with a cold supper, which Miss Evangeline ate alone in the dining room. "At least my husband is enjoying a hot meal at his mother's table," she said with forced contentment as Joanna set her plate before her. She retired early, unknowingly giving Joanna the treat of an extra hour alone to work on her Birds in the Air quilt.

All the slaves went to bed early, tiptoeing out the back door and across the cobblestone walkway so that the mistress would not wake up and decide they were shirking their duties. George, who always tried to catch Joanna's eye at bedtime, must have been emboldened by the novelty, for as Joanna undressed down to her muslin shift, George brushed by her and spoke for her ears alone: "We both alone," he said. "You a pretty girl. Why don't you come with me?"

"I'm married," she replied shortly, in an undertone. "Why don't you ask Sally?"

"I don't care for Sally. I like you."

"I got a husband."

He regarded her, not with the anger of rejection but with sympathy. "How long it gonna be before you see him again? He probably got himself another wife by now."

"Not Titus," Joanna shot back, not caring who overheard. "Not my Titus."

George shrugged as if to say that he knew better but considered it unkind to say so. "You change your mind, you let me know. I'm here, and I ain't going nowhere."

Without another word Joanna pushed past him and climbed into bed, drawing the unfinished Birds in the Air quilt over her. How long would it be before Titus abandoned hope of reuniting their family? How long before another girl caught his eye, a girl without a scarred face?

He'll be true, she told herself. Titus is a good man. He'll find a way to bring us back together.

But new worries nagged her now, doubts where before there had been only certainty.

When the handyman came the next morning to fix the stove, Miss Evangeline could not resist letting him know how greatly the wait had inconvenienced and upset her. "And look what the explosion did to my girl," she exclaimed, indicating Joanna's burned cheek. "If she had been standing any closer when the pipe exploded, it might have killed her!"

The man eyed Joanna's scar. "Your girl heals mighty quickly."

"Indeed she does. It's a peculiarity of her tribe. Nevertheless, you shouldn't be surprised if my husband presents you with a bill for the damage to our slave."

The man nodded — only to avoid arguing with a lady, or so Joanna thought — and presented the mistress with a bill of his own. Paying him proved to be no easy matter, since Miss Evangeline and Joanna had to search the marse colonel's study for the pocketbook he said he had left in a desk drawer but which turned up hidden behind a dictionary in a bookcase on the other side of the room.

The following morning, the two young stable boys became ill from eating spoiled fish, and after paging frantically through her recipe books in a fruitless search for a remedy, Miss Evangeline hastily wrote out a pass and sent Joanna running to Aunt Lucretia's house for a purgative. Every day brought another crisis, another household calamity to set before a mistress entirely unprepared to solve it.

On the morning before the colonel was due to return, Miss Evangeline collapsed into her chair in stunned astonishment upon discovering she would have no milk for her tea, nor butter for her bread, nor even bread for that matter, since she had neglected to give Sally orders to go to the market.

"Why didn't you tell me we were running low on supplies?" Miss Evangeline cried.

"I did," protested Sally. "You told me to go on back to the kitchen and not to bother you."

Miss Evangeline drew in a breath sharply as if preparing to scold her, but then she went suddenly still. If she didn't remember the exchanges, Joanna could have reminded her, for twice she had witnessed Sally coming to her for instructions and being sent away. But the mistress seemed to need no reminders. Her shoulders slumped and some of the life seemed to go out of her.

"Joanna, fetch my husband's pocketbook," she said. After Joanna returned with the small leather pouch, Miss Evangeline withdrew a handful of coins and counted them out into Sally's palm. "Go to the market and buy whatever you need to sustain us until my husband returns — and also get everything you need for his favorite meal. I want you to serve it on his first night home.

He mustn't suspect that anything was amiss."

"Yes, missus. What meal his favorite, missus?"

"I couldn't possibly say. Don't you know? You've been his cook far longer than I've known him."

"Yes, missus." Sally hurried away as if worried that if given too much time to think it over, the mistress would amend her instructions and force them to go hungry. Joanna didn't blame her. Whom would the colonel punish if he came home and found nothing to eat? Certainly not his darling bride. Colored folks took the blame even when everyone knew the buckra were at fault; sometimes, even if the colored folk had nothing to do with it, they were punished just for being unlucky enough to witness the buckra making a mistake.

Miss Evangeline inhaled deeply, rested her elbows on the table, closed her eyes, and pressed her fingertips to forehead, nose, beneath the eyes, as if smoothing out lines of worry that she dared not allow to form. "I'm beginning to see why my father married her," she said, mostly to herself but perhaps also to Joanna. "She has neither beauty nor charm nor grace nor wit, but she does know how to manage a household.

'Practice embroidery!' she told me. 'Translate Greek!' What use are those to me now? I need to know how to manage servants, how to keep a larder stocked. What sort of teacher fails to teach me the things I most need to know?"

Suddenly she let her hands fall to the table, and she regarded Joanna plainly as if expecting an answer. "I don't know, missus," said Joanna. "Maybe Mrs. Chester thought you could figure it out on your own."

"Or maybe she wanted me to fail."

Joanna knew better than to criticize one white lady in front of another. "What about your friends? They mothers teach them how to do all these things?"

Miss Evangeline thought for a moment. "No, I suppose not. Their educations were much like my own. Surely if they were learning how to make tallow candles and bake bread, they would have mentioned it." She let out a small laugh of astonishment. "I don't know how to cook. Do you know I've never cooked a meal in my entire life?"

The image of Miss Evangeline red-faced and perspiring in the kitchen, up to her elbows in bread dough or testing the heat of an oven, was so absurd Joanna almost laughed. "You don't need to cook," said

Joanna. "You *have* a cook."

Miss Evangeline smiled, suddenly light-hearted. "Yes, you're right. And Sally did try to warn me that I was neglecting my responsibilities, but I didn't listen. My father is not above taking advice from slaves. He listens to Aaron regarding the field hands and the cotton, and he seeks Titus's opinion regarding horses. I shall follow his example." She slapped her palms flat on the tabletop and pushed herself to her feet, her confidence restored. "And you, Joanna, you must help me. If you hear servants fretting about this or that not being done the proper way, you must tell me promptly."

"Yes, missus," said Joanna, concealing her dismay. She had never carried tales to the big house at Oak Grove, though some in the quarter believed all house slaves spied for the master. She didn't want any of the Harper Hall slaves to think ill of her, nor did she think Miss Evangeline was likely to heed her warnings when she ignored Sally's.

She would have to be careful, but with any luck, helping Miss Evangeline learn to manage the household would send her off on many other errands around Charleston. In two days she had been sent out twice, the first times she had been truly on her own since her recapture at Elm Creek Farm. It was a heady feeling, almost as if a wind might sweep in off the ocean and carry her far away. She saw the ships in the harbor, dodged wagons rumbling over cobblestones, heard trains chugging in the distance, and knew that some of them carried cotton and rice and oranges to northern shores. If they could carry bales and sacks and crates, they could carry far more precious cargo, if she could just find a way, if she could just get her family together and make a plan and go.

She would learn the city and the ways out of it, so that when she and Titus and Ruthie were finally all together again, she would be ready. Her Birds in the Air quilt was nearly complete. She had saved the pass Miss Evangeline had written for the errand to Aunt Lucretia's. All she needed was her family and a plan.

Miss Evangeline must have realized that she couldn't rely upon her busy husband for amusement, for she befriended several young wives who lived nearby and eagerly accepted her aunt's invitations to gatherings at her house on East Bay Street near the Battery. Joanna usually accompanied the mistress when she went visiting, and she came to know the back rooms and kitchens of most of the houses on Meeting Street from hours spent sewing and talking with the hostesses' slaves while listening for her mistress's summons. Afterward, Miss Evangeline would query and probe and question Joanna until every scrap of slaves' gossip about their masters' families had been wrung from her. Joanna always felt exhausted afterward, as if Miss Evangeline had put her through the mangle. Although the other families' slaves never demanded that she keep their secrets, they surely assumed she would. Eventually word would get out that Joanna told her mistress everything, and no one would talk to her anymore.

After an outing, Joanna had to scramble to make up for the work neglected during her absence. She learned to wash clothes at a breakneck pace and to sew everything right the first time so she did not have to waste time picking out stitches. Once, as she was sewing in the kitchen while Sally started the fire for breakfast, she heard Miss Evangeline call for her, so early and so unexpectedly that Joanna bolted to her feet and jabbed herself with the needle. The thread snapped and the button she had been sewing to the marse colonel's new shirt rolled away and fell between a crack in the floorboards. Sally tsked her tongue in sympathy, knowing Joanna would be punished for the lost button.

Joanna had only a moment to crawl on hands and knees to see if she could spy the button before she had to hurry away to dress the mistress. All that morning worry gnawed at her. She could not substitute a button snipped off another shirt, not even one he rarely wore. The mistress had purchased these brass palmetto-shaped buttons especially for her husband's new uniform, a Christmas gift from his wife.

All day long as she worked and waited on the mistress, her thoughts were on the shirt and how she might rearrange the buttons so that no one would notice one was missing. It was impossible, and she knew it. She would have to tell the mistress and take her punishment.

Then, as the slaves were gathering in the kitchen after the Harpers' supper for their own meal, Joanna felt a tug on her sleeve. Hannah, the little girl who never spoke, peered up at her solemnly, the shiny brass button pinched between her thumb and forefinger.

"How did you find that?" Joanna exclaimed. Hannah made no reply but to drop the button into Joanna's palm and scurry

313

over to the stove, where Sally filled her gourd bowl with rice and okra.

"I saw her down cellar this morning," Sally told Joanna in an undertone when she went forward with her own bowl. "That button must've fallen clean through. Lucky for you it wasn't stuck somewhere in between."

"Lucky for me Hannah think to look for it," said Joanna, watching the little girl scoop rice and okra into her mouth with her fingers. She sat on the floor in the corner, cross-legged, hunched over her gourd bowl as if expecting someone to snatch it away before she finished. Joanna had never taken much notice of the girl before except to wonder why she never spoke. She obviously wasn't simpleminded, and she followed Miss Evangeline's directions, so the problem wasn't that she understood only Gullah talk.

Later, as Joanna sewed the rescued button onto the marse colonel's shirt, she noticed Hannah watching her from the doorway. "Come closer," she said. "You know how to thread a needle?"

Hannah shook her head, so Joanna snipped a length of thread and demonstrated. "Now you try," she said, pulling the thread from the eye and holding out needle and thread to Hannah.

Hannah hesitated before taking them. She threaded the needle properly on her second attempt and held it out to Joanna solemnly. "Good," Joanna said. "Now watch and I teach you how to make a knot."

By the time Hannah was called away to help in the kitchen, she had made five good, strong knots, spaced evenly along the thread.

From that day forward, whenever Joanna sat down to sew, she found Hannah at her elbow, watching intently, memorizing the motions of her hands as she worked the needle. Joanna trimmed a few patches into squares and set the girl to work on a Nine-Patch block, correcting her mistakes, praising her successes. Perhaps because she could not ask questions, Hannah hung on Joanna's every word and practiced every gesture, and Joanna was amazed by how quickly she learned. "If you learn to sew good, mistress might train you up as a seamstress," Joanna said. Hannah's eyes darted to her face, then back to her sewing, another Nine-Patch block for her growing pile. "It's not bad work. Better than scrubbing floors —"

Joanna stopped short. Many years ago, as a much younger girl, as she had ridden back from the Ashworth plantation, she had listened eagerly as Josiah Chester's loyal groom told her that her sewing could lead to her salvation. The money she earned would keep the Chesters from selling her down south, he had said, and Marse Chester might let her keep a portion so that she could buy her freedom someday. Now she was farther south than she had ever been before, and Miss Evangeline valued her services so much that she refused to hire her out.

Joanna could not bring herself to give Hannah false hopes.

And yet sewing was a skill that might serve the child well someday. So Joanna continued their lessons, and though they were brief, infrequent, and often interrupted, Hannah learned like dry earth soaking up rainwater. Joanna was proud of her, and yet it pained her to think of how she might have, should have, passed on her knowledge to her own daughter. Who would teach Ruthie the things she needed to know while Joanna taught another little girl?

Titus will see to it, she told herself firmly. *Tavia will teach her to cook. Auntie Bess will tell her stories. Pearl will teach her pride and strength.* Ruthie would learn. Even without Joanna there beside her, Ruthie would learn.

Over time, Joanna's curiosity compelled

her to ask Sally why Hannah couldn't speak. "Nothing's wrong with her mind," Joanna said, as if daring Sally to contest the point. "She always been like this, or she get a sickness?"

Sally opened the oven, held her hand inside, and counted silently, testing the temperature. "Nothing wrong with her until about three years ago," she said, placing another stick on the fire and closing the door. "Before the colonel marry your mistress, his widow sister live here and keep house for him. Her name Missus Givens, and Hannah's mother her maid."

"Hannah could talk back then?"

"As good as any child. Maybe more than most." Sally wiped her hands on her apron and took a sack of cornmeal from the pantry. "She still too young to work much but she help me out from time to time, help her mother, too. The Givens boys her playmates. You know how buckra children and colored children play together till they grow up and figure out one's the master and one's the slave."

Joanna nodded.

"One day —" Out of habit, Sally glanced through the open doorway for eavesdroppers. "Hannah and the boys playing on the low piazza, stacking up the boys' wood

317

blocks and knocking them down. They laughing and having a good old time. Then all a sudden, Missus Givens put down her knitting and calls Hannah to her. She say she got a very important job for Hannah, 'cause she gonna send Hannah to fetch something from the store. Hannah so proud. She never been out on her own before like that and she felt like such a big girl. So Missus Givens write out a pass, and she write out a note, and she give both to Hannah along with the money. Then she say, 'You give that note to the storekeeper, and you tell him to read it and fix up what I ask for, then you pay him and bring my parcel back to me.'

"So Hannah run off, and soon here she comes back carrying something wrapped in brown paper. She ran smiling all the way, and she want to give the parcel to the missus, but the missus tell her open it herself."

"What was it?" asked Joanna.

"A leather whip. Wood handle, braided fringe. Before Hannah knew it, the missus was whipping her, not saying a word, just whipping her over and over. Hannah cried and screamed and begged to know what she had done wrong, but the missus don't tell her. Hannah's mother hear her and come running, and she beg missus to stop. She even tried to grab the whip out of Missus Givens's hand, but she just got whipped herself." Sally measured four handfuls of cornmeal into a bowl and took two eggs from the basket on the table. "Hannah never say another word after that."

Sickened, Joanna pressed a hand to her mouth. "Why?" she managed to say. "Why she beat a sweet child that way?"

"Them wood blocks she was playing with, you recall, with the missus's sons." Sally gestured awkwardly, forming a shape in the air. "They got letters carved in the sides."

A flash of rage shot through Joanna. It was unfair, so terribly unfair. "But Hannah wasn't trying to read. She stacking blocks and knocking them down! Could've been any picture carved on them blocks for all it meant to her."

"It meant something to the missus." Sally cracked eggs and set the shells aside. "After that, Hannah wasn't good for nothing. She hide when Missus Givens call her, she jump at the tiniest noise. I hear the marse colonel tell Asa his sister ruin a perfectly good slave and their father not too happy about it. When Marse Colonel marry your mistress, his sister and her boys go back to live on the James Island plantation with their folks. Missus Givens take her maid, but she leave

Hannah here. Say the marse colonel can sell her or keep her, she don't care what he do with that useless thing."

"And now Hannah so scared of words she don't even say them."

Sally nodded. "Marse Colonel understand why she that way. He won't sell her for it." She seemed to be reassuring herself as much as Joanna. "He don't mind a quiet slave. He say at least she never sass no one."

That was what he said now, Joanna thought. But masters changed their minds, or died, or forgot promises when a change in fortune compelled them to sell slaves to pay debts. No slave was safe, and a frightened child who could not speak was more precariously placed than most.

One day when the mistress was in a particularly cheerful mood, Joanna asked her if she might train Hannah as a seamstress. "You mean the mute girl?" Miss Evangeline asked, surprised. "My sister-in-law says she isn't suited for anything but the simplest of chores."

"Maybe that's how she was when Marse Colonel's sister here, but she older now, and she can learn. I seen it." Joanna tried to sound as if she didn't care too much one way or the other. Seeming to want something too much was a sure way to convince the mistress not to let you have it. "This way, if you need me to dress your hair or sew you a fancy gown, there's someone else to do the little things like mending and darning. That work always got to be done even when other, more important things come first."

Miss Evangeline considered the proposal and agreed that Hannah could learn to sew as long as her lessons did not interfere with her other chores.

That same day, while Miss Evangeline was out with her aunt Lucretia, Joanna sat down with the colonel's shirt and waited for Hannah to come to her with her pile of Nine-Patch blocks. As the girl sat down at her feet and threaded a needle, Joanna strained her ears for the sound of approaching footsteps. All she heard were carriages and wagons passing on the street outside, Sally singing in the kitchen, a loose shutter banging in the wind.

"Look here." Joanna snipped a long thread off the spool and arranged it on her lap until it formed the proper shape. "This here the letter *A*."

Hannah's eyes went wide and she backed away.

"It's all right." Joanna beckoned to her, but Hannah stood rooted to the spot, just beyond arm's reach. "Marse Colonel and missus gone. And look. Anyone come in, we do like this." She brushed her fingers across her skirt, and at once the letter was no more than a snarl of thread. "See? Don't be afraid. Don't never be afraid of words."

Hannah looked terrified, but she took one step forward, and then another until she stood so close she touched Joanna's knee.

"This here's the letter *B*," Joanna said, and arranged the thread.

That night, a rustling of coarse blankets and a sudden stir in the air woke Joanna. Invisible in the darkness, Hannah climbed into bed beside her, pulled the covers back over them, and promptly fell back asleep. Joanna sat awake for a while, her hand resting on the girl's head, thinking of Ruth back at Greenfields and how safe she had felt curled up beside the larger woman, even when her presence did not protect her from Josiah Chester's predations.

Joanna rolled over on her side, put her arm around the sleeping child, and drifted back to sleep.

Winter came, and when the master and mistress weren't discussing secession, they were debating Christmas. The colonel wanted to spend the holiday on the James

Island plantation as he had always done, as every Harper had done since the first Harper came to South Carolina, but the mistress was equally determined to celebrate Christmas with her father and siblings at Oak Grove. Joanna hoped and prayed that the mistress would have her way, because Miss Evangeline would certainly expect Joanna to accompany her home. Joanna longed for Ruthie and Titus so deeply that she could almost feel her husband's arms around her and the weight of her baby in the sling. But instead of indulging his bride, the colonel proposed that they invite both families to Harper Hall. Joanna's heart sank as Miss Evangeline threw her arms around her husband, kissed him, and declared him "as wise as Solomon." Joanna might still see Titus, for he would surely drive the coach that brought the Chesters to Charleston, but Ruthie would just as surely be left behind.

The decision sent Sally and Minnie into a frenzy of alarm, cleaning, cooking, preparing for a houseful of guests. Joanna was so busy helping them whenever she could spare time from her regular duties that she had to set Hannah's sewing lessons aside. Joanna wondered, but could not ask the mistress, if the colonel's sister would be among the guests. Joanna felt a strange, angry eagerness to see the woman who had stolen Hannah's voice. She imagined Mrs. Givens as a monster, imperious and terrifying, and she fretted over little Hannah, who had become less jumpy and fearful in recent weeks. If Mrs. Givens tried to hurt the girl again, Joanna did not think she could stand by and watch it happen, but what could she do? Best to keep Hannah out of her sight altogether. With so many houseguests bringing slaves of their own, Joanna hoped she could shield Hannah within the crowd.

Suddenly she remembered that Hannah might not want to hide from the visitors. Joanna had forgotten that Hannah's mother was Mrs. Givens's maid. Hannah's desire to see her mother again would surely overcome her fear. If Joanna had been offered a chance to see her mother again, she would have left Ruth's side in a heartbeat. It was only natural that Hannah would just as easily forget Joanna when her mother appeared.

But Joanna couldn't help feeling a twinge of regret, which she quickly chased from her thoughts. How could she, who had been taken from her own mother and missed her own daughter so desperately, begrudge young Hannah a visit with her mother?

A few days before the Harpers and Chesters were expected to arrive, Joanna and Minnie were receiving Miss Evangeline's instructions for their guests' sleeping arrangements when the pealing of bells interrupted her. First a church bell rang somewhere in the distance, and then another and another until it seemed every steeple in Charleston swelled the chorus. Joanna gasped as a low boom rattled the china in the cabinet. "Cannon fire," said Miss Evangeline in wonder, and suddenly she clasped her hands together as her face lit up in fierce joy. "The vote. They've taken the vote!"

Snatching up her shawl, Miss Evangeline raced outside. Joanna trailed after her, curious and half-afraid, to find men and women pouring from the houses into the streets. Men threw their hats in the air and cheered; women waved handkerchiefs and embraced one another. "Mrs. Ames," Miss Evangeline cried out, spotting her neighbor. "Tell me, what's the news?"

"The convention vote was unanimous," Mrs. Ames declared, dabbing at the corners of her eyes with a handkerchief and beaming. "One hundred sixty-nine to zero. The Union is dissolved!"

Cold fingers of dread brushed against Joanna's heart as all around her the jubilation multiplied. Ever since she had come to Harper Hall, she had overheard speculation that South Carolinians might get so fed up with the federal government that they would leave the Union and go their own way. Now it had happened. Most of Miss Evangeline's friends had said that they expected the Union to let them go without a fight, but Joanna couldn't believe it. In all her life she had never known buckra to let go of something they thought was rightfully theirs. They never stood on the front porch waving good-bye to a runaway. They set the dogs on him.

Joanna left Miss Evangeline celebrating with Mrs. Ames and went inside to finish her work.

All day long, Charleston celebrated. Miss Evangeline dashed off letters to her father and to friends, and when she sent George to East Bay Street with a note for Aunt Lucretia, he returned carrying Aunt Lucretia's invitation to a secession party to be held at her home the following day. The colonel came home early to escort his wife to Institute Hall for the formal signing of the declaration. Abner drove the newlyweds in the coach, Asa and Joanna rode along on the drivers' seat, and the newlyweds arrived just in time to witness the delegates marching in procession from St. Andrew's Hall. The General Assembly awaited them within, or so Joanna heard the colonel say as the master and mistress joined the throng of jubilant Charlestonians who had come to witness the historic event. The Harpers managed to work their way through the crowd and through the front doors; folks took once glance at the colonel's uniform and instinctively stepped back, clearing a narrow path for them. Hundreds of people who could not squeeze inside milled about on the stairs, the balconies, the sidewalks, but when the clock on a cupola high above the tall white front columns approached half past six, a hush fell over them, as all strained their ears in a vain attempt to hear what passed inside.

Joanna, Abner, and Asa waited outside near the coach. "So quiet," Joanna said, uneasy, drawing her shawl around her shoulders although the evening was unseasonably warm. Such a change from the noisy celebration of the day.

"Each of them men got to sign his name," said Abner. "That vote don't mean nothing until they make their mark."

Joanna imagined the buckra inside, holding their breath, leaning forward eagerly as one by one each of the 169 men signed the paper. The clock hands slowly moved; Joanna paced near the coach and thought of Ruthie and Hannah. Two hours passed. Then, suddenly, a roar erupted within Institute Hall, the doors burst open, and all at once it seemed that from every direction people filled the streets, shouting and whooping and singing. "South Carolina is an independent commonwealth!" a voice rang out above the din, and was swallowed up by cheers.

Joanna pressed herself against the coach, wishing the colonel would return so they could go back to Harper Hall, wishing Miss Evangeline had not required her to come. Somewhere a band struck up a merry march; fireworks popped and crackled; celebrants formed impromptu parades. The horses shied and stomped their hooves while Abner tried to calm them. Joanna spotted Miss Evangeline passing between the building's tall white columns and descending the stairs, beaming and clinging to her husband's arm as they worked their way through the crowd to the coach. Joanna sprang forward to help her inside, tucking in her long skirt, assisting her with her wraps. The sooner the mistress was settled, the sooner they would reach the safety of Harper Hall.

It took them nearly an hour to make a journey that on an ordinary day would have needed only a few minutes. At last they passed through the wrought iron gates, and a laughing, exuberant Miss Evangeline pulled her grinning husband from the coach and danced with him on the lawn. Abner was tight-lipped, concerned about the jittery horses, which shied at every burst of fireworks and cannon shot; Asa was sober and silent.

Joanna put away the mistress's wraps and went to the kitchen, where Sally and Minnie peppered her with questions as they hurried to serve the Harpers' delayed supper. Joanna answered as best she could, but when they asked her what secession meant for colored folk, she did not know what to say. It could not possibly mean anything good for them. Secession would bring war, and war meant trouble, and when trouble came, the colored folk always got the worst of it.

She was sick at heart when she considered that Elm Creek Farm was now within another country. It was no farther away than it had been before the convention voted, but somehow it seemed more impossible to reach.

"What a merry Christmas this will be,"

the colonel declared as Asa helped him undress for bed and Joanna undressed Miss Evangeline. "Just think of it: our first Christmas as a free and independent commonwealth."

"Let's hope the New Year doesn't bring us a war." Miss Evangeline pulled back the quilt and climbed into bed. "Federal forces are too close for comfort. I wish we could drive them out of the harbor and out to sea."

"They won't trouble us," her husband reassured her. "Major Anderson is no fool. He has only a handful of men at Fort Moultrie, hardly enough to start a war, especially one he himself doesn't want. He knows Charleston is well protected as long our men hold Fort Sumter."

"But after that loathsome Mr. Lincoln takes office, if he should give orders —"

"He won't. If he should threaten war rather than let us leave the Union peacefully, Great Britain will intercede. They'll rally to our cause rather than allow their cotton supply to be cut off."

"Of course you're right," said Miss Evangeline, but Joanna recognized the familiar lightness that meant the mistress was not telling the whole truth of what she felt.

Three days later, Christmas guests began to

arrive. Joanna rushed around tending to one newcomer after another, but always she listened for horses' hooves on cobblestones and the rattle of a familiar coach. Hannah listened and waited too, eagerly peeping out the front window at the sound of each new arrival. "Your mama comin' soon," Joanna promised her, and the silent girl rewarded her with the quick flash of a smile.

The James Island Harpers were among the first to arrive. Hannah was helping Joanna make beds in a guest bedroom when the coach pulled up with the Marse Colonel's parents, widowed sister, and nephews. Hannah raced downstairs to greet her mother, and after a moment Joanna followed, curiosity overcoming her caution, for she knew she would be punished if she did not have their guests' rooms ready in time.

She caught up with the girl on the front porch, frozen in place, staring at the wagon that had pulled up behind the James Island Harpers' coach carrying slaves, trunks, and parcels. "Which one your mama, child?" Joanna asked, watching the female slaves, wondering why not one face lit up in recognition, why no one cried out in joy at the sight of Hannah awaiting her.

Suddenly Hannah turned and darted back inside.

"Hannah?" Quickly Joanna followed and, rounding the corner, barely avoided crashing into Minnie and sending the housekeeper's armful of linens flying. "Where Hannah go? Why she run away from her mama?"

Minnie went to the window, peered outside, and shook her head. "None of them's her mama."

"Ain't her mama maid to Marse Colonel's sister?" No buckra lady went for an overnight visit without her maid.

"She was, but she ain't here." Minnie indicated one of the slave women with a jerk of her head. "That one there, I ain't never seen her before. Maybe she Mrs. Givens's new maid."

Joanna's worries were confirmed later that day after Minnie showed the newcomers to the slaves' dormitory and hurried back to tell Joanna what she had learned. The unfamiliar slave woman was indeed Mrs. Givens's new maid, purchased after Hannah's mother died of malaria. "She been gone three months," Minnie said, shaking her head and glancing at Hannah, who gave no sign of hearing or understanding a word as she went to the kitchen as if intent on some errand for Sally.

But Joanna knew better.

■ ■ ■ ■

While unpacking the colonel's mother's bags, Joanna heard the familiar rattle of carriage wheels at last, and her heart leaped as she raced to the window to confirm her hopes. Her eyes filled with tears at the sight of Titus, tall and strong in the driver's seat, pulling up to the carriage house and looking around eagerly for her. Forgetting the open trunk, the folded dresses, she raced downstairs and outside. "Titus," she shouted. "Titus!"

He pulled the horses to a halt and swiftly climbed down from the high seat. A moment later, his arms were around her, his mouth seeking hers. "Don't cry," he murmured in her ear. "I'm here. It's all right."

"How's Ruthie?" she said, breathless. "My baby girl all right?"

"She's good." Titus kissed her and held her so tightly she almost couldn't breathe. "Why don't you see for yourself?"

With a gasp, Joanna whirled around and watched as a wagon pulled up behind the coach, the bed loaded with parcels and slaves whose services could not be done without even for a short visit. Mrs. Chester's maid climbed down from the wagon bed, and when she unwrapped her shawl, Joanna spotted Ruthie in her arms. She ran to her daughter, snatched her up, and held her close, convincing herself that it was only her imagination that Ruthie squirmed and reached for the maid. "It's Mama," Joanna told her. "I'm your mama. You remember me."

"I thought you would be pleased," said Miss Evangeline, who had come outside to greet her father, brothers, sister, and stepmother as they emerged from the coach. "I meant it to be a surprise for Christmas, but I suppose it would have been impossible to hide a baby, even in such a busy house as ours."

"Thank you," Joanna said, voice trembling. Miss Evangeline had never shown her such kindness. "Thank you for not waiting for Christmas, missus. I get two more days to visit with her now."

"This isn't a visit," Miss Evangeline said. "Julia will be staying with us."

Joanna hardly dared speak. Surely this must be one of the mistress's cruel amusements. "For good?"

"For good, and if she's anything like her mother, I know one day I'll wonder how I ever managed without her. I know you're training Hannah as a seamstress." Miss

Evangeline smiled and laid a hand gracefully on her abdomen. "But my daughter shall need a maid."

"You mean our son shall need a servant." The colonel seized his wife's hands and raised them to his lips. "What do you say, Titus? Any plans for a boy?"

Any reply Titus might have made was lost in the sudden exclamations of joy and flurry of embraces as Harpers and Chesters celebrated the couple's happy news. "A grandson," Marse Chester proclaimed, shaking his head in wonder and delight. "My dear, I haven't been so happy since —"

"Since South Carolina became an independent commonwealth?" Miss Evangeline broke in. Everyone laughed — except for the colored folk, who were busy unloading packages, minding children, tending horses, making sure the masters and mistresses wanted for nothing. Nothing must spoil their holiday. "I can't promise you a grandson, Papa, only a grandchild."

"How are you feeling?" her stepmother inquired politely.

"As well as can be expected," the mistress replied. "Aunt Lucretia has been very attentive and our neighbor, Mrs. Ames, shows me great kindness. The servants see to it that I don't want for anything." She turned a fond glance Joanna's way. "I only hope that Julia will be as good and faithful a servant to my daughter as you have been to me."

"Yes, Mrs. Harper," Joanna managed to say. "Me too."

"You mean to your *son*," the colonel and Marse Chester corrected in unison, and all the buckra burst into laughter.

Unhitching the horses, Titus looked Joanna's way, and when his eyes met hers, he gave his head the tiniest shake. She knew what he was thinking. He could not wish a lifetime as Miss Evangeline's maid upon their baby girl. The only dream good enough for her was freedom.

Hannah took to baby Ruthie immediately. While Joanna unpacked the visiting women's trunks, Hannah lay Ruthie on a quilt spread on the floor and dangled a hair ribbon for the baby to seize and tug with her tiny fist. Joanna watched the two girls while she worked. Ruthie's legs kicked busily as she beamed up at her new playmate; silent Hannah made amusing faces and bent forward to give Ruthie's round cheeks tiny kisses. It probably did not occur to Hannah, who had no one and expected nothing for herself, to be jealous of the baby.

All day long, Joanna blissfully cuddled her daughter whenever she could steal moments from her work, whenever Miss Evangeline could not observe them. She dared not remind the mistress why she had once accused Joanna of allowing her child to distract her from her duties. Titus had to keep to the stable and the carriage house most of the day, but when all the servants came together at mealtimes, they could be together. Joanna sat on the floor with her side pressed close to her husband's, his arm around her shoulders, baby Ruthie on her lap. Hannah sat nearby, scooping rice into her mouth from her gourd bowl, eyeing Titus warily as if waiting for him to shoo her away.

"Look like she think she belong to you," said Titus, amused.

"She understand everything you say," Joanna warned lightly. People often made that mistake and spoke freely in front of the silent girl. If Hannah could speak, Joanna could only imagine the secrets she would spill. "She don't got no one else."

As Joanna lifted Ruthie to her shoulder, Titus cupped her little head in his palm. "You got your own girl now."

Hannah appeared to be preoccupied with picking the last grains of rice from her bowl, but Joanna knew better. "Maybe I got two."

Almost imperceptibly, Hannah smiled, but at the same time, a shadow darkened Titus's eyes. "You mean Miss Evangeline got two."

His words took the merriment from her like an exhalation of breath. He was right. Hannah couldn't ever be Joanna's. Not even Ruthie could ever be truly hers, not when the master or mistress could part them forever with a single word.

That night, after Ruthie fell asleep in the narrow rope bed beside Hannah, Joanna crept down the stairs and slipped outside, the cobblestones cool and smooth on her bare feet. Silently she stole away to the carriage house, where she found Titus waiting for her in the hayloft. They embraced as if they were once again alone by the riverbank on Oak Grove, and she slept that night in his arms, peaceful, free, until he woke her by stroking her hair and murmuring a warning of the approach of dawn. Brushing straw from her dress, Joanna slipped back into the kitchen building and upstairs to the dormitory, where she found Ruthie wide awake, peering curiously up at the sloped ceiling. Beside her Hannah slept on, her arm curled protectively around the baby.

The days passed in a blur of work and

stolen moments of happiness in Titus's arms. Christmas Eve came. Joanna wondered how many slaves back at Oak Grove would receive their annual clothing ration and how many would do without. She could not imagine Mrs. Chester finishing the work Joanna had left incomplete. Perhaps Marse Chester had bought another seamstress from the Charleston slave market. Or perhaps Josiah Chester had sent another incorrigible runaway down south, another problem for his more responsible brother to fix. They probably thought they had fixed Joanna, that they had driven the yearning for freedom from her forever. Marse Chester had assured his wife that marriage and motherhood would settle Joanna down, and she had let them believe that. What they would not know until the day they found her missing was that marriage and motherhood had made her even more desperate to see her family safely to freedom, where no one could ever separate them.

How she and Titus would bring this to pass, she did not know, but when the time came, she was determined to take Hannah with them.

The Harpers and Chesters made merry Christmas Eve and Christmas morning, their celebrations infused with an eager anticipation and bold promises of what the New Year would bring the new commonwealth. The colonel and Marse Chester expected other Southern states to follow South Carolina's lead and withdraw from the Union. As their numbers increased, the men said, the Northern states would recognize the futility of holding the old nation together and let the Southern commonwealths go without argument. In the meantime, the colonel said as he raised his glass in a Christmas toast, he would train his soldiers and wait.

Two days after Christmas, the colonel was proved entirely wrong when a messenger came running to Harper Hall and breathlessly repeated the news that had shocked Charlestonians waking early on December 26.

The Stars and Stripes flew over Fort Sumter.

Chapter Six

1860–61
Charleston, South Carolina

"How can this be?" Miss Evangeline cried, pacing back and forth while Asa swiftly dressed the colonel in his uniform. "How could Major Anderson have slipped past the harbor guards?"

"Perhaps those guards indulged in a little too much Christmas cheer," her husband replied grimly, holding out his arms so Asa could slip on his coat. "I have to give the major credit. It was a brilliant maneuver. If he'd remained at Fort Moultrie, he would have been vulnerable to an attack from the rear, but now —"

"Now he's in the middle of the channel, probably turning his guns upon us as we speak."

"Dearest." The colonel cupped his wife's face in his hands. "Don't worry. This city is well out of range of their cannons. Anderson's bought himself some time, but that's all. He'll run out of provisions eventually on that island, and then he'll have no choice but to surrender."

"I suppose so," said Miss Evangeline, with a frown that suggested she could not believe resolution would come so easily.

The colonel smiled. "Darling, remember, this is Major Anderson in command. He's married to a Georgian, for goodness' sake. He's owned slaves. He doesn't want a war any more than I do. He's taken Fort Sumter, but he can't hold it. We'll starve him out, send him back north, and that will be the end of it."

Joanna kept her face studiously impassive as the colonel kissed Miss Evangeline good-bye and strode from the room. She figured Miss Evangeline was right to be doubtful. Josiah Chester had owned many other slaves, but when Joanna had run off, he hadn't contented himself with the slaves who remained but had hired Isaac and Peter to hunt her down. He had lost money recapturing her, for she had seen his brother's ledger and knew Stephen Chester had bought her for less than Josiah Chester had paid in slave hunters' fees and expenses. How much more would a nation do to regain a rebellious state?

Miss Evangeline occupied herself entertaining her guests while the colonel was out seeing to a soldier's business, but Joanna knew she was distracted. All day long the Chester and Harper women left behind at home murmured worriedly and started at any loud noise from the street. The colonel's sister — Mrs. Givens, the same woman who had beaten the voice out of Hannah — wrung her hands and lamented that Major Anderson would surely fire upon the city at any moment, and that they would all be much safer back on James Island. "You must come with us too," she told Miss Evangeline. "Our father has enough room for your entire household. You can return to Harper Hall after the Union men are driven from the harbor."

Joanna's heart quaked until Miss Evangeline shook her head in refusal. "Nonsense," she replied briskly. "Robert says we're perfectly safe in the city, and I trust in his judgment, both as my husband and as a military man. In fact, it might be wiser for you to extend your visit."

Apparently the colonel's sister was not convinced, for she persuaded her parents to return to the James Island plantation the next day. To Joanna's sorrow, the following morning Marse Chester announced that his family too would be cutting their visit short. When Miss Evangeline protested, the colonel tried to persuade his father-in-law that such precautions were unnecessary. "Anderson will surrender Fort Sumter when his men run out of food," he said. "We'll take the fort without firing a single shot. You've heard what Colonel Chestnut's said."

Marse Chester gave a rough chuckle. "That he'll drink all the blood spilled in this 'war.'"

"He must have a prodigious thirst," remarked Mrs. Chester.

Both Marse Chester and the colonel regarded her in surprise for a moment, but then the colonel smiled. "What the colonel meant, Mrs. Chester, is that he expects there to be so little bloodshed —"

"Oh, I understood his remark perfectly," Mrs. Chester interrupted. "What I don't understand is how he could have reached such an astonishingly optimistic conclusion."

At last someone was talking sense, Joanna thought. Mrs. Chester was a Northerner herself and understood Northerners better than those boastful men did. They ought to listen to her. But even though she was white and had once been a teacher, they were likely to ignore her because she was a woman — and because she was saying what they did not want to hear. They would gladly agree with a woman who echoed their own certainties.

Despite his son-in-law's reassurances, Marse Chester was determined to return to Oak Grove before the day was out. Joanna was sent scurrying to dress ladies and pack trunks, with not a single moment to slip away to bid her husband good-bye. Titus found her in the laundry, searching for Mrs. Chester's petticoats that had somehow gotten mixed up with her stepdaughter's. They embraced, but Joanna held back her tears, unwilling to make Titus's leave-taking any more difficult for him.

"I meant what I said before," he told her, covering her face in kisses. "Now you got Ruthie with you, there ain't nothing to hold you back. Abner's gonna show you how to ride and how to drive the wagon. First chance you get, you run."

"And leave you behind at Oak Grove?"

Titus nodded, his gaze locked on hers. "I'll find my way to you somehow. You got to have faith in me."

"Take my quilt," Joanna blurted. "I don't need it. I got the pictures right here, in my heart." But Titus shook his head. "Why not? You know I can't run off unless I know you follow after."

"Joanna, those pictures don't mean nothing to nobody but you. You the only one who understand what they mean and what order they follow."

"I can tell you what they mean," she persisted. "If you get the chance to run, you got to be ready and take it, just like you said I should do."

"When I run, I can't carry a quilt with me. But I don't need to. I remember every word you ever tell me about Elm Creek Farm. I know I can find it even without your quilt. You keep it, and you teach Ruthie its secrets." Titus scowled as from somewhere around the front of the house, Marse Chester shouted his name. "Devil take that man. Someday, Joanna, I swear —"

Joanna tightened her grip on his hands. "Don't go just yet." She flung her arms around him and kissed him as if she might never see him again. Perhaps she wouldn't. With Union men occupying the harbor and South Carolina militiamen marching and drilling with rifles, it was impossible to say when the Chester family would return to Charleston.

"Listen," Titus said, his lips searching hers. "Keep breathin'. No matter what. Keep breathin', keep livin'. Long as you and

I keep breathin', we got a chance. We always got a chance, long as we stay alive."

Marse Chester shouted for Titus a second time. Soon Abner would be sent to find him, and the white master would think twice about letting Titus visit his wife again. They both knew it. With one last, fierce kiss, Titus tore himself from her arms and hurried off without looking back.

She wished he had agreed to take her Birds in the Air quilt with him. Since she was keeping Ruthie, when he returned to Oak Grove there would be nothing left to remind him of his wife. She wished she could think of him comfortable and warm as he slept in the hayloft, the quilt embracing him as she wished she herself could do.

More troubling than her loneliness was Titus's insistence that she must teach Ruthie the secrets of the images hidden in her quilt. Ruthie was just a baby, unable to understand. Titus must believe that they would remain enslaved for years, long enough for Ruthie to grow old enough to make sense of words and pictures, long enough that she might have to make the journey north to freedom on her own.

Keep breathing, she told herself. Keep breathing.

What else could she do?

■ ■ ■ ■

After her houseguests departed, Miss Evangeline paced through her lovely, empty home, stroking her abdomen absently even though she had not even the tiniest bump yet. Soon, Joanna suspected, the mistress would have her making over old dresses so they would accommodate the growing baby. Joanna wondered if she would need a new dress for herself. She had spent every night of Titus's brief visit in his arms, and maybe Ruthie was not the only child he had left behind. She did not know whether to hope for another baby or pray that her womb would remain empty. She wanted Titus's children, but she could not wish them to be born into slavery at such times, with their escape plans so fragile and the buckra at turns jittery and exultant.

The work of the holidays ended and the New Year began. The Union soldiers still held Fort Sumter, but since they hadn't turned their guns on the city yet, it seemed increasingly unlikely that they would do so. Joanna knew their provisions wouldn't last forever, just as the colonel said, and something would have to happen. But even as the colonel assured his wife that he doubted even a single shot would be fired over South Carolina's secession, he prepared as diligently as if he expected bullets to rain down like hail upon Meeting Street. He was often away from Harper Hall from before dawn until after dusk, and when he was at home, he was ensconced in his study with other officers clad in the uniforms of the various state militias, or with men in fine suits who could be businessmen or politicians or both. Once the colonel got into a shouting match with a distinguished older gentleman who stormed from the house without bothering to put on his coat and hat until he had reached the street.

"Mr. Petigru is the only man in South Carolina who hasn't seceded," the colonel remarked ruefully when Miss Evangeline hastened to the foyer to see what was the matter.

"I wish you could have made him see reason," said Miss Evangeline, watching through the window as the man strode away. "I did so enjoy Jane's company."

"Our political disagreements shouldn't prevent you and his daughter from remaining friends."

Miss Evangeline offered him an arch smile. "You forget we women take sides as firmly as you men do. You men weren't the only ones who seceded. Besides, I don't expect the Petigrus to remain in our commonwealth if they love the Union so dearly, do you?"

"They'll have to decide which they love more — the Union or South Carolina."

Before Miss Evangeline could reply, the colonel smiled indulgently and disappeared into his study, where the other men waited. Joanna knew this annoyed the young mistress and she resigned herself to an hour of grumbling and ill-temper. Miss Evangeline understood that her husband was busy with the affairs of state and had few idle moments to pass in his pretty bride's company, but that didn't mean she liked it. Sometimes Miss Evangeline complained about his negligence, knowing that Joanna dared not repeat her complaints to anyone who mattered.

In her husband's absence, the mistress found other ways to occupy her time — managing her household, calling on friends, and waiting attentively on her husband at the one time of the day when she could command his attention, over supper. There she drank in every word as the colonel spoke of the militia's preparations. Joanna dreaded each new revelation. More soldiers in the city meant more eyes to spot a fleeing slave, more guns to wound a fugitive. Once, when the mistress was in a reflective mood, Joanna suggested that they might be safer at Oak Grove. Miss Evangeline responded so promptly that Joanna knew she had considered the idea herself. "I couldn't leave Charleston," she said. "My place is with my husband, especially now that we're going to have a child."

Joanna almost replied that she too had a child, and that her place was with her own beloved, but she held her tongue. Miss Evangeline could take back her Christmas present as quickly and unexpectedly as she had given it. If Joanna were not careful, Ruthie could be sent back to Oak Grove, or even sold off.

Joanna often accompanied Miss Evangeline on her rounds of friends and family, and while sitting in the back rooms and kitchens, sewing and awaiting her mistress's call, she learned that other families were just as anxious about Major Anderson's presence in the harbor as the Harpers and Chesters were. On one occasion, Miss Evangeline's friends mulled over rumors that a ship from the North might bring provisions to the Union men holed up at Fort Sumter; a few days later, all of Charleston buzzed with the reports that a newspaper in far-off New York had announced that a Union steamer had set out from the city, bound for Charleston with supplies for Anderson's men.

The colonel warned Miss Evangeline to stay close to home when the ship was expected to arrive, but when a message came from Aunt Lucretia that a crowd was gathering on the Battery, Miss Evangeline ordered Abner to prepare the carriage and set off as soon as it was ready. Joanna rode along beside Abner, almost forgetting her apprehension in her determination to learn all she could about driving horses. Her beloved had told her to learn and she would not disappoint him. Once Abner let her take the reins, joking good-naturedly that he hoped she didn't learn too well or the colonel might order them to trade work, and his fingers were too callused and clumsy for a needle.

When they reached the Battery, Miss Evangeline managed to find her aunt in the crowd, and arm in arm they looked out across the harbor. "Anderson's run his guns out," Joanna overheard a man say, but even when she shaded her eyes with her hands, she couldn't make out anything different about the small fort perched on the island in the middle of the harbor.

Suddenly a thrill of excitement sped through the crowd; a ship had been spotted entering the channel. Joanna held her breath and knotted her apron in her hands, wishing she were back at home, praying Ruthie was safe in Hannah's care.

"Colonel Harper ain't gonna like us being here," said Abner, shaking his head at their young mistress, who stood well out of earshot. "He told her to stay home."

"Next time he'll remember to tell you too," said Joanna. The master's orders always trumped the mistress's.

Slowly the ship moved into view — just one lone merchant steamer as far as Joanna could see, and not a decoy with a string of gunboats behind it, as some of the rumors had warned. Suddenly puffs of white smoke appeared at the tip of Morris Island; the sound of gunfire took a few moments longer to reach Joanna's ears. On the Battery women cried out; a man whooped and threw his hat in the air. More bursts of smoke from the point where Charleston's defenders were stationed, more pops like distant fireworks. And yet nothing, nothing from Fort Sumter. It was as if Major Anderson and his men had already fled.

Almost imperceptibly the Union steamer pressed on, closer to Fort Sumter, closer to the hail of gunfire from Morris Island. Sometimes the smoke grew so thick in the distance that Joanna couldn't discern what was happening — if the ship had fired upon Charleston's defenders or if it had been sunk. But then a breeze wafted the drifting smoke aside, and again the ship came into view, pressing ever onward. Joanna silently willed it along, praying for the blue expanse between ship and fort to swiftly narrow, her heart pounding as the ship came fully into the range of the guns.

And then all at once a cheer went up from the men and women watching spellbound from the Battery. Slowly, so slowly that Joanna could almost convince herself it wasn't happening, the ship was turning — away from Fort Sumter, back toward the open ocean.

"What are they doing?" Joanna cried, standing. "They're so close, so close!"

Abner seized her arm and yanked her back to her seat. "Hush up," he muttered. "Don't let the buckra see you upset."

"But the ship —"

"It got hit. Don't you see? On the mast and the rudder. They got to turn back before they get sunk."

Joanna bit her lips shut, mindful of the cheers and celebration surrounding the carriage. The steamer looked sound enough to her. How could those few guns endanger a ship that size? They had turned tail and run, and why, Joanna couldn't imagine. It sickened her to watch as the steamer grew smaller in the distance and finally disappeared in the lingering smoke.

She had not realized until that moment that she had expected salvation to arrive on that Union ship.

"Those were my husband's men," Miss Evangeline told her aunt triumphantly as they returned to the carriage. "Those were his cadets. Think of it — students, boys really, driving off a Union invasion."

Joanna didn't think it had been much of an invasion, considering the ship had never even dropped anchor, but she knew better than to say so as she helped Miss Evangeline and Aunt Lucretia into the carriage, tucking skirts and shawls around them, shutting her ears to their exultant retelling of the events they had all witnessed. Abner let off Aunt Lucretia at her home before returning to Harper Hall, where Miss Evangeline ordered Sally to prepare a grand feast to celebrate the victory, which the young mistress seemed to believe was entirely her husband's doing. In later days, Joanna overheard Miss Evangeline boast that her husband had fired the decisive shot that had struck the *Star of the West*'s mast and sent her fleeing to safer waters — although by then, Miss Evangeline knew perfectly well that her husband had not been within four miles of Morris Island at the time.

Weeks passed. Somehow, even without reinforcements, Major Anderson clung stubbornly to Fort Sumter, unwilling to provoke a war and unwilling to leave. Other states quit the Union — Mississippi, Florida, Alabama, Georgia, Louisiana, and Texas — and in February, Miss Evangeline held a grand party to celebrate the forming of their own nation, the Confederate States of America. She hosted another in early March, on Mr. Lincoln's inauguration day, to celebrate that he was not *their* president.

Joanna knew she could no longer hope for Union soldiers to bring her freedom on a merchant steamer. While Miss Evangeline celebrated and Colonel Harper drilled, Joanna waited — and prepared. She memorized the streets of Charleston as she ran errands for the mistress; she befriended free colored merchants and craftsmen whom she might one day be able to call upon in a time of need. Slowly but certainly, she taught Hannah to read, forming letters from thread, spelling simple words. She praised

Hannah when she pointed to the object the thread letters named, but she was not satisfied. "It ain't enough to know what the word look like. You need to say it too," she told the girl, but Hannah did not reply.

Marse Chester did not bring his family to visit Harper Hall again, but on one joyful day, Titus appeared unexpectedly, sent from Oak Grove with letters and gifts for Miss Evangeline and the colonel. He stayed only long enough for the newlyweds to write their replies, which was barely enough time to marvel at the changes in their daughter since he had last seen her. Though it was almost more painful than joyous to see him so briefly, Titus left Joanna with a hopeful secret: He had heard Marse Chester and the mistress talking, and he knew their letters urged Miss Evangeline to return to Edisto Island until it was certain that the Union would let the Confederate States secede peacefully.

But Joanna's hopes were short-lived. Miss Evangeline was determined not to leave her husband, although she was reluctant to choose him over her father. "Papa must understand that it makes no sense for me to return to Edisto Island just in time for the malaria season, when in every year past he has sent me to Charleston to avoid it," she told her husband as she tucked the letters into a desk drawer. The colonel nodded, and as far as Joanna knew, they never again considered evacuating the city.

Hiding her bitterness, Joanna counted her blessings and bided her time. Ruthie spoke her first words. Miss Evangeline outgrew her gowns and grew increasingly impatient for her husband's attention. For the first time, the newlyweds argued; Joanna, Hannah, and the other house slaves hid out in the kitchen listening and waiting for the furor to subside. They flinched at the sound of china shattering as someone, probably the mistress, flung a teacup against the wall. "He married himself a fiery sweetheart but want a docile wife," Sally said, shaking her head. "Can't you say something to make her sweet again, or least make her *act* sweet?"

The last was directed at Joanna, who regarded the cook with astonishment. "You mean for me to walk into that?"

"Not now. Later, when you alone. You her maid. You supposed to keep her in a good temper."

"She ain't mad at me," Joanna pointed out. "I can make her fine dresses and fix her hair pretty, but that won't make the colonel forget those Union soldiers in the harbor."

"Mistress jealous of Major Anderson," George said in mock sorrow, and the slaves muffled their laughter. Joanna might have laughed more gleefully than the others. She had no interest whatsoever in helping Miss Evangeline cultivate a sweeter disposition. The more Miss Evangeline and the colonel argued, the more likely the mistress was to remember her father's indulgent affection and the comforts of Oak Grove.

Winter faded and spring arrived. Miss Evangeline resigned herself to lonely hours and Joanna to remaining in Charleston. Ruthie took her first hesitant, unsteady steps on the lower piazza; Hannah was so delighted that Joanna hoped for a moment that she might speak to praise the younger girl, but she only clapped her hands. Miss Evangeline set Joanna to work on a whole-cloth quilt made of her father's finest Sea Island cotton for her unborn child. Joanna could not put a stitch into it without imagining Ruthie as a young woman, dressing the golden curls of an impetuous young mistress who slapped her if she pulled the comb too hard through a tangle of hair. And that would be the best Joanna could hope for Ruthie in slavery. In her nightmares she saw her daughter the favorite of some insatiable master, sold off far away when the mistress discovered her carrying the master's child.

The next time Titus came and stayed the night, the very next time, she would convince him to steal the carriage and they would flee.

One night she finished her Birds in the Air quilt — large triangles and small, each pointing north to freedom. In whispers after the other slaves had fallen asleep, Joanna traced the quilted images with her fingertip and told Hannah their secret meanings. Hannah listened, wide-eyed and solemn, but if she were curious or eager or frightened, Joanna could only guess. Hannah said nothing, asked no questions. Maybe she had truly lost her voice forever.

Sometimes, instead of whispering over the quilt, Joanna feigned sleep, her arms curled protectively around her two girls while George lay on his side watching her from around the half-wall partition. She had come to know him better since the day he had first invited her to share his bed, and she had grudgingly come to like him. He was quiet and rarely smiled, but then unexpectedly he would pass by her and murmur a stingingly accurate and disrespectful observation about the colonel or the mistress or their guests that had her biting the inside of her cheeks to stifle laughter. She knew he hoped she would forget Titus and turn to him, and if she had not loved Titus so much, she might have welcomed George's affection. But she loved Titus completely, and no distance between them could make her love falter. According to the ledger downstairs and the law, she belonged to the Harpers, but in her heart, she belonged only to herself and to Titus. She felt only kindness and sympathy for George, and privately wished he would look to Sally, who lit up whenever he entered the room and always saved him the best parts of the leftovers from the master's table. The fool man never seemed to notice.

Sometimes she fell asleep remembering the feel of Titus's hands upon her, and as she drifted between wakefulness and sleep, she breathed deeply and almost thought his scent lingered on her skin and in her hair. But she knew it was only a memory and not the man.

For a time the colonel seemed correct about the Union's willingness to let the rebellious states go easily. Anderson's occupation of Fort Sumter remained a nagging thorn in the side of the new Confederacy, or so Joanna gathered as she overheard the dinner conversation of the Harpers and their frequent guests. Until Anderson and his men were evacuated, which everyone seemed to believe was the inevitable outcome of their stubborn, slow starvation, the young nation had no credibility with either the North or with foreign powers, who surely wondered why a so-called sovereign nation tolerated another country's presence on their free and independent soil.

Then April came, and with it rumors that President Lincoln was sending a fleet of ships to bring food to Anderson's men. The plans were supposedly secret, but the *Courier* reprinted stories of troop movements that had appeared in Northern newspapers, so all of Charleston knew of them. Joanna glimpsed headlines on stacks of newspapers on street corners as she ran errands for the household, and invisible as Miss Evangeline's maid, she listened to heated conversations from the colonel's study and witnessed all manner of soldiers and messengers and politicians racing to and from Harper Hall day and night. The colonel reassured Miss Evangeline that Lincoln could send an armada of ships but it would make no difference; he and his fellow South Carolina soldiers were merely waiting for Anderson to run out of food so he could surrender honorably. Once Joanna overheard the astonishing suggestion that Anderson was not merely stalling for time until reinforcements could arrive but had fixed the date and time of his upcoming surrender with General Beauregard. Joanna was torn between hoping Anderson would surrender and praying that he and his men could hold out until the Union ships arrived. All around the city, men drilled and paraded in a variety of uniforms; every day brought new ships into the harbor, filled with Confederate troops. If war came, it would bring chaos and bloodshed, it would endanger Ruthie and Hannah — but the frenzy and fire of battle might cover their escape.

If only Titus would return. If only Marse Chester would send the carriage and insist Miss Evangeline leave for Oak Grove at once, but Joanna could not count on that. She had to make her own plan, a plan for her and her girls.

A week later, or maybe more, a low boom like a distant roll of thunder shook her awake. In the early morning darkness, she saw George at the small window on the east wall, looking out toward the harbor. As she climbed carefully from bed to avoid rousing the girls, George glanced her way, shook his head, and returned his gaze to the misty, charcoal gray sky outside. "Bet those Union soldiers came at last," he said. "That's cannon fire for sure. Marse Colonel had Asa sleep outside his room last night. He know this coming."

Shivering, Joanna wrapped her shawl around her shoulders and peered out the window. In the distance she saw flashes of light in the mist, heard more low rumbles, but Harper Hall was too far from the harbor to discern what was happening. But surely the attack had begun; what else could it be?

Suddenly the low rumbles turned into furious reports, and the sky flashed baleful fire. A shiver of fear and anticipation ran up Joanna's spine, but before she could crane her neck and try to see what was happening, Miss Evangeline rang the bell for her, a barely audible summons she couldn't pretend she had not heard, even considering the distance and the din. Miss Evangeline might believe her, but she would punish Joanna for disobedience just the same, and perhaps demand that Joanna sleep on a pallet outside her door in the future, away from her girls.

The shouts and cannon fire had woken the others. Ruthie sat up, whimpered, and reached for her, but Joanna could spare her only a brief, hasty cuddle before turning her over to Hannah and hurrying downstairs and across the cobblestones to the big house, lips pressed together to hold back bitter recriminations. War had come, and Joanna could not even comfort her baby girl. What need could Miss Evangeline possibly have that was greater than Ruthie's? Joanna could not bear it, but she had no choice except to go when and where she was summoned.

In the Harpers' bedchamber, Miss Evangeline ordered Joanna to dress her, because sleep was impossible. Joanna helped her into her gown, quickly noting that the colonel and Asa were nowhere to be seen. "To the roof," Miss Evangeline instructed, mouth in a tight line, hand on her rounded belly. "I must see what is happening."

Joanna obeyed, willing to risk the danger of the roof rather than the greater peril of the Battery, relieved that the impetuous mistress had not sent orders for Abner to prepare the carriage. Up the stairs onto the roof they climbed, the young mistress's awkward gait making Joanna fearful that she would tumble backwards and knock them both to their deaths. At last they reached the top, breathless from alarm and exertion, and looked out over the city to the harbor, which lay shrouded in heavy mist that nearly obscured the outlying islands. Joanna flinched and drew her shawl tighter around her shoulders as the cannon fire increased in fury, but Miss Evangeline's face was alight with eagerness and alarm.

The South Carolinians were bombarding Fort Sumter, and as far as Joanna could see, no Union ships were speeding to the rescue.

On other rooftops throughout the city, others gathered, watching the fierce spectacle. For hours every other fort in the harbor unleashed its fury upon the starving men holed up in Fort Sumter, but not a single shot came from the Battery. More than two hours had passed since the shot that had awakened Joanna, about two and a half hours of constant cannon fire. At daybreak, Anderson's men struck back, but Joanna could see they were no match for their attackers.

"Not Fort Moultrie. Not Fort Moultrie," Miss Evangeline murmured, clutching her hands together as if in prayer.

Joanna knew at once that the colonel was there. "Maybe you should go back down," she said. If Fort Moultrie were reduced to rubble, Joanna would not grieve for her dead master, but she didn't believe Miss

Evangeline ought to be there to see it.

But the young mistress refused to go. She did agree to let Joanna return inside and bring her food and drink, but she kept her gaze fixed on the distant harbor even as she broke her fast. Joanna remained with her, since she had not been given permission to leave. By midday the mists had lifted and Joanna could easily make out three dark shapes off the bay, warships from the North, but they remained out of range of the cannon fire, their captains unwilling or unable to bring relief to Anderson's men.

On and on the fighting continued, but it was late afternoon before Joanna could persuade Miss Evangeline to come back into the house. The mistress sat in the parlor brooding, unfinished knitting on her lap. Once she sent George to her aunt's house for news, but when he returned, he reported only that three Union warships sat out in the harbor, Fort Moultrie seemed undamaged, and Fort Sumter was being hit hard.

The colonel did not return all that day.

The next morning Miss Evangeline was determined to take the carriage to the Battery, but Joanna managed to talk her out of it, for her unborn child's sake. Thus they did not witness the firebombs explode in Fort Sumter and set it aflame, nor were they among the thousands who stood watching and waiting for the three Union ships to enter the harbor and join in the battle. The ships never moved.

Miss Evangeline learned all this from rumors that flew through the streets of Charleston after the cannons subsided, rumors confirmed when Colonel Harper finally returned home, filthy, exhausted, triumphant, on the same day Major Anderson surrendered. Miss Evangeline waved off Asa — who was just as weary and bedraggled as the colonel, having endured the same harrowing firefight as the man he served — and tugged off her husband's boots herself, then removed his soiled uniform while Joanna drew him a bath. As he washed off the filth of battle, the colonel recounted the formal evacuation of Fort Sumter, how Anderson and his men had been allowed to withdraw honorably to one of the Union ships sitting in the bay. His voice rang with pride and Miss Evangeline exclaimed in admiration over every detail. Later Abner drove the couple to the Battery, where — as the coachman reported later — South Carolinian buckra of every age and social station, men and women alike, took to boats and filled the harbor to see for themselves the destruction wrought on the former stronghold, to exclaim over the piles of debris that had once been the fort's upper story, to study the traces of cannon shot on the parapet, to marvel at the smoking ruin.

It's begun, Joanna thought wearily as she went about the duties neglected during the young mistress's vigil. It was impossible to guess how it would end.

The buckra of Charleston reveled in their glorious victory. Miss Evangeline threw party after party, even as her husband cautioned her that they must now prepare to settle down to the hard business of war. This time his predictions proved true. Soon after Anderson's surrender, Union warships blockaded the harbor, immediately shutting down the transport of goods and food in and out of the city. Often Joanna found the shelves of the mistress's favorite shops empty of the items she had been instructed to purchase, and she was forced to search from street to street until she found what was needed rather than return to Harper Hall, basket empty, punishment certain.

Military camps formed throughout the city; slaves were put to work setting up cannons and barricades and fortifications. Once a pair of soldiers with accents Joanna did not recognize detained her outside the fish market and ordered her to return with them to their encampment to work at the battalion's laundry.

"My mistress expect me home," she gasped as the taller of the two seized her upper arm in an iron grip, nearly lifting her from the ground. "She don't hire me out. I got a pass in my apron pocket."

The soldier grinned, baring yellow teeth. "I'm sure your mistress won't mind you serving the defense of her city."

Joanna struggled and protested, but the pass fell from her pocket and fluttered into an open sewer as the soldier pushed her stumbling along to one of the many encampments that had sprung up along the edge of the city. There the armed soldiers forced her to join three other slave women in bright headscarves toiling over large kettles set upon the fire. Each of the others wore a small, hexagonal copper badge pinned to her blouse with the name of her master and a license number, showing that they had been hired legally. None of the other soldiers milling about with guns slung over their shoulders seemed to notice or care that Joanna had no badge. She was colored, so she would do.

Joanna's eyes darted around the encampment as she stirred lye into a bubbling kettle. She knew she could not sneak away yet, not with so many eyes upon her, so she worked without complaint alongside the other women, waiting for the soldiers to relax their guard. As soon as they did, she would flee.

Before an opportunity came, Abner and George arrived. A familiar wagon pulled to a hasty stop just beyond the last row of tents, and while Abner held the horses steady, George leaped down from the back and quickly approached a group of soldiers polishing their boots not far from the working women. "That there girl needed at home, suh," George said deferentially, handing one of the soldiers a folded paper.

"That there wench is busy, boy," drawled the solider, but he unfolded the paper and read it, frowning. Then his glance darted to Joanna, who feigned obedient disinterest as she hung shirts on the clothesline. "You mean to say she's Colonel Harper's wench?"

"Yes, suh, and Mrs. Harper needs her right now. She say if you don't let her come home right this minute, I'm to find Marse Colonel and —"

"No, no, that's all right. You, there. Girl," he snapped to Joanna. "Collect your wages for your mistress and get home. Thank her for her trouble and be sure to tell her we treated you fair. Can you remember that? You a sensible wench?"

Joanna looked at the ground and bobbed a nod, silent. A few minutes later, she was sitting in the back of the wagon beside George, coins jingling in her pocket, heart in her throat. "How did you know?" she managed to ask as the encampment disappeared behind them. If they had not come after her, if they had not found her —

"Missus Ames's Jenny saw you picked up by them soldiers. Missus Harper go into a fine fury when she get the news." George shook his head. "I thought you smarter than that, girl. The missus plenty mad you go off with them soldiers."

"I didn't go off with them! They drag me along all the way from the fish market. Jenny don't see that?"

"You shoulda got away. I hear you know how to run."

"They had my arm," Joanna said, but she knew it would do no good. Miss Evangeline was sure to blame her just the same.

Sure enough, before Joanna could slink in through the back door, Miss Evangeline met her outside and slapped her twice across the face, so hard that Joanna knew her palm stung almost as badly as Joanna's scarred cheek. "Your duty is to this household," the young mistress snapped. "If the soldiers need your services so badly, they should consult your master. You are never to go off without my permission ever again, even to serve the Confederacy, is that understood?"

"Yes, Missus Harper," Joanna mumbled, eyes downcast to conceal her anger.

"Take care you remember that." Miss Evangeline's blue eyes narrowed. "If you should fail me, I'll sell your baby and that girl Hannah so quickly it will take your breath away. Do I need to rid you of all distractions so that you'll remember your duties, or can your sorry little nigger mind carry more than two thoughts simultaneously?"

Joanna's heart burned, anger and fear searing her chest. "I can carry as many thoughts as you need me to, missus."

Miss Evangeline put her head to one side and regarded Joanna through narrowed eyes, suddenly calm. "That was a very good answer. Get inside. There's mending waiting in your basket."

Joanna obeyed, closing her fist around the coins in her pocket so the mistress would not hear them jingle.

Miss Evangeline did not let Joanna leave

the house for two weeks, but eventually necessity overcame her resolve and she sent Joanna out to the market for a spool of thread and a packet of needles. On her way home, a man in a long brown coat stopped her and asked to see her badge. "I ain't got no badge, suh," she said, showing him Miss Evangeline's handwritten pass, praying he would not order her to some other task. "My master don't hire me out."

He studied the pass. "You belong to Colonel Harper?"

I belong to myself was her first thought, and then, *I belong to Titus.* And to Ruthie, and to Frederick so far away but never forgotten. And to Hannah. *I am my beloved's and my beloved is mine.* "Yes, suh."

He folded the pass and scrutinized her face, his gaze lingering as everyone's did on her scar. Then, to her relief, he handed her the pass and waved her on her way.

She saw the man again at the market a few days later; he gave her a tiny nod and looked away before she could drop her glance. Later that same week, she could have sworn he followed her as she went from street to street searching for the items Miss Evangeline had requested. The Union blockade led by the fearsome warship *Niagara* had successfully prevented ships from entering the Charleston port, and though a few swift blockade runners had managed to elude capture and bring in some supplies, the markets were all but depleted of their usual goods. But the brown-coated man did not demand to see her pass, nor did he speak to her again. He must have some official position in the city, she decided. A secret policeman, or a patroller. Nearly every other able-bodied buckra man his age in Charleston wore the uniform of one militia or another. He did not, so he must serve the Confederacy in another fashion.

With the blockade in force, Fort Sumter taken, and Charleston under siege, Harper Hall became a sort of military compound, with messengers running back and forth with sealed letters and officers gathering at all hours to meet in the colonel's study. Joanna and the other slaves were constantly in motion, scrambling to attend to their usual duties as well as the extra work the unexpected guests required. With so many buckra eyes and ears around, Joanna had to abandon Hannah's reading lessons. The girl silently continued on her own, studying the letters on a sack of flour, peering at the cover of a book left open on a chair. Sometimes Joanna had to whisper a warning that she must take care not to seem too interested in the written word, and Hannah would gaze steadily up at Joanna, silent but sure, as if to say that she, of all people, knew the danger.

Summer settled in, and the blockade continued. As Miss Evangeline neared her time, she wrote reams of letters to her father at Oak Grove, to friends scattered on plantations around the low country, to her aunt Lucretia a few short blocks away. Joanna dressed the mistress's hair, listened to her complaints, and prepared the Harper baby's layette, wishing she could fashion the soft, gentle fabrics into clothing for her own children. Hannah had outgrown her best dress long ago, and Ruthie grew so quickly Joanna had to make over her dress nearly twice a month. But whenever she asked the mistress for fabric, Miss Evangeline would shake her head and make vague excuses about the difficulties of obtaining goods because of the blockade. Joanna, who had seen the bales of cotton piled up on the wharf for the lack of ships to carry them away, knew that Marse Chester surely had stores of his own going to waste. Surely some could be spared for Joanna's girls and all the Harpers' slaves. Joanna was willing to learn to weave homespun to clothe the entire household. But when Joanna hesitantly suggested this, Miss Evangeline merely sighed, interlaced her fingers over her rounded abdomen, and said she would ask her father.

One day Joanna was sewing in the back room off the kitchen when she heard the rattle of a familiar wagon — Marse Chester's wagon. "Titus," she murmured. Leaping to her feet, she ran outside only to find an unfamiliar slave driving Marse Chester's wagon up to the carriage house.

"Where Titus at?" she cried, clutching her sewing so tightly that a needle pierced the fleshy base of her thumb. "Why didn't he come?"

"Titus sick," the man said, climbing down from the seat as Abner and the stable boys came to help him unload the wagon. "Yellow fever hit the quarter hard. His sister die yesterday. His auntie, two days before that."

Dizzy, Joanna slumped to the ground. "Pearl?" she said faintly. "The children?"

"They still all right when I left." The man peered at her quizzically, then drew back, chagrined. "You that yellow girl, Titus's woman."

Joanna nodded.

"Titus strong," the man said quickly, too quickly. "He prolly be sound by time I get back. You want me carry him a message?"

"Tell him I love him." Joanna's heart seemed to splinter in her chest, cutting her to the quick as the shards fell apart. Tavia. Auntie Bess. Titus, her beloved Titus. "Tell him he got to get better, for me and for Ruthie. Tell him to keep breathin'."

The man nodded, his eyes full of sympathy that offered Joanna no comfort.

The wagon had brought cotton from Oak Grove, some in bales in hopes that Colonel Harper might be able to arrange for a blockade runner to speed them past the Union ships and earn Marse Chester some sorely needed cash. A smaller portion had been woven into coarse homespun, which Miss Evangeline presented to Joanna with a warning not to waste it. "Use the scraps for your patchwork," she suggested. "I'm sure our other servants would be pleased if you furnished each bed with one of your creations, and the colonel would certainly approve of such frugality. Perhaps something like that other quilt you made, the one with the triangles and the intriguing stitches. It's very quaint, quite lovely in its way."

Joanna was so terrified that the mistress might ask for a closer look that she almost forgot to thank her for the homespun. From a distance the quilted images blended in perfectly with the coarse muslin, but a careful inspection would reveal each unexpected irregularity, and Miss Evangeline had too sharp a mind to dismiss them as mistakes. But the mistress promptly forgot the Birds in the Air quilt, out of sight in the slaves' dormitory above the kitchen, and Joanna soberly beckoned Ruthie to come closer so Joanna could measure her with a long strand of yarn. She blinked away tears as she cut out the pieces for the girl's new dress, heart heavy with grief, imagining Titus tossing and turning in his hayloft bed, sweating and groaning with pain and fever. Or perhaps he was in Tavia's cabin, tended by his niece. Pearl would care for him. Though she was young, she was strong; she had learned to be strong in the cotton rows, and now she would care for her brother and sister as her mother had done —

It was too much to bear. Sewing allowed Joanna too much time alone with her thoughts. She welcomed errands that sent her from the busy house with its constant coming and going of soldiers and into the streets of Charleston, where she could forget her heavy heart in the challenge of finding the scarce goods Miss Evangeline craved.

Midmorning one day in mid-July found Joanna running to the fish market to procure something for the colonel's supper. "For once we won't have guests, so get the best of whatever they have," Miss Evangeline instructed Joanna and Sally, counting out coins into Joanna's palm. "There must be nothing unsavory to distract my husband from the pleasure of my company."

"Should've sent you first thing this morning," Sally grumbled after the mistress left the kitchen. "Everyone know best fish all gone by now."

"Just pour a lot of sauce over it and they won't know no better." Joanna adjusted her headscarf and snatched up her basket. The mistress was becoming increasingly capricious as her frustration with her confinement — and her husband's inattention — grew, and the slaves bore the brunt of her bad temper. As Joanna hurried down the street, rain-soaked and muddy from a recent downpour, a painful flash of memory struck: Titus fishing in the river just beyond the quarter, Titus bringing home a string of trout for Tavia to fry up, Titus watching Pearl and the younger children licking juices from their fingers and beaming at their uncle as they filled their bellies. Not a word had come to her about how her beloved fared, and in her desperation for news, she had begun sneaking into the colonel's study whenever it was unoccupied and searching desk drawers and pigeonholes for letters from Oak Grove. She read about thriving crops, destructive storms, admonishments for Miss Evangeline to exercise moderately for her health, and countless other minutiae, but nothing about her own dearest ones. She tried to convince herself that the absence of her husband's name from the letters was a good sign. Marse Chester so prized Titus that if he had been obliged to purchase a new driver, he surely would have mentioned it.

Joanna reached the fish market and inspected the nearly empty stalls with a sigh, resigned to failure. She ought to just drop a line in the harbor herself for all the good this would do her. She made her way down the block, looking for something decent enough to please the mistress, when she spotted a small, handwritten sign tacked to a barrel of redfish: "All redfish and speckled trout half-price after noon."

Joanna glanced at the sky; noon could be no more than thirty minutes away. Sally was right that all the best fish were sold by morning, but if she waited and the fishmonger didn't sell out, she could keep the difference for herself. The mistress would never know how much she had paid, and the blockade had sent prices soaring so high that she would not expect Joanna to return with change. The pass in her pocket did not say what time she was expected home, and given the scarcity of goods in the city, Miss Evangeline would never think to wonder why Joanna had taken so long to find what she needed. Joanna could conceal the unspent coins under her bed with her wages from her day at the soldiers' laundry, her tin cornboiler, and her few other treasures. She would need money when she ran.

Joanna made a show of considering the redfish before shaking her head and moving off through the crowd. Other colored folk milled about, some with badges pinned to their clothes showing they had been hired out, others with the same sober, wary look of slaves she was sure they saw in her own eyes. Free people of color worked their shops, their smiths, their fruiteries — and how Joanna envied them. It appalled her that some of those free colored folk owned slaves of their own, something she had never seen before coming to South Carolina. Colored folk should lift up other colored folk, not spend their hard-earned freedom working other slaves. To Joanna, that made them worse than the cruelest of the buckra.

Joanna finished her other errands, and as

soon as a bell in a distant church tower struck noon, she returned to the fishmonger and purchased a string of fine redfish. She wrapped the unspent coins in a bit of cloth so they would make no sound as she went about her work back at Harper Hall. She probably wouldn't be able to sneak them from the big house to the slaves' dormitory above the kitchen until much later, and until then, she had to be careful.

"You there, wench."

A hand on Joanna's shoulder spun her around, and she faced the man in the long brown coat. There was a glint of intelligence in his green eyes, but she quickly remembered to drop her gaze to his boots. Buckra hated being looked in the eye; they thought it impudent. "Yes, suh?"

"Come with me," he said, his voice low, his grip on her shoulder firm. "Don't make me drag you."

Heart pounding, she allowed him to steer her away from the busy market, away from the confusion and down a secluded alley. Her hands clenched around the basket, but she forced herself to remain calm, clear-headed. As soon as he released her to unfasten his trousers, she would strike him with the basket and run.

But he did not let go. He guided her into

a doorway, glanced over his shoulder, and regarded her appraisingly. "You read that sign."

Her heart was in her throat. "No, suh, Marse. I can't read."

"Don't lie to me. I've been watching you. You read that sign, then you bided your time and came back when the fish were half-price."

"His fish always half-price after midday. Everybody know that."

"You're quick-witted but wrong. That lie could be easily disproved." He released her and took a step back, searching her with his eyes. She held the basket in front of her as if it would keep him at bay, but she no longer feared he meant to molest her. But if he reported that she could read, it would be far worse for her. She could be beaten or killed, separated from Ruthie and Hannah and Titus forever. No matter what this strange man said, she would not admit she could read.

"I'd like to hire you."

Hire her? "My marse don't hire me out, suh."

He shook his head, impatient. "This has nothing to do with your master, do you understand? You help us, and we'll help you. If we succeed, we may help all of your kind."

Joanna risked a quick look at his face and saw only clear determination there, no malice, no deceit. Still . . . "Don't know what you mean, suh," she mumbled, looking to his muddy boots again.

"You're sensible, you're well placed, and you can read," the man said as if she had not spoken. "You could be our eyes and ears within the headquarters of the military defense of Charleston. You can intercept letters, overhear conversations, gather information, and I'll pass it along to those in a position to use it. You can help end this siege, Joanna, and bring a swift conclusion to the war. Wouldn't you like to see the Confederacy fall? Wouldn't you like to see an end to slavery?"

How did he know her name? "You could be anybody," she said, meeting his gaze boldly. "Maybe you think to trap me, get me to defy my marse, and get me killed."

"Why would I bother? You're just one housemaid. What would I possibly have to gain?"

"What *I* got to gain?"

He smiled grimly. "Aside from freedom for your people if we succeed? I can pay you a little. The rest of your reward will have to wait until after the war is won."

She had not given any thought to a reward. "That ain't what I want. I got two children here with me, two girls. I get you your secrets, but you got to help me when I need you. I get caught in the marse colonel's study and he kill me for it, you buy my girls and get them north to freedom. My marse try to sell them, you buy them and set them free. He try to sell me, same thing. My family never get split up, never get sold away down south. That's it. That's my price."

He needed little time to mull it over. "Agreed."

Joanna nodded and let out a deep breath she had not realized she had been holding. "What I got to do?"

Quickly the man explained that she should gather information about troop movements, supplies, and defenses, and report to him once a week, every Friday in that same alley. If she could not get away from Harper Hall at the appointed time, she should set her basket on the kitchen windowsill as a signal. If she discovered news so important that it could not wait, she should go to the market and drop her basket in front of the stall where she had purchased the redfish. "I'll be watching you," he said. "I'll know."

He tugged on the brim of his hat and turned away.

"Wait," she said. "Who you be? What your name?"

He smiled. "I'm with Mr. Lincoln's army, and you may call me Mr. Lewis."

With that, he strolled from the alley as if utterly unconcerned and melted into the busy throng of craftsmen, slaves, gentlemen, and passersby. By the time Joanna reached the street, he was gone.

Joanna's theft of Marse Chester's letters to Miss Evangeline had trained her well for Mr. Lewis's assignment. She had learned when Colonel Harper was most likely to be away from the study; she had trained herself to wake in the middle of the night, leave the dormitory without waking anyone, and creep silently across the cobblestones and through the darkened house. She had learned how to open the second desk drawer, the one that stuck and opened with a loud squeak, without making a sound by lifting the handle just so, and she had discovered a nook between the bookcases where she could quickly and invisibly read the news from Oak Grove, unseen by anyone who might cross the hallway or pass outside the windows. In the day, she worked upon her sewing and mending on the front porch instead of the back piazza so she could monitor the comings and goings of messengers and eavesdrop through the open window on discussions in the colonel's study. She silently repeated unfamiliar names of people and places until she knew them by heart, for she dared not steal paper and ink and write down the secrets she discovered. If even a single sentence on a scrap of paper were found on her, it would mean her death.

Friday came. She concealed her impatience as she waited for the mistress to send her on an errand, and when no errand appeared, Joanna hid the last spool of black thread and said that she had used it up mending the colonel's trousers and needed more to finish the job. A few minutes later, pass in hand, coins jingling in her apron pocket, she ran off to meet Mr. Lewis in the alley off Market Street.

At first she thought she was alone, but a movement in the shadows suddenly revealed him. "Good girl," he greeted her in a murmur, then took her elbow and steered her deeper into the alley.

He listened intently as she told him everything she had learned since their first meeting — new fortifications being built around the city, the appointment of a Cuban soldier of fortune as General Beauregard's chief of artillery, the names of Charleston's most successful blockade runners and their ships. Mr. Lewis kept his face impassive, so she could not discern whether he considered her news good or bad, helpful or worthless. For all she could tell, he already knew everything she told him.

"Have you seen any maps?" he asked when she had finished. "Anything to indicate troop movements, future offensives, plans of attack?"

"Only what I already told you, suh," Joanna said, wishing she had more to offer.

She feared for a moment that she had displeased Mr. Lewis so much that he would cancel their agreement, but just then he dropped a few coins in her palm and told her he would see her the following week, if not sooner. Without waiting for a reply, he strode away and melted into the crowd, his brown coat blending into the mud of the streets, the storefronts, the passing wagons and horses.

The weeks passed. Joanna grew bolder, venturing into the colonel's study in daylight while he was away, glancing at the papers scattered across his desk while dusting or sweeping. Once she smuggled a map to Mr. Lewis, pressing herself into the darkened doorway and willing herself invisible while he copied it into a sketchbook. Her heart did not stop pounding until hours later when she returned it to its pigeonhole in the colonel's desk, rolled and tied with brown string as if it had never been disturbed.

Ruthie was walking confidently now, chattering and laughing as she toddled around the workyard, faithful Hannah chasing after. Joanna saw her beloved Titus in the curve of her smile and the shape of her head, and though she tried to find comfort in these signs of his earthly presence, sometimes they pained her so much that she had to look away. Sometimes it seemed as if her brief moments of happiness in Titus's arms had never happened, that it had all been a dream, that he himself had been a creation of her own longing and loneliness. Ruthie was the only sign that he had ever been, that he had ever loved her.

The colonel bought a new slave, a midwife and nurse from one of the barrier islands who understood every word she heard but spoke only Gullah. Mattie had sharp, observant eyes and her Gullah talk disguised a keen mind, and Joanna knew she couldn't continue her daylight excursions into the colonel's study until she knew whether this newcomer could be trusted to keep her mouth shut. The other slaves would look the other way and say nothing if Joanna ventured into places where she really had no business, but she could not be sure about Mattie.

Thus only at night when she was certain she would not be observed did she move through the house like a ghost, haunting the study, moving aside books to see what loose pages they weighted down, unrolling documents, slipping letters from envelopes. Every detail she discovered, no matter how simple or seemingly unimportant, she passed along to Mr. Lewis, who never failed to reward her with a few small coins. But that was not why she did it, why she took the risk. Mr. Lincoln's army had to win. A Union victory was Joanna's best chance for freedom, for reuniting her scattered family, for finding little Frederick so far to the north. If any of the secrets she passed along to the mysterious man in the long brown coat hastened the end of the Confederacy, it was worth the risk to herself a hundred times over.

In August Miss Evangeline labored for fourteen hours before giving birth to a robust, dark-haired little boy. The colonel had been away from home for two weeks, and as Miss Evangeline was seized by contractions, she raged at him for being so far away, for sending no kind word of comfort, for abandoning her to her travail. She gasped out curses as she paced the floorboards of her bedroom, Mattie the new midwife on one side, Joanna on the other. "My papa was always present when my mother gave birth," Miss Evangeline gasped out between curses. "He never left the plantation during her last month. Never!" She added a few curses for Mr. Lincoln, whose selfish aggression she blamed for her husband's absence.

When Miss Evangeline could no longer stand, Mattie helped her into bed and checked between her legs, nodding and murmuring that all was well. Eventually pain and exhaustion rendered the young mistress incoherent, but then came one last push, one last groan of pain, and Mattie caught the baby. Joanna quickly helped her clean the child — the boy, a future master — and stepped back as Mattie swaddled him, declared him the best baby child in all of Charleston, and placed him in his exhausted mother's arms. Miss Evangeline's anger vanished as soon as she held her child, and the next day, when the colonel returned home in a storm of horse's hooves and dust from the road, she offered not a word of rebuke but rather praised him as the best of all possible husbands for racing to her side despite the needs of the young Confederacy and the overwhelming call of duty.

"If he been here a day ago, he'd know the missus's shouts can drown out any call of duty," George remarked to Joanna in an undertone. She smothered her laughter, wishing she were brave enough to tell the colonel all the terrible things his sweet wife had said about him in his absence. She had her own reasons for mirth, beyond George's joke: Miss Evangeline had borne a son, not a daughter. Ruthie would not be compelled to be this child's maid. Her future remained unwritten, and perhaps she would be able to write it herself, pen firmly within her own grasp.

Mr. Lewis remained a mystery. As the summer waned, Joanna learned nothing of him, his past, or his people, but his questions and requests for certain documents eventually revealed his most urgent desire: He desperately wanted to close the Port of Charleston permanently and decisively, so that not even the smallest blockade runner could slip through. He queried her constantly about which ships were the fastest — Thomas Lockwood's *Kate* was the answer that promptly came to her lips — and which were the most successful — again the *Kate* — and what they were smuggling in and out. "You can see for yourself what the market holds," she retorted when he grew impatient. "You can see for yourself the cotton piled on the wharf. Everybody feeling the strain, most of all my people. Colored folk always got the smallest piece of the loaf. Now we get just the crust. Your blockade hurting those who want to help you."

Like me, Joanna thought, watching him pace back and forth across the narrow alley. She had put her trust in him, had come to rely upon his extra coins to buy food for her girls, which she smuggled into the attic and fed them under the covers after the others had fallen asleep. Only George knew — he was alert to any movement she made in bed at night, as if ever hopeful that she might suddenly change her mind and lie down beside him — but he said nothing. He never even asked how she came by the food or asked her to share.

He wasn't Titus, but he was a good man.

Mr. Lewis stopped pacing, folded his arms, and regarded her sternly. "Everyone's feeling the strain, and yet the forts never seem to run out of arms, and yet the Charleston aristocracy feasts and dances and celebrates without a care in the world instead of practicing thrift and preparing for a long siege."

It was true. The wealthy buckra threw lavish parties where officers and ladies mingled until dawn, sometimes coming in boats from the barrier islands held within the blockade. Sometimes they stayed too late and the tide went out, leaving their boats stuck in the mud. Miss Evangeline teased her becalmed friends that they conveniently forgot the tides whenever they especially enjoyed a soldier's company and wanted an excuse to remain overnight in the city. But there was a frenzied quality to their celebrations, as if they knew their merriment couldn't last. "Them buckra never had to ration nothing," Joanna said. "They don't know how. Or they don't think they got to. They all say the war be over before Christmas."

Mr. Lewis snorted. "Your rebel officers don't believe such nonsense."

That was also true; Joanna had read the correspondence herself, the exhortations that they must prepare themselves for a long fight, that a change of command was coming. "They ain't my officers," she retorted.

"I've thrown my lot in with you. You lose, I lose."

Her vehemence startled him. "Of course. I misspoke. Forgive me."

Joanna did not know what to say. No white man had ever asked for her forgiveness. Unable to speak, she waved a hand and shook her head to tell him it didn't matter. She needed this strange, unpredictable, unknowable man. She trusted him to rescue her and her girls from the auction block, and yet she had no idea if he was worthy of that trust. If she did get caught with her fingers on the seal of one of General Beauregard's directives, Mr. Lewis might shrug, turn his back as she climbed onto the auction block at the slave market, and walk away. If she could no longer spy for him, she was of no use to him. Why rescue her when she could no longer serve his cause?

"You remember your promise, don't you?" she heard herself say. "What you got to do for me if my family gonna get split up?"

He regarded her steadily. "I remember every word, and I will stand by that promise until my dying breath."

She held his look with equal steadiness, but she could not read him. He spoke pretty words, but he was a practiced liar. The security he offered her might have no more substance than the air between them.

But she had no choice but to trust him.

October came. Young Master Thomas Harper grew round and robust, dressed in gowns of the the softest Sea Island cotton, his tiny pink mouth sucking greedily at Mattie's dark breast. Ruthie hung back and stared at him, fingers in her mouth, unsure what to make of this strange new creature who had thrown the household into such upheaval, whose arrival had heralded so much celebration. A week after his birth, Miss Evangeline squeezed into her most accommodating dress from before her pregnancy and threw the exact sort of party Mr. Lewis had found so inexplicable. The colonel was obliged to sell some precious family silver to pay for it all, but he insisted upon only the best for his son and heir. Joanna thought of Ruthie's welcome to the world — a coarse blanket, small gifts of food from Tavia's and Titus's friends, sorrowful glances from the other women in the quarter who knew the bleak fate that awaited the girl. But Joanna turned her thoughts from bitterness and grimly went about her work, tending to Miss Evangeline by day, collecting priceless information for Mr. Lewis by night.

War abruptly returned to Harper Hall in the form of a congratulatory letter bringing new orders from General Beauregard. Colonel Harper had been reassigned to Fort Walker on the tip of Hilton Head Island, about fifty miles from Charleston, to help with the defense of Port Royal Sound. Although he would have preferred to have been placed in command of one of the many South Carolina regiments that had been sent north to battle Union forces in Virginia, he was pleased to accept.

Within a day he was gone, and he might as well have been on the other side of the world as far as his wife was concerned. Miss Evangeline sat listlessly in her parlor as if all the air and sunlight had been sucked out of the room. Gone was the luxury of seeing her husband every day, or even every other day, a luxury she had taken for granted and criticized as insufficient. Now she was as lonely and bereft as any other soldier's wife, although one with a fine home, a beautiful new baby, and servants to take care of her every need.

When the colonel's lengthy deployment began, Aunt Lucretia spent two weeks at Harper Hall to distract Miss Evangeline and keep her loneliness at bay. Aunt Lucretia's suspicious gaze darted everywhere, and

Joanna never knew when she might turn a corner and find the woman eavesdropping on the slaves to be sure they weren't shirking their duties. Worse yet, she was an inconsistent and light sleeper; twice when Joanna sneaked into the house to riffle through the colonel's desk, she discovered Aunt Lucretia, first sighing and staring out the front window, fanning herself with a book, and then in the kitchen opening cupboards in search of a bite to eat. On both occasions Joanna managed to steal back outside to the slaves' dormitory without drawing the older woman's attention, but she decided with great misgivings to curtail her work for Mr. Lewis until the interloper left.

Eventually Aunt Lucretia departed, but although Joanna was once again free to examine every document on the colonel's desk, she found little new information to offer Mr. Lewis. There were no more officers' meetings in the study, no more messengers coming and going, and few letters from Fort Walker. Even those carried little of military significance; the colonel wrote as a husband would speak to a beloved wife, lavish in his praise for her beauty and goodness, guarded in his description of his work lest the letters fall into enemy hands. But just in case the smallest, least significant detail might aid Mr. Lincoln's soldiers and sailors, Joanna memorized the letters and recited them to Mr. Lewis. Sometimes a word or phrase would evoke a glimmer in his eye, and Joanna knew she had offered something useful. "What you do with all this I tell you?" she was compelled to ask him once, when he smiled grimly at a somewhat amusing story the colonel had shared about his men's search for oysters.

"I calculate their positions, their troop strength, their will to fight," he replied. "They're searching for oysters, therefore they must be hungry, though I never met a soldier who wasn't half-starved most of the time. They snuck off picket duty to do it, which shows that dissatisfaction is high and discipline lax. Port Royal might be the place to strike."

Joanna stared at him in disbelief. Mr. Lewis had never shared so much of his intentions with her, nor had she ever imagined that the colonel's warm, affectionate letters could become the very weapon that would destroy him. And she had placed that weapon in Mr. Lewis's hands.

Mr. Lewis studied her. "You don't regret divulging your master's secrets, do you?"

She shook her head.

"Perhaps you regret only what I intend to do with them."

"No," she quickly replied. It was war, and Colonel Harper fought for those who wanted to keep her and those she loved forever enslaved. He had made his choice and Joanna had made hers. She would not regret it, nor would she cease until the narrow stream of information trickling into Harper Hall dried up entirely. Her freedom, her children's safety, her very life depended upon it and demanded that she press on.

Mr. Lewis's confirmation that her efforts were not in vain should have been enough to encourage her, but it wasn't. She needed more. She prayed for hope, for courage, for a sign that someday the war would end and her family would be reunited.

And at last a sign came.

On the first day of November, Marse Chester wrote to his daughter to tell of hard times on the plantation, her eldest brother's increasing fascination with the military, and his own purchase of land further inland in case the family should have to evacuate Edisto Island. "Our bountiful harvest is next to worthless if I cannot sell it," he wrote. "If the war does not end by springtime, I shall consider turning over more land to corn. Our stores are running low and I have little time for hunting. There are days when our table would be bare indeed if not for Titus's skill as a hunter and fisherman."

Joanna's heart soared, leaving her so faint and breathless that she had to sit down and compose herself before she could read on. Titus lived. He had survived the fever and was strong enough to hunt and fish. One day, she hoped, he would take the master's hunting rifle and keep going, across streams and through forests, until he crossed over into Union territory and found freedom. They could use a man like him, strong and wise and a crack shot. He would fight for the Union his way, and she would fight hers.

But of course that was only an ambitious, impossible dream. Titus would not abandon Tavia's children, even though Pearl was old enough to look after her younger brother and sister. And even if Titus found a Union camp, they would put him to work digging ditches or pounding tent stakes. They would never let a colored man point a gun at a white man, even if that man were a rebel.

Less than a week later, a massive fleet of Union warships, transports, and supply vessels sailed into Port Royal Sound and launched a ferocious attack on Fort Walker. Within hours the surviving Confederate defenders abandoned the ruined fort and fled inland, and later that night, the defenders of Fort Beauregard at Bay Point on Eddings Island to the north of the sound followed. When word of the defeat came, Miss Evangeline frantically tried to get some official account of her husband's fate. Days later, when word finally came that he was safe and uninjured in a camp west of Charleston with his surviving men, the young mistress immediately decided to pack the wagon with supplies and join him. Joanna was content to let her, thinking that she and the girls might slip away in her absence, and she hid her eagerness behind a mask of dutiful obedience as she helped Miss Evangeline prepare for the journey. But Mattie spoiled everything. She watched Abner load the wagon, shaking her head and muttering that the missus was in no fit condition to travel and shouldn't leave young Master Thomas. Before Joanna could stop her, Mattie strode next door and brought back Mrs. Ames, who managed to stall Miss Evangeline long enough for Aunt Lucretia to come racing over to dissuade her. "You can't become a camp follower," said Aunt Lucretia, scandalized. "If Robert were injured and needed you to nurse him, that would be another matter altogether. As it is, you will only distract him. He can't protect you and lead his men both." Reluctantly, Miss Evangeline agreed, and Joanna could only fume silently over Mattie's inopportune caution.

The colonel's survival and location were the only bits of information Joanna passed along to Mr. Lewis that week, but if he were disappointed, he did not show it. If anything, he seemed especially pleased to see her, which told Joanna that he — and the information she had given him — had played an important role in the success of the Port Royal mission.

In the days to come, the talk of the streets swirled around a new commander assigned to defend Charleston now that the Union forces had established a foothold on Port Royal, a general named Robert E. Lee. Mr. Lewis urged Joanna to discover all she could of his intentions, but only one letter came from the colonel in all that time, and it said nothing of the new commander. "I don't got nothing for you," Joanna was forced to admit one Friday when they met in the alley. It was the second week in a row she had failed to find even the smallest detail that might help him. "Things ain't the same as they was before the colonel go to Port Royal. Officers don't come to Harper Hall no more and we don't get much news."

Mr. Lewis said that he understood, and to Joanna's disappointment, he said that he would not meet her weekly anymore, but if she acquired any information, she should signal him by placing the basket on the kitchen windowsill. She agreed, as she had little choice, but her heart was heavy. She had needed those clandestine meetings even more than the coins Mr. Lewis paid her. Somehow every secret she passed along had made her feel one week closer to freedom, and now that she was no longer useful to him, Mr. Lewis might not feel obliged to save her and her girls from the auction block.

December came, and although Joanna searched Miss Evangeline's letters in vain for scarce details that might benefit Mr. Lewis, she did manage to find a bit of good news when Marse Chester wrote to broach the subject of the upcoming holidays. This year he wanted Miss Evangeline and her family to come to him. The house he was building on his new acres further inland would not be as grand as the big house at Oak Grove, but there would be room enough for everyone, and with all but the finish work completed, there was no reason why they could not pass a perfectly comfortable Christmas there. What more did they need in those troubled times but four walls, a roof, plenty to eat, and those they loved? He would be delighted if the Harper and Chester families would celebrate the holidays there in a rustic fashion suiting their troubled times.

Miss Evangeline must have replied that she had hoped for the Chester and Harper families to reunite at Harper Hall as they had the previous year, for her father's next letter expressed his regrets that such a thing would not be possible. Elliot, the elder son, was now fifteen, and too besotted with the military to be trusted near the dozens of various militias that marched in the streets and camped outside the city. Back home he could only gape in wide-eyed admiration at the officers who came to Oak Grove, but in Charleston he would be sorely tempted to run away and join the first regiment he could persuade to take him on as a drummer boy. A letter that quickly followed admonished Miss Evangeline not to even consider passing Christmas or any other day on the Harper family's James Island plantation. Should the Union invaders swarming over Port Royal decide to attack Charleston, James Island lay directly in their path. Even if the Harpers avoided having their lands taken over by Confederate forces setting up a defense, they would surely be forced to evacuate the moment the Union soldiers began to march. Marse Chester was certain Colonel Harper would agree with him, but even if his son-in-law did not, Marse Chester would not allow his daughter and infant grandson to risk such unimaginable danger.

Joanna didn't care where the Chester and Harper families finally decided to spend the holidays as long as Miss Evangeline required Joanna to accompany her and Titus drove Marse Chester to whatever location they settled upon. It was always possible that the whirl of holiday gaiety would distract the buckra long enough for Joanna, Titus, and the children to run off. It wasn't likely, but it was possible, a gentle breath of wind on the fading embers of her hopes.

One night two weeks before Christmas, Joanna was asleep, dreaming of Union warships anchoring in Charleston Harbor, blue-coated Union soldiers pouring onto the docks like a wave of indigo, the church bells reformed from Confederate canons and restored to their steeples and ringing out freedom. The bells pealed on as someone shook her awake. "Get up," said George.

"Whole city burning. Get up!"

Joanna scrambled out of bed and hurried to the window. The sky was red with flame; she smelled smoke and tasted ash.

"We on fire?" cried Sally, throwing back the covers.

"Not yet," said George. "Not yet."

Heart pounding, Joanna stood on tiptoe and peered through the leaded panes. The sky was a lurid, swirling gale of red and black, of smoke and fire. As the other slaves scrambled into their clothes, she stood transfixed, craning her neck, pressing her face against the glass, trying in vain to discover the fire's location, its distance and direction. The window was too small, the palmetto trees too close. Did walls of flame surround them? Could they flee to the river?

Ruthie's wail roused her. She snatched up her daughter, seized Hannah's hand, and hurried down the stairs and outside. Miss Evangeline was already there, standing before the carriage house and studying the smoke-filled sky with Abner. The strong wind carried the sound of the horses' terror-filled whinnies, their stomping hooves.

"We got to run," George said, close by her side. "We got to get to the river or we be burnt up like dry straw."

Hannah's grip on Joanna's hand tightened. "Which way?" Joanna asked George, gesturing to the north, to the south, in every equally uncertain direction. "We run away from the fire or into it?"

Before George could reply, Miss Evangeline spotted them. "Fetch water," she screamed into the wind, her golden curls whipping about her face. "Soak the house. Every inch of it!"

"Missus Harper," George called back, incredulous. "We got to go. Joanna go fetch young Marse Thomas while Abner get the wagon ready."

"I will not abandon my husband's house to the flames," Miss Evangeline shouted over the clamor of bells and sirens. Her eyes were wild and red-rimmed. "He must have a home to return to."

"He must have a wife and baby to return to," Joanna retorted. "What good this house to him if you and young marse dead?"

Suddenly Miss Evangeline raced across the garden, nightdress trailing ghostly in the smoky air, to slap Joanna hard across the face. "Fetch the water! Your impudence will kill us all."

"Your stubbornness kill us first," Joanna snapped. Miss Evangeline slapped her again, harder, then shoved her toward the laundry, toward the pump. Joanna stumbled, nearly dropping Ruthie and releasing Hannah's hand. George caught her by the arm and kept her on her feet. He gave her a long, grim look before racing off to the pump.

Joanna shifted Ruthie on her hip and beckoned to Hannah. "Come on."

They hurried after George, but before filling a single bucket, George soaked the two girls from head to toe. "Take the baby into the kitchen," he ordered Hannah. "Kick the logs out of the way and stand in the big fireplace. You understand me?" Hannah nodded, reached for Ruthie, and darted back inside.

For hours they kept the house and yard soaked, filling buckets, flinging water upon the whitewashed brick walls of Harper Hall, trying in vain to discover from people fleeing through the streets, buckra and coloreds alike, where the fire line was, how much of the city had burned, if the fire department or army had mastered any control over the conflagration, if the flames were heading their way. Rumors whirled about like the ashes that fell like snow and settled over the Harpers' garden, black and gray and glowing red. Some said that the fire burned in a single north-south line across the peninsula, and where they stood on Meeting Street, they were cut off from the mainland. Or that Union spies had set fire to multiple targets throughout the city, and the fire was burning toward the center, destroying everything in its path. Or that rebellious slaves had set fire to the slave market and were passing out stolen rifles to any colored man willing to fight. There was no discerning truth from fiction, no time to make sense of the hysterical and contradictory tales shrieked or shouted from tear-streaked, sooty faces — men and women on foot, on horseback, in carriages, on wagons loaded with all their worldly possessions —

We should run, Joanna thought, watching them. The Harper slaves were many, and Miss Evangeline was but one. In the chaos the other buckra would never guess they fled their mistress as well as the fire. But where would they run? Where? She had no idea if the people fleeing down Meeting Street were running away from the fire or toward it. Sometimes her gaze met George's, and she knew he shared her thoughts. She knew from the set of his jaw that he thought they should flee anyway, that running was better than roasting alive all for the sake of saving Colonel Harper's house. Suddenly, startlingly, she also understood that as much as George wanted to run, he would never run without her.

Hours passed. Joanna's shoulders ached from hauling water, from beating out small fires that sparked into small blazes on the piazza, on the grass. On the roof. When Miss Evangeline spotted the first flames high above them, she screamed for George and gestured wildly. George nodded and hurried inside, his eyes catching hold of Joanna's before he disappeared through the doorway. In another moment he reappeared on the roof with a bucket of water and a soaked gunnysack, beating out the flames.

Her eyes and nostrils stinging from acrid smoke, Joanna watched as Miss Evangeline's glance traveled wildly from the roof to the street jammed with people and horses and wagons. Her attention lingered on an elegant carriage packed with trunks and valuables, a gentleman in suit and hat unexpectedly at the reins where his colored driver ought to be, a lady with a fur wrap over her shoulders by his side but looking back whence they had come, where their fine house was likely burning.

"We should go," Miss Evangeline said. Joanna could not hear her over the din, but she recognized the words the rosebud lips formed. Then, suddenly, the mistress ran to Abner as he flung water upon the tall front doors of the stable. Miss Evangeline gestured frantically and shouted something Joanna could not make out. Abner shook his head, gesturing helplessly toward the choked street — wagons loaded with furniture, buckra on horseback, hired-out slaves carrying the tools of their trades on their backs, their metal badges still carefully displayed on their coat fronts. The Harper household wouldn't get far, Abner was surely telling the mistress. Too many people in flight, frightened horses — the time to escape had passed. They must it stick out and save the house or perish.

Abner raised his hands to defend himself when Miss Evangeline began beating him about the head and shoulders, but he was not injured; without her whip, the mistress's blows were merely a shameful nuisance, a distraction when he could not afford to be distracted. He ducked away, took up his bucket, and sprinted for the pump. Joanna knew he cared more about saving the horses than any punishment that might descend later, if they survived the night.

From time to time Mattie appeared at the back door, plump face creased in worry, shawl around her shoulders as if she awaited the order to flee, young Master Thomas in her arms. Suddenly a man on horseback pulled hard on the reins just outside the gate and came to a clattering stop. "Cousin Evangeline," he called out. "Why on earth are you still here?"

With a glad cry, Miss Evangeline forgot Abner and raced to open the gate. Joanna recognized the fair-haired man despite his soot-streaked face — Gideon, Aunt Lucretia's youngest son, the only one who had not yet joined a Confederate regiment. He rode into the yard and swiftly dismounted, but his boots had scarcely touched the cobblestones before Miss Evangeline flung herself into his arms. "We sent Sam for you," Gideon said, looking her over to reassure himself she was unharmed. "Mother's evacuated to the Battery. Sam was supposed to escort you and the baby there hours ago."

Miss Evangeline shook her head. "I've seen neither hide nor hair of him all night."

Gideon scowled. "Likely he's taking advantage of our distress to run off. Father never did trust him." He glanced back down Meeting Street. "There's no time to load the wagon. Run inside, tell your nurse to bring the baby, and fetch whatever valuables you can carry on horseback. We have to leave at once."

"But the house," said Miss Evangeline.

"The furniture, our china —"

"Your servants can stay behind and save what they can."

Miss Evangeline hesitated only a moment before nodding and hurrying inside. Joanna's heart leapt. Their chance perhaps was only moments away. Once Miss Evangeline and Mattie departed, those left behind would be free to run. She continued working, stomping out fallen cinders, splashing water on the piazza, working as if she had no thought but saving her master's home. The time to run might have come at last.

Over Abner's protests, Gideon flung open the stable doors and pushed the groom ahead of him inside. Gideon soon reappeared holding the reins of two horses, saddled and bridled, just as Miss Evangeline emerged from the house carrying an overstuffed satchel. Mattie followed on her heels, young Master Thomas in her arms, but she balked when she realized she would have to ride on horseback. She didn't know how, she protested. She had never ridden but in a wagon or carriage.

Miss Evangeline threw Gideon a desperate, beseeching look. "The wagon?"

He shook his head. "There's no time."

Gnawing on her lip, Miss Evangeline turned back to Mattie and seemed about to order her into the saddle when her gaze fell upon Joanna. "Joanna. Has Titus taught you to ride horseback?"

Joanna's heart thumped. "My husband a groom, missus. That don't make me one."

"Mind your tongue," Gideon barked. "Can you ride or can't you?"

Joanna couldn't speak. She shook her head.

"She can too ride," Mattie shrilled. "Abner shown her. I seen her in the workyard helping him."

"Even if you ride only a little, you'll be safer with us than here," said Miss Evangeline. "Mattie, give Master Thomas to Joanna."

Before Joanna knew it, Mattie had fit her with a makeshift sling and had bound the sleeping boy firmly to her chest. "My girls," Joanna gasped as Gideon all but threw her onto the back of the horse. "Please, missus. Let me take Ruthie and Hannah too."

Miss Evangeline snapped out a laugh as Gideon lifted her onto the back of her horse; she was too distracted to notice that Joanna had used the forbidden name. "Absolutely not. You'll have your arms full with your young master." She hooked the handle of the satchel over the pommel of her saddle, took a deep, shaky breath, and nodded to her cousin. "All right. I'm ready."

Miss Evangeline called out some last-minute instructions to Abner as Gideon led the way through the open gate onto the street, his grasp firm on the reins of Joanna's horse. "Sally," Joanna shouted, but the cook was nowhere to be seen. "George!" In the eerie semidarkness she did not see him, but she thought she saw a shadow move on the roof. "My girls! Watch over my girls!"

She could do no more. The three horses set off down Meeting Street, but Joanna was insensible to the press of the crowd, the strange distant explosions, the crash of wood and showers of sparks as roofs caved in, the howling wind, the acrid stench of burning. Her precious, precious girls, cowering in the kitchen fireplace. They were waiting for her, depending upon her to save them, but she was riding away.

It seemed ages until they reached the Battery, where Aunt Lucretia and thousands had already gathered in some measure of safety to watch in horror as their city burned, bracing themselves against the fierce wind that whipped the waves into whitecaps as the tide rose. Flame cast a lurid red glare against the clouds of smoke rising to a clear blue velvet sky. Women shrieked as a church steeple collapsed, but

Joanna only stared at the flickering light. Somewhere within the smoke and heat were her girls, the beloved children she would have given her life to protect, and yet here she stood with their future master curled peacefully against her bosom. Were they crying for her, Hannah and Ruthie? Were their charred bodies even now mingling with the ash of the kitchen fireplace?

Wordlessly, soundlessly, Joanna watched the city burn, shaking from fear and rage and exhaustion. Her girls. Tears streamed down her face, but they could not obscure the nightmare scene before her. How could she have left them? She should have leapt from the back of the horse and fled to the kitchen, flung her arms around them, protected them or perished with them. What was the worst Miss Evangeline could have done to punish her disobedience? Beaten her? Sold her off to the Georgia traders? She could have endured a beating more easily than this agonizing waiting, wondering, and bearing witness, and the separation of distance was nothing to the final parting death would bring.

"The Yankees will see this as God's vengeance," said Gideon, scowling. Aunt Lucretia shook her head and pressed a perfumed handkerchief to her nose, but Miss

Evangeline nodded absently.

Vengeance? Perhaps not, but the chaos and disruption had been a stroke of grace, an opportunity that Aunt Lucretia's Sam had seized and Joanna had let slip from her grasp. *Please, Lord Jesus, watch over my girls and protect them,* she prayed. *Let the stone fireplace stand cool and strong. Let the flames part around the kitchen like Moses parted the waters of the Red Sea. Protect my girls, preserve them, and the next time You open a path before me, I won't miss it. I won't misunderstand Your signs a second time.*

If her girls lived and they were granted a second time.

Keep breathing, she imagined Titus murmuring in her ear, his breath tickling her hair. But the air was thick with smoke and despair, and she could not breathe for choking.

The sun rose; the fire burned on.

Eventually Gideon received word that although some parts of the city were still engulfed in flame, the fires on Meeting Street had been extinguished and it would be safe to return to see what remained of Harper Hall. Aunt Lucretia urged Miss Evangeline to stay with her while Gideon went on ahead alone to investigate, but Miss

Evangeline insisted upon accompanying him. They left Aunt Lucretia at her house, which had escaped the fire unscathed, and continued on into the charred ruins of the city.

Joanna shut her ears to the rumors that darted and flew through the smoky air like a flock of disoriented barn swallows. She feared the worst, and the sights along the route back warned her to prepare herself for the most devastating, cruelest shock she had ever endured. But there could be no preparing herself for the worst, if her prayers had not been answered, if her girls were dead.

The horses picked their way down streets littered with shattered glass and smoldering trunks and furniture, abandoned by their owners as they had fled. Gideon led them past smoldering ruins, a forest of blackened chimneys planted in dusky gray ash. Market Street was gone; only a single stone archway remained of the alley where Joanna had once met Mr. Lewis. Institute Hall, where the Ordinance of Secession had been signed, had burned to the ground, as had the Catholic cathedral, the theater, the Congressional church, and more businesses and dwellings than Joanna could count. In the sling a hungry young Master Thomas squalled for his nurse, but Miss Evangeline did not seem to hear, and Joanna had nothing to offer him. The mistress's pale face betrayed no emotion as her gaze skimmed the ruins, pausing to linger on clusters of survivors who sat on stone steps leading nowhere, huddled under borrowed blankets, sipping numbly at tin cups of coffee. Joanna knew Miss Evangeline wondered if she too had been reduced to such a state.

They rounded a corner, and suddenly the Ames's house stood before them, whole and sound but for a blackened north wall. Just beyond it was Harper Hall, entirely undamaged but for a section of the wrought iron barricade that had been knocked into the street by a fallen palmetto tree, which even now smoldered on the front lawn.

It was not until they passed through the open gate that they saw any sign of life within the house. Minnie and Mattie burst through the front door as they approached, and a moment later, Abner came running from the stable. Mattie didn't wait for Joanna to dismount before taking an unhappy young Master Thomas from her and putting him to the breast. Without waiting for Miss Evangeline's permission, Joanna slid down from the horse and ran around back to the kitchen building.

It seemed undamaged, but suddenly George was there, and he put out an arm to stop her. "You all right," he exclaimed. "God bless you, girl, I thought you got burned up."

Joanna clung to him. "Ruthie? Hannah?"

"They in the kitchen with Sally. Don't you worry none. Not a hair on their heads is harmed. Didn't I tell you I look after them? Have a little faith, girl."

In all the confusion, Joanna had not heard his answering shout from the rooftop, nor had she known for certain if George had heard her plea. "Thank you," she choked out, and embraced him quickly before breaking into a run for the kitchen.

She found the two girls sitting on the floor, Hannah soaking bread in milk for Ruthie to eat. Joanna fell to her knees and embraced them. "Thank the Lord. Thank the Lord you safe and sound."

"Mama," Ruthie said as she patted Joanna's cheeks. "Mama."

"Mama's back," Joanna confirmed, and as she held the girls close, she made a silent promise that she would never leave them again.

In the days that followed, Joanna learned that two blocks of Meeting Street had burned in the fire that had miraculously spared Harper Hall. In a broad swath from northeast to southwest across the peninsula, almost six hundred homes had been consumed and many businesses lost. Rumors abounded, but most reports concurred that the blaze had begun in a shed near the Russell machine shop and had rapidly spread to Cameron's foundry, where an enormous quantity of Confederate arms had been destroyed. Some folks said Yankee spies had set the fire, while others blamed rebellious slaves, and still others came up with even more outlandish explanations. As Gideon had predicted, Yankee newspapers proclaimed that the hand of God was visible in the destruction, and the fire was the manifestation of His divine judgment upon the Cradle of Secession. Joanna was unable to read the stories herself, for Miss Evangeline tore up and burned the pages of the Charleston paper that reported on their Northern counterparts' glee, but Miss Evangeline indignantly repeated the stories so often to her friends that Joanna soon knew every phrase by heart.

A week later Joanna contrived an excuse to venture down Market Street and through the remains of the alley where she had often passed information to Mr. Lewis, but although she had hoped he would appear, she did not expect him to, nor did he. She considered leaving the basket in the kitchen window to signal to him, but she doubted he would approve of her summoning him merely to discover whether he had survived the fire. She had no new secrets to offer, and therefore no good reason to trouble him. So instead she waited and wondered and eventually concluded that he must have left the city either on foot or up in smoke and she could not count on him to rescue her or her girls from the auction block.

They were on their own — and, Joanna admitted to herself, they probably had been all the while.

CHAPTER SEVEN

1862
Charleston, South Carolina

After the disastrous fire, other Confederate states sent food and clothing to Charleston, and those residents who had not lost their homes took in friends and families whose homes had burned. Colonel Harper's relations showed up unexpectedly the day before Christmas, the letter they had sent having gone astray in the confusion. The family led the way in the carriage, a wagon loaded with most of their worldly possessions following close behind. Joanna realized before Miss Evangeline did that they intended to stay indefinitely. Most planters had evacuated James Island after Port Royal fell, and now that the island had been almost entirely given over to military defenses, old Marse Harper couldn't hold out any longer.

Joanna's heart hardened when Mrs. Givens, the colonel's widowed sister, stepped from the carriage. She resisted the urge to run into the house and warn Hannah to hide, knowing Hannah had surely seen her former mistress arrive, knowing hiding would do little good if a mistress took it into her head to vent her frustration and rage on a slave child. Fixing her practiced, impassive expression in place, she carried the Harpers' belongings inside, followed Miss Evangeline's instructions for sleeping arrangements, and helped Minnie with fresh linens and unpacking. Hannah kept out of sight for most of the day, and only occasionally did Joanna glimpse her minding Ruthie in the workyard or in the laundry. As the days passed, Hannah grew bolder and returned to her usual routine, and Mrs. Givens never gave her more than a passing glance. As far as Joanna could tell, the colonel's sister had either completely forgotten what she had done to the child, or she remembered but suffered not the slightest pangs of conscience. Joanna could not decide which was the greater outrage.

Christmas came and went; the New Year began. The novelty of entertaining house-guests faded, and Miss Evangeline grew snappish at every implied or imagined criticism from her sister-in-law. "I'm spending a fortune to keep her in cordials and cakes," she complained as Joanna dressed her hair one morning, referring to Mrs. Givens's favorite delicacies. "And what are my husband's people contributing to the household save their delightful companionship and insightful critiques of my housekeeping? If they had brought some cotton bales with them instead of burning everything in the gin house, they might have been able to sell them and live off the profits."

"If Marse Harper could sell it," said Joanna, twining a golden lock around the curling iron. "If he get it past the blockade."

"Where there's a will, there's a way. England wants our cotton. Not badly enough to go to war with the Yankees for it, apparently, and that's a lesson learned too late, but they still want it and they'll pay for it. But my father-in-law let that opportunity go up in smoke, and now my husband's kin are spending my son's inheritance as if there's no tomorrow."

Old Marse Harper wasn't the only one to burn his cotton rather than allow it to fall into Yankee hands, nor was Mrs. Givens the only South Carolinian who lived in defiance of the hardships of war. She accepted every appropriate social invitation and begged Miss Evangeline to throw parties, and the young mistress, eager for diversions, usually assented. But what Miss Evangeline wanted most was news from her husband and from her relocated family, and when too much time passed between letters, she grew peevish and fretful. What troubled her most, she confided to Joanna, was her pervasive feeling of utter uselessness. Her husband could take up arms and lead his men on the field of battle, but what could women do? Some became nurses, others took jobs preparing armaments, a privileged few with the right connections acquired desirable positions in the government, but a young woman with a baby in arms could do little for the Confederacy besides supporting her own husband, encouraging other able-bodied men to enlist, and raising funds.

As the winter passed, Miss Evangeline became ever more preoccupied with contributing to the Confederate cause. She visited wounded soldiers recovering in hospitals, read to them or wrote in her crisp, elegant, practiced script while they dictated letters to mothers and sweethearts far away. She joined the Charleston Soldiers Relief Association and helped organize charity concerts and association fairs, with the proceeds going to buy provisions for the soldiers at the front — everything from bandages to shaving kits to underwear. If raising as much money as possible was the goal, Joanna thought, the association fairs were impractical. As far as Joanna could tell, it was mostly the association members themselves who browsed the tables trimmed with bunting and flowers, and association members who bought handicrafts and cooked delicacies from one another. Joanna figured they could have saved themselves a lot of work and made a far greater profit if the ladies had merely donated the money they spent to make their cooked briskets and embroidered table runners. But the organization and management of the fairs kept the buckra ladies busy, and maybe that was just as important to them.

As impractical as the association fairs seemed to her, they weren't as odd as another favorite benefit event, the *tableau vivant.* The buckra ladies would dress up in costume and pose on a stage, not dancing or singing or playacting but holding perfectly still, recreating a famous scene from history, literature, or art while music played. Sometimes they would stage an elaborate scene; more often they would enact several different tableaus, lowering the curtain while the ladies rapidly changed costumes and assumed other poses. Naturally Joanna

429

sewed most of the costumes, not only Miss Evangeline's but often her friends' as well. Sometimes the ladies she fitted offered her a few coins as a token of their gratitude, which they probably assumed she would turn over to her mistress. Instead she tied them up in her oldest, most threadbare headscarf with the rest of her carefully saved money and hid them beneath her bed with her tin cornboiler and other treasures.

Fancy ladies' costumes were not the only sewing Joanna contributed — grudgingly, reluctantly, delaying as much as she dared — to the Confederate cause. On several occasions Miss Evangeline's friends gathered at Harper Hall to turn bolts of cloth into uniforms and flannel shirts and drawers for Confederate soldiers. While they sat in the parlor chatting and cutting out shirtsleeves and measuring palmetto buttons for buttonholes, their slaves worked outside on the coarse sewing, fashioning yards and yards of canvas into tents. Some of the slaves had never sewn before, and Joanna found herself giving impromptu lessons, just as she had done with Hannah, who had progressed so well that Miss Evangeline had assigned her to help the more experienced slaves with simple tasks. Hannah seemed proud to have been trusted with the sewing instead of merely minding Ruthie, and she took her place in the sewing circle, stitching diligently while Ruthie toddled about from one new face or comfortable lap to another. Joanna couldn't help feeling an occasional stab of guilt whenever Ruthie didn't favor her own mother over someone else with a quicker smile or a more soothing voice or a treat such as a carrot or slice of dried apple in her dress pocket. Joanna had not wanted to give Ruthie to the wet nurse so she could work in the big house at Oak Grove; she had not wanted to leave Ruthie behind when she was sent to Charleston as Miss Evangeline's wedding gift; she would much rather tend her own child than pass her off to Hannah and tend to Miss Evangeline, who was more of a spoiled baby than Ruthie could ever be. And yet it seemed as if Ruthie, though surely too young for such judgments, wanted to punish her mother for every moment of absence, every measure of protection denied, although none of her neglect had been Joanna's choice.

"You should be in the house doing fine sewing," said Rebecca, another slave seamstress who had long admired Joanna's deft hand with the needle. "You sew a better seam and fit a better coat than any of them buckra ladies."

"I'd rather be outside with you," replied Joanna. "I don't want to sew no Confederate uniform unless I get to sew a target on the front, right here." She made a circular motion in front of her chest, and the other slaves muffled laughter. She'd rather not make tents either, but since she had no choice, she used the biggest, loosest stitches she dared, hoping the wind would drive the rain through the seams, soaking the inhabitants so that they took a chill and became too weak to fight.

From sewing and benefit performances and fairs of dubious value, Miss Evangeline turned her attention to a more ambitious project — raising enough money to purchase a gunboat to protect Charleston Harbor. With her friend Mrs. Hoskins, a Meeting Street neighbor and wife of a colonel with the Seventh South Carolina Infantry regiment, she founded the Charleston Gunboat Society, and together the two military wives went door-to-door recruiting members and soliciting donations. There were more *tableaux vivants,* more musical performances on the piazza, more benefit dramas where ladies who only a few years before would never have dreamed of doing anything so unladylike as performing in public took to the stage and recited heartfelt historical speeches or Shakespearean soliloquies. Joanna knew from the colonel's rare letters that he did not entirely approve of his wife's new public role, and she guessed from subsequent letters that Miss Evangeline had told him, not altogether truthfully, that she remained behind the scenes organizing the bolder ladies and rarely took to the stage herself. If he could see her glowing and basking in the audience's admiration as she pretended to be Ophelia or Cordelia or Juliet, he would marvel at the transformation war and necessity had worked upon his wife. But that was because he had never truly known the real Miss Evangeline the way the slaves of Oak Grove knew her. The way Joanna saw it, Miss Evangeline had been an actress all her life.

Spring came, and one morning in April Joanna realized that Frederick's birthday was only a month away. He would be, if he yet lived, three years old, still much too young to be sent to the fields to pick hornworms off the tobacco. She caught herself, rebuked herself for such thinking. Her boy was in Canada, safe and free, hundreds of miles from Greenfields, his cruel white father, and the tobacco fields. He was safe and sound, and someday Gerda Bergstrom would tell her where.

Keep breathing, she told him silently, squeezing her eyes shut against tears. *Keep breathing, stay alive, stay safe, and someday I will find you.*

For weeks the older Marse Chester didn't come to Charleston, never mentioned Titus in his letters, never said anything that might prompt Joanna to put the basket in the window in the slim hope that Mr. Lewis might still be around. Then one day a letter came from Mrs. Chester, a frantic lament that Miss Evangeline's brother Elliot had run off to join the army.

Joanna learned what had happened as Miss Evangeline did, from the hasty flurry of letters that followed, from explanations wrung out of reluctant, unfortunate messengers. "He was supposed to be safely out of the way at school," Joanna overheard the mistress tell Mrs. Givens and her mother-in-law as she paced the front foyer, awaiting an overdue messenger from her father. "He's only fifteen. Have we come to such desperate ends that we must send children to fight the Yankees?"

The school that was supposed to have kept young Elliot Chester out of the military in fact helped him find his way to it. Marse

Chester, who had strongly advocated secession but did not want to sacrifice his own offspring to the subsequent war, had enrolled Elliot at a private boarding school in Walterboro about fifty miles west of Charleston, twenty-five from the marse's new plantation, West Grove. Marse Chester thought that if his son's mind were turned to Greek and Latin and mathematics, he would have no room for thoughts of uniforms or parades or rifles. He had chosen the Vogler Academy because of its schoolmaster, a learned doctor from Germany and reputed pacifist who had opened his school in order to avoid the draft. The physician would not tolerate romantic notions of soldiering in his pupils, and he would surely curb Elliot's enthusiasm with a dose of stark reality and a course of vigorous study.

All was well until Port Royal fell, but after that, either newly discovered patriotism, concern for the soldiers wounded in battle, or a combination of the two compelled Dr. Vogler to close his school and enlist as an army surgeon. His pupils were understandably delighted; few boys their age preferred a dry and dusty classroom to the battlefields upon which the brave won honor and glory. If Dr. Vogler had notified his former students' parents that his school had closed, the letters must have gone astray, for only a handful of the boys returned home. Most followed their headmaster's example and enlisted in whatever regiment would have them.

When Marse Chester discovered that his son was training with the Beaufort Volunteer Artillery, he raced to Elliot's commanding officer, explained that his son was only fifteen, and demanded his immediate discharge. Apparently Major Powell was unimpressed by the planter's bluster, for he summoned Elliot and asked if he wanted to be relieved of his duties. Elliot flatly refused, and although Marse Chester threatened to bring charges against Major Powell for allowing Elliot's illegal enlistment, the major remained unmoved, pointing out that if he let Elliot go, the boy would in all likelihood seize the first opportunity to run away from home and join up with another militia. Major Powell needed men, and if Elliot was going to serve anyway, he might as well serve with the Beaufort Volunteer Artillery.

Marse Chester, accustomed to having his orders obeyed, did not give up so easily. The letters that flew back and forth between West Grove and Harper Hall were matched by others attempting to reach Colonel Harper in the field. It was days before the colonel learned of his brother-in-law's enlistment, and days more before he could get leave to call on Powell's commanding general, Robert E. Lee. General Lee ordered Elliot's discharge on the grounds that he was underage, giving Powell no choice but to release him. Elliot was furious, and only Colonel Harper's promise that he could enroll at the South Carolina Military Academy appeased him.

To escape Marse Chester's fury, Elliot convinced Colonel Harper to bring him to Harper Hall instead of escorting him to West Grove until a place could be found for him at the military college. He had grown several inches since Joanna had last seen him at Oak Grove, filled out, acquired a deeper voice, but he was still a boy, chagrined that he had been found out but incapable of concealing his delight that his punishment — if it could be called a punishment — was to train as a military cadet.

Miss Evangeline was visibly relieved to see her younger brother safe and sound. After scolding him for deceiving and distressing their family, she embraced him, kissed him soundly on both cheeks, and praised him for his patriotism and courage. "If I had been fortunate enough to be born a boy, I would have done the same thing," she declared, and immediately put Joanna to work on sewing Elliot a cadet's uniform. As she took his measurements, Joanna remembered the boy she had known at Oak Grove — brown-haired like his father, freckled, boastful, a boy who hid in the bushes and watched while the women slaves bathed in the river, who took pleasure in pranks and pratfalls and blamed whatever unfortunate colored child was nearest when he got caught. Now he would be drilling, marching, and learning how to kill Mr. Lincoln's soldiers. Chances were good he would get shot himself before he did anything to advance the Confederacy, but Joanna could not make herself care about his fate. Let the soldier boy die and teach Marse Chester what it was to be separated from one's child. Then he would know. Then he might understand.

A few days after Joanna finished the new cadet's wardrobe and Elliot had been settled in at the Academy, Colonel Harper returned to the war. Miss Evangeline begged him to linger one day more, but the colonel was determined to return to his men. Already the war had aged him, put gray in his hair and furrows in his brow. He said little about the battles he had fought, but the few details he let slip about Port Royal and its aftermath convinced Joanna that he had witnessed more gruesome brutality than he had expected, and far less valor.

For the first time, Joanna overheard him encouraging Miss Evangeline to consider evacuating Charleston and joining her father at West Grove. The ongoing naval blockade, the continuous shelling of the city, the restrictions of martial law, the increasing scarcity of food and goods, the gambling and vice that had flourished and spread after General Pemberton had taken over, the potential for another disastrous fire — alone, each was a compelling reason to leave the city, and in the aggregate, they were overwhelmingly persuasive.

But not persuasive enough. "I will not abandon your family home," Miss Evangeline replied firmly after he had made, in Joanna's opinion at least, a convincing argument. "You've already lost the James Island plantation, and my father has been forced to abandon Oak Grove. Although my father is generous and I know he would welcome us, as he and my stepmother describe the new house at West Grove, I don't see how it could accommodate all of the Harpers and Chesters comfortably. Even if our families will be able to return to the old home places after the Yankees are defeated, so many of our cherished heirlooms will have been destroyed in our absence. This house is that last repository of our family history. I won't leave it."

"No house and no possessions are more precious to me than you and our son," the colonel said, and repeated his reasons more emphatically, as if perhaps his wife had not heard him properly the first time.

Miss Evangeline seemed moved by his emphatic passion, but she held fast. She assured her husband that she would obey his wishes, of course, but with him away so often, she felt much safer in the city. If her husband's family preferred to evacuate to West Grove, they were welcome to do so, but she would remain behind at Harper Hall with the servants. West Grove was not her home even though her father and younger siblings lived there, and she would feel lonely and bereft in unfamiliar surroundings without her husband. In Charleston she had her friends, her caring neighbors, and her work with the Charleston Soldiers Relief Association and the Charleston Gunboat Society. She could not abandon the important duties she had assumed. The colonel could not ask her to be less of a patriot than he was.

Thus Colonel Harper was persuaded to let her remain.

"All that stage actin' pay off for her," George muttered as he and Joanna eavesdropped from the hallway. "She always get her own way."

"I think she mean every word of that fine, fancy speech," said Joanna, her hopes of reuniting with Titus at West Grove receding like the tide, slowly and inevitably, but sure to return. She could not stop hoping, no more than she could make herself stop breathing.

Though the colonel had agreed to allow his wife to remain at Harper Hall, he was apparently not entirely convinced of her safety, for on the eve of his departure, he wrote lengthy instructions for her to follow for managing the household during his prolonged absence. He wrote another, shorter letter explaining what she should do in the event of his death. Miss Evangeline didn't know about the second letter; Joanna found it a week after the colonel's departure while riffling through his desk, searching for news from West Grove. The colonel hoped in death to secure what he had not in life: He ordered Miss Evangeline to sell Harper Hall, or rent it out if she could not find a buyer, and return to her father until the end of the war, at which point she had his blessing to remarry. When Thomas came of age, he was to be enrolled at the South Carolina Military Academy unless he demonstrated another particular aptitude for something suitable, such as medicine or law. Joanna almost felt sorry for the colonel as she returned the letter to its envelope. She knew that Miss Evangeline would follow her own inclinations no matter what. If she would not obey the living, breathing man standing in front of her, why would she obey his words on a page?

Over his sister's protests, the colonel also sold an antique cherry bureau and a grandfather clock that had been in the family for generations. He refused Confederate bills and insisted upon being paid in silver federal dollars from before the war, and Joanna soon learned that his preference was not only due to the decreasing value of Southern currency. On the morning he left, he instructed Joanna to sew a quilted petticoat for his wife, and to tuck a silver coin into each of the small, square pillows as she created them with crosshatch quilting stitches. When Miss Evangeline laughed in astonishment at the thought of wearing such a garment, the colonel replied that if the city should be overrun with Union troops, she would need her money safely hidden but close at hand. He had seen the ruins of once-grand plantation homes the Yankees had pillaged, taking everything of value and burning the rest. Yet even Yankee soldiers respected genteel Southern ladies, and they would surely not search Miss Evangeline's person. Furthermore, if her other funds ran out, with the simple snip of a few threads on the underside of the garment, she could remove the coins from as many of the quilted pillows as necessary without disturbing those that remained.

The unusual project gave Miss Evangeline a much-needed distraction during her husband's first morning away, but she alternated between admiring the ingenuity of his idea and berating his concerns that Charleston would be invaded. "The Yankees can't invade by land, not with General Lee's forces moving so admirably along the railroad lines," she said, "and they couldn't possibly invade by sea while our brave soldiers hold the forts so securely. It's a pity that a weak woman like myself has more faith in our military than one of our own officers."

"If they hold the forts so good, why you need to get them a gunboat?" said Joanna through a mouthful of pins.

"I wouldn't expect you to understand," Miss Evangeline retorted. "You'd like our boys to do without a gunboat, wouldn't you? Then your precious Yankees can swarm into South Carolina and bring you darkies your freedom. Well, I assure you, you'll have it far worse under the abolitionist Yankees than you do today. You'll have no one to look out for you, to feed you, to clothe you, to keep a roof over your head. You'll have to earn your own keeping for the first time in your lives, and you'll discover it's much more difficult that you ever imagined. Oh, yes, your beloved Yankees might set you free, but they wouldn't care a fig for you after that, you mark my words."

Joanna knew it was wisest to let Miss Evangeline have the last word, but she couldn't help herself. "The free colored folk in Charleston seem to do fine."

"That's only because there are so few of them, and each has a white guardian." Miss Evangeline gave the soft folds of muslin an impatient shake. "Enough nonsense. Keep your mind to your task. And there had better not be a single silver dollar missing when you're through. I counted them ahead of time, so you may be sure that I'll know if you've stolen from me."

Joanna nodded and made her face a mask

of perfect obedience. Miss Evangeline had counted the coins, all right, but not until after Joanna had slipped two into her apron pocket.

Not long after that, Joanna learned from Mrs. Ames's Jenny that a few days before, in the very early hours of the morning while the buckra officers were ashore, a slave harbor pilot named Robert Smalls had commandeered a Confederate transport steamer. He brought his family and a dozen other slaves on board, turned the ship toward the open sea, blew the proper whistle signal to each Confederate fort to secure permission to pass, and sailed out to the Union blockade, where he raised the white flag and turned over the ship to a Union captain. Joanna was thrilled by his story of daring and courage, and she wished with all her heart that she had known Robert Smalls and could have joined those families on board the *Planter*. What a treasure he had given those fortunate few who had escaped with him, and what a fine prize he had turned over to the Yankees — not only the ship itself, but armaments intended for the Confederate forts and Mr. Smalls's extensive knowledge of Charleston Harbor, its navigation channels and currents, and the position of the Confederate defenses.

Joanna hoped Mr. Smalls would find a man like Mr. Lewis among his Yankees, someone who would listen, someone who would not dismiss valuable information because it came from a slave, someone who would recognize the pilot's courage and reward him accordingly. Maybe, even though he had not taken them aboard the *Planter,* Mr. Smalls would help bring Joanna and her girls to freedom just the same.

June descended, hot and sultry. The laundry was unbearably warm and steamy, so that as Joanna labored over the washtubs, she thought she must drink the air or drown. On washdays, hanging the clothes on the line in the workyard was her only respite from the labor that seemed never-ending. The Harpers' prolonged stay resulted in so much more laundry that Joanna could scarcely keep up with it. If not for Hannah, she probably would have fallen so far behind on her work that she would never catch up.

But while her laundress's duties had increased, her work as a seamstress had sharply declined as fabric, thread, and needles grew more difficult to come by, for the needs of the military increased demand

and the harbor blockade reduced supply. Miss Evangeline requested no new ball gowns or summer dresses, making do with what she had in the spirit of patriotism, so except for the occasional project for one of the mistress's relief organizations, Joanna sewed very little except for a bit of mending now and then. The quilted petticoat was the only new garment she made all that spring and early summer.

Perhaps that was why sometimes, tired though she was from the work of the day, Joanna's fingers itched to hold a needle. Some evenings, when Miss Evangeline was preoccupied elsewhere with the Harper ladies, Joanna would sit outside in the work-yard beneath the magnolia trees with Hannah and Ruthie, savoring the relief of cool breezes, shade, and her girls' company. There she would work on her own quilts, so different from those Miss Evangeline admired. Instead of appliquéd flower baskets or neat rows of precise, identical blocks, the quilts she had made since coming to Harper Hall were bolder, covering the entire surface of the quilt, with squares and bars that often bore little resemblance to traditional quilt blocks. Sometimes she added some of the leftover Birds in the Air blocks, placing them here and there, wherever she pleased, without giving any thought to the order or symmetry that Miss Evangeline believed were essential to true beauty. These were quilts no buckra mistress would claim for herself, so they were quilts Joanna knew she would be able to keep forever — if forever meant anything to a woman whose life was not her own.

Her thoughts and dreams and fears were too big to be contained within the small neat boundaries of a traditional block, her life too strange and unique to be represented by the repetition of the same pattern. She collected everything that was inside her — all the thwarted love, the rage, the anger, the fear, the uncertainty — and cast it upon her quilts like paint upon a fence. She would let it spill over the edges, collect in pools on the ground, soak into the earth. She could not be contained.

At night the slaves sweltered in the dormitory above the kitchen, crammed two and sometimes three to a bed, while others slept on quilts spread on the hard wooden floor. Mrs. Givens's and old Mrs. Harper's maids slept on pallets in the corner of their mistresses' bedchambers, the Harpers' groom had joined Asa and the boys in the stable, but the rest had been squeezed in with

Colonel Harper's slaves in the dormitory. Often Joanna couldn't sleep despite her exhaustion, stifled by the heat and the smell and the press of so many bodies. George had given up his bed to a newcomer, a woman and her two young children, and he now slept on the floor beside Joanna and her girls. At first his closeness had annoyed Joanna, but she eventually grew accustomed to his presence, even glad for it. She knew that George had kept her girls safe from the fire and he would not hesitate to protect them from whatever dangers the future might bring. And what did Joanna give him in return? She would not let him into her bed. She mended his clothes, but she helped all the slaves in this way. She laughed at his jokes, but only because they were truly funny. She did not talk to him more than to the other men, nor flatter him, nor speak admiringly of him, although there was much to admire about him. And yet he slept beside her bed at night and would protect her and her girls and would never demand anything in return. Joanna knew this, as certainly as she knew that she should not allow herself to grow too fond of him.

One night as Joanna slept, Ruthie's hand tangled in her hair, Hannah's breath warm against her shoulder, a soft tapping sound roused her. Groggy, she sat up and traced the noise to the stairwell, just as it ceased. A moment later she heard the door at the bottom of the stairs easing open.

She glanced at George lying on the floor beside her bed; he had not awakened. As worry stirred in her chest, she carefully extricated herself from between the girls and made her way to the stairwell, gathering herself to scream if some buckra soldier had come looking for trouble.

Instead, silhouetted in the doorway was a familiar figure — her beloved, her Titus.

Stifling a gasp, she tore down the stairs and threw herself into his arms, finding his mouth with hers, kissing him breathlessly. "What you doin' here?" she gasped softly when she could finally speak. So late at night, so stealthy his arrival, Marse Chester couldn't have sent him on an errand.

"Been too long since I got to hold you." Titus's embrace tightened. "Oh, Joanna. I been missin' you so much. How our baby?"

"She a big girl now, walkin' and talkin' a little bit. She smart, Titus, she and Hannah both." Her heart pounded and the hairs on the back of her neck tingled as if a cold wind swept over them. "Titus, you run off?"

In the dim light, she saw him nod. "Two days ago Marse Chester gave me his rifle to go hunt dinner for the buckra. I set out on foot but double back and take a horse from the stable, and then I just lit out. I stick to the woods, stay out of sight. I come straight to you."

Joanna marveled that he had made it so far without being captured by patrollers or shot by soldiers. She shivered to think of the dangers that must have threatened his every step — but he was here now, here and safe. The time had come. At last, they were going to run. "I got all my things bundled in the quilt. Money too." She squeezed his hand and turned to dash upstairs. "Let me get the girls and we can go."

But Titus held her back. "Joanna, no. I can't take you with me."

"What?"

"I'm not runnin' north. I'm going south, to Hilton Head."

"But — but that don't make no sense. That right into the fighting. We got to go north."

"Joanna, I ain't running for freedom. I run to fight." He picked up the rifle, which until then Joanna had not seen propped up in the corner of the stairwell. "I hear about a Yankee there, General Hunter, who makin' up a colored regiment. Negro men, Joanna, fightin' for our own freedom. Most of them

I reckon never held no gun. I'm a crack shot. They need me."

"I ain't heard nothing about no colored regiment." Joanna shook her head and drew a deep breath. It made no sense, no sense at all. At last they were all together, Titus even had a gun and a horse, and he meant to leave her and the girls behind?

"It all true. A man I trust seen them with his own eyes — marchin' in uniform, red trousers, blue coats, blue caps."

"Titus, you know the buckra don't give no guns to colored folk." In response, he shifted Marse Chester's rifle in his hands, but she waved that off impatiently. "That ain't the same. He sent you out to fetch his dinner. That different from training up a lot of colored folk as soldiers."

"Joanna, I got to go. If they gonna let colored men fight, I got to be with them. I got to get my freedom."

"Get it by running north with me and the girls! What use you gonna be to us if you get yourself killed?"

"Don't talk like that. I fight for you and the girls too. You ain't seen what it like out there, outside Charleston. Armies here and there, you never know when a scout party turn up and start shootin'. Four of us run north right smack into a war, we likely all of

452

us get shot. This way no one in danger but me."

Joanna stood, hands clasped, trembling, as all of her dreams and plans crumbled into dust. "Fine. You go to Hilton Head. We go with you."

"Joanna —"

"Armies got their women, too. I seen it in the camps all around the city. They got women to cook and do laundry and every other thing. You fight, and I do the same work I always do but I do it for Yankee soldiers. We go together."

"No. Army camp no place for Ruthie and Hannah. That no life for two little colored girls, or for you either."

"At least we be free."

"It won't be freedom for me if I have to fear every day I might lose you." Titus pulled her into an embrace. "I got to go. Kiss me, Joanna, be sweet. Don't know when I see you again."

Her anger was not yet spent. She wanted to argue, to persuade him to see sense, but all at once her will to fight evaporated. He had made up his mind, and he thought he had chosen what was right. Nothing she said would persuade him otherwise. She would only delay his departure, risk his capture, and make what could be their final parting ugly and bitter.

So she swallowed hard and flung her arms around him. The butt of his rifle brushed against the back of her calf as he held her tightly. "Remember to keep breathin'," he murmured in her ear, but then he released her and stepped from the open doorway into the night.

Joanna stood rooted in place for a long moment, her eyes filling with tears. Then she blinked them away and eased the door shut, holding on to the latch and resting her forehead against the door.

"That your man?" George asked quietly from the top of the stairs.

Joanna didn't turn around. "That Titus, my husband."

"An army of colored men." George's skepticism stung, though it was but an echo of her own. "Your man likely run off to get himself killed."

"He go to fight for his freedom," Joanna snapped. "Mine and yours too. Slavery got to end and look like this the only way to do it."

"Someone tell your man a wild fib. No way no buckra general gonna make a colored army."

"If Titus say it's true, I believe him."

George made no reply. Silence filled the

stairwell.

"You best come to bed," said George eventually. "All your work still gonna be there in the morning. Your husband ain't made us free yet."

Without a word, Joanna climbed the stairs, brushed past him, and climbed into bed. She put her arm around her girls and drew the thin blanket over them, her back to George and his pallet on the floor.

Two days later, Miss Evangeline summoned Joanna to the parlor. Joanna had heard the messenger at the door, and when she saw the letter in the mistress's hand, she knew it had been sent from West Grove.

"Joanna," said Miss Evangeline sternly. "Have you seen Titus?"

"Yes, ma'am. Last time he brought letters from your pappy Marse Chester, before they move to the new place."

The mistress's blue eyes narrowed icily. "And not since then?"

Joanna furrowed her brow and shook her head, but not too much, just enough to suggest confusion. "No, ma'am. You know I ain't never been to West Grove."

"I've heard from my father." Miss Evangeline tapped the folded paper lightly on her palm. "Your Titus seems to be missing."

Joanna hesitated. "Sorry, ma'am. What you mean, missing?"

"I mean he's run away."

"Run away? No, ma'am, not Titus, he —"

"He's run away, and my father believes he is on his way here. Unless he's been here already." Miss Evangeline studied her. "But I don't suppose he would have continued on without you. You're a runaway. You know more about running away than he does. For that reason alone he would have taken you."

"Mrs. Harper, Titus ain't the sort to run off."

"He was sent out hunting with my father's old rifle. He never returned and a horse is missing."

"Maybe he don't find no game close, so he take the horse to look far off." Joanna pressed a hand to her throat. "He don't know the land 'round the new place like he know Oak Grove. Maybe he got lost. Maybe he fall off the horse and layin' hurt somewhere. Maybe them Yankee soldiers kill him for the horse and rifle." Joanna fell to her knees and clutched the hem of Miss Evangeline's dress. "Missus, please, you got to ask your father to send folks out to look for him. He could be close to death in those woods somewhere."

"Oh, not to worry. My father has certainly

sent people to search for Titus, and I have no doubt that they will find him, wherever he might run." But a slight shadow of doubt clouded her pretty features as she gave her skirts a twist to release them from Joanna's grasp. "In the meantime, if your husband does turn up here, you must inform me immediately or you'll find yourself without a husband or a daughter."

Anger churned, but Joanna ducked her head and nodded. "Yes, ma'am."

When Miss Evangeline dismissed her, Joanna quickly left the room, only to find George standing in the hall. "You almost as fine at playactin' as her."

"Better," Joanna retorted. "I got to be."

She stormed from the house and across the cobblestone path to the laundry, where the steaming kettles and stinging lye boiled and burned as if with her own simmering resolution.

In mid-June, the Harpers rejoiced at the news that the heavily outnumbered Confederate forces had successfully fought off a Union attack on Secessionville on James Island. If the Yankees had won, and if they had overrun the Confederates' yet unfinished earthwork fort, they would have flanked the defenses of Charleston Harbor and would have been perfectly placed to invade the city. Instead, after suffering heavy losses, the Union forces had withdrawn from the island. Colonel Harper's family eagerly sought out news about the battle, debating and pondering every new detail, imagining the scenes of battle that had taken place on the lands they knew so well. Old Marse Harper even declared that he was glad to sacrifice his plantation to such a glorious purpose even if it meant he would be raking grapeshot out of his rice fields for years to come. Mrs. Givens gave voice to what was probably the unspoken hope of the rest of the buckra in the household: Surely this stunning victory meant that the Confederates would soon bring about a decisive end to the war.

But the family's jubilation was short-lived.

The letter that brought word of Colonel Harper's terrible injury was written in an unfamiliar, feminine hand — a nurse, perhaps, a young belle who tended the sick and injured instead of dancing at balls, a widowed plantation mistress numbing her grief through useful work. The colonel had been shot, his right leg amputated below the knee. Considering what had befallen him, he was in fair spirits, though not sufficiently recovered to write to his dear wife on his own, and if the wound did not fester, he had a good chance of surviving. His body servant had been killed on the battlefield at his side, faithful to the last.

The colonel's mother collapsed in a faint after Miss Evangeline read the letter aloud. George was sent running for the doctor, Joanna for smelling salts. Mrs. Harper was conscious but dazed by the time the doctor arrived; he ordered her to bed and dosed her with laudanum. He offered Miss Evangeline a bottle too, but she waved him off and assured him it was not necessary. He did not press her, perhaps seeing as Joanna did that although the mistress was pale and trembling, there was nothing anxious or hysterical about her mind.

After the doctor left, Miss Evangeline and her father-in-law fell into urgent debate. They agreed that no nurse would tend the colonel better than his own devoted wife, and she resolved to go to him at once. But she would not allow her husband to languish in an army hospital tent, "those cesspools of filth and putridity," as she called them. As soon as he could travel, he must be removed to a more healthful location.

Mrs. Givens entered into the discussion; Joanna, Minnie, and George listened from the fringes. Over supper Miss Evangeline, old Marse Harper, and Mrs. Givens concluded that they must impose upon Marse Chester's generosity and evacuate the entire household to West Grove. The Harpers would be responsible for transporting household goods and slaves and would go directly to the new plantation; Miss Evangeline would take only the necessities in the carriage, with Abner to drive her, so that she could proceed as quickly as possible to her husband. As soon as he regained enough strength to make the journey safely, they would join the others at West Grove.

Once the decision was made, preparations proceeded swiftly. Miss Evangeline ordered Sally to pack a hamper with food, medicine, and bandages. The colonel's father decided what possessions must be brought along and what could be safely left behind — what they could, if they must, do without. Joanna and Hannah raced to pack trunks with clothing and valuables; whenever buckra eyes were not upon them, the slaves stole away to say their good-byes to friends and to bundle their own few belongings into kerchiefs or worn blankets.

Once Joanna found George alone in the slaves' dormitory, folding his extra footman's coat and tucking his clothes into a faded feed sack. "Faithful to the last," he muttered. "That's what they think about Asa now he dead and gone. He got a wife and child, you know that? Before you come here, Marse Colonel sold them both to buy that fine black horse he rode off to war on." He shoved a pair of trousers into the sack. "Faithful. Only reason Asa not leave Marse Colonel to face those bullets on his own 'cause he know he get shot in the back if he run."

Joanna did not know what to say. "Asa gone to a better world."

"Better world. You sound like that buckra preacher they make us listen to Sunday after Sunday. Asa don't want no better world, not yet. He want his wife and son." George slung the feed sack over his shoulder and stormed past her to the staircase. "Now his bones lie in some trench with all the other faithful servants who go with their marses into war, covered over with dirt and not even a stone to mark the place."

She watched him go, wishing that her attempt to comfort him had not gone so badly awry. George was right. Asa had faced every danger his master had faced, but the buckra would soon forget him. When he was well enough, Colonel Harper would buy a replacement, and perhaps even change the new slave's name to Asa so he did not have to trouble himself to remember a different name.

Joanna spread the Birds in the Air quilt over her narrow bed and rolled her extra clothing, her tin cornboiler, and her few other treasures into the center. The knotted kerchief that held her carefully hoarded coins she tied around her waist under her skirt. Her quilt, her kerchief, and her girls — she was packed and ready to go to West Grove. If only her beloved awaited her there.

Moving day came, chaotic and sudden. Miss Evangeline and her father-in-law tried to keep order, shouting instructions, distributing people and cargo and slaves between two carriages and two wagons, one apiece for Miss Evangeline's household and her in-laws'. The Harpers' slaves and the possessions they had brought from James Island filled their wagon, along with other treasures from Harper Hall they could not bear to leave behind. Although Miss Evangeline had declared that they should take only the most precious, cherished heirlooms, she had been unable to pare down her selections to fit in one wagon, so at the eleventh hour she sent George out to buy another. He soon returned with the only conveyance he had been able to find on such short notice, a small, rickety cart, with a loose axle and charred boards as if it had barely escaped becoming kindling in the December firestorm. When Miss Evangeline learned how much he had paid for it, she cuffed him on the ear and upbraided him for wasting their money. Joanna looked away so the buckra would not see her scowl. If the wretched woman thought she could have found something better at a lower price, she should have gone on the errand herself. It would serve the temperamental mistress right if George had lied, if the price had been half of what he had reported and he had kept the rest of the money for himself.

Miss Evangeline was the first to depart, wearing a dark brown traveling dress over the quilted petticoat padded with cotton and silver coins, setting off in her carriage with Abner at the reins, making haste to her husband's bedside. "Watch that one," the mistress called through the window as she pulled away, gesturing to Joanna. "She can't be trusted. She runs."

And even though Joanna had never given the Harpers reason to doubt that she was any less a faithful servant than Asa, the buckra eyes narrowed as they shifted to her, measuring her, suspicious. They would watch her constantly all the way to West Grove.

Miss Evangeline had been gone almost half a day by the time the caravan was loaded and ready to move out. The curtains drawn, the shutters latched, the doors locked, Harper Hall was shut up tight until better times might allow the family to return. Old Mrs. Harper dabbed her eyes with her handkerchief as her husband helped her into the Harpers' coach. Mrs. Givens climbed in after her parents and sons, carefully cradling her nephew and murmuring that he must not miss his mother too much, because his auntie would care for him tenderly in her absence. From her place on the driver's seat next to old Marse Harper's coachman, Mattie looked down upon the exchange pensively, seeming bereft and distracted without baby Thomas in her arms.

Joanna sat in the back of Miss Evangeline's wagon with the rest of the grown slaves, her back pressed uncomfortably against a steamer trunk, a knot of dread tightening in her stomach. There had not been enough room in the wagon for Ruthie and Hannah, even though Joanna argued that they could both ride on her lap, even though Minnie and Sally had insisted they didn't mind a tight fit. Ignoring their pleas, Mrs. Givens had ordered them to ride in the cart, so Hannah perched precariously on top of the luggage, with Ruthie on her lap.

"It ain't safe," Joanna had protested.

"Nonsense," Mrs. Givens called through the window of the carriage, entirely missing the point. "Together those girls don't weigh fifty pounds soaking wet. The cart will hold together long enough to get us to West Grove."

Joanna had made a soft nest for them out of her newest quilts and begged Hannah to watch over Ruthie, but that was all she could do for their safety and comfort. It would be a long, hard, hazardous ride, and she knew she would feel every jolt and jarring bump in her heart.

When old Marse Harper gave the order to move out, the stable boy holding the reins to the carthorse quickly scrambled onto the seat and, out of longtime habit, made himself as small as possible to make more room for the driver. Though her gaze was locked on her girls as she silently willed them to hold on tight, out of the corner of her eye Joanna saw a smile flicker on George's lips as he gathered up the reins and obeyed old Marse Harper's command to start the wagon.

But the carriage and wagon moved forward only a few paces before old Marse Harper called the caravan to a halt. "What's wrong with you, boy?" he shouted. "Get that cart moving!"

Adam, who, Joanna knew, was no more than nine years old, gulped and ducked his head. "Don't know how, Marse Harper, suh."

"What nonsense is this?" shrilled Mrs. Givens, unseen within the carriage.

"Adam tend the horses and clean stalls, missus, but he don't drive," George answered. "Marse Colonel don't let boys drive his horses till they twelve year old."

The carriage rocked slightly as old Marse Chester rose from his seat. "I'll drive the blasted thing then."

"No, Father," said Mrs. Givens. "It's a deathtrap. It's not safe."

Safe enough for my girls, thought Joanna, studiously looking away so that the buckra would not see her glare.

"You can stay put, Marse Harper, suh," said George. "This girl Joanna, she can drive, and she light enough for the cart." He shot her a look that set her in motion, a warning that she should not delay long enough for the buckra to think of a contradictory argument.

"The laundress can drive a horse?" asked Mrs. Givens, her narrow, suspicious face appearing in the carriage window.

"Yes, ma'am. Her husband Marse Chester's groom. He taught her all he know."

They must not have heard of Titus's disappearance, for Mrs. Givens and her father exchanged a glance, and then old Marse Chester said, "Very well, get to it, girl. We've delayed long enough."

Quickly Joanna scrambled to her feet and swung the Birds in the Air quilt over her shoulder.

"What's that you're holding?" Mrs. Givens called out.

"Just my things, ma'am."

Mrs. Givens's mouth thinned into a suspicious frown. "That bundle holds all your earthly goods? Everything most precious to you in the world?"

Her children, Titus, and her dream of freedom were infinitely more precious, but of course Joanna could not tell the colonel's sister that. "Yes, ma'am."

"Then leave it be. You can have it back when we reach West Grove." Mrs. Givens settled back into her seat, and Joanna heard her add to her father, "You heard what Evangeline said. The wench isn't likely to run without her belongings, is she?"

Joanna could part with any of it in a heartbeat, except the Birds in the Air quilt, with its hidden symbols that would one day lead her back to Elm Creek Farm and Frederick. But she dropped the bundle, thanked Sally when she promised to look after it for her, and climbed down from the back of the wagon. She took her place on the cart seat next to Adam and gathered up the reins.

"Missus Givens, Marse Harper," said George. "Don't she need a pass?" He held up his own, a requirement for any slave traveling without his master present, but all the more essential since the declaration of martial law.

"Confound these endless inconveniences," old Marse Chester grumbled as he climbed down from the carriage and set Minnie and Sally searching through trunks and valises for paper and pen. He scrawled a note, thrust it at Joanna, and ordered Minnie to repack everything as they rode. Joanna surreptitiously read the pass as she slipped it into her pocket: "This slave wench, Joanna, is the property of Colonel Robert Harper and is en route to his father-in-law's plantation at West Grove transporting his goods and property including 3 young slaves. Please allow her to proceed unmolested.

Signed, Wilberforce Edward Harper."

At a word from old Marse Harper, Joanna guided the cart into place behind the carriage and the wagon and followed them through the wrought iron gates onto Meeting Street. No one had thought to tell her how to get to West Grove, so she followed the wagon closely, worried that she would lose sight of the others in the crowd of soldiers and businessmen and slaves, or that the fragile, creaking cart would fall apart beneath her and the children. Once George glanced over his shoulder, shook his head slowly and deliberately, and raised a palm, so Joanna pulled back on the reins to slow her horse and give the wagon more space. But the street was so busy that she couldn't allow the gap to widen too much, or another wagon might cut in front of her, obscuring her view. She feared the cart wouldn't hold together if she were forced to yank on the reins and bring the horse, a gentle mare that the colonel had kept past her prime for sentimental reasons, to an abrupt stop.

"Slow down."

Joanna had never heard the voice before. She glanced at Adam, but he had turned in his seat and was staring into the back of the cart. She followed his line of sight but glimpsed only her girls, Ruthie in Hannah's lap, sucking on one fist and clutching the front of Hannah's dress with the other, Hannah studying the wagon and carriage ahead of them.

Just then, Hannah's lips parted and Joanna heard the unfamiliar voice a second time, pure and sweet. "Slow down."

All at once Joanna understood.

"Right, Hannah," she murmured, as if the Harpers might overhear. "Thank you, baby. You such a smart girl."

She gave the reins a gentle tug, and the mare obediently slowed her pace. The carriage pulled farther ahead, the wagon not close behind it. Amidst the cargo and slaves Joanna spotted her Birds in the Air quilt, holding her belongings as safely as it sheltered the secrets of the way to Elm Creek Farm. Once she had believed that those landmarks would be sealed in her memory forever, but so much had happened since she had been snatched back into slavery, so much grief and pain and upheaval, that she sometimes could not remember the route. Sometimes at night she needed to study the patterns worked in thread before the images floated to the surface of her memory, before she could remember the order the landmarks followed. Without the quilt, she could not be sure she would ever get back to Elm

Creek Farm, to the Bergstroms, to Frederick.

But Ruthie and Hannah were with her now, and Titus was out there somewhere, fighting for their freedom. He needed her even if he couldn't admit it.

Another few streets, another imperceptible slowing of the cart. Her heart tore painfully as she lost sight of the Birds in the Air quilt. She could urge the mare into a trot, call out to Sally to throw her the bundle — but of course that was unthinkable, impossible. She would only draw attention to their escape.

The distance between the cart and the wagon increased. Another block. When a peddler's wagon moved into the gap, Joanna slowed the cart and ducked her head in a show of allowing the white driver precedence.

George glanced over his shoulder at her and smiled. Then he turned back around and urged his horses into a slightly quicker pace.

Joanna held the mare to a walk as other carriages and wagons and men on horseback sped ahead of her and obscured her view of the Harpers' carriage and wagon. "Joanna," Adam said worriedly, "we fallin' behind. We gonna get lost."

"Hush up, Adam," said Hannah, low and urgent. "Mama know where we goin'."

Adam fell silent, and Joanna bit her lips together so that she would not cry. Hannah was speaking. Hannah had called her mama. It was surely a sign.

When she could no longer spy the high top of the Harpers' carriage, Joanna turned the cart down a side street and made her way south. No one cried out, no one pursued them.

At the edge of the city, they arrived at a camp of Confederate soldiers. A sentry party standing guard at the foot of a bridge challenged them, but when Joanna produced the pass, they questioned her briefly before waving her along, their attention already drawn to another approaching wagon.

"Where we goin', Joanna?" asked Adam plaintively as the horse's hooves clomped over the wooden bridge.

Hilton Head, Joanna thought. *Hilton Head and Titus.* She knew only that it was south of Charleston along the coast, but she would put her trust in the Lord that he would guide her, perhaps sending sympathetic colored folk to tell her the way. Hadn't he already given her a sign? Hadn't he made the mute speak? But she couldn't tell Adam her plans in case they were stopped and questioned again. "Don't worry," she said instead. "I'll look after you."

They traveled all afternoon, Adam wary and full of questions, Ruthie sweet and curious, Hannah inexplicably calm and speaking only rarely. But at least she spoke.

They were challenged only once more that day, by a party of four very young soldiers who seemed vexed to have been left behind to guard a little-used road when the excitement of the real battle lay only a dozen miles away. They studied Joanna's pass, poked around the cargo for a while, and queried her about the location of West Grove, which was too new to have garnered any fame. Eventually they grew bored with her vague replies, and having found nothing threatening about her or a cart full of miscellaneous household items and skinny slave children, they let her go.

They stopped for the night in a small clearing in the woods, just off the road. In a stroke of good fortune that Joanna recognized as another divine blessing, Sally had packed many of the kitchen supplies in the cart, including sacks of flour, a tin of oil, dried apples, cheese, bread, and a peck of beans. Joanna was afraid to build a fire and take the time to cook, so she unhitched the mare, fed the children apples, cheese, and bread, and made a bed of quilts for them beneath the cart while they devoured every crumb. Exhausted though she was, she stayed up all night watching over them and listening for sounds of pursuit. Occasionally she heard explosions in the distance and knew that somewhere nearby the war raged on. She feared that she might be leading the children straight into it, but she could think of nowhere else to go but to Hilton Head.

She knew the Harpers would begin the search for her soon if they hadn't already. She had almost no head start to speak of and very little time. She would never make it to the North, not even with a horse, a cart, and a pass whose value diminished with time and distance from Charleston.

Her only hope was to reach a place where Northern freedom had come to South Carolina.

All through the next day they traveled southeast, slowly and cautiously, pulling off the road into the thick underbrush at the sound of other travelers. Joanna alone stepped out from hiding twice to speak with colored folk — once to a slave traveling on an errand for his master, another time to a free colored family evacuating in advance of the approaching army. Both told her that Hilton Head wasn't a safe destination. "You want Port Royal," the free colored man told her. "That's where all the freed slaves from the barrier islands are going. That's your best bet. Yankee soldiers and abolitionists setting up things right nicely for freed slaves, so I hear."

"Have you heard anything about a colored army?" Joanna asked him. "You know where they might be?"

The man shook his head. "I heard something about that in late spring, but not much since. If there's a colored army, I don't know where you might find it."

But he had heard of it, which meant that Titus hadn't been chasing some fool story. She would find the colored regiment, and there she would find her beloved.

In midafternoon the clouds burst open and rain poured down in sheets. The children huddled in the cart beneath a canopy of her quilts, but the soft covers quickly soaked through and did little to keep the rain off. Before long the cart wheels slowed and churned through ruts in the muddy road. Joanna walked alongside to lighten the load and urge the mare forward, but it was a long, hard slog through ankle-deep mud, and they made little progress.

Eventually she was forced to admit defeat. Although she was anxious to get as far away from the Harpers and Charleston as quickly as possible, she knew they could go no further until the cloudburst ended and the muddy roads dried.

She found a rocky place more or less free of mud beneath a cluster of oaks a few yards off the road. After managing to coax the mare over to it, she unhitched the harness, picketed the mare near a patch of grass, and urged the children to take shelter beneath the cart. They obeyed without complaint, shivering and gobbling up the last of the bread and cheese as they sat cross-legged on the hard-packed earth. Exhausted, Joanna joined them, though the shelter would do her little good, soaked through as she was. Ruthie climbed onto her lap and clung to her so tightly that Joanna doubted she had the strength to pry her loose. Eventually the children slept, and Joanna, overcome with fatigue, felt herself drifting, fading.

She woke to the sound of voices and rustling underbrush. The rain had stopped and night had fallen. The children were awake and alert, watching her, waiting for her to tell them what to do. Adam began to speak, but Hannah slipped her hand over his mouth before he uttered a sound.

"Wheel ruts," a man called out. "Fresh. They go into the bushes."

Joanna's heart pounded at the sound of branches being forced aside, heavy boots in mud. *Please let them pass,* she prayed. *Please don't let them see us.* Torchlight flickered on the ground, and she knew all was lost.

Four pairs of boots halted in front of the cart; rifles cocked.

"You, under the cart," another man said. "Come out from there with your hands up."

Shaking, biting her lips together to keep from sobbing, Joanna rocked onto her knees, kissed Ruthie, and passed her to Hannah. "You listen good," she whispered. "You the oldest, so you got to take care of these little ones. You understand?"

Wide-eyed, Hannah nodded.

"Soon as I go, you take Adam and Ruthie and run fast as you can the other way through them bushes there. Get far away but go quiet. You hide yourself good until morning, then you get these children to Port Royal. Don't trust nobody but other colored folk until you get there. Stay out of sight. When you get to Port Royal, find a nice Yankee lady and she'll get someone to look after you."

"What about you?"

"Time's running out," the man called. "Come out now or we'll drag you out."

She could not let the men see the children; it was their only hope. "Do as I say," she told Hannah, and waited for the girl's answering nod. She touched each of the children's faces briefly. Oh, Lord, protect them. The fear and confusion in their eyes —

Joanna took a deep breath and extended her hands into the open. "Don't shoot. I'm comin' out." With one last warning glance to Hannah, she crawled out from beneath the cart. She stood and instinctively straightened her skirts and headscarf. Then, though her heart was pounding so fiercely she was sure the men would hear her terror, she planted her feet and wordlessly faced the four soldiers, who slowly lowered their rifles.

"Looks like we found ourselves some contraband," one of the men said, his grin a flash of white behind a dirty red beard.

"Evening, miss," said another. Joanna recognized his voice as that of the man who had ordered them to come out from hiding. "I expect you're a runaway."

Joanna thought of the crumpled pass, soiled and soaking wet in her pocket. If the ink had not smeared beyond legibility, he might accept it. He might believe her if she told him that she had become hopelessly lost in the rainstorm, that she was trying desperately to get back to her mistress. But if they believed her, they would send her off toward West Grove. They might even insist upon escorting her there in order to collect whatever reward they might have coming. Then what would become of the children? Miss Evangeline would order her beaten until she revealed where they had gone, and eventually the overseer might drag the truth out of her.

Her only hope was to delay the soldiers long enough for the children to make their escape. And if she provoked these soldiers into killing her now, before they questioned her, before she was bound and gagged and pulled along behind a horse all the way to West Grove, before the Harpers could summon the overseer with his whip — so be it. The children would be free, and she would no longer be a slave.

"Yes, suh," she said defiantly. "I am a runaway. I'm on my way to the Yankees at Port Royal. I'm done with bein' anyone's slave. I am a woman. I don't belong to no one but myself and the Lord."

"Is that so?" drawled the man with the red beard, but he fell silent at a sharp gesture from another soldier.

Joanna was beyond caring what happened to her. She had to buy time for the children to flee. They would carry her hopes with them. They would keep breathing, long after slavery ended and all colored folk were free.

"Yes, that's so," Joanna shot back. "Maybe today you can keep me from getting to freedom, but you can't stop freedom from comin' to me. The Union army be comin' this way soon, and they got colored men fightin' too. You can try but you can't stop so many folks all fightin' for their freedom. It's coming because it's got to come. You can be sure of that. And the only way you can stop me from runnin' is to kill me right here and right now, because I ain't goin' to stop. Take me back and I just run again. I gonna run and run and run until I get my freedom. Long as I keep breathin', I gonna run for my freedom."

She glared at the astonished men, breathless and defiant, listening for her children, hoping they had slipped away into the forest, that they had obeyed her, that somehow through some miracle she would see them again.

Keep breathing, she told herself, her thoughts an echo of Titus's voice. She wanted to, but she feared her next breath or the next or the one after that would be her last.

She had held out as long as she could.

"I don't doubt for a moment that you're determined to be free." The soldier's voice had lost its sharpness, and his eyes were kind. "But you can stop running now. I'm James Conner of the Sixth Connecticut Infantry. This is Union territory, and you're a free woman."

EPILOGUE

Seated at her father's oak desk, Sylvia spread out the documents Summer Sullivan had sent from Chicago, printouts of old census records the young historian had found online through a genealogy website. Summer had found Josiah Chester in federal census records from 1850, 1860, and 1870, but had been unable to locate a slave census for Greenfields. Summer had also found many Chester families in South Carolina and Georgia, but it was impossible to determine which, if any, were the relatives to whom Josiah Chester had sold Joanna. Indeed, as Summer had pointed out in her accompanying letter, those relations might have had a different surname, in which case searching for other Chester families would be a wasted effort.

"I'm not going to give up," Summer had written. "I'll ask some of my professors to recommend other resources. If I uncover anything new, I'll let you know."

But Summer was busy with her graduate studies, and Sylvia knew she didn't have much time to devote to Sylvia's request. She had already found so much: the census records, the map of Greenfields, a few slim leads that might lead to answers. Sylvia resolved to be patient. Summer never gave up on an intriguing puzzle once it captured her interest, and Sylvia knew she would explore every possibility until she either found the answer or determined that the historical record could not provide it.

Sylvia had waited years for the fresh leads the bundle of letters in the antique desk had unexpectedly discovered. She could wait a little while longer.

She was arranging Summer's documents into a neat pile, preparing to file them, when Sarah entered the office carrying a slender, sturdy cardboard envelope that was so flat it appeared to be empty. "Grace Daniels overnighted this to you," said Sarah, "but I'm not convinced there's anything inside."

Sylvia took the envelope, which was so light that she was inclined to believe it was indeed empty. "Goodness. I can't imagine what Grace would need to send me so urgently that she would go to this expense. Camp registrations aren't due for months."

Sylvia peeled back the tab and withdrew a colorful brochure for a quilt exhibit. Grace was a museum curator as well as a quilt artist, and it wasn't unusual for her to let Sylvia know about new, intriguing shows, especially if she or one of her friends were directing them. But the postal service or email had always served Grace perfectly well before.

"The Quilts of North Freedom," Sarah read over Sylvia's shoulder. "I think I've heard about them. In *Quilter's Newsletter Magazine,* maybe?"

They sounded familiar to Sylvia as well. She studied the photographs, admiring a series of scrap quilts that seemed improvisational rather than carefully planned, with bold colors and striking arrangements of squares, bars, and triangles. Then she turned to the front of the brochure and read the story of the quiltmakers, members of an enduring quilting circle from the small rural town of North Freedom, South Carolina.

The quilting circle, the Freedom Quilters, had come into being shortly after the end of the Civil War on an isolated barrier island that had once been the site of a prosperous cotton plantation. The founder of the group, Joanna North, was a former slave who had worked for the Union army as a laundress, nurse, and literacy teacher from 1862 through the end of the war. Afterward she accepted a government grant of forty acres of land on Edisto Island, where she raised five children and helped create a thriving community of former slaves. After the boll weevil destroyed the Sea Island cotton industry, Joanna North trained her daughters and other neighbor women as seamstresses and laundresses so that they could become self-supporting. The Freedom Quilters evolved from her early lessons, as the women continued to meet for quilting, literacy classes, prayer, and friendship even after they had finished their training. As the years passed, the women brought their daughters into the circle, and then their granddaughters, and on and on up to contemporary times. Since until recently the community had been relatively isolated, their quilting evolved in a unique style, departing dramatically from popular quilting trends elsewhere in the country. Perhaps most significantly, every quilt completed by a Freedom Quilter since the founding of their circle contained one important, identifying feature whose symbolism had been lost to memory: a pattern of four triangles, one large and three small.

Sylvia gasped in recognition as she examined close-up photos of several examples of the signature motif.

Though the arrangements varied from precise to abstract, the triangles were unmistakably minor variations upon the Birds in the Air block.

"What is it? What's wrong?" Sarah asked. Wordlessly Sylvia passed her the brochure and waited, dumbfounded, for her young friend to reach the same conclusion. After a few moments Sarah placed her hand on her gently rounded tummy and sat down. "Birds in the Air."

Sylvia nodded.

Sarah studied the brochure, shaking her head in disbelief. "Do you think this Joanna North is the Joanna that your great-great-aunt Gerda knew, the woman we've been calling Joanna Frederick?"

"If not, the appearance of the same block is a striking coincidence." Sylvia remembered the envelope, checked to see if Grace had included anything else, and discovered within a single sheet, a letter from her friend.

"Dear Sylvia," Grace wrote, "there's so much more to this story than any show brochure could possibly contain. It defies letters, emails, and phone calls too. How would you feel about meeting me in

Charleston so we can see and hear it for ourselves, together?"

Two weeks later, Sylvia and Sarah arrived at the Charleston International Airport and rented a car for the forty-mile drive south and west to Edisto Island. Grace Daniels had arrived the previous afternoon with her daughter, Justine, and they were waiting to meet Sylvia and Sarah in the lobby of their lovely inn, a restored antebellum plantation house. Sylvia was pleased to see that her friend was in good spirits and in even better health than the previous August, when Grace had returned to Elm Creek Quilt Camp for her annual reunion with a special group of beloved quilting friends. Her doctor had placed her on a clinical trial for a new treatment for her multiple sclerosis, and it appeared to be going remarkably well. Two years ago Grace had required a wheelchair to move from room to room, but the next year she had gotten by with only a walker, and now it appeared that she could make do with a single cane and an occasional assist from Justine, a strikingly lovely woman in her thirties, who had been blessed with her mother's strong cheekbones, sharp intellect, and rich brown skin. Unlike Grace, who favored short, natural curls, Justine wore her hair in dozens of fine, long braids tied back in a batik headwrap. She kept a protective watch over her mother but balanced carefully between stepping in when needed and letting Grace complete tasks she could handle just fine on her own. Only Grace herself seemed prouder of each bit of independence she had regained.

The women exchanged news about mutual friends, the manor, Grace's work at the de Young Museum in San Francisco, and Justine's son, Joshua, but catching up quickly was all they spared time for in their eagerness to meet Grace's colleague from the local historical society. As soon as Sylvia and Sarah checked in and left their suitcases in their rooms, they climbed into Sarah's rental car and set out for the Edisto Island Folk Museum to learn more about Joanna North and the Freedom Quilters.

"Sophia Lawrence told me that the Quilts of North Freedom have been part of a touring exhibit for the past four years," said Grace. "They return to Edisto Island only one month out of the year."

"We're fortunate the timing worked out so perfectly for us," Sylvia remarked as Sarah pulled into a parking spot in front of the museum. Her heart fluttered and she took a deep breath to calm her nerves. The answers to all her questions — and the questions that had plagued her great-great-aunt Gerda until her death — could lie just beyond those museum doors.

Her eyes met Sarah's as they climbed out of the car. Sarah, her long shirt all but concealing her early pregnancy, threw Sylvia an encouraging grin as she hefted her tote bag to her shoulder and gave it a protective pat. Sylvia smiled, knowing Sarah would allow no harm to come to its precious contents.

Sophia Lawrence greeted them in the vestibule, embracing Grace like a long-lost friend and clasping Sylvia's hand as if she were an honored guest. "I admire your work very much," she said, her salt-and-pepper dreadlocks brushing her shoulders. "I keep an old American Quilter's Society calendar open to *Sewickley Sunrise* on the wall of my office."

"So within your museum it's always May of 1982," Sylvia remarked.

"May of 1982, December of 1861 — we try to preserve all significant eras here," replied Sophia. "But from what Grace has told me, it's the years of the Civil War and Reconstruction that interest you most."

Sophia led them into a spacious gallery where the quilts from the brochure as well as several others fashioned in the Freedom Quilters' unique style were displayed. As they toured the exhibit, Sophia shared what she knew about the creator of each quilt, the materials she had used — almost always scraps preserved from worn clothing or remnants from a now-defunct local fabric mill — and the quilt's provenance. Most of the contemporary quilts had come from the artists' own personal collections, while the antique pieces had been donated or loaned by the quiltmakers' descendants. In recent years, media attention and the respect of the art world had brought the current Freedom Quilters a measure of national success that the founders of the quilting circle would have found astonishing. They had quilted to beautify their homes, to make frugal use of worn clothing, and to take pleasure in creative work. They never would have imagined that their handiwork would be displayed in museums, sold for astonishing prices, admired by collectors, and praised in art reviews in magazines and newspapers from coast to coast.

"If not for Joanna North's vision," Sophia said, "these quilts would never have been created, their unique style would never have evolved, and so much beauty would have been lost to the world."

"Tell Sylvia what you've learned about Joanna North," Grace asked. "But please start at the beginning. I wanted her to hear the story from you."

"There's so much to tell," said Sophia, smiling. "We're fortunate that Joanna was literate, that she taught her children to read and write, and that she kept a journal."

"A journal?" exclaimed Sylvia.

"Yes, but unfortunately only a few pages have survived the years." Sophia indicated a glass display case on the opposite wall. "They're very precious to us, as you can imagine. But even so, most of what we know of Joanna's history has come down through the oral tradition, stories passed down from daughter to daughter."

Born in Virginia, Sophia explained, Joanna had been sold down south after a failed escape attempt. She worked as a seamstress and laundress in the household of Stephen Chester, one of the most prosperous Sea Island cotton planters in South Carolina. On the Chester plantation, Oak Grove, Joanna married and had a child, a daughter named Ruth. Given to Chester's eldest daughter as a wedding gift, Joanna and Ruth were brought to Charleston to serve her new master and mistress, Colonel Robert and Mrs. Evangeline Harper. Family lore told that during the early years of the war, Joanna had served as a spy for the Union by passing along valuable military secrets gleaned from Colonel Harper's office. However, she had not known her Union contact's real name and thus after the war she was unable to prove her record of service.

"We have court documents detailing her fight to receive the military pension which she had rightfully earned," Sophia said. "Eventually the government awarded her and her heirs a modest annual stipend for the years she spent working for the Union army at Port Royal as a laundress, but nothing for her time as a spy in Charleston, which was by far the more dangerous duty. But I'm getting ahead of myself."

At some point during the spring or summer of 1862, Sophia continued, Joanna's husband ran away from the Chesters and managed to get word to Joanna that he intended to join the African-American regiment formed by General David Hunter on Hilton Head after the fall of Port Royal. Joanna had never lost her thirst for freedom and she was determined to reunite her family, so when the Harpers decided to evacuate the city, she managed to slip away in the chaos, bringing with her Ruth and her two adopted children, Hannah and Adam. They managed to make their way to Port Royal, where Joanna discovered that her husband had indeed joined Hunter's African-American regiment, but that it had been disbanded under charges that Hunter had acted without authorization and that his soldiers, former slaves all, had not volunteered but had been forced to enlist.

For years afterward Joanna had struggled in vain to discover what had become of her husband. All that was known for certain was that for many months he had served the Union army as a laborer, the only service available to African-American men at the time, but inconclusive evidence suggested that he had later joined up with the Fifty-fourth Massachusetts Volunteer Infantry, an African-American regiment led by Colonel Robert Gould Shaw, and had died in the ill-fated but valorous attack on Fort Wagner.

"According to family tradition, Titus Chester was an expert hunter," said Sophia. "He would not have been content to dig ditches and pitch tents when he knew how to handle a rifle so well. In one of Ruth's surviving letters, she recounts a visit from Lewis Henry Douglass, a sergeant major from the Fifty-fourth, and says he told

493

Joanna that Titus had fought bravely and died with honor."

"Lewis Henry Douglass," Grace said. "Frederick Douglass's son?"

Sophia nodded. "That's correct. Apparently he kept in touch with the family for several years afterward, and Joanna probably would not have received her government stipend without his intervention."

As Sylvia listened, tears of joy and wistful discovery gathered and threatened to fall. She wondered if Joanna North had ever met Frederick Douglass himself. The Joanna that had come to Elm Creek Manor had learned to read after being inspired by Douglass's *Autobiography*. If these two Joannas were one and the same, it would have been fitting if she had eventually met the man whose life had helped shape her own.

Sophia continued the astonishing tale. Alone at Port Royal with three young children in her care, amidst ten thousand other slaves abandoned by owners fleeing their barrier island plantations ahead of the Union advance, Joanna found work as a laundress and seamstress. Although those were her official roles, she served however she could be useful, sometimes as a nurse, as a cook, and often as a teacher, helping other newly freed slaves learn to read.

She served faithfully throughout the Civil War, and later, as the head of her household, she was granted forty acres of land as part of the Port Royal Experiment, wherein property that had once belonged to the rebellious planters was divided up among the newly freed slaves. Joanna accepted forty acres of the Chesters' abandoned plantation, Oak Grove, perhaps believing that her husband would think to look for her there.

He never came, but others did: Titus's two nieces and a nephew; Sally, a cook from the Harpers' Charleston home; and George, another house slave who had been instrumental in arranging Joanna's escape. In 1868 Joanna and George married, and since Joanna refused to accept George's surname — Harper, that of their former master — he changed his last name to North, which Joanna had assumed upon her escape.

Joanna had named the farm North's Freedom, and as the years passed and the community grew, the possessive was dropped and the small town that sprung up became known as North Freedom. "Most people believe it refers to a direction," Sophia said, shaking her head in amusement. "Or they believe it's the northern part of a town called Freedom. That's not the case at all. The town and the quilting circle that arose from it were named after Joanna. She lived out the rest of her years in North Freedom, and according to family stories, she both appreciated the blessings of her hard-won liberty and endured difficult times throughout Reconstruction, when the promises of slavery's end failed to materialize. For most African-Americans in the South, the struggle for true freedom had only just begun."

"Did Joanna ever leave North Freedom?" asked Sylvia. "Didn't she ever travel north once she was free?"

"According to a family history her eldest daughter, Hannah, wrote, Joanna often spoke of traveling back to the Pennsylvania farm where she had once found refuge. But in the early years, she felt compelled to remain on Edisto Island in case Titus came searching for her. Later, after Titus was gone and she remarried, she had two more children by George, not to mention so many other responsibilities that travel became impossible." Sophia smiled ruefully. "Travel was also prohibitively expensive for a family that struggled to get by on very little. But Hannah's family history offers another suggestion."

"What's that?" asked Justine.

Sophia hesitated, thinking, weighing her

words. "It's a cryptic passage, one I never could quite puzzle out. Hannah says that once, when an opportunity to travel north came her way, Joanna mulled over the opportunity for days before finally deciding to remain home. When Hannah asked her why, Joanna replied, 'Everyone I knew from those days has gone on to make better lives for themselves. They probably wouldn't thank me to come to them carrying tales from unhappy times. Sometimes the past is best left alone.' Or at least that's how Hannah remembered the conversation."

"How sad," said Sarah. "I would think her former protectors would have been thrilled to have heard from her, to know that she was alive and safe."

"Perhaps they knew," replied Sophia. "Joanna was reputedly a prolific letter writer. Perhaps Joanna had informed them of her safety and was only awaiting an invitation to return, an invitation that never came. We'll probably never know."

Sophia led them on through the gallery, pausing to study and admire individual quilts, each of which retained the traditional characteristics of the Freedom Quilters while also expressing each woman's unique artistry. Gazing upon them, Sylvia could imagine the Joanna she had discovered in the pages of her great-great-aunt Gerda's memoir persevering through unimaginable hardships, doggedly pursuing her freedom, and going on to teach and share and inspire those around her. Could there have been two such courageous, amazing women in the world at the same point in history?

She knew the answer already: There had been hundreds, even thousands, of such remarkable women in every era, but their stories had gone untold or had been forgotten. It was up to current and future generations to preserve the fragments of women's history that remained, to mend the frayed edges, to tell everyone who would listen about the strength in the warp and the beauty in the weft so that no one could dismiss their unsung contributions as mere scraps of faded fabric.

Even if she never confirmed that Joanna North was the brave runaway who had found shelter with her great-grandparents, even if she never discovered why that runaway had never returned for her son, even if Gerda's long-lost quilter were never found, it was enough to know that such a woman had existed, that she had faced loss and hardship with courage and faith, and that she had remained undaunted. If one such woman or two or thousands had lived, it should give all women hope that they too could live as bravely, *would* live as bravely, whatever dangers or sorrows confronted them.

At last Sophia brought the tour to a stop before what appeared to be the oldest quilt in the collection. Though the pieces were worn and faded, the pattern had retained its striking boldness — a Courthouse Steps variation surrounded by an outer border of solid squares occasionally replaced by a Birds in the Air block. Beside her, Sylvia heard Sarah draw in a sharp breath of recognition and excitement.

"We're certain that Joanna North herself made this quilt," Sophia said proudly, pleased by Sarah's reaction, though she could not possibly suspect its cause. "It's the jewel of our collection."

"How do you know Joanna made it?" asked Sarah, although she surely knew that Sophia's conclusion was true.

Surely Sarah must have recognized the size of the Birds in the Air blocks, the blue-and-brown homespun fabric used in the large triangle in the lower right corner, the double pinks scattered here and there in the smaller triangles, the dark wools, the soft faded cottons. Sylvia had known them the moment she saw them, for she had seen those same prints and patterns in another quilt, studied them and wondered about them and the woman who had sewn the small pieces together for so long that they were engraved on her memory.

"Yes, how can you be sure?" Justine asked. "Did Joanna sign the quilt or embroider her initials?"

"She wrote about it in her journal," Sophia explained. "One of the few extant complete passages describes how she enlarged a quilt that had turned out too small by attaching borders made from blocks left over from an earlier project. I only wish our collection boasted that first quilt, the quilt that influenced all the Quilts of North Freedom that followed, but I'm afraid that treasure has been lost to history."

"Perhaps it's not lost after all," said Sylvia, beckoning Sarah to open the tote bag, to show Sophia the tattered Birds in the Air quilt that had set her upon a quest to discover what had happened to Gerda's lost quilter, a quest that seemed, at last, to have reached its end.

ABOUT THE AUTHOR

Jennifer Chiaverini is the author of the Elm Creek Quilts series as well as three collections of quilt projects inspired by her novels, and is the designer of the Elm Creek Quilts fabric lines from Red Rooster fabrics. She lives with her husband and two sons in Madison, Wisconsin.